FINGLE'S TRIAL

FINGLE'S TRIAL

M. A. HOWLAND

CLAYBORN
PRESS

They say the best things in life are worth waiting for, so I waited for my remarkable wife to walk into mine.

I dedicate this tale to her, whose belief in me never once faltered, even when mine had floundered like a health and safety representative inspecting one of Pat Thogen's meat pies.

I must also dedicate this work to Goblinkind, in the hope of changing our understanding of this largely misunderstood race. However, a cautionary note must be added at this point. While you read these pages, it would be wise to pay particular attention to the shadows that may cavort around the corners of your eyes. For once Goblins have fully merged with your imagination (wittingly or otherwise), they will never leave you...

Chapter 1

"Liar!"

Before Fingle could protest, his gaping mouth was crammed full with rotten wrangleroot, which in all honesty tasted just as foul when fresh. In a normal court of law, open practice of food hurling at the accused was punishable. But this was no ordinary court of law and Fingle was no ordinary prisoner. In all consideration, he was far from being an ordinary Goblin too.

After spitting out the blockage in the most unmannerly way possible, Fingle directed his plea to the high council, "I 'int dun nuffin wrong, I mean right, I int dun nuffin right like wot yer are saying I 'ave dun, wif respect, m'lod."

"Litigants should address the Court as, 'my Lord," blurted the haughty judge, "and silence in the gallery. Should anyone else feel compelled to declare their opinions above mine, I will be compelled to fling their carcass into a sanitised cell for a whole moon cycle, am I clear?"

The ragged assembly of Goblins nodded awkwardly, staring down at their shuffling feet. Fingle looked anxiously towards the gallery and was extremely relieved to see Clump had managed to find the courtroom unaided.

"Fingle Froglick, regardless of your whining protestation and due to the alarming volume of irrefutable evidence stacked against you, the court sees no other alternative than to place you into further custody. A final court hearing will take place one cycle from now to consider your fate, but I must warn you, it does not look promising, not one bit of a blot!"

A loud cheer arose from the goblic gallery, then quickly withered as the Judge raised his menacing brow—prompting his oversized monocle to slip from its greasy socket. Wheezing heavily, Judge Peeper Pickles unsteadily hauled himself onto his swollen feet, wobbling perilously with the girth of his impressive waistline. Cautiously, he shifted down from his bench with each enormous hand clamped tightly upon the groaning skulls of two devoted clerks struggling beneath him. As three burly guards approached Fingle, he shouted considerably more coherently, "Clump, yer need ta get me help, legal help and be snip-snap about it!"

"Who?" mouthed the giant with his usual vacant expression.

"Anyone yer big oaf, anyone!" shrieked Fingle as he was dragged away to his sparkling and exceptionally hygienic cell, which would have been repugnant to any self-disrespecting Goblin, but not to Fingle, secretly to him it was divine.

Clump waved while his best friend was led away to the court's dungeon. Besides Fingle's uncle Merlock, Fingle was his only friend. Oddly, Clump and Fingle could not be further apart in nature and stature—a solitary salty winkle fastened to a lustreless grey and clammy boulder—which is probably why they gravitated so well together. Unlike Fingle, Clump lacked in the communications department, having few words at his disposal. It hadn't helped his cause that the emotional expression of his words had also become AWOL and hung at high noon for deserting its post. However, that did not mean that Clump lacked the capacity for thought and feeling. This is something that Fingle regularly overlooked, usually to his detriment. Quite often, Fingle would find himself thrust against a wall, being throttled by one of Clump's mammoth hands while staring into those depthless puddles Clump had for eyes. Clump left the courtroom and slowly made his way to the busy entrance of the courthouse, stepping outside to where the cool dungy air filled his lungs once more. He stood, a tall dark obelisk set against a granite sky, glumly pondering which direction to take.

As Fingle was dragged to his cell, an inflamed guard left in a hurry, after having vigorously scrubbed and polished the surfaces from top to bottom. Gagging violently, he applied the finishing touches of perfuming the cell with the rich scent of lavender.

In retreat, he fixed his livid stare upon Fingle, "See how you like *that,* Goblin hater."

Fingle shrank as the guard stumbled around him, disappearing into the gloom of the dank, unlit corridor, wincing as the receding jangle of keys and cleaning products were accompanied with heavy retching sounds. The remaining two guards both held a grimy hand to their equally grimy, appalled faces and threw him inside. As Fingle lay face down, his reflected grin widened upon the highly polished floor tiles as the cell door slammed shut. He slowly got up and ran a long spindly finger across the immaculate surfaces while breathing deeply of the heady fragrance. *Wonderful* he thought, eyes closed, savouring the civilised sumptuousness he had so deeply yearned for. Fingle's eyes blinked open—although in truth they were so beady the distinction was difficult to discern. Regrettably, his lavish accommodation would not last forever, he was in serious trouble this time; he had simply gone too far. He sank to his knees wailing in the realisation that Clump, although his best friend, was also his only salvation. His small sinewy body shook as he sobbed. Fingle slumped further to the sanctity of the polished floor once again, his whimpers pausing briefly to allow for licking of the pristine tiles, while repeating, "Lavendeeeer..." over and over.

*　　*　　*

Still standing at the entrance to the courthouse twenty minutes later, Clump's decision making prowess had been mercifully accelerated by a frantic guard who came reeling from the court's entrance, holding his gagging mouth and carrying a lavender scented mop. The collision between them was sufficient enough to force Clump to embark upon his weighty mission by lurching slowly to his right, as the bewildered guard rebounded heavily, crashing down the steps to his left. The guard's aggressive vomiting was barely perceptible to Clump, as he wandered past a circle of stone statues depicting the city rulers of bygone eras, resplendent in moss and bird plop. This was not anything unusual for Goblins and certainly not in the city streets, outskirts, or the whole of Goblindom.

An angry growl demanded Clump's attention from its lofty, sparingly comprehending heights, down to his heckling belly. *Nosh* he thought and decided to pay a well-earned visit to the city's shimmering jewel that boasted the finest grog, hot bread, and savoury meat pies that could be purchased or stolen. After hastening through the busy cobbled streets, Clump arrived at the doorsteps to the highly regarded, yet remarkably un-magnificent 'Pye Shoppe'. The shop's title and wares bore little in imagination, but atoned for its banality by being continually packed to the rafters with gluttonous Goblins. The pies themselves, although of hearty size, had nothing of the spectacular about them. They were at best, bland in flavour and appearance and highly suspicious in content. But there was something uniquely imponderable that kept repeat customers in their vast numbers deeply gratified. Of course it was of little coincidence that every pie and grog purchased came with an extra pie and grog unconditionally free. Every Goblin worthless of his or her weight would tell you that nothing *ever* came free. You either paid for something or you stole it and yet somehow against all Goblin tradition stood a squalid little enterprise, nested in the centre of the great Goblin City giving away grog!

A large sign in the steamy window proudly displayed:

BUY ANY PIE AND GROG
FOR THE PRICE OF TWO
AND GET ANOTHER PIE AND GROG FREE!

Clump rubbed his prodigious belly and lowered himself through the doorway, hitting the door-bell with his forehead—as was customary due to his colossal size. Instantly, the hot acrid air and noise rushed to meet him in equal measure.

"Usual, Clump?" cried Maw Wallop—the shop's sweaty scullion—above the near deafening babble while shifting her enormous dappled breasts, one to each side of her whelp bearing hips.

Clump nodded and walked over to his seat, the seat he had *always* sat on. Clump was a creature of habit; he chose what seemed right and stuck to that. This simple philosophy removed the need to make any further unnecessary decisions upon the matter, or any other matter for that matter. Clump stood impatiently over a large, inebriated Goblin city-guard who happened to be occupying his chair. Before the King's enforcer could slur out a protest at Clump's impudence, he found himself hanging upside down from a rusted meat hook dangling from the central beam that ran the length of the muggy shop. This amused the dregulars to no end, dregulars who knew better than to ever sit in Clump's chair but had neglected to inform the unfortunate newcomer. Clump sat down, contemplating where he might find help for his best friend. Fingle would have known who to ask or where to go; he was always dealing with other Goblins. He didn't know exactly what Fingle did, but he knew it was important as he was busy all of the time. Clump was just happy to tag along; he wasn't ever doing anything especially special. The shop's shrill bell heralded more custom, followed by an unwelcome rush of fresh air and a band of merry males singing deplorably out of tune with one another.

"You're in high spirits today, Pilf, why so?" enquired Maw, tucking a rebellious bosom beneath her right armpit.

"We is celebrating, Maw, celebrating justice dun on Fingle."

Clump's awareness was stimulated sufficiently to turn around upon hearing his friend's name. He immediately recognised them as the same gaggle of Goblins that had thrown rotten wrangleroot and decaying gurnips at Fingle from the court's goblic gallery. Clump stood up and although emotionally ill-equipped to harbour personal vendettas, a fierce sense of loyalty for his friend remained. He plodded purposely towards the riotous assembly, sidestepping slightly to avoid the gently swaying guard—who, still suspended from the central beam, was now fully unconscious and dribbling like a Pekingese with a peppermint.

"Hey, isn't that Fingle's—"

Before the lubricated muckraker could finish his sentence, at least two of Clump's knuckles smashed their way through the sneer to find the fatty throat tissue surrounding the spine. A loud crack was heard before several dislodged teeth had plopped into the sawdust that covered the grog-stained floorboards. The lifeless Goblin would have joined his rotted enamel evictees, that is, if Clump had decided to lower his extended fist...

"Anyone else wants to hang their coat?" said Clump impassively.

The crowd responded exceptionally well to Clump's deadpan humour, although he himself felt nothing, at least not initially. Clump lowered his colossal forearm, but the Goblin's mouth was still impossibly stretched around his fist. Clump then attempted to shake him off, resulting in a horrific marionette parody of a flopping torso and flailing limbs, creating yet further entertainment for the boozy crowd.

Eventually he freed his fist—ignoring the collapsing cadaver—and casually picked out any remaining teeth that had embedded into his fingers. An elderly customer presented Clump with a tankard of frothy grog for the impromptu performance from which the old Goblin was giggling and wheezing heartily away. As Clump accepted the fizzing accolade, a change in his stoical countenance emerged. It was barely perceptible, but any change from his detached expression was so significant, it was as if night had become day, or perhaps a Goblin had become Human, ever dread the notion! A faint chuckle rippled along Clump's black lips from his previous remark, then the flames of realisation 'snuffed out' as swiftly as they had been fanned into life.

Clump looked down upon the frail figure dancing before him and asked, "Can you help Fingle?"

"What's that, lad? What did you say? Holler up." croaked the grizzled Goblin, crinkling up his mottled face like a decomposing lime sucking upon itself.

Clump gently lifted him high above the floor and raised a wrinkled ear flap to his twitching mouth, "I said, *can, you, help, me*?" roared Clump.

Great flecks of spit sprayed upon the bewildered Goblin as his straggly yellow-white hair blew gracefully from the foul smelling tsunami. In the silence that followed, the catatonic customer simply remained staring into the abyss through the fully raised portcullis of Clump's gaping jaws. Realising any further attempt at communication was futile, Clump respectfully placed him into a vacant seat and taking his own tankard, prised it into the Goblin's rigid fist. Clump surveyed his handiwork and thought it prudent to leave before he too was imprisoned by the King's guards. After all, Goblins weren't completely uncivilised, just mostly. Clump sighed as the door-bell danced upon his skull once more, causing a clattering coalition of dissonant clangs. Turning right into Lostleg Street, he felt a sharp tug upon his tunic. Peering skywards crouched an anxious looking Goblin dressed in reasonable finery, clutching an enormous leather case stuffed untidily with parchments. Nervously, he beckoned for Clump to follow, so follow he did. As Clump entered a backstreet, a hooded figure skulking in a nearby doorway watched his movements intently. Several twisty turns later, they stopped in a quiet alleyway. Aside from the muffled cries of the distant street sellers, the general bustle of the main drag was left far behind. The only company they shared was with numerous plump rats that overran the rotting vegetation and animal carcasses, dumped from the rear entrances of various enterprises.

"You're Fingle's friend?" said the Goblin in hushed tones, laced with urgency.

"Yes." replied Clump.

"I understand he requires legal representation?"

"Yes. Can *you* help him?" asked Clump.

"No and yes." replied the furtive Goblin.

Clump was confused, what offer of help was this? Sensing impending doom as Clump's smooth forehead rapidly became a sheet of corrugated iron, the Goblin quickly continued.

"What I mean to say, is that although I am a soullessisitor, *I* unfortunately cannot help you, nor indeed would *any* other Goblin, as it would undoubtedly mean certain death to do so in accordance to Goblin law and for the crimes that Fingle is accused. However, in the extremely unlikely event of proving Fingle *was* of a rotten nature and therefore innocent, then both Fingle *and* his legal representation would be fully pardoned."

Clump's forehead relaxed a little, "Who can help?"

"Well anyone, anyone who practices law and who isn't a Goblin I suppose?"

Clump remembered Fingle's parting words; his friend had said much the same. Fingle had also taught him to be highly suspicious of generosity.

"Why are you telling me this? What do you want?" interrogated Clump.

The Goblin visibly trembled and looked ready to bolt, "No reason, other than helping out Fingle, he is an old friend." stammered the skittish solicitor.

Clump reckoned he looked desperate and terribly afraid, but knew from past experience that he had an uncanny effect on folk that often made them apprehensive. Still, it was the only advice he had been given on the matter and was ever likely to. *So be it,* thought Clump.

Chapter 2

Robin Swindlar was mildly astonished he had the nerve to spit the thickest phlegm he could muster into his manager's premium deli breakfast sandwich. In truth, the consumption of nearly an entire punnet of peculiar mushrooms—with their strange effects still paddling gleefully around his addled brain—may well have been the deciding factor. Rob had almost dropped the soggy snack while replacing it, convinced he would be caught in the act. *Asshole,* he thought, *not only am I paid a pittance, I have to listen to this moron criticise me too!* Outside the office, he could hear one of the supermarket's security guards being reprimanded. Rob felt the sting of guilt, but found solace knowing the security team unilaterally agreed it had been a night to remember. Feeling suitably smug, he watched as Mr. Cornfoot—the store's manager—burst back into his office, stormed behind his desk and allowed his diminutive elderly frame to collapse into his large executive swivel chair. The chair itself was a status symbol, defining the vast power that could be wielded at the occupant's discretion. It reminded Rob of those fancy command and control positions on board the 'Star-Trek Enterprise', audacious and futuristic. It had numerous levers, knobs, and dials. Rob wondered if the seat could eject.

"Well, have you thought any further on *why* you did it, Rob? How it affects the company? How it affects *me*? Despite your father's assurances, I knew employing you would be a grave mistake. And not two weeks later, I arrived at work earlier this morning to find you fast asleep, slumped over a dismembered mannequin, butt-naked in the store's front window display!"

Rob could see Mr. Cornfoot approaching critical mass and prepared himself for the perfect storm.

"The head of day security provided me with some extremely disturbing C.C.T.V. footage taken from last night." hissed his seething employer.

As Cornfoot frantically fiddled with his computer monitor, Rob noted in particular how his manager's voice had elevated to a falsetto pitch and marvelled at the steady transformation of engorged veins that swiftly became a pulsing frenzy of subcutaneous tendrils, swarming his neck and licking vehemently around his deeply ploughed forehead.

"At precisely 23:01, *you*, with the night security guards are seen admitting three unauthorised personnel via the rear delivery door. At 23:09 all of you are then seen filling a shopping trolley with *stolen* goods from the wine and spirits section."

At this juncture, Rob felt genuinely aggrieved; it was unfair to suggest the majority of stolen goods were alcoholic in nature. Memory serving, he was reasonably confident that due diligence had been exercised at the delicatessen and baked goods section. He was about to object but hesitated as Cornfoot's eye-lids stretched alarmingly to the rear of his capillary streaked eye balls. Sensing Rob's interjection, the manager decided to share with Rob the condemning on-screen evidence, but over zealously swivelled his computer monitor, causing a huge tear shaped leaded crystal trophy—for "Retailer of the month"—to be knocked down from its pride of place and embed deeply within his groin. Rob ruptured into peals of delight. The spectacle of Cornfoot's weak arms wrestling with the weighted prismatic award and his miserly face contorted in humiliating pain was too much to withstand. Cornfoot sacrificed his remaining dignity by wedging his left hand beneath the multi-faceted glacier to offer his aching scrotum a temporary reprieve from the biting torture. Using his free right hand, he snatched up his computer mouse and threw it directly towards Rob. The device sadly never reached its target. Instead the cord had recoiled back with venom, striking the bridge of Mr. Cornfoot's nose with surprising force. Rob watched in horror as the manager's nose suddenly resembled a scaled down volcanic eruption, with hot magma spraying indiscriminately around his beloved Pompeii. Cornfoot's eyes performed a complete reversal by clamping shut, although the liver spotted seals gradually relented to a surging tide of tears, tears of pain and contempt for the young imbecile standing before him.

"Get out! Get out!" spluttered the blood soaked manager, his flailing hand desperately seeking another projectile to launch.

Rob felt the rise of panic take root as the surrealism had forced his capacity for logical reasoning to re-ignite. Cornfoot located his keyboard and after several slippery attempts he grasped it tightly. Reaching backwards, he hurled it within the general direction of where he last saw Rob standing. In his outrage, he had neglected to realise this too was attached to something else and only succeeded in pulling his computer monitor from off its stand to impale itself—screen upwards—upon the apex of his crotch nested shimmering prize. This resulted in an impressive display of multi-coloured sparks and billowing clouds of acrid smoke. Groaning loudly, imprisoned within his own inner Abaddon, Cornfoot sank further into his hi-tech throne as the computer monitor's extra weight encouraged the translucent traitor to burrow itself yet deeper into his redundant appendage. Rob stared in disbelief at the gyrating monitor screen. Although inordinately cracked, the C.C.T.V. footage still displayed his nocturnal movements in surprising clarity. At 00:26 Rob was seen hurtling down the frozen meat aisle seated backwards in a trolley at breakneck speed, while a night security guard sat cross legged in his underwear, painting the freezer doors in complimentary hues of organic yoghurt. Rob's artistic appreciation of his captivating on screen appearance was rudely interrupted as the overhead sprinkler system activated itself—sensing the toxic plumes of smoke from the monitor—accompanied with a deafening alarm. Cornfoot entered a delirium as every one of his heightened senses were under siege. The damaged monitor screen had one more insidious trick up its polymer sleeve. During the electrical shortage the room's safety fuse relay system had also malfunctioned…

This inadvertently allowed the monitor and his beloved hi-tech chair to be the *only* electrical devices that remained operable in the entire building, while the emergency sprinkler system continued to spray wildly. This was considerably unfortunate for Mr. Cornfoot as he abruptly discovered when a huge surge of electricity coursed through his crippled body. His right leg instantly reacted to the electric shock by jerking violently against his burr-walnut leather top desk, sending his chair into an uncontrollable spin. The remaining cables that hung loosely from between the computer tower and the collection of I.T. equipment that had accumulated in his lap, were now roping tightly around him, binding Cornfoot to his state-of-the-art recliner.

The whirling chair jolted to a stop once the tightened cords had reached their limits. Mr. Cornfoot was once again facing Rob, but now unconscious. Rob instinctively approached his fallen nemesis, gently wiping away the blood around his eyes using a waterlogged deli napkin, becoming deeply moved at how paternal he felt in the precious moments of intimacy they now shared. Another blinding flash crackled across the pathetic torso of Cornfoot, immediately reanimating him, replacing Rob's reverie for fractured mental images of Frankenstein's monster. The second electrical pulse had unsympathetically invoked the chairs integral heating system and motorised back massager, which were both now operating hideously beyond their maximum pre-programmed levels! Terrified, Rob stumbled back as Cornfoot took on a whole new demeanour. Despite the congealing blood and relentless sprinkler droplets invading his eyes, his glare remained transfixed upon Rob with undiluted malice. What began as a deep guttural rumble soon escalated to a sickening scream. Rob could only stare in undisguised horror as Cornfoot was brutally beaten by the red-hot vibrating plate hammering against his back. While his manager squealed an array of appalling expletives in an oscillating high pitch, it appeared to Rob that his voice was now fully electronic in nature and somehow, in this oppressive little office, he alone had witnessed the hallowed birth of trans-humanism, a beautiful symbiosis between man and machine.

Flashing blue lights abruptly appeared, increasing in their intensity, while Rob ceremoniously raised his arms in sincere adulation to have had this unprecedented honour bestowed upon him by the universe. The office door burst open as two firemen attempted to comprehend the bizarre scene laid out before them. Rob approached the sacred witnesses in religious entrancement, anointing the firemen's foreheads using a sachet of low-fat mayonnaise, nodded devoutly then proceeded out into the corridor, pausing long enough to cast a loving glance upon the night security guard sitting once again cross-legged and facing the wall. The guard, quite oblivious to the proceedings, fervently scribbled esoteric symbols into the aging plasterwork using his company issued biro pen. The firemen looked at each other, then back to the elderly man convulsing heavily, tied to a smoking chair that was shaking itself apart. They then looked towards the large diaphanous object implanted within his genitalia, refracting a strobe of emergency blue light in a three hundred and sixty degree arc. Lastly their disbelieving eyes collapsed upon the gyrating, flickering screen lanced by the crystal strobe, displaying five naked bodies simultaneously surfing upon the stores checkout conveyor belts at precisely 03:33. Gliding down the humid corridor, Rob rejoiced in the fresh deluge of forest rain falling gloriously upon his upturned face from the overhead sprinkler valves, agreeably astounded in how Cornfoot's diminishing robotic gargles had somehow transformed into an exotic mating call of a Norfolk black turkey. *I must sober up*...mused Rob, smiling enigmatically in preparation to greet the early morning sun outside.

* * *

Mr. Swindlar strode into Chipping Norton police station that had custody of his son. As he approached the front desk the sergeant nodded somberly toward the cells and shrugged. Rob's father could hear his son before he saw him.

"Two aces! Can you believe that? I can't. Who can be *this* lucky? It's unnatural." laughed Rob, collecting his winnings.

Mr. Swindlar entered the cell. Immediately two police officers stood, dropping their cards to the floor.

"Hello, Sir, we were just—" spluttered the reddened officer.

"I can see perfectly well what you were doing, Constable, although I strongly doubt that gambling is inclusive within the budgetary requirement for this department. I am confident my son's enthusiasm is due to having earned some small part back of what I pay in my taxes."

"Dad! It was my fault, not theirs, I was just passing the time until, well, you know."

"Until I collect my disobedient child again, you mean?"

"Something like that."

Rob's father signed the necessary discharge papers and routinely apologised for his son's behaviour. The pair walked out of the police station to their car in silence. His father's car was another symbol of high office, large and powerful, a subtle warning for all to take him seriously or reap the consequences. A highly respected and accomplished solicitor, Rob's father had earned such recognition after many years of hard work and laborious networking. Rob admired his father, loved him of course, but never felt close. He had always assumed after his mother's death during his birth, his father had harboured deep regrets towards him, despite his father's insistence otherwise.

Rob stared out of the car window at the blur of images flashing past. "Dad, why didn't you ever remarry?"

As soon as he had asked the question, he regretted it. After an uncomfortable pause his father sighed deeply, "Rob, you know I don't like to talk about it. Your mother meant everything to me and I could never betray her, I mean betray her memory."

His father was about to question why his son betrayed her with his actions, but he accepted his son's behaviour was simply a result of his failings as a father and of a son deprived of a maternal presence in his life.

"Look, Rob, I understand why you do the things you do—"

"You mean don't live up to your expectations."

"I didn't say that."

"You didn't have to."

The rest of the car journey was quiet and awkward. They were too tired to carry the conversation to its usual conclusion where they would inevitably end up shouting at each other and regret their words without reaching a conciliation. As the car lurched into a long gravel drive, Rob unfastened his seat-belt, eager to escape and slam the door shut on his pain as he had always done.

"Chinese?" asked his father, pulling up the parking break.

"Yes, that sounds good, Dad."

Mr. Swindlar watched his son trudge over to their empty house in the retreating daylight. *If only I could tell him the truth,* he thought, picking up his heavy briefcase. He walked slowly to the front door that Rob had left open as the first drops of rain began to fall.

Chapter 3

Clump sat down upon a pile of wooden crates, watching the well-dressed Goblin scurry through the dark alley back towards Lostleg Street. Clump would never have seen him nod to the hooded figure, who slipped away into the shadows, disappearing altogether from sight. Clump picked up a flabby rat and began to stroke its greasy fur. He wondered how he would get help, he hardly knew anyone and talked to virtually no one.

"Right," he said, "I *will* save Fingle."

Clump vowed to sit within the clammy confines of the litter strewn alley until he hatched a suitable plan, no matter how long it might take. His face, although largely inscrutable, began to moisten with the effort, his tense body shook. Clump was in deep thought, deeper than he had ever been, he was in un-chartered territory. Minutes went by, then an hour, then three. Eventually an eyebrow arched and a foot scraped the slippery cobbles beneath his bulky frame. A thought bubbled up to enter the gloom of his cavernous mind.

"Merlock!" he barked triumphantly.

This was accentuated by a loud squeak and a popping sound as his fists squeezed tightly together. Clump looked down at the gelatinous remains of the poor rodent, then proceeded to devour the remnants from off his open palm, licking meticulously between his grubby thickset fingers.

Fingle's Trial

"Wilful waste makes woeful want." he said dutifully to himself.

It was decided, he would travel to Whisperun Forest to meet with Fingle's uncle Merlock. He didn't understand Merlock at all, meaning Fingle's uncle was much smarter than he was. He was genuinely surprised he hadn't thought of seeking out the old wizard much earlier, perhaps after two hours of contemplation. Clump stood up amidst a flurry of oily brown fur darting in every direction and made his way back to the clamour of Lostleg Street while maintaining a watchful eye for any City guards. Although he knew Merlock lived in Whisperun Forest and had visited him many times before, it had not registered to Clump to pack provisions for the journey; he had forgotten it took three days travel by foot. Usually Fingle would have reminded him, he was really quite lost without him. Although Clump was always walloping someone that Fingle had double crossed, in truth it was Fingle that looked after him.

Famished after a three days uneventful march, the dusty track finally brought the great forest into view. Clump scanned the immense treeline of Whisperun, searching for the opening he and Fingle had used on many occasions to gain entry. It was seldom ventured from outwards to within and less so from within to out, for city types and woodland types were vastly different creatures. Clump eventually happened across a large pink granite rock protruding from the vibrant gorse that lined the forest's edge. Instantly he recognised its lichen colouring and distinctive character, as no two rocks were ever alike if you bothered to study or ask them—in actuality, they can become inherently huffy by uninformed folk overlooking their individuality and refuse to communicate any further; a stony silence would undoubtedly ensue.

His lessons in tracking taught by an inexhaustibly forgiving Merlock had thankfully paid off. This particular rock, although insignificant to any ignorant 'townie', was a crucial marker to one of the few rudimentary pathways through the dark forest. Clump was exceptional at spotting things as his mind was largely uncluttered from the barrage of incessant dap trap and distractions that poke, tease and coerce 'greater' minds.

After forcing his bulk through the camouflaged opening—considerably less concealed than before—he found the primitive path and followed.

The forest rapidly grew dark as he ventured deeper into its leafy domain, the crowded canopy high above allowed for little light to trickle through. This lent a distinct chill to the air and encouraged mist to gather in large swathes of swirling grey bitterness. It was suicide to enter Whisperun without possessing the necessary skills that Clump had gained over the years. Skills cultivated by Fingle and Merlock and some that he had already possessed naturally. Whisperun Forest was an enormous entity. To navigate your way through its labyrinth without previous familiarity or receiving assistance would be quite impossible. And if by sheer dumb luck you somehow managed to escape, you could rest assured that your sanity would remain held captive within its gloomy dominion forever. The un-dead that roamed the dark forest could quicken a soul to flee from its body through relentless fearful torment. But of course, the un-dead knew better than to try and ensnare Clump, for he was beyond entrapment. When Clump heard the disembodied whispers, he could block them out easily if he so wished. If he saw no one, then why should he pay any attention to a silly 'mind whisper', other than passing the time with trivial chit-chat? After all, even the roaming dead became lonely and eternity can be a real drag. The restless spirits could read the future to an extent, making small talk even more depressing, but in a murky ocean of oppressive green silence, small talk, no matter how preconceived was preferable to none, but only marginally. Naturally the spirits could commune with one another, but due to the stifling melancholy they all possessed, the flow of conversation was often stemmed quite abruptly...

"How are yooooooou?"

"I am deeeeeead."

"Niiiice weather weeeee are haviiiiiiing."

"What does it matteeeerrr, I am deeeeeeead."

Suddenly, an invisible wavering voice manifested from within the shadowy trees and seeped into the fogginess of Clump's head.

"Hellooooo, Clump, long tiiiime no seeeeeee."

"I could say the same." replied Clump, oblivious to the quality of his riposte.

"Yooou offf to vissssit Merlock, I supposssse?"

Clump replied to the undead, his huge form causing eddies to swirl in the icy shroud as he lumbered onwards, "Yes, Spirit, I am here to see Merlock, Fingle needs his help."

"Sorrryyy to hear it, I wiiiiill inform Merrrrrlock of yourrrrrrr arrival, so looooong."

"Bye, un-dead Spirit." said Clump matter-of-factly.

Time here was redundant. A sleepy stillness infused with an intoxicating blend of heady pine and decaying wood, which despite the chill, could entice a weary traveller to lower their guard and perhaps rest for a short while. Every forest was a place of potential danger and held their own inimitable mysteries, Whisperun was no exception. To qualify as a resident you had to be prepared to hunt, or be hunted, usually both. Clump was aware of this, unfortunately not all of the forest's predators were aware of Clump. The remainder of his journey—aside from being urinated on by a rowdy clan of inebriated winged Faux—was otherwise pleasant. Eventually Clump recognised a steep descent to his right, leading away from the secret path and down towards a small trickling stream.

From here it was only a short way across the shallow water, back up a small rise, round a coppiced corner, and beneath a gnarled Yew tree—that looked as if it would shake the shekles from you given half a chance. Merlock's domicile was impressively well hidden, built entirely beneath ground with a small peep hole just above, hidden by scrub and holly. If you had no prior knowledge of its existence, you would have walked straight past, on top even and be none the wiser. Even the chimney had been funnelled into an enormous hollowed out tree trunk to allow smoke to exit high above the canopy and out of sight.

A Boggle smelt Clump long before it had heard him, which in fairness was hardly surprising. Not that Clump was dreadfully smelly, not by Goblin standards, but Boggles have a marvellous sense of smell making them the perfect choice for Merlock's early warning system. The Boggle began noselling irritatingly loudly. A 'nosel' is essentially a yodel, but performed through both nostrils simultaneously, something a Boggle learns to do as an underling, as they are muzzled immediately at birth. The other unique ability besides their supernatural sense of smell, can only be experienced once its muzzle has been unwisely removed. A Boggle is approximately twelve inches tall, resembling an oversized meat ball with a short muzzled snout and baleful violet eyes. Once the muzzle's removed, they instantly transform to resemble whoever confronts them in size and appearance, but with one significant advantage. If you are ever unfortunate enough to be engaged in a conversation with a Boggle, they will literally bore you to death. As a matter of fact, many of the forest's 'Un-dead' were originally victims of a Boggle encounter and now fine hone their newly acquired trade of boring unwary travellers to dribbling dream-drumbles by studying further Boggle encounters. The un-dead will tell you the only difference between the whispers of the forest spirits and a Boggle encounter, is that the un-dead prefer to lace their banality with a dash of terror. But in reality, a Boggle conversation makes the un-dead utterances unreservedly sublime to withstand. Once dialogue commences, a Boggle's magickal charm ensures the victim is utterly compelled to endure the most insipid of trite-tales to the point of madness, then far, far beyond. They have literally *boggled the mind*. This is precisely why all Boggles are referred to as simply *Boggles,* for to call them by their true name would imply a previous conversation had taken place, which is supremely unlikely.

Clump bent down and picked up the little squealer before it could scamper away. It continued to nosel loudly, bothering Clump to queasiness. He shook it vigorously, while the poor Boggle impersonated an indecisive siren with acid reflux.

"Put him down!" commanded a voice directly behind him.

Clump dropped the warbling Boggle, watching it stagger towards the rise he had just climbed. It leapt over the edge while enfolding its snout and stumpy legs into its fat underbelly and rolled away at high speed while belching noisily. Clump searched the surrounding area but could see no one.

"Do you realise just how dangerous that could have been?" said the disembodied voice, now originating some distance away in the opposite direction.

Clump spun around to face Merlock's hidden home and still no sign of anyone.

"If you *had* begun talking to that Boggle, it would have meant insanity at the very least, but not for you, Clump, for the Boggle!"

This time the voice came from above, followed by loud cackling laughter. A large bush twenty feet in front of Clump parted and out walked a short elderly Goblin chortling merrily.

"Hello, Clump, it's been quite a while, lad. Did you enjoy the voice throwing?" asked Merlock proudly.

"Yes." replied Clump.

"I suspect you are longing to know how it's done, eh?" said Merlock, scratching his feral beard.

"No."

"Well let me tell you. I create a small sphere of energy, then, by placing it to my lips simply speak. When I am done, I hurl the ball to wherever I wish and where it collides with solid matter, the energy of the words spoken into it are released *and* with the intended cadence."

Merlock was most delighted and began to perform an awkward jig, becoming caught up in his oatmeal robes while Clump looked on dispassionately.

"Please forgive me, my boy, I don't receive many guests. Where are my manners? You *must* join me for lunch, come in, come in."

Clump followed Fingle's strange uncle, as he beckoned him over to a large bush. On approach, the bush parted for Merlock and Clump to enter. Merlock led the way with Clump crouching close behind. As they descended the worn stone steps, the bush swiftly closed behind them, whipping at Clump's backside. Clump suspected it was always deliberate and rubbed his stinging rump without further comment. They continued to descend, sensing the ambient temperature becoming much more agreeable and were grateful for it.

Lunch had been a lengthy affair. It was apparent to the old Goblin that poor Clump had been without food for quite some time. He did not mind that the giant had depleted his supplies by nearly half, while he continued to fetch plate after plate of cured meats, cheeses, bread and nuts, washed down with a torrent of foamy grog. When Clump had eventually showed signs of slowing, he expressed his satisfaction with a loud continuous belch from both ends.

"So, where is my Nephew?" enquired Merlock, surprised Clump had made the solo journey.

"Oh yeah, that's why I'm here. Fingle's in trouble, he needs help, legal help."

Merlock leapt up, "Why didn't you say, boy?"

"I just did."

"No, I meant earlier."

"You didn't ask earlier."

"What do you *mean* legal?"

"He's in a cell in the Goblin City's Courthouse. He will have a try-all in one cycle."

"Crom! What did he do?"

"He was caught doing something good." said Clump, shaking his head while licking his plates clean.

"Hmmm, that'll do it alright. Well, we are stuck between a rock-Trolls buttocks, we shan't find a Goblin brave enough to defend him. I could try, but I know nothing of legal-tea and un-awful behaviours. Finding someone stupid enough is another matter entirely, but where?" said Merlock, pacing the room.

"That's what the Goblin in the alley told me."

"What Goblin?" said Merlock, studying Clump closely.

"A small friend of Fingle's with a big book. He said it must be someone who knows lore and who isn't a Goblin."

"Hmmmm, I once knew of such a soul and he knew lore. He wasn't exactly a Goblin either, but he was brave and noble, but that was long, long ago. Clump, I have an idea..."

Merlock retreated to his inner sanctum to formulate his plan in greater detail, leaving Clump to his own company, who promptly fell fast asleep.

Several hours had passed before Merlock re-emerged beaming triumphantly.

"Wake up, boy; we have some packing to do."

After securing his home with magickal charms, Merlock led Clump through a heavily wooded path, which looked no different from any of its surroundings. After several hours of bramble rambling, Clump noted the ambient light finally brighten and the heavy woodland air taking on a fresher, lighter note. In the near distance the trees thinned, giving way to a broad expanse of lush wetland.

"We have arrived, young Clump, welcome to a most formidable place, 'Pardonme Marsh'."

"Why? For saying Marsh?" queried Clump.

"No. Pardonme Marsh, that's its full title, Pardonme Marsh." said Merlock grinning.

"Why?"

"Well, all that's known of this cursed place, is that several hundred long-cycles ago, a Gnome King's army had decided to enter these wetlands to escape the wrath of an Orc army they had upset. Something to do with defiling the Orcs heritage. The Gnomes could only see Orc gold, instead of the priceless antiquity it was and mountains of it if you believe the legends. Sadly, only a single Gnome had ever managed to make it out alive and it was this lone survivor, 'Appollo Jemaid' who named it Pardonme Marsh."

"Why call it that though?" pressed Clump.

"Appollo refused to say any more on the matter and I don't suppose it does matter, only those that go in together, do not come back out together..." cautioned Merlock.

They continued to walk towards the marshland until they were forced to stop at the Oodles riverbanks, a deep course with powerful currents that carved its passage between the forest and marshlands. There was an old rusted ferry that bobbed at the water's edge with an iron chain suspended above it, stretching across the river to the far side. Vegetation had weaved its way through the corroded linkage all along its squeaking, swaying length.

"Best get to it, boy." smiled Merlock.

They hopped aboard and Clump gripped the chain tightly. After a few sharp tugs, the ferry scraped away from the muddy shore. Aside from the links rattling through the ferries hull as Clumped heaved away, it was eerily quiet. The force of the rivers under currents could be felt as the ferry pushed hard against the chains, making Clump work harder. For an instant, Merlock thought he had seen something unnervingly large swim beneath the creaking vessel. He knew the river ran deep and held many myths; he edged a little closer to Clump until they had safely reached the other side. Once disembarked, Merlock set his travelling point to the correct direction. Clump took it, then proceeded to wade through the sodden grass and spongy peat with vigour. All that mattered to him was helping Fingle and if he died trying so be it, but he would not give up without a fight, a good punchy one at that! Very soon the marsh became hard going and their feet were sinking with every step. The visibility was atrocious, considerably worse than the misty forest they had just left, as an impenetrable fog now enveloped them. Though only a couple of feet apart, any discernible features were largely muted, smudged outlines were all that were perceived at best. As Clump ventured onwards he let out a *parping* sound, followed by an obnoxious smell.

"Crom, boy, that's bad." coughed Merlock, close behind.

Clump ignored his comment and continued following the travelling point.

Paaaarrrp!

Merlock was rendered totally blind, covering his face from the foul stench, "Clump, *please* consider my refined sensitivities, I'm not a cave dwelling clan Goblin. Your expulsions are beyond hideous!" spluttered the ailing magus.

Clump did not feel anger exactly, but he was not without irritation and found Merlock's trumped up allegations increasingly irksome.

"Please let me walk in front, Clump, my delicate wizard's constitution is taking a right royal battering back here."

Clump allowed Merlock to take the lead, handing over the pointer and responsibility which suited him fine. Several steps later, *paaaaarrrrrp*.

Clump steadied himself as the repugnant cannonade slapped him mercilessly. "It was *you* all along, Merlock, say sorry, say sorry now!" demanded Clump.

Merlock was as equally affronted, "I will *not* say sorry, how dare you suggest that my body harbours such malignant imps, they are clearly yours and not mine."

Clump lurched forwards to wring out an apology, but Merlock anticipated this, splodging away from the giant's grasp as fast as he could through the marsh reeds. Clump gave chase, but the added momentum combined with his extraordinary weight forced each step to sink deeper still into the squelching mire. As they both ran, every step issued a loud *parping* sound, immediately followed by a diabolical odour. Merlock made the connection long before Clump and as his pace slowed, so did the frequency of trumps. Clump had now caught Merlock, suspending him upside down, while the magus was hysterical with laughter.

"What's so funny?" demanded Clump.

"Ha ha ha, Clump, hee hee, start, ha ha, start walking." giggled Merlock.

Clump walked forwards.

Paaarrrp.

Clump paused for thought.

"Lift me up, you big clod!" spluttered Merlock.

The wizard's face hung in the firing line and had taken a direct hit with his maltreated nostrils just inches above the rotting vegetation. As Clump raised Merlock he wondered how the wizard could have made the sound when it seemed to come from him...?

"Genius! It's the marsh, boy, it was always the marsh. Those hog headed morons with swords would rather have cut each other's throats than apologise for something they didn't do. This is precisely why the Gnome King's army had attacked each other."

Clump stood motionless in the reeking fog allowing for the realisation to seep in.

"*That* is why the marsh is called Pardonme Marsh!" exclaimed Clump.

"Yes, yes, and the *only* way to escape it alive is to accept any blame that's spuriously cast and politely apologise, thus avoiding the very justifiable bloodshed, it's insidious." cackled Merlock.

Clump slowly nodded, feeling considerably more appeased by this explanation and a smite more buoyant in managing to digest a revelation of this complexity and magnitude.

"Clump, you can put me back down." said Merlock dizzily.

Although they had solved the mystery of the marsh, they had not yet beaten it. Each step demanded a ransom of strength from their exhausted muscles and slithers of hope from their sinking spirits. Clump saw Merlock falter, without hesitation he scooped him up into the fold of his bulging arm.

"You're a good boy, Clump, Fingle doesn't deserve you." said Merlock weakly, his smile straightening as he succumbed to the inescapable lure of sleep. Clump continued to follow the travelling point as he wandered further and further into the cold white abyss.

Clump had lost all track of time and sense of self until his feet began to scuff instead of sink. He roused sufficiently to recognise he was walking uphill. As he climbed, the fog slowly dispersed, allowing the glorious night sky to occasionally peek through. Clump picked up momentum and in turn awakened Merlock from his deep slumber. He marched forwards until at long last he had reached the apex, the ground had now levelled out and was considerably firmer. The pair stared in wonderment at the ancient stone circle standing tall before them, partially bathed in silvery moonlight, set against a breath-taking backdrop of twinkling stars with lazy platinum plated clouds.

"It's real." said Clump, his deep voice sonorous around the enormous stones.

"I never doubted its existence, I have travelled here several times, but only using tri-ocular sight, never in body." replied Merlock, rapidly regaining his faculties.

Clump lowered Merlock and they both walked over to the nearest of the three stone megaliths.

"Why is it called a circle of stones when there are only three?" enquired Clump.

"Quite right, it's actually a triangle isn't it," chortled Merlock, "to have a circle you need at least five stones, four stones make a square, three a triangle and two is simply not enough. Without a centre point the magick cannot be focused. In truth, Clump, you can find the centre in circles, squares and triangles, so why hump around *more* than three stones, when three will do just fine. After all, isn't a Goblin's creed to get away with doing as little as possible?" winked the wily wizard.

"I forgot to thank you, Clump, for carrying me earlier, so thank you. But for now, we must hasten our work as the celestial architecture favours our intentions this very night."

Fingle's Trial

Clump sat down upon the dry grass pulling off his wet boots, allowing the cool night air to dry his swollen feet and tickle his wriggling toes. He watched as Merlock produced a large ball of twine from his knapsack. The magus secured it firmly around the first stone then walked the twine out to the next stone, fastening it tightly. Then repeated the same for the last stone.

"This will be our perimeter, Clump, it will harness the focused energies within the...circle."

Clump watched Merlock walk out another line from each stone again, but this time to the centre of the opposing perimeter line. When Merlock had completed it for a third and final time, Clump could now see a large star shape with six points formed on the inside of the perimeter line.

"Why—" began Clump, but Merlock cut him short.

"Because we need a doorway and six points make a door. The travelling pointer I gave you has only four points, four directions, but with six points we also have above and below, or rather spirit and the underworld."

"But how—"

"I'm glad you asked, we need to vitalise this doorway. I have created a web for what we want from the universe, but without vital essence it is nothing more than twine." Said Merlock, his bright eyes easily mistaken for the twinkling stars framing his jubilant form.

"How do we—" started Clump.

"With 'Whatwewantweavers' of course, for the wishing web we have just created ha ha, hee hee." Sang Merlock gleefully.

The small wizard reached into his leather satchel and produced a sealed earthenware jar. He walked over to the centre of the star shaped web and unfastened the perforated lid. Hundreds of small glossy blue spiders escaped, running along the lengths of twine in all six directions. The spiders were instantly busy at work, coating the twine with their portal-silk. As the night's

31

breeze caressed the twine, the star-shaped web began to shimmer into life; it was a remarkable sight to behold. When all the twine had been fully coated, Merlock held his jar back at the centre point, waiting patiently for the tiny cobalt weavers to begin their return journeys, until all were safely back and sealed away.

"Now what do we do?" said Clump hurriedly, determined to finish his question.

"Now we wait." Smiled Merlock, sitting down next to Clump.

They brewed up a small pot of Tar, a traditional Goblin refreshment enjoyed in the quieter of moments. It contained only a small amount of grog, but was hot, sweet and comforting. They sipped gratefully while gazing skywards, losing themselves within the wondrous expanse, extending out to infinitude.

Chapter 4

Rob sat staring at his computer screen. One web page open listing universities specialising in Law and another advertising employment in some faraway destination, where the lure of adventure was painfully compelling. His father as usual was right, he *had* to knuckle down and take ownership of his destiny, with all the repellent responsibilities that came with it. Mr. Swindlar was a hard man, but not devoid of compassion. He held high expectations from everyone and this had always placed considerable pressure upon Rob's young shoulders, particularly as an only child who found law as appealing as a fish felt wrapped in seaweed, then expected to pose beguilingly upon a sushi board. He moved away from the flickering glare and collapsed upon his bed face down. He *would* show his father that he was not a complete failure and at the very next opportunity he vowed he would prove beyond any doubt that he was a Swindlar to be proud of.

* * *

"Wake up, it's time, it's time!" shrieked the wizard.

Clump rubbed his puffy eyes and pulled on his boots. The clouds had finally parted, revealing a spectacular full moon. Its pervasive silvery light now shone brightly between the formidable stones and onto to the wishing web. The winds howled as air elementals danced excitedly around the ancient rock, assisting the magickal work. Clump stared in amazement at the azure radiance that sparkled upon the swaying twine which held against every urgent gust.

"Now it's vitalised!" sang Merlock, hopping from foot to foot.

The sorcerer raised his voice above the blustery winds, his robe and hair blowing wildly, "Clump, you *must* think of his name and his location, then the closest mirror in his world will become the opening. Think hard while I raise the energies, snatch him as quick as you can."

Clump nodded, standing at the glowing centre, while mentally repeating the name and location they had agreed upon back at Merlock's home. Gradually, a portal began to shimmer into life…

"Hurry, my boy, this won't stay open for long, be as swift as the spring salmon!" cried Merlock.

Clump peered through the rippling portal and just as Merlock had foretold, the Human lay fast asleep only a short distance away. Clump reached forwards, but still fell short. Nervously, he edged his way through the opening until he was just inches away. Rob began to stir. He was partially aware of a pulsing light within his room and cursed inwardly for leaving his computer on again, but that hadn't accounted for the cold winds.

Rapidly, his sluggish mind reclaimed its focus as he fully awakened, "Bloody hell!" screamed Rob, as an enormous green paw swiped at him.

The room was illuminated in a scarlet haze, pulsing from a huge rupture where his mirror should have been. Confused and terrified, Rob's thoughts were scattered like the memories of a disturbed nightmare. Somehow, the mirror at the base of his bed was alive and *grabbing* at him! Clump leaned closer still as Rob edged further back against his headboard, cramming himself into a corner.

"Fingle needs help!" shouted Clump, stumbling into the room and crashing upon the bed, smashing its wooden frame into splintered upright shards that penned in Rob.

Clump's determined features loomed between the broken timbers as he attempted to calm Rob by smiling as best he could. Rob screamed louder as Clump's black lips stretched fully, revealing an alarming uneven array of razor sharp teeth that resembled steak knives for dwarves, complimented by a tusk on either side. Clump slapped Rob gently, more in frustration than anything else and watched him fall into unconsciousness. He hoisted the limp Human over his shoulder and rushed back through the fading portal.

"Hurry it's closing!" shrieked Merlock.

As Clump returned back into his own world, he caught sight of a tall man running into the bedroom towards him before the portal sealed itself shut.

Merlock joyfully skipped around the stones, "We have our champion, Fingle will be free." he squawked.

The more Clump thought on this, the more he became uncertain, "Merlock, it *was* 'Rob Swindlar' we wanted wasn't it?"

"Yes, yes, he shall be our victor, he will save our beloved Fingle." sang Merlock in dissonant tones.

"Merlock, does the shiny red hole make Humans young again?"

Merlock froze and slowly looked over to where Clump was holding Rob.

"Clump, you *did* concentrate on his name and his location, *didn't* you? You did say, 'Robert Swindlar' didn't you?" asked Merlock with deep concern in his voice and on his face.

"Yes…I…did! I thought of 'Robert Swindlar', or maybe it was just 'Rob Swindlar'? And where he lived, really hard, really, really, really hard." said Clump defensively, worried he may have somehow stolen the wrong Human.

Merlock's features sagged, "You did say 'Robert' and *not* 'Rob', Clump?"

Rob began to stir as he breathed in the cool night air, Clump slapped him back to sleep, this time more from despair than anything else.

"Maybe, I said 'Rob' and *not* 'Robert'. But it's the same thing isn't it?" mumbled Clump.

"Quick, let me see him. Crom! We have the wrong Human. There must be two 'Rob Swindlar's' in the same house." wailed Merlock, dropping to his bony knees while muttering incoherently to himself.

Clump thought it better than to interrupt greater minds at work, especially as he had little to offer anyway and he had done quite enough by the look of things. Merlock eventually raised his head and heaved himself onto his tired feet, "Well, either way we cannot return him now as the portal has closed. We shall have to wait until the next full cycle to be able to put him back. I feel terrible for ruining Fingle's last hope for freedom." murmured Merlock, becoming more despondent with the passing of each moment.

There was no alternative but to take the stranger with them, he was their responsibility now, regardless of his identity or origin. Clump continued to carry the snoring Human over his shoulder while Merlock untangled the twine and packed away his things in silence. They stood together, surveying the majesty of the heavens for the last time before they embarked upon their arduous return journey with mixed emotion.

The stench was not easily ignored regardless of how long you suffered it. Save for the sploshing footfalls and corresponding marsh trumps, the silence was deafening.

"What's that filthy smell?"

Merlock splashed over to Clump, peering through the fog. The captive had awoken and looking the worse for wear. The small party stopped while Rob thrashed around, fearful and confused.

"Put me down you freak, what are you? Help, somebody help me!"

Clump leaned backwards and let him slide off, landing him face first into the squishy bog. Rob looked upwards, his wild eyes—encircled by stagnant peat—searched everywhere, desperately seeking out an escape.

Before he attempted a run for it, Merlock spoke reassuringly to him. "Rob, my name is Merlock and this is Clump. Please believe me when I say we wish you no harm and any attempt at escape in this damnable place would be sheer folly."

Clump added his agreement by nodding his massive oval head ludicrously slowly. Rob sat twitching in the mud, hyperventilating and completely unable to respond as his face went into spasm. Merlock smiled warmly, then placed his palm gently upon Rob's crown applying a bliss dressing. Instantly Rob relaxed and his breathing slowed.

"I suspect you have many questions?" said Merlock softly.

Rob's eyes glazed over, his head gently lolling from side to side.

"Ahem, I said you may have some questions for me, my boy?" repeated Merlock a little more brusquely.

Rob's eyes wobbled upwards as he giggled, dribble escaping freely from his idiotic grin.

"Hmmm, I may have used too much bliss, it seems young Rob is very susceptible to magick here. Stop!" yelped Merlock, sensing Clump about to add his own unique contribution to the matter. "Pick him back up would you? With any luck he will soon become more coherent." said the wizard, his doubtful eyes betraying his reassurances.

After several hours of marsh marching, Rob had regained enough composure to address some nagging concerns, "My goodnish, Mr. Greeeen Giant, what *ish* that smell?"

"That, is Pardonme Marsh." replied Clump in his regular monotone.

"Ha ha ha, Pardon me, no, pardon you, for 'inverting the burp' you shtinky green giant."

Merlock and Clump stopped, looked at each other for a moment, then both howled with laughter. It was a much needed tonic and Rob was ecstatic he had made such an impression with his newfound friends, even if they were green and smelly. With their spirits raised they felt renewed and continued to apologise theatrically as each foot *parp* announced itself. Although the novelty had eventually worn off for the Goblins, Rob continued in earnest, for an excruciatingly long time…

* * *

Clump had been the first to see it as the other two were snoring loudly, buried into each of Clump's rounded shoulders. As the fog thinned, the rising morning warmth touched his face. Finally free of the chilly shroud, his bloated feet found solid ground once more. He drank deeply of the amber light perforating the dark forested horizon. Clump may have been a simple Goblin, but his simplicity enabled him to truly appreciate the finer things in life, which were of course always the simplest. Ignoring the snorting couple, he closed his tired eyes, enjoying the suns caress. He let escape a protracted sigh and began choking as a band of giggling Faux pissed into his gaping mouth, again... Clump waved his arms frantically above his head, determined to swat the pesky vermin and then remembered he was carrying his two companions, but only after he watched them fall to the floor with a jolting thud.

"Crom! What's happening? Where are we? Damn those Boggles." grumbled Merlock in a befuddled daze.

In a spectacular encore, Rob landed on his head again and continued to snore away, despite his face buried in the dew dressed grass.

"Sorry, Merlock. It's those mean sprites, they follow me and pee on me and laugh at me whenever I come to see you." said Clump miserably.

Merlock squinted against the rising sun to see the troublesome troupe of male Faux sharing their high pitched squeals of drunken delight; as well as the small brown bottles they swigged upon while pointing at Clump's despair. Their leader had waged a long standing vendetta against Clump, ever since his first visit to Whisperun Forest. Clump had been fishing for tea in Shadow Lake, not far from Merlock's place, when he had accidentally hooked upon a revelling Faux while casting his line. Clump could only watch as the unfortunate Faux was hurled towards the lake's centre and into the yawning maw of a grateful Happeem-eel. The poor sprite was never to be seen again. There are two types of faeries that inhabit Clump's world, the 'Fae' and the 'Faux'. The Fae, although devastated by such a tragedy, would have accepted the loss and moved on with their lives, littering their infernal glitter where ever they saw fit.

Unfortunately for Clump, it was the latter. The Faux were a hard bunch. They were well aware of the general goblic perception regarding faerie folk and were determined to offer an alternative interpretation. Persistent grog consumption was integral to this plan. In all honesty, it was entirely inconsequential that Clump had unwittingly sent one of 'theirs' to his watery doom. Withholding any vendettas, Clump had made a fine target for the airborne hooligans to amuse themselves.

"Shoo, move away fluttering vermin and bother us no more." wailed Merlock.

The intoxicated bother-hood approached Merlock, but decided to keep to a healthy distance upon hearing the familiar crackle of magick dance between Merlock's outstretched fingers. Everyone's attention turned to Rob as he writhed upon the ground scream-gurgling, desperately trying to avoid a breakaway group who were wishing Rob a good morning in their own inimitable style. Clump marched over and swiped angrily at the hooligans, each time narrowly missing them while they laughed at his clumsy attempts. The leader landed upon Rob's head standing proudly, grinning at Clump while latching his thumbs high inside his tiny tunic's chest pockets. Before Merlock could intervene, Rob took a belting right palm to his skull from an exasperated Clump, then promptly returned back to his snoring while the cruel Faux flew away in peals of burpy laughter. Clump could barely hear Merlock's tongue-lashing, such was his irritation as he stood dejectedly over the Human hostage. The familiar wet warmth returned, trickling down the back of Clump's neck. He knew the aerial antagonists would never relent in their campaign, until he *made* them. Clump's belly grew white hot as a rising surge of anger that had been forged from an eternity of gnawing frustration built within him. One of the Faux had seen his vast knuckles tighten, but alas, it was too late. In a single movement he turned, leapt upwards and bellowed out a war-cry that delivered an enormous gust of rancid air from the depths of his being, sending chills to all those in ear shot. As several Faux immediately passed out, Clump positioned his mouth so that they fell inside. Crunching down harder than he probably needed to, his sharp black teeth gnashed away in unrestrained satisfaction. Merlock shook his head from sympathy rather than judgement, at the sad yet necessary action Clump had been forced to mete out against his adversaries of old. The remaining thugs were reduced to cinder ash mid-flight by Merlock's arcing wizard-fire. The wizard abhorred the taking of life, but knew in circumstances such as these, without intervention, the vendetta would have escalated to involve a much greater number of casualties, as regrettably vendettas always do. Feeling a mixture of relief and remorse—erring on the relief—Clump carefully picked up Rob, trying to ignore the obvious lump now throbbing on his head.

The weary three entered the murky forest of Whisperun and back to the mind waffle of the roaming dead welcoming their return. But strangely in some small way, the sense of familiarity, no matter how irritating, still afforded them a measure of comfort.

Chapter 5

A jostling mob of noselling Boggles greeted the small party upon their return to Merlock's home. They jumped up at Rob, slumped over Clump's shoulder.

"Shoo, get away, you are supposed to alert me to intruders, not to ourselves you imbecilic meatballs." hissed Merlock.

Clump followed the wizard through the hidden opening and down into his subterranean lair, dolefully rubbing his rump. There were innumerable twists, turns, and long unlit passageways. Without prior knowledge of the layout, an intruder would unquestionably fall foul to one of the many deadly traps that lay in wait. When they had finally reached the living quarters, Clump lowered Rob onto Merlock's bed, watching while Merlock made him comfortable.

"Do you think he will be able to help us?" asked Clump.

"Let's hope so, for Fingle's sake *and* ours, otherwise we will have lost Fingle and likely end up as fertiliser for the King's gurnip fields." replied Merlock scratching his chin, while looking down at their last and only hope snoring his dribble in and out.

*   *   *

Fingle's Trial

Almost a quarter cycle had passed since Fingle had last seen his best friend Clump. Even the shiny tiles had become lacklustre of late. He knew the routine, at the cockcrow each sunup, he was vigorously scrubbed down with lavender soap in a hot tub, while his cell was polished and fragranced. Fingle would feign his usual displeasure by eliciting overly dramatic groans and gripes, all the while ensuring his external features did not betray his inner pleasure. To writhe around in hot soapy bubbles was positively divine, but wearing a mock expression of excruciating torment was critical, torment he so aptly deserved for betraying his own kind...

For betraying his own kind, scoffed Fingle, staring up at a hanging basket of fresh potpourri attached to the bars of his cell window. *When were Goblins ever interested in each other's affairs anyway?* The answer was of course found in the Goblin City itself. The city, the *only* Goblin City, was originally established on a large peninsula jutting out into to the Great Wet, taking full advantage of the lively trade ports and warm southerly winds that made for the highly favourable living and working conditions. As legend dictated, a clan Goblin known as 'Shuffles'—a name coined by his clan members due to his poor eyesight and constant shuffling, while always carrying a large block of stone somewhere—had personally waged a war against the biting winds of the North. Shuffles had taken it solely upon himself to erect a huge stone wall in an attempt to shelter from the disagreeable northerly winds. However, no matter how high or wide he built his wall, he could still feel the cutting breeze taunting him. So he continued to build and never stopped building, until one fateful day he had fallen off the edge of the peninsula and into the Great Wet, ironically weighted down by the final block of stone he would ever carry. Sadly, he was never to be seen shuffling anywhere ever again.

Had he decided to shuffle a little *inwards,* away from the towering outer edge—that he was always building from—at *any* point in time after he had embarked upon his unattainable crusade of lunacy, he would have duly noted the chilly winds would not have reached him at all! So there it was, Shuffles had built a huge wall spanning the entire peninsula where he had lived so many long cycles ago. And as he built, other clan Goblin's had discovered for themselves that the great wall afforded them much in the way of protection from the elements *and* protection from invaders, while harnessing a markedly more agreeable climate from the south. However, of much greater import, this had encouraged the clan Goblins to herd together within a single location and in vast numbers for the first time in the whole of Goblin history.

The increasing trade that flourished around the city's ports, coupled with the promise of great wealth, was just enough distraction to keep them from cutting each other's throats, at least for the most part. Ethical principals were naturally immiscible with Goblin principals, which consisted of maybe one or two at most and rightly so. As such, introducing a judicial system was a complete façade! How could a city heaving with Goblins who knew nothing of morality be expected to thrive within a society that imposed law and order? Regardless, the first legal framework had been implemented not long after the first Goblin council had been formed. The City's reputation had spread far and wide, to all root races across the mainland and far beyond due to its unprecedented citizenry and astonishing success in commerce. As it transpired, Goblins—when the conditions were propitious—made for formidable traders in everything from coffins to coins, of which were both in abundance. In fairness, within a relatively short time, the Goblins that had settled within the city walls had begun to change and for the better, although none would entertain such a notion. They co-existed with some reluctance, unsurprisingly, but conditioned suspicion was replaced quite organically with an elementary form of increasing tolerance. So, if this was indeed the case, then *why* had Fingle been persecuted for advancing just that little bit further? Why shouldn't he be allowed to partake of a cream tea instead of dung-fly soup? Why not be allowed to parade in regal finery, draped in exotic silks imported from beyond the Great Wet, instead of stinking leathers and rusted chain mail? If Goblins were predominately a capricious bunch of dullards and braggarts conforming to a stereotype of their own creation, why did venturing outside of that mouldy mold for the betterment of all brand *him* a traitor to his own kind? On the contrary, Fingle was a keen enthusiast of supporting his kin, a true Goblin philanthropist, forever on the lookout to con, swindle, and cheat his way to the bottom. If Fingle was able to tell you the truth, he would be the first to admit the game was rigged heavily in his favour, as the majority of his reprehensible lowbrow peers had only half a gnat's brain between them at best.

The exception was 'Dingle Dogspit', his arch nemesis. A ribald, rival trader who had spied upon him that inauspicious evening after he had ineptly bolted his window shutters, not quite shut. Less than a quarter candle burn later, the city guards had burst into the living quarters of Fingle's small cargo vessel anchored at port, to discover that Dingle's Daliesque allegations were regrettably well founded. Fingle had been caught green-handed, devouring a sugar dusted pastry and sipping elderflower tar from a delicately ornate clay cup. That alone sent shivers up the malformed spine, but it was the manner in which he lay on his chaise lounge, dressed decadently in silk stockings and a finely embroidered Basque. This was complemented by a towering powdered wig with rouge plastered disturbingly all over his gratified grin. Two of the arresting guards were forced to vomit over-board and for quite some time.

Fingle's thoughts returned once more to his final court hearing due the next full moon and as providence would dictate, upon the exact same day the City was celebrating its 'Build-Wall day', in honour of Shuffles, the late City's founder. Fingle had long given up hope from any attempt at rescue by Clump. He knew that for all of his friend's loyalty, Clump was simply incapable of such a thing. No, he would have to devise a particularly cunning means of escape and Build-Wall day with all of its nauseating pomp and ceremony would make for the perfect cover.

* * *

Rob awoke to hushed conversation nearby. As he lay in a bed of animal skins, fleeting images of recent events flooded his awareness. He sat bolt upright and wished he hadn't. As he cradled his pounding head in his hands, he became aware that the voices had now stopped. In a panic he attempted to get out of bed, but Merlock entered his sleeping chamber, holding up both palms in surrender as he spoke softly.

"Rob, I understand you may be confused and frightened, but rest assured you are quite safe here, but now you must rest."

"Green! Why are you green?" blurted Rob, "Where am I? How did I get here?"

Rob went into shock, Merlock moved in quickly to help.

"Stop—" was all Rob could manage before he threw up.

Clump had been ordered to remain outside for everyone's benefit and was glad he had. While Rob continued retching, Merlock kept reassuring Rob he was in no danger and when he had calmed himself sufficiently, all of his questions would be answered. Looking like a lost child, Rob looked up into Merlock's kind eyes and to his unintentional credit, wearing a queasy appearance that was not entirely incongruent with his captors' complexion. Rob's caution had long been surpassed, replaced by surreal resignation and sheer exhaustion. As Merlock explained their exceptional circumstance, Rob became more respondent. His glazed stupor subsiding, allowing for curiosity to percolate. When Merlock had eventually finished, there was a lengthy pause while the information trickled into his fragile mind. Without warning Rob sniggered, which soon escalated to borderline hysteria. Merlock tentatively chuckled; after all, laughter was a powerful healer and a supreme conqueror of fear. Outside the room Clump grinned, eager to join the merriment and barged open the rattling door.

"Bloody hell!" screamed Rob in unconcealed terror, disappearing beneath the animal skins. "That's…that's the monster that grabbed me from my bedroom." spluttered Rob, quivering from beneath the bedding, adding, "*and* that's the monster that hit me too."

Clump felt genuine remorse for his earlier misjudgement with the taunting Faux, "I'm very sorry, Rob, it was an accident, the Faux kept pissing on us." offered Clump dejectedly.

Rob slowly peered over the animal skins he was holding up. Two long, flat, furry legs hung down from where his head emerged, suggesting a bizarre hybrid experiment and sending the two Goblins into fits of giggles. Rob felt brave enough to protest, but looking down he realised how ridiculous he must have looked.

After a pause, Rob said, "And he was the monster who carried me all night, keeping me warm and safe."

Clump beamed proudly and Rob managed a sober smile for the first time since his abduction, although he knew it would take a considerable while to become fully accustomed to the giant's terrifying grin.

*   *   *

The meaty tendrils had found their way to Clump's snout from the kitchen, where Merlock had been preparing the evening stew for the three of them. They all sat around a large rustic table and ate heartily, sharing knowledge of their worlds. As the grog flowed, so did the remarkable conversation. Rob was amazed in how at ease he now felt within the company of Goblins, *real* Goblins! Similarly, Merlock and Clump's perception of Humans—being a comparatively treacherous and highly dangerous horde of blood thirsty warriors—had been justly placed into serious question by Rob's kindly demeanour and infectious personality. Rob sympathised in Fingle's predicament and with his new found friends. After talking at length, Rob realised their lives were shockingly similar. They all shared commonalities in the demands, fears and hopes that life brought about, regardless of which world they inhabited. He also realised that as insane as it all was, this was *still* an opportunity to prove to his father and to everyone else that he was able to accomplish something meaningful, *heroic* even.

Rob knew enough of law, but was it enough to liberate a condemned Goblin from certain death? He assumed that Goblin law— due to its infancy—must be a little disorganised and that Fingle's prosecution would be poorly prepared, he hoped…

During their incredible discussions, Merlock stopped talking and looked directly at Rob. "Rob, there is something I must ask of you before we can go any further with Fingle's rescue attempt." Merlock leaned in closer, his solemn face lost in shadow, save for his piercing eyes framed by flickering firelight, dancing wickedly around the underground lair. "Rob, in order for this to work, you will need to become…a Goblin…"

Rob sat blinking as his jaw dropped, then howled with laughter, spilling his frothy tankard over the table. Merlock and Clump looked at each other and erupted too.

"And if we get caught stealing Fingle, they will hang us dead too." said Clump wide-eyed, extending his arm then pretending to tighten an invisible rope around his neck.

Rob stopped laughing, until an undignified snort of grog-froth from both nostrils prompted tears of pickled pleasure to stream down their flushed cheeks. All were lost in the moment and quite unable to fathom the critical nature of the mission that lay ahead. The jamboree continued well into the early hours, until tiredness eventually forced sleep upon them all.

Chapter 6

Rob awoke, the lump on his head no longer hurt, but the rest was chiming like a church bell at a royal wedding.

"Oh my sweet Lord..." he groaned, refusing to open his eyes to the invading light.

Stumbling over to where he remembered Merlock's wash bowl had been, he reached in and splashed his face clumsily with cool water. Peeping between his wet fingers he noticed something was wrong, something terribly wrong. His screams awoke Merlock. Clump was already awake and came bounding down the tunnels towards the commotion.

"What's the matter, boy?" asked Merlock, concerned and bleary eyed.

"Green! I'm bloody green! And weird! What have you done to me?" stammered Rob, almost forgetting his headache.

Clearly his addled mind has forgotten the oaths we all took, mused Merlock. In truth, Merlock could not recall ever casting a change-form spell. He thought it best to omit his recklessness, as any oath forged by Grog was *always* a deplorable idea and he should have known better.

After a robust breakfast of cheese, sausage, bread and nuts, the passing of a few hours and Merlock's ceaseless insistence that Rob's transmogrification was completely reversible, *without* any adverse effects, Rob accepted his new, *temporary* appearance. He accepted that remaining in Human form would end his journey in a very abrupt and final way; he had scant choice given the circumstances.

"We have little time to bring you up to speed, young Rob, so we must begin your education immediately. Education in the ways of our kind and also our legal-teas that is if we are to have any chance of freeing Fingle."

Merlock disappeared into a back room. When he returned, he brought in two tomes, one significantly smaller than the other. He placed the largest down with due care and respect. "In this book, you will begin to forge an understanding of what it means to be a Goblin, it is a collection of our entire history as a race. It is known as the 'Gobbledebook'."

He then tossed the other tome—explaining legal-teas—aside with disdain, sending a puff of dust mushrooming upwards, triggering a sneezing fit from Rob. Watching the proceedings Clump sniggered, as Rob's newly acquired and overly generous ear flaps— eminently long for any Goblin—repeatedly slapped the sides of his face, like two belligerent leather chamois.

"Do you think something went wrong with the spell, Merlock? These flaps are awfully long? When did you cast it anyway? Was it last night as I don't remember?"

Merlock grew uncomfortable beneath Rob's glare, impatient for an answer.

"Everything went just fine, the effects of the spell are different for everyone. Now please, let us continue as we have much to do." scolded Merlock, hoping that was the last of the interrogations.

Casting his suspicions aside, Rob regained his composure. He realised that passing for a Goblin may prove to be a greater feat than succeeding in court. Fortunately after a quick perusal, it appeared Goblin law was lacking in anything particularly law-like. *This may be to my advantage,* he hoped. "Merlock, are there any other legal systems for any other race that you know of?" enquired Rob.

"I don't believe so, only the *laws of the land*. Generally speaking, most races respect one another and respect the land, but if a race, creature, or individual upsets that balance, then higher forces come into play and folk get what's coming to them."

Rob nodded and continued, "Is it commonly known that Goblin law is modelled upon Human law?"

"Yes of course. It's widely known the only other race we have knowledge of that co-exist in vast numbers *and* have a proclivity for brutality and violence—particularly amongst themselves—is indeed the Human race. We recognise that this is why Humans require a legal framework, for their own survival. The Goblin council adopted a similar, loosely based system within the Goblin City." replied Merlock, wondering where Rob was leading his line of enquiry.

"Okay, Merlock, we all accept I am not the man you wanted. You wanted my father, the great Robert Swindlar, the incredibly successful legal luminary. But in fairness, I like to think I have acquired no small amount of knowledge in this arena. Four years of laborious study and twenty two years of living in my father's shadow does not account for nothing!" enthused Rob, extending aloft his avocado finger for emphasis.

"And it's quite possible your father would not have adapted to this rather unique situation as well as you have?" offered the old wizard, his eye's twinkling playfully.

Rob laughed aloud, imagining his father as a Goblin, realising this was *his* golden opportunity to shine, to prove he could be his own success. Meanwhile, Clump wandered off while the others were engrossed in important matters. Clump was feeling hopeful. Like Rob, he had also been given an opportunity, to prove to Fingle that he could do something without his guidance, or more often than not, his orders.

* * *

After several weeks had passed, Rob's adjustment had not been entirely without incident. There was the time he had strayed a little too far into the forest alone and encountered a bevy of Truth-Trolls. Fortunately for him, his cover was not blown as they had only gotten as far as to ask him his name. As Rob was utterly compelled to tell the truth—as such was the charm that Truth-Trolls held over anyone—he could only answer to *Robin Swindlar*. Rob's answer was sufficient enough to allay any further questioning, as the Trolls were completely beside themselves, unable to imagine who could be as callous as to call their offspring by such a thing. Although it had to be said, by Goblin standards it captured the true essence of all Goblin aspiration.

And then there was the unfortunate incident he incurred while out foraging. The whispering dead had pounced and proceeded to diminish Rob's annoying optimism to a melancholy so deeply entrenched, that by the time Merlock had rescued him, it took four whole days before he could manage a spurtive quarter smile, despite Clump's best efforts of juggling noselling Boggles, badly. Ironically, his recovery had been largely impeded by Clump's inept juggling, causing a full Boggle transformation to occur after it had managed to escape its muzzle. Merlock then re-rescued Rob after happening upon Clump and the Boggle debating the taxonomy of differing shades of grey, while Rob wept, rocking back and forth.

The departure day for the great Goblin City had arrived much sooner than they would have liked. Rob was satisfied he had absorbed enough information to survive in court, providing he followed every statement with 'my lord' and adhered to the bizarre court rituals, he felt able to present his argument with some success. Should all else fail they always had a plan 'B' to fall back on, nonetheless, Rob had prayed in earnest every single night since his learning of the contingency, that it would never, ever come to pass.

After packing all they would need for several days travel, Merlock cast a boundary spell around his home, before the brave, determined band of heroes set off. Clump was dressed in his battle tunic, with his heavy shield and axe slung over his broad back, while Merlock wore a satchel and carried his yew staff. Rob turned around as sonorous trumpet calls from the guardian gobbets bade them farewell. He took in a deep breath and ventured forth to meet his fate. Had Rob looked behind a second time, he may have caught sight of a small winged creature emerging unsteadily from the concealed chimney, flying up into the tree canopy heading north. Smidge had managed to keep his presence unknown ever since he had first found himself in a bag the giant had been carrying. He recalled several weeks ago when a repugnant blast of fetid air from the giant's mouth had caused him to fall into Clump's backpack. He remembered peering over the drawstring, helpless as he watched his beloved Faux clansmen vaporised by the wizard's magick. He made a vow upon that day that he would seek his vengeance against these disgusting barbarians. As Clump had returned to pick up his bag, Smidge had buried down deeper, where he would bide his time. He would hatch a plan so contemptible, they would be begging for mercy, but only after he had found where they kept their grog first. Merlock had become so preoccupied with Rob's tutelage over the passing weeks, that he was unaware of little Smidge's presence, or if he had known, he had sensed no danger in it. Why should he? As far as he was aware, the only Faux that were of any real threat had all been dealt with near the marshes that fateful day. In truth, Smidge knew he would struggle to enlist the help he needed for his retribution and considered cutting his losses after a good drink. But upon the first night at Merlock's place, Smidge had borne witness to a dreadful and dark magick, a magick that was strictly forbidden within the Kingdom. He had seen a repulsive Human...transmogrify into a Goblin *with* unnatural earflaps! This had provided the perfect leverage he would need to convince the shadow Goblin government to hunt them all down and destroy them slowly. So, Smidge had stayed hidden, watching, listening—boozing when possible—and was further astounded to learn of a scandalous plot to free Fingle, another usurper! After the Goblin impostor and co-conspirators' had left for the Goblin City, Smidge had left for the Goblin council. The Goblin council was located to the south within the Goblin City itself, but he knew of another Goblin council. A dark and powerful entity from which all decisions were really made and he felt assured they would mete out the punishment he craved, free from trial and more importantly free from mercy.

*   *   *

The brave trio avoided the main thoroughfares since leaving Whisperun Forest, opting to travel over fields and woodland, in favour of sleeping outside at night within the cover of trees opposed to busy Inns and the problems they create. Rob's transformation was convincing enough, but his behaviour was still highly unpredictable, impeded by the excessive frequency of ethical choices he made. After a final night of mild discomfort and broken sleep, they awoke with the sunrise and pressed onwards. It was still morning when they at long last reached an opening in the trees. Stretched out below them stood the vast Goblin City, bathed in amber-gold from the early sun. Rob gasped at its enormity. Beyond the City, the warm southern waters of the Great Wet spanned the horizon, its enticing sapphire waters shimmering; crammed full with commercial sea vessels of infinite variety.

"It's incredible…" murmured Rob, awestruck.

"Yes, yes it is. Our crowning glory. Something that was once considered impossible and yet against all opposition, has been made manifest. What say ye now naysayers?" said Merlock proudly.

"Pies." said Clump rubbing his belly, confused at Rob and Merlock's laughter.

They began the long and winding descent towards the noise of the outer city ghettos. Rob heard the vigorous clanging of anvils—accompanied with its leathery scent of singed hooves—complaining livestock, hungry babies, heated bartering and drunken disputes scattered throughout. It was a sprawling hive of dubious activity. The buildings did not conform to any specific style, shape, or size and everything was jammed tightly together, cracked by misshapen streets and innumerable shadowy alleyways. This was a Goblin shanty town. It had developed outside of the City walls to encircle it as far as the land would allow. The Goblins looked mean and hungry, Rob could see why they were kept outside but held genuine pity for them, reminding him of the problems his own society still faced. Rob stared up at the colossal stone wall as they approached the City's main gates.

"Remember, let me do the talking." whispered Merlock as the city guards blocked their passage.

"Halt!" screamed the central guard, his spiked helmet—which was ridiculously oversized—wobbling from side to side.

"State your business and code." he yelled, constantly adjusting his head-dress.

Merlock stepped forwards holding both arms out in front, palms facing upwards. The guard placed a tattered wooden box on Merlock's hands, which had been fashioned to resemble a large block of stone. As the wizard spoke, he respectfully shuffled his feet on the spot.

"We wish to enter, to leg-alley represent a prisoner of the City in the Grand Court tomorrow, his name is Fingle Froglick. My code is to the Great Goblin Council, the Goblin elders, the Rule of Three and to the mystery of the Never-ending Sky Spiral. I pledge my life and coin-bag on my vow. If I utter a falsehood, then may my gold be stolen, my eyes plucked and my giggleberries squished by a rockstomper."

With the introduction and oath proclaimed, Merlock returned the wooden block and shuffled backwards solemnly. The diminutive guard marched forwards and stood to attention, propelling his helmet over his eyes this time.

"You have stated your business and sworn your oath as witnessed by us, the City-guard."

He turned about—almost collapsing under the weight of his ill-fitting armour—then shouted, "Open the City gates!"

Nothing seemed to happen. Rob looked at Merlock, the wizard shrugged. Rob looked at the angry little guard who looked back at Rob, then back towards the gates.

"Open the fracking gates!" he screamed louder, yet still nothing happened.

The other guards did not look particularly interested by his crotchety commands. One casually polished his dagger by spitting on it, far more than was necessary. Two others were playing a game that consisted of throwing unmarked stones at more unmarked stones, while a fourth was suspiciously slumped against the wall with a shoddily concealed bottle beside him. Trying to appear professional, the Chief guard half marched, half jogged over to the enormous gates and began hammering his fists against them, which had absolutely no other effect than bruising his hands and disputing his authority further.

"Hmmm, they don't seem much organised here do they?" commented Clump, watching the guard stab and slash at the wooden gates with his sword.

Eventually the gates creaked loudly. The guard stiffened and tried to limp away, but his cumbersome armour had betrayed him. The gates, which didn't open outward as one would expect, came crashing downwards as a drawbridge would.

"Change the guard." advised one of the apathetic armoured Goblins.

As the trio were finally escorted into the magnificent Goblin City, the gates were noisily raised again. Rob looked over his shoulder to see the twitching guard was still alive and gurgling angrily, until a drunken gate sentry conveniently let slip the chains that raised the enormous gate. The deafening impact included a closing yelp.

Through clouds of swirling dust, the grinning sentry looked at Rob, "Oops!" he hiccupped, winked, then took an appallingly obvious swig of grog from behind his shield.

Upon entering, the noise, smells and sights immediately assailed them. The buildings were surprisingly elaborate and well built. In sympathy to the shanty town architecture, the construction this side of the wall was also tremendously varied, but considerably grander with permanence as a constant in the overall design. Beyond the main streets, the lesser, narrower avenues were noticeably more modest as most cities often were. In the far distance, reaching high above the rest of the City, stood a central series of towers shining brightly, plated lavishly with gold. Rob smirked, half expecting a Faerie princess and her cohorts of animated characters to appear from the balcony windows, singing some awful song to camera-snapping tourists at regular intervals—if Rob were to wait until dusk, he would have seen droves of opportunistic gold-drunk Goblins, forcibly being removed by the City guards. Excitement rippled throughout the teeming streets as thousands of Goblins prepared for Build-Wall day, where the festivities were to begin at next dawn. As providence would dictate, the exact same day as Fingle's trial…

*   *   *

Fingle stretched out upon his luxurious prison bed gazing upwards. He was as prepared as he would ever be. The brightly coloured feathers were thankfully easier to obtain than he had originally thought. No one had noticed him secreting them away inside his sumptuous mattress—already stuffed generously with goose-down. He knew precisely when to strike. After the farce of his trial had concluded, he would be led back to his cell, upon which a traditional 'last grog' would be offered for those facing the penalty of death. This would be his only opportunity to break out and head towards the lesser guarded rear entrance to the courts, on account of a skeleton crew on shift during Build-Wall day. Fingle maintained a reasonable amount of confidence and consolation in knowing the success of his escape plan relied crucially upon the idiocy of his fellow Goblins and allowed himself a satisfied smile. As the intoxicating filaments of sleep entwined about him, he snuggled deeper into the prison bed's decadent cosiness.

Chapter 7

Merlock led the way to the Courthouse entrance as Rob wrestled with the rising surge of apprehension by convincing himself he stood out as an impostor.

"Calm yourself, lad." Merlock reassured, patting his arm.

Rob nodded, drawing in deep relaxing breaths, until he saw a bloated Goblin swinging from the gallows outside the front of the building.

"Bloody hell! What did he do?"

"Ah yes, that's Gimple Fleablotch. Nice fellow, shame about the crime, was caught stealing moss."

"Moss! Did you say moss?"

"Well, he actually stole one of those statues out front. Nothing wrong with that of course, but he failed to see the moss on it. If something has moss growing upon it, it is technically un-pinchable. However, if Gimple *had* seen the moss, he could have scraped it off and his life would have taken a very different turn. But sadly he didn't. For any object to have moss upon it implies it has stood 'un-pinched' for quite some time, therefore it cannot be stolen and must no longer be considered in *thefting* circles," Merlock walked Rob away from the harrowing scene and continued, "it is no exaggeration to say that any object without moss can theoretically be in the possession of every Goblin that has ever existed and will ever exist. This cycle will proudly continue until the object is either lost, damaged beyond repair, or—"

"Grows moss on it, yes I get it. So are you telling me this poor soul was hung because of moss?"

"Goodness no. Whatever gave you that idea? He was hung because he'd killed his seventh Gawk."

"Gawk…?"

"Forgive me, Rob, we didn't cover this did we? For all lesser crimes such as Gimple's mossy statue robbery, you are allowed to leave the court until the day of trial, but only on the condition of taking a Gawk with you. A Gawk is an unusual creature. I suppose it resembles an upside down broom, but the body is wider and taller and the head is not as wide as a broom-head. In fact, forget the broom analogy. All you need to know about a Gawk is that it follows you *everywhere*, standing only a Faerie's fart from your face." the wizard ushered Rob to the courthouse steps and proceeded to climb and educate. "The court enlist Gawks, because they remember every single thing they see and hear, their memories are phenomenal. The court then interviews the Gawks regularly to see if the accused has breached their bail conditions, while a fresh Gawk is reassigned to those still out on bail. From what I recall of Gimple Fleablotch, he was a highly disrespected burglar with a bright future, but like many of the great career criminals, the Gawks had simply got the better of him and after killing seven of them, Gimple's punishment had increased from the rack to the rope. Having a Gawk breathing in your face for several cycles is not something I would ever wish for, particularly as a Gawk's breath reeks of honesty and integrity. Such an unnecessary waste of life and innate talent."

"Hmmm, don't you think this whole moss growing thing is, well, just a bit silly, Merlock?"

"Not at all. Over the short time I have known you, you have *grown* on me. I wouldn't want to have you stolen away from me, would I?"

After entering the main entrance, Merlock told Clump to sit in the waiting area while he and Rob made their way to the front desk. A steely clerk sitting above a considerably higher platform stared down at the pair before speaking.

"What is your business?" he said quietly, allowing his razor edged teeth to partake in his sneer.

"We represent Council for Fingle Froglick during tomorrow's try-all." replied Merlock authoritatively.

The clerk's black eyes narrowed, "Name?"

"I bring Defence Councillor, Robin Swindlar." said Merlock, with a hint of defiance.

The clerk's gaze slid over to Rob, burning into his resolve. Rob sensed small beads of perspiration erupt all over his face and was genuinely grateful for his kale complexion, concealing what would have otherwise resembled a heavily spanked baboon's backside.

"You *do* realise the gravity of his crimes?" warned the clerk, looming closer.

"Yes, of course he does!" snapped Merlock impatiently.

The clerk's stare never left Rob as he spoke, "Your Councillor can surely speak for himself?"

Rob felt like bolting, as the room slowly devoured his trembling body. His vision clouded over until all that remained were those interrogative onyx cracks that seized his own. Had he reached this far only to fail? What would happen to him and his new found friends? What of Fingle's fate? His thoughts raced to his father, he realised just how much he needed his help, needed him, missed him. What would his father do?

Rob stiffened, cleared his throat and noted the intimidating clerk's name tag.

"Hear me well, Throttlebottom. I am fully aware of Fingle Froglick's *alleged* crimes. I am also fully aware of the manner in which he is being mistreated and you may rest assured that this Court *will* find Fingle Froglick absolved from all charges and leave a free maaaa—, Goblin tomorrow!"

Merlock's relief was palpable and the clerk sat back looking significantly less smug, "Very well, Lawyer, I will require you to sign forms A2, B2, B3, C6, C6a, B2b, B and D2aand 3b/3c respectively. Go to the third door down the corridor on the left and approach the clerk there. He will provide you with the case file, for what it's worth." balked the clerk, refusing to look up any further while he scribbled fastidiously with his squeaky quill.

As they both turned away from the front desk, they exhaled a huge sigh of relief.

"Did you hear that, Merlock? He called me a *lawyer*."

"Quiet, you fool. Now start acting like one."

"A fool, lawyer, or Goblin?"

"A *lawyer*. Although I concede there is very little difference…"

After three excruciating hours of mind-mincing paperwork, interspersed with painfully prolonged periods of waiting—presumably to allow for the gallons of ink to dry—they were finally free to go on their way. Rob had been handed a huge case file to pick apart with less than twenty four hours to prepare Fingle's defence, leaving him disheartened and doubtful.

"Don't look so glum, Rob," said Merlock, as they left the oppressive Courthouse, "have a little faith in yourself, after all, you *really* fooled them and let's not forget, we always have plan 'B'."

"That's what worries me." groaned Rob, as the others cheered a mock victory.

"I will look for a quiet place to stay tonight. Clump, can you see to it that Rob has a good meal, where do you propose?"

Clump thought hard, then eagerly replied, "Pye Shoppe, on Hepy Titus Street."

"Ah yes, I know it well, who doesn't? I will see you both there in less than a Boggle's bugle and remember boys, *please* keep your cons-sealed." Merlock pulled his cowl over his head, then vanished into the long shadows staining the tangled streets as light rapidly renounced the day against his best efforts.

* * *

This looks pleasant enough, thought Rob as they approached the Pye Shoppe. It reminded him of those old Victorian Christmas cards displaying shops in wintry towns, casting their warm inner glow through opaque, snow dusted windows and onto the busy cobbled streets outside, humming with excited shoppers and horse drawn carriages. Before Rob could warn Clump, the doorbells familiar discordant clangs danced upon the giant's mottled dome, synonymous to an obsessive bell swingers' therapy group left unsupervised. Cursing aloud, Clump opened the door a little too enthusiastically, sending two nearby sozzled Goblins to become obscenely intimate with the crumbling stucco on the far right wall.

"The usual, Clump? Same for your friend?" shouted Maw Wallop.

Clump nodded, then led Rob over to his table. Rob sat down and looked around, utterly dumbstruck. The noise was deafening and the smell putrefying, but the behaviour! *My God,* he thought and *this is their interpretation of progress? A fully armed riot squad would have been ill equipped to deal with this tawdry bunch*. His Christmas card image quickly devolved into photographic evidence for a colossal crime scene. Clump was happy to wait while Rob ploughed through the large stack of case papers. In fact, he was in his happiest of happy places, with a meat pie in one hand and a large tankard of frothy grog in the other. The pair had become so preoccupied in their endeavours that they had failed to notice a table of murderous looking Goblins which had been watching them intently ever since they had first arrived. Rob looked up at Clump and after waiting to be seen between two vast pistons pumping up and down towards the goliath's jaws, he finally caught Clump's attention—for what it was worth.

"Clump, have you ever heard the name Sly Slaughter?"

Clump paused for thought and in doing so, neglected to close his heavily laden mouth. As time passed—painfully—a small puddle of partially chomped pie had built upon itself between his propped up elbows. Rob was forced to look away, the stink hole he was in had already weakened what he had initially thought of as an iron constitution. Rob tentatively returned to face him after he finally heard Clump issue a gargled grunt from his slack jaw while shaking his head—encouraging the increasing mound of congealing mouth matter to expand its foamy colony in an easterly and westerly direction beneath him.

Trying to ignore the spumy spillage, Rob held up a file, "What about this symbol, it's stamped next to his name every time?"

The symbol consisted of three circles, all with a single dot in their centres. One circle was larger than the others and all three were all grouped tightly together.

Once again Clump had intimated much the same, but thoughtfully added, "Slibber-sauce?"

Feeling quite unsettled, Rob declined the offer while Clump continued to devour his sixth pie and eighth grog with extreme prejudice. While poring over the remaining paperwork, Rob realised Fingle was going to be made an example of in court. Rob also knew the preposterously diverging evidence provided by key witnesses' was downright slanderous. They had even denied Fingle his own statement, stating that he had 'forfeited the right due to his treasonous crimes'. This comment was signed by 'Sly Slaughter'. *That name again?* thought Rob and with that same peculiar stamped symbol. Rob shuddered as plan 'B' was fast becoming a reality. He would give it his best shot; he had little choice either way. He was not only fighting to keep Fingle alive, he would also be fighting for his own life. Rob resigned himself to whatever fate had in store and glugged down the rest of his grog.

"That's more like it." praised Clump.

Rob grinned, "Another?"

* * *

"Crom! What's the time?" shrieked Merlock, jumping off the creaking bed. The warmth of the crackling fire he had prepared for their return had unfortunately gotten the better of him. Judging by the glowing embers and two and a half notches missing from the bedside candle, he was terribly late in meeting the boys. After tugging on his warm boots he had left by the fireside, he pulled over his heavy cowl and left the warmth of the Inn, shivering his way through the crisp night air.

When Merlock arrived outside the Pye Shoppe, he recognised Rob's voice instantly, only it was singing and in a very peculiar way. He pushed open the door to find the crowd cheering for Rob while he sat on his knees plucking away at some imaginary object and singing loudly, "*I was born, born to be wild, never climbed so high, never gonna dieeeeee, born to be wiiiiillld*!"

Although unusual to witness, Merlock couldn't deny it was an infectious melody. Everyone applauded, including

Clump who saw Merlock enter and eagerly beckoned him over to his table. Clump frowned as Merlock pointed frantically behind him. One of the hostile Goblin's that had been glaring at the pair all night had sensed his opportunity, racing full tilt towards Clump holding a knife. He vaulted onto the table to leap onto Clump's back but had failed to factor in the coagulated pie dribble that Clump had amassed, causing his foothold to swerve away aggressively. The stunned Goblin crashed heavily upon the table and careened into Clump's concrete legs, then slumped at his feet groaning pathetically. Clump turned and looked downwards at the crumpled heap. Before he could respond; a further two Goblins launched towards him like a pair of rabid snarlers. Clump raised both hands and caught them spectacularly by their throats mid-flight. Merlock forced his way through the drunken horde and dragged Rob away from his heckling audience. Merlock knew Clump was more than capable in a bar brawl and felt genuine pity upon those foolish enough to try and best him. Rob however, was no match and barely able to stand.

Clump looked blankly at the two pairs of bulging eyes before bringing them together with a satisfying scrunch. The spent opportunists' joined their fallen comrade at Clump's feet. As a further five assailants were hesitantly poised to join the attack, Clump snatched up his grog and drank unhurriedly, eyeing up the growling Goblins as he did so. When he had finished, he brought his tankard down so violently, that the robust wooden table practically disintegrated into a shower of splinters. He glowered at his quarry and in well-oiled fashion, his eyes narrowed, his colossal shoulders rounded and his mighty jaws tightened as a terrifying sneer stretched taught across his maddening face.

"Rob, are you okay?" asked Merlock, concerned.

The fresh night air violated Rob's lungs, punishing him for his overindulgence. Grimacing, he managed back a tentative nod, aware the slightest of movements were sending his head and belly into a spin. "Where ish Clump?" slurred Rob, trying to maintain his focus upon the middle Merlock in a kaleidoscope of troubled wizards.

"Oh, he's just fooling around, you know Clump. Simple Goblin, simple pleasures."

A loud shatter announced the arrival of an unconscious airborne Goblin, eventually crashing against the cobbled stones not three feet from Merlock amidst a shower of broken glass, bringing with it the boisterous clamour from inside the shop. Squinting, Rob appraised the casualty, concentrating his wavering focus on the meat pie stuffed grotesquely into its mouth. The expunged Goblin appeared to look directly at him from an eye that hung perilously loose from its fractured socket. Rob retched violently while Merlock rubbed his arching back, muttering something unfavourable regarding Clump. Two more bodies were flung into the street, somehow knotted together in a manner that limbs should never be able to achieve. Merlock knew they could not present much of a case for Fingle's defence if they were thrown into an adjoining cell, so reluctantly he left Rob and ventured back inside to fetch Clump, while stepping warily around the increasing carnage.

"Psst! Psst! Look up you disgusting Human."

Somewhere within Rob's befuddled mind the word 'Human' was sufficient enough to set muted alarm bells ringing. Rob looked up unsteadily and gazed upon a small fluttering object.

"Listen to me very carefully; you and your friends will be arrested tomorrow. You will be taken to the Fortress of Eternal Darkness and tortured mercilessly. It is my entire fault and I am sorry, but you had killed my clan and I sought revenge." confessed Smidge solemnly.

Rob hazily recalled being attacked by the Faux several weeks ago outside the marshes and assumed the matter ended there.

Smidge could see confusion upon Rob's fizzled features, "Listen to me you aborted dump, they know everything, they know who you *really* are. This isn't about revenge or you being a Stinky-Pink, or even about Fingle's release. After I had asked the Shadow Goblin Government to kill you, they agreed and then sent me on my way, only I didn't leave straight away. While sneaking around searching out a little liquid livener, I overheard a terrible plot, such a fiendish and dreadful scheme created by the Shadow Goblin Government that involves *both* of our worlds!"

Rob sobered, despite his throbbing head and turbulent stomach. He managed to sit upright, oblivious to the cold wet stone beneath him, "What plot? *Who* is doing this?" he stammered, desperately trying to regain his faculties.

"The plot involves bridging the three peaks, look for the three peaks and you will know your enemy. But first you must send urgent word to Buttercup, only she has the power—"

Before Smidge could finish, somebody yelled, "Watch out!"

They had just enough time to duck, as a large ball of green fire seared the air between them and exploded violently against a nearby wall, scorching it black.

Immediately from inside the Pye Shoppe, Merlock had sensed the use of dark magick and spun around to see Rob shielding his face amidst a burst of blazing emerald sparks. "Clump, move!" yelled Merlock.

Clump quickly scanned the shop. The only Goblins trying not to claw an escape from Clump, were the two dozen or so littered around his feet, feet which hadn't once moved from where he first stood. The giant reeled around; the look on Merlock's face had said enough. The remaining customers frantically parted the way as Merlock and Clump bounded from the shop—the doorbell sadly resounding its final chime before it was wrenched free, plopping inelegantly into a nearby tankard—and back out, into Hepi Titus Street, where Rob was managing to raise himself back onto his wobbly legs.

"Rob!" screamed Merlock, sensing a further use of unlawful dark enchantment about to be released.

Clump leapt forwards, snatching Rob out of the line of fire as a second fireball narrowly missed the pair. Clump held Rob behind him, then using his other arm, reached behind his back unfastening his battle shield with deadly speed and launched it into the shadows, while Rob threw up over Clump's feet. Clump stared downwards while Rob returned an idiotic grin by way of an apology. A black robed body fell from within the shadows, while its bearded head rolled awkwardly towards a grateful pack of emaciated snarlers, wasting no time with formalities. Rob felt his stomach churn again, but managed to compose himself after Clump raised a cautionary eyebrow. Merlock ran over and bent down, attempting to identify the dark magician's body.

"Do you know him?" Clump called over.

"Not the easiest of tasks, Clump, particularly when the facial features are missing." criticised Merlock. He searched the garments and found nothing as he had expected. He was about to leave when he noticed an emblem. It was embroidered upon the magi's robe, consisting of three silver circles each with a dot in the centre. It was identical to the stamp mark in Fingle's case file.

"Thanks for warning me, I would have been burnt toast." slurred Rob, giggling nervously.

"I only warned you the second time. Someone else must have helped you." replied Merlock puzzled.

In the distance clanging bells were heard.

"Clump, the City Guard are on their way and we cannot be caught, we must move now, quickly follow me."

Clump dragged Rob away, disappearing down a dark alley in pursuit of Merlock. Rob had just enough time to look around at the scene they had left. He wondered if the Faux was still alive, but could see no sign of him. The Pye Shoppe was in total disarray. The front of the premises now lent to a more alfresco charm and the in-fighting had heartily continued between the remaining Goblins, never wishing to waste an opportunity. For when the scent of blood was high upon them, Goblins *always* succumbed to fighting, they simply couldn't help themselves. The only Goblin Rob could see that was still conscious and *not* fighting, was an elderly customer with a look of permanent shock etched across his weathered face. He sat hiccupping against the broken doorway holding an empty tankard and with each hiccup a faint chime would follow. As they fled from the scene, a second cloaked figure emerged from the shadows to follow them, taking great care to remain undetected.

Fortunately, the distance between the Pye Shoppe and the Inn they were staying was sufficient enough to be unconcerned with any repercussions from their nocturnal activities. As they entered, the innkeeper inspected them over his fizzling tankard and nodded gracelessly. Clump helped Rob up the stairs, while Merlock opened the door. Rob immediately fell through and plunged onto his bed. As Merlock pulled off his boots, Rob made a feeble attempt to sit upright, but utterly exhausted, fell back upon the straw mattress. In a series of broken slurs, he tried desperately to impart Smidge's warning of the insidious plot and how they had to find someone called Buttercup, but the warm enticing glow and gentle sputter from the fire's embers prevailed. Promptly, Rob slid into a deep slumber, snoring unashamedly loudly.

Chapter 8

Clump burst through the door clutching a huge block of hollowed out wood fashioned to resemble stone. He shuffled into the room grinning inanely, "Happy Build-Wall day!" he boomed.

Rob buried his pounding skull beneath his straw stuffed pillows. Clump put down the block reverently and opened the curtains wide, instantly the room sang with light. Rob threw a pillow towards Clump, stirring up dust motes that danced between the lancing rays of the sun. There was no escape from the rawness beyond the confines of his aching skull, so Rob resigned to crawl out and face it like a Goblin. Outside their window, a confusing jumble of sounds assaulted Rob. In every direction, Goblins young and old were seen running and shuffling around in preparation for the day's festivities. Merlock also shuffled into the room, struggling with a teetering plate, stacked high with greasy hog bacon—still spitting and sizzling—with large chunks of fresh bread slathered in rich salty butter. Rob retreated beneath his scratchy pillow to hide from the intense meaty aroma and mocking laughter.

*　*　*

Merlock was reasonably confident they would not be recognised from the previous night's events as they wandered through the lively streets towards the courthouse. Clump had all but forgotten about his Pye Shoppe shenanigans, devoting a far greater interest in the colourful decorations hanging from buildings and lining the streets. Everyone was high spirited; giggling whelps weaved between their joyous parents, who sang in cheer and made merry. Rob's thoughts however, were preoccupied with the case. Everything else was numb and distant, until he approached a pack of hungry snarlers feuding over a heavily gnawed mandible. The unsettling spectacle instantly triggering fractured images that replayed from the previous night. Rob's apprehension increased as they neared the courthouse. It hadn't helped that their progress was continually hampered by half of the City shuffling around, carrying absurd wooden blocks. He couldn't shake off the nagging notion there was something terribly important he had to remember.

"Rob, will you be alright in there?" asked Merlock.

Rob snapped towards the watchful wizard and nodded unconvincingly. As they turned into Lostleg Street, they were ill prepared for what awaited them. In front of the daunting courthouse, scores of jeering Goblins waited impatiently, eager to witness the full clout their justice system could impose upon a traitor. The court's guards struggled to maintain the pandemonium and almost collapsed beneath the jostling crowd when Fingle's defence attorney was seen to arrive—during a trial this scandalous, extra troops from the city guard would normally have been drafted in to maintain the decorum, but they were already stretched to their limits during the capital's primary day of celebration.

Rob began to perspire, his mouth feeling as dry as if he'd sucked a salted sponge to dust. Merlock held his arm and instantly Rob felt his courage return as a strange heat arose from within. He looked down at Merlock puzzlingly, the wizard smiled back warmly. Clump strode boldly to the front and stared down the unruly assembly, wisely they responded. As they climbed the steps and passed through the imposing doors, Rob managed in a sarcastic tone, "I never knew Fingle was so popular."

Merlock added, "Fingle, is the most devious, cunning, and downright mendacious Goblin you will ever meet, that is why he is this City's most successful and notorious tradesgoblin."

As the heavy doors slammed shut behind them, the crowds continued to shout and push against it. Rob dearly hoped the ageing timber would withstand the barrage. A clerk guided them to a waiting room by way of extending a highly polished cane in the appropriate direction. He was taller in stature than most Goblins and as thin as a winter's twig. Bowing in questionable solemnity, he looked in very real danger of snapping.

"I presume you are here to represent Fingle Froglick?"

Rob nodded.

"In that case, remain here until the Court is available. Do familiarise yourselves with the Court's etiquette. I will summon you when the Judge is ready."

The angular clerk handed them a well-thumbed list of court rules, then wheeled about to saunter down a dark corridor. They opened the first page of many, Rob's eyes widened.

"Is this a joke?"

1 - Everyone is guilty one way or another, do not expect you are any different. If you do presume otherwise, then you are guilty of breaking rule number one, ergo guilty!

2 – You are limited to throwing soft to firm inanimate *or* animate objects from the above goblic gallery. If the animate object is a Goblin, then he/she must be a full grown, not a whelp—preferably a small elderly one that does not contribute much and is less to scrape up.

3 – By sitting in the goblic gallery, you have submitted your agreement to be thrown by either the general goblic *or* by the Court staff. Please see rule number two for further details.

Before Rob could read past the first page the clerk re-appeared from the gloom, "Please follow me, the Court is now ready." he said authoritatively.

They followed him down the musty corridor, until he stopped at a set of double doors displaying a depiction of smiling Goblins sitting on chairs, holding what might have been vegetables.

"This is the entrance to the goblic gallery, if you are not representing the accused please enter."

The wizard took Rob's hands, "Well, this is it, Rob. I wish you the best of luck, my boy and whatever happens from this point onwards, I just want to tell you, to say how much…"

Rob swallowed as Merlock struggled. Merlock had been like family since his arrival. He realised in that singular moment that love was truly universal, bound not by time, place, colour, or smell.

He choked his reply, "Hey, we always have plan 'B'."

Merlock smiled, then walked through the swinging doors wiping his eyes.

"Good luck, Rob." offered Clump.

As Rob turned, he caught his breath as their eyes met. Clump held such a gaze of honest warmth, he felt as though they had become like brothers. Without warning, Clump picked him up and hugged him tightly, "Save Fingle please…" whispered the giant.

Rob nodded frantically as he fought to breathe, hearing several vertebrae realign. After he released him, Clump followed Merlock up the stairs. The clerk, not immune to such open displays of genuine affection pivoted around, croakily summoning Rob to the Court's main entrance.

"Are you ready, Defence?"

"Yes, I think so."

"I shouldn't say this, Lawyer, but good luck. Fingle and I, well, we have very similar tastes, a certain proclivity for the finer things you understand." sniffed the clerk, plucking a delicately embroidered handkerchief from his cuff and dabbing it against his eyes—eyes which had the tendency of appearing closed at all times on account of his eminently upturned nose that cut through the air like a predatory shark fin.

The clerk rapped surprisingly hard three times against the large wooden doors using the gilded hilt of his slender black cane—which could have been easily mistaken for any one of his limbs—then bowed gracefully as the doors creaked open. It was the first and hopefully last time Rob would *ever* taste rotten wrangleroot! Unbeknown to him, the gallery had been waiting to express their pent-up outrage. Why hadn't he been warned? In retrospect, he should have taken the courtroom rules more seriously. As Rob tried to avoid another face full, he slipped upon a spoiled coliweed and dropped his paperwork, becoming sodden with sour dingleberries and decaying gurnips. *Ah well,* he thought, *I didn't have much prepared anyway.*

Rob scooped up what he could and battled his way to the defence bench amidst an onslaught of organic missiles. Rob managed to steal an upwards glance, the gallery was packed to the rafters with heckling Goblins, baying for justice and intent on perfecting their aim.

"Not you as well," shouted Rob, shaking his soggy head in despair while Clump held aloft an entire harvest of decomposing vegetation. Merlock slapped Clump, causing him to release his noxious bounty on those unfortunate enough to be seated below.

"Order, order, order in the Court!" screamed the Clerk, his face blotchy with the alarming level of volume he accomplished.

With harmony marginally restored, he straightened himself, "Please be upstanding for the Judge." Raising his cane high, he brought it down forcefully against the floor.

The door to the Judge's chamber opened while a fanfare was being crucified, heralding the attending V.I.G. An enormous Goblin squeezed his generous midriff through the doorway and despite a gouty limp, swaggered over to his bench as two grovelling Goblins offered their tilted heads for support while he waddled up the steps. After collapsing into his protesting chair, he raised a gleaming brass monocle to his bulbous left eye and surveyed his Court menacingly, rasping loudly after the strenuous climb. Rob looked in horror at his adversary; he resembled an enormous asthmatic bull frog with proptosis, which served only to amplify his murderous agenda.

"Would the Defence and Prosecution approach the bench." commanded the Judge with a notably nasal timbre.

Rob stood—wiping away the remaining lumps of perishables from his hair and case file—then walked towards the bench in a professional manner, the prosecution did the same. As previously instructed, he avoided all eye contact with the Judge and remained looking down at the floorboards as he stepped closer. The short distance seemed to take an inordinate amount of time, until eventually he was ordered to halt.

"You may now look upon your Judge…"

Rob didn't want to; he was facing a nightmare, a nightmare that held his life in its sweaty fat palm. As he raised his head, his vision anchored instantly to a grossly enlarged eye that drilled deeply into his quaking essence. The judge's left eye was so obscenely magnified from the monocle he wore, that even the slightest of movements from the pulsing capillaries to the fluctuating pupil was petrifying to behold. Rob *had* to know if his right eye was as grotesque and simply couldn't help himself but to snatch a glance, then, with all his heart he wished he hadn't. Rob had of course seen people with askew eyes before, but *never* as severe as this. As if in sheer terror of its own monstrous twin, the Judge's right eye seemed to permanently search out an escape route.

"Your statements of claim please, Lawyorrrs."

Utterly powerless to look away, Rob raised his dripping document. He felt like inevitable road kill, transfixed within the headlights of an oncoming, dangerously over-inflated hovercraft. The appalled Judge snatched up the soggy offering, then mercifully looked towards the prosecution, but the respite was short lived as the Judge's askew right eyeball was now looking directly at him. No! It hadn't wished to escape its evil twin at all; it was part of a foul collaboration, a vigilant sentinel that provided the Judge with an enormous scope of peripheral vision. Every couple of seconds it would twitch disturbingly—no doubt an unfortunate spasmodic payoff for possessing almost three hundred and sixty degrees of vision.

Rob shrank further inside himself as the Judge's fat lips curled in delight at the look of despair upon Rob's face. Feeling a huge blister of terror burble up, it punctured as hysterical giggling, in response, the twitching watchtower twisted away to face the southern quadrant, while the glaring left oculus returned and narrowed its obsidian lens to a perilous point, a ballistic 'Judge-to-Lawyer missile' prepping for launch.

"You dare to laugh at me? I, am the personification of Justice. Perhaps you regard treason as innocent horseplay?"

"No. I mean no, *M'lod*. I'm afraid I am not used to being saturated with stale fruit and veg before a trial." replied Rob, discovering some pluck.

"And how about the prosecution? Are you aware of the gravity of these heinous allegations?"

"Yes of course, M'lod, it is no trite thing to be un-Goblin like."

As the prosecution spoke, the first thing that struck Rob was the voice, it was assuredly female. The other observation was that the voice sounded, well, wonderful. Rob turned to look at his opponent. Something happened, something quite unexpected. A small inner voice insisted this was all very wrong, but he was completely enamoured by her. He had no idea a Goblin could look so lovely. Rob admired her auburn hair tussling loose about her shoulders, with just a hint of where her ear flaps lay beneath. Her honey eyes were lighter than any he had seen before, with an enduring twinkle of impishness. She smiled deliciously as she caught him gawping at her.

"Is *everything* as long as your ear-flaps, Lawyer?" teased the prosecution.

Rob realised he was ogling. She was green, of course she was, but she was hot! Did he say *hot*? Rob looked away immediately, feeling his face burn with embarrassment. "I am so sorry, I had no idea you could be so….attractive…" mumbled Rob in a mild delirium. The Court gasped and the Judge's monocle slipped from its podgy holder as his toad like features inflated fully to display complete disbelief.

"Whaaaaaat? You come into *my* court, *my* domain, you hand me little more than pulp for your statement, you proceed to openly mock me and *then* make advances of a romantic nature towards my prosecution, *directly* in front of me. If it wasn't for Build-Wall day, I would have you thrown immediately into a sanitised cell for contempt of court. If you cannot control your urges, Lawyaar, I will see to it that you *and* Fingle Froglick will join our City's founder at the bottom of the Great Wet, *crom rest his soul* and not before you're stripped, strapped, and strangled. Now take your damned seat before I change my mind!"

Rob walked back to his chair confused. He desperately wanted to steal another glance at her, to make sure he still felt that way. Perhaps it was a by-product of the change-form spell? He was Human, *not* Goblin. He *was* Human…wasn't he? *Shit*, he thought, *who am I?* It had been so long he wasn't certain of anything anymore and more worryingly, he was beginning not to care…

The clerk brought down his cane again, sending a small blur of dust to rise from the worm riddled boards, "Bring in the defendant, Fingle Froglick." he announced dramatically, sniffing into his handkerchief.

After numerous bolts had clunked and copious locks clicked, the door to the Court's dungeons finally groaned open. A lean, hunched over Goblin with excessive chains wrapped about him hobbled in, shouldered by a burly guard either side. Immediately the gallery was in uproar.

"Goblin hater!"

"Traitor!"

"Look, look at him dragging his feet, why it's ol' Shuffles himself."

The entire gallery burst into cruel laughter, Fingle's head lowered further.

"Leave...him...aloooooone!" roared Clump.

A deathly silence filled the humid courtroom for the first time, save for the clinking of chain metal as Fingle slowly looked up. *I know that roar,* thought Fingle. He searched the goblic gallery and sure enough, there stood the giant with a beaming grin from flap to flap. Fingle was overcome with a bittersweet mix of gratitude and guilt. Guilt for losing faith in his closest friend and yet here he was and with his uncle too. Tears rolled down his perfumed, exfoliated cheeks. Fingle was a resilient character, but his vulnerability had gotten the better of him on this occasion.

"How very touching, but we have a court case to decide. Prosecution, please begin, Defence remain seated." sneered the condescending Judge, although rattled by Clump's thunderous threat.

Fingle's razor sharp mind kicked into overdrive. *Defence he said? Me old chum has somehow managed ta get me a Defence attorney?*

A rumbling of optimism tentatively developed. Fingle accepted he was to be made an example of and only crom knew how many enemies he had, but what if he managed to pull this off? He would be a free Goblin once more, a far greater prospect than becoming a fugitive, spending the remainder of his days scratching out an existence in some dark and smelly cave—although desirable to most Goblins no doubt—while avoiding capture because of an enormous bounty placed on his notoriously famous head, obviously... The Prosecution sauntered over to stand before the Court. Everyone was entranced by her obvious beauty and wanton charm, that is, all except Fingle.

This was not by chance, he mused; it was an additional measure to help bury him. Not only did she win the gaze and goolies of every green blooded male in the Jury, Fingle was certain she was also employed to soften his Defence solicitor. He scoffed at their desperation, only a complete imbecile would succumb to such an overt and dire tactic. Fingle leaned forwards to see who was defending him. Rob sat drooling, utterly oblivious to everything but the heavenly creature standing before him. Fingle's grin deflated, then buried itself into his sympathetic palms. Fingle peered through his fingers at Clump, who simply shrugged back. *Stupid oaf, he's brought me a simpleton who thinks with his knackers and not his noggin!* Demoralised, yet hardly surprised, Fingle felt around for the coloured feathers secreted within the waistband of his breeches. He knew his escape now relied solely upon his own efforts, as was everything else in his life.

"My Lord, I call upon Fingle Froglick for cross examination." requested the Prosecution, flashing a devilish smile at Rob, causing his elbows to slip from beneath his chin.

She let out a small giggle and proceeded to drift over to where Fingle was seated. Fingle was rubbing his wrists after the manacles had been removed, then looked up at her with a menacing smirk, *not* what she was expecting.

"Fingle Froglick, I do not need to remind the court of your crimes and of their severity, as it is quite the talk of town. Or call into question the validity of the evidence, as you were caught green-handed, powdered and scented too, as I understand."

The gallery reacted well to her remark, Fingle did not, "Yer are quite correct lore-yer, I do not need reminding of something I did, because I did it and as fer severity? Am I ta understand that I cannot privately purfle meself ta alleviate me offended senses of which are under constant barrage by me fellow Goblins, you madam being no exception!" snapped Fingle, dramatically pinching his protracted nose.

Clump cheered, alone. Merlock's face went from lime green to laurel. He knew Fingle and he knew where this was going.

"I see, so we are far from repentant and yet you do not deny the charges brought against you?" pressed the Prosecution.

"Listen up, lady lore-yer, if indeed yer are either. I can see that we are having difficulty in communicating here. I have never once denied the facts, but I do not accept being branded as a traitor and certainly not by a Tirliry-puffkin such as yerself," spluttered Fingle, his eyes darker than coal, "and if yer realised this excruciatingly simple crinet of information, yer may just get by as a soullessitor, but since yer wouldn't know the facts if they jumped up and yanked off yer earth-apples, I strongly doubt it."

Everyone began laughing, except of course Merlock, the Prosecution and the Judge, who was demanding order between hackling wheezes. The comely lawyer had now completely changed her countenance to that of a threatened animal.

"You think this is amusing do you, Fingle Froglick? Let's see how funny it is when your hanging around with Gimple Fleablotch in about, oh, one candle burn from now!" seethed the Prosecution.

"Objection, your Honour, Prosecution is not questioning, instead she is being argumentative." petitioned Rob.

Finally! He has seen this wallydraigle for who she truly is, thought Fingle, *we may at last get somewhere...*

"Objection denied, she is merely stating the outcome, I mean *possible* outcome." croaked the Judge, extremely agitated by the proceedings so far.

Merlock sat up, Rob had managed to snap out of his stupor, wondering how he could have been so easily affected considering his earthly origins? He decided the change-form spell was considerably more potent that he had initially thought.

"Fingle Froglick, as you lack the capacity to see my point of view, let alone respond to it, I see no further need for cross examination." said the lawyer formally.

"Lady, I would love ta examine things from yer point of view, but it would be unfeasible ta wedge me head that far up yer fat arse." remarked Fingle dispassionately.

"Order! Order!" cried the flustered Judge as the surviving vestiges of decorum completely disintegrated.

Fingle continued, "My honourable Lord, I beseech yer, why in the whole of Goblindom is it acceptable fer *her* ta be a lame brained dullard, yet unacceptable fer me ta bring this ta the attention of the Court?" implored Fingle, feigning deep distress.

"Fingle, enough of this!" fumed the floundering Judge.

Fingle was far from finished, "Yer Honour, I agree. We have progressed little more than a pissed one-armed Gnome, pushing a wheelbarrow laden with Troll turds up the Cone of Certainty, while deficient of its wheel."

Even Merlock sniggered, while Rob made odd snorting sounds attempting to conceal his amusement.

"This Court is now in recess until order has been restored!" screamed the Judge, stumbling down from his seat and slapping the lowered skulls of his devoted clerks aside as he limped back to his chambers.

Rob walked over to Fingle who looked up innocently. The first thing Rob noticed were the nose rings he wore, like a gold spring spiralling down his impressive proboscis. "So you're Fingle, Clump's best friend and Merlock's Nephew. I heard you were troublesome, but that doesn't really come close, does it?" said Rob smiling.

"Yer were correct on three counts and as fer trouble, well it seems ta find me," replied Fingle with a wink, "so tell me, Lore-yer, where is yer business located and how exactly did they persuade yer ta risk yer rump, or are yer just extraordinarily dim-witted?"

Rob chuckled then replied, "Well it was fairly straightforward really. Clump and Merlock knew they could not convince a Goblin to defend you in court as it would result in certain death, so they decided to enlist help from another realm of existence altogether. After crossing a marshland that farts constantly, they opened a portal into the Human world and snatched me out of it. They then magickally changed me to look like a Goblin and proceeded to teach me your history and way of life. I agreed to all of this because not only am I dim-witted, but most likely insane too."

There was a long pause while Fingle studied him, "That's a fine tale indeed, Lore-yer, I can see why yer were chosen." Then Fingle leaned in closely, raised one of Rob's inordinately long ear flaps and whispered, "I strongly suggest yer keep that ta yerself from now on, Rob of Terra, if yer are discovered, then death will be a luxury for us all."

"How did you know my name?" gulped Rob.

"That's my business, let's just say I see things differently. It's also me business ta know who I'm dealing with. So tell me, Rob, what is yer winning argument, how do yer propose we will leave this Court with our freedom and fruitcake's intact?"

Rob splayed his fingers on the desk and exhaled, "I have an idea in how to spin this, Fingle, but it will not be favoured by everyone, especially toady up there."

"Well, that sounds like a jape, I'm in. But be careful, they have assigned the worst Judge in the city for this trial, 'Pickled Peeper' has wanted to sink his claws into me for years."

"Fingle, if this fails and let's put our cards on the table, it most likely will, we have a contingency, what we call plan 'B' to aid our escape. Look to Merlock if all seems lost and then you will know what to do."

Rob was deliberately ambiguous, as the plan itself was highly dangerous and saw no value in telling Fingle more than he needed to know.

"Will the Court please be upstanding for the Judge, again!" shouted the clerk, the conversation simmered down as everyone stood.

The chamber doors re-opened and the Judge stumbled out. His appearance was dishevelled and his gait hesitant. Eventually, he arrived back at his bench, slapping each hand on his helpful clerks as he gingerly ascended the steps. Everyone gasped as the Judge fell backwards, but managed to regain his balance with a sweaty paw grasped firmly upon the face of a clerk who struggled to breathe until he had flopped back into his chair.

A garbled fanfare began from a quartet of Goblins high up in the gallery.

"Too late, you're too fracking late, I'm already sitting you fools and you sound appalling, get out of my Court!" screamed the judge.

Rob was deeply concerned; it was fair to assume that whatever transpired in the Judge's chamber during the short recess was most certainly to involve grog and lots of it.

"Defence, your turn and get on with it." hissed the Judge, his bleary eyes swivelling everywhere and refusing to settle on anything.

Rob stood and walked to the centre of the Court amidst the various heckles.

"Shut the frack up!" roared the Judge, "The next Goblin to interrupt will be hung from their seed bag."

An agonizing silence unfurled, until Fingle decided it was a splendid opportunity to break that silence, by issuing an exorbitantly loud and prolonged backdoor breeze that sent reeking reverberations to all cardinal points. Far and wide, quivering ear flaps and bulging cheeks were painfully preserved as a primed explosion of restrained laughter rapidly rose towards its critical mass. The Judge yawped incredulously at Fingle's shocking display of gross insubordination, while Fingle casually picked his nose. Time ground to a stop, all eyes were transfixed upon this impasse, a power struggle between two opposing forces, then Fingle leaned forwards ever so slightly and released a further two unemphatic farticles. The very ramparts seemed to raise with deafening laughter. The Judge had long given up trying to be heard and had quietly taken himself back to his chambers. Rob walked back over to Fingle, before he could protest, Fingle looked up pleadingly while holding out his hands and wrapping his spindly fingers about themselves. Rob could see the corners of his mouth betraying his sincerity and caught a glimpse of undiluted mischief buried within Fingle's piteous eyes and in spite of the dire situation, he found himself laughing too. Fingle was an oddity, a rarity, an imponderable. Never to be underestimated or understood. To believe you had the measure of him was precisely what he wanted. Rob looked up at Clump, who was busy chomping on something but otherwise content. Merlock was smiling too, but the concern he held for his Nephew's fate could still be seen.

Sometime later, an exasperated clerk announced the Judge's third arrival. The Court was astonished to see the chamber doors burst open, followed by the rotund Judge sprawling disgracefully across the floor. Inconsolable, the ingratiating clerks ran to their fallen chieftain. After a humiliating struggle, the Judge was finally hauled onto his feet and began to walk unsteadily back to his chambers, until an apologetic clerk deftly steered him towards the direction of his bench. As he sloped passed Fingle he tilted his head and breathed, "I'm watching you, Flingle Figlick."

Up close, Fingle saw the folly in such a grog soaked statement, for his right eye was all but closed and his left pupil was completely irretrievable, forfeiting any sensible juxtaposition to its inebriated neighbour. The clerks were obligated to enlist reinforcements in order to heave the woozy reptile into his seat. It was an embarrassing spectacle to bear witness. Whatever dignity and respect the judge possessed before the trial, had now plunged between the cracks in the dusty floorboards, forever lost. All that remained was a repulsive, gelatinous, quivering sneer.

"Prostitution, my lovely, finish him." slurred the Judge.

"My Lord, I have already finished my cross examination." replied the alluring lawyer quizzically.

"Very well, Defensh, you're up and be quick you wretch of a Goblin."

Rob took his position and shrugged at Fingle. How could he proceed in a case where the Judge was completely incapable of making any decision, let alone a fair and just one? Fingle simply shrugged back, smiling a long and gratifying smile.

Rob had little choice but to continue, hoping that despite the conditions and after he had proven Fingle to be innocent, the Court would see sense, a high hope he knew.

"Thank you, M'lod. Fingle Froglick, how long have you lived in this great City?" questioned Rob.

"Hmmm, let me see, well I have been here long enough ta do business with nearly every Goblin and most of them's were still suckling on their mothers' teats when I first arrived." offered Fingle.

"More like *cheat* every trader." came a cry from the gallery, followed by further giggling.

"Shut the frack up! Throw that piss in a cell." shrieked Peeper Pickles and then issued forth a volley of acidic hiccups that bubbled down his amphibian chin.

Fingle ignored the comment and the two Court guards tossing the heckler from the upper balcony.

Rob continued, "Would you say that you were one of the early settlers?"

"Yes. Although I never saw old Shuffles himself, the wall had just been completed when I first arrived."

"Okay, thank you, may I also ask, why is it that you chose to live here, within the confines of such a place?"

A silence hung over the Court as Rob's line of questioning was puzzling and unsettling to the Prosecution who had since lost her smugness, realising that the Defence, may actually have one.

Fingle thought about it and replied, "Well, there is the obvious advantage, the wall helps ta keep the City warm. Also, I soon discovered that I could engage in free commerce without resorting ta fisty fights fer a change.

Not that there's anything wrong with a healthy ding-dong, but gold's more important so it is."

A murmur of agreement rippled throughout the court.

"Thank you, Fingle Froglick. So would you agree that this City and all of its new-found rules has helped to unite a previously warring race and enabled it to evolve, to exist in a civilised way even?"

Everyone looked at one another, some in shock, others in confusion, some began to nod.

The Prosecution stood, "My Lord, the defence is clearly leading the defendant. My Lord, My Lord?"

The judge was snoring and had to be nudged awake, forcibly, several times.

"What, what ish it now?" mumbled the toady tyrant.

"I said…never mind." the soulessisitor sat back down looking just as frustrated as Rob had earlier.

Fingle's keen mind had swiftly grasped where Rob was leading his argument and quickly took his cue, "Yes, Lore-yer, I would say that with all certainty, this great City of ours is the crowning achievement in all of Goblin history. Those I once saw as me enemies, are now me business competitors. I have lived 'ere long enough ta see great changes. It's almost as if a new, enlightened race of Goblins has evolved and continues to do so." Fingle stood, opening his arms wide to the entire Court, "And let us all 'ere and now during Build-Wall day, our most sacred of days, celebrate our expanding existence, an existence born anew by every male, female and whelp Goblin in the pursuit of becoming better Goblins and wealthier too!" Fingle looked to the sky with arms raised as the cheering and enthusiastic applause continued.

"Shilence you blithering poshtules. This ish all fracking nicey, but Flaplick ish unnatural, he's shnivilised!" snarled the Judge, trying to insert his monocle into his forehead.

Rob spun around to address the Judge with an air of confidence and conviction, "I put it to the Court, that *if* Fingle's crimes were indeed *unnatural*, then by association of this logic, this entire City is a perversion of the Goblin code, is it not?"

The Judge's eyes had opened for the first time since his return, rolling around in sickening conduct. He almost fell from the platform as he heaved his faltering frame upwards in protest. "You dare call thish City a pervert? On Build-Wall day? You do *not* come into my Court and call ush all snivilised! There are rules yesh, but we shtill fight, drink, and shteal like any indecent downshtanding Goblin is born to dooooooo..."

During his drunken diatribe, Judge Peeper Pickles had lost his balance then spectacularly burst through his desk and balcony rail, falling several feet to crash heavily upon his distended face. Rob rushed forwards to help the jerking judiciary, but was held back by a guard. A flock of faithful clerks and guards rushed over to assist. Giggling was heard throughout the Court, as were the pitiful groaning hiccups of the squirming Judge. After he was raised back on his feet, smirks were replaced by revulsion. Somehow, his monocle had wedged deeply within his left eye socket, forcing his eyelids to stretch grotesquely over its entire circumference. The judge's bulbous eye—now squashed against the magnified glass—squeaked abhorrently loudly whenever it moved. Peeper Pickles was hauled away through a cheering crowd amidst dust and splintered wood. As Rob finally sensed hope for Fingle, the main doors flung wide open. The Goblins that were picking up rotten fruit released it immediately. Fingle's eyes narrowed, while everyone else's widened.

"I, am an emissary of the Goblin high council and as such my authority here and pretty much everywhere else is incontestable. I will take over the proceedings from this point. Oh, and some may recognise me, *or* perhaps my name. For the Court's records, I am Sly Slaughter…"

Merlock, Rob, and Clump looked at each other as the tall masked stranger entered the Courtroom, followed by menacing Goblin guards in full battle dress. Rob had seen his name in Fingle's case file and here he was in person. Sly kicked away the debris and sat down in the Judge's seat. The Goblins sat in silence while he scrunched his leather gloved hands together tightly. He fixed his gaze upon Rob and merely stared. The air became stifling. Rob tried to look elsewhere, convinced the masked Goblin knew who he really was. Rob's gaze lowered to the emblem that shone brightly on Sly's black uniform, it was identical to the symbol used in the documents, three adjoining circles each with a dot in the centre—Sly's initials were also embroidered beneath it, 'SS'.

"Well, Lawyer, have you finished? What I heard before I opened the door, were words of wisdom imparted by a high ranking judicial servant. I believe you tried to convince him that Fingle is as pure as the City itself and therefore innocent? Forgive me, but what I find intriguing, is how can a *Goblin* such as *you*, state that another Goblin, in fact the whole of Goblindom is anything but impure and by being good little Goblins we are now a civilised race? Isn't that treasonous also?"

Rob's head swam in a storm of scattered thoughts, somehow Sly knew he was masquerading as one of them. He knew when he was being teased, only this was not in jest, this was deadly. *He was right though,* thought Rob, *no Goblin would ever perceive themselves as un-Goblin like, for they were simply incapable of doing so, because to do so would mean you were not a Goblin at all, unless of course, you were…not a Goblin!*

Rob choked, berating himself for such a foolish mistake. He was not dealing with Humans here, *no,* he had to 'think' like a Goblin and think quickly.

"Well? We are all waiting, Lawyer." pressed the sinister inquisitor, his voice as penetrating as his stare.

Rob looked to Fingle and for the first time he saw fear in Fingle's eyes. Fingle shook his head to dissuade him, but Rob hadn't come this far to back down, especially to someone who did not have the courage to face the world without hiding behind a mask.

Rob inhaled and continued, "I am glad you saw through my disguise, Darth-Vader." shooting Sly a contemptuous wink—the leather gloves scrunched tighter.

"You are correct, Sly, no Goblin could ever be considered pure, dread the thought. I was just, well, you know, being deceptive; after all it's in my nature isn't it?"

Sly did not comment, but instead leaned forwards, never once removing his gaze.

Rob continued, "Frankly, my Client is soooo Goblin-like, so despicably deceptive, so filthily scurrilous and debauched, not to mention *uniquely* depraved, it would be a catastrophic misfortune to ever cross paths with this most malodorous of all scat-syphoning nematodes!"

"Steady on." hissed Fingle.

"And to prove it, my client has completely altered his own personality in the fearless pursuit of the ultimate deception, that he no longer even knows himself. In his relentless *service* to goblinkind, Fingle's self-sacrifice can be considered no less than absolute, in honourable, or rather dishonourable intention, that he has remarkably somehow even managed to deceive himself. This is no mean feat considering his past transgressions, of which many have become legendary in a City bursting its seams with rotten conniving slopsuckers like all of you here today, crom bless you all!"

The Court was now upstanding, filled with whistling and rapturous applause. Fingle's name was chanted aloud with renewed respect, in awe of his astonishing sacrifice to the hallowed trade of dishonesty. Rob took a bow and

Fingle tipped his coif cap in recognition of Rob's quite brilliant recovery. Sly had not budged an inch, he simply sat watching intently. Finally, after the applause had died down, one hand clap remained. The slow clap came from Sly Slaughter, it had the unsettling effect of sounding deeply sinister instead of appreciative.

"Bravo! Oh, well done, Lawyer. I concede you have won over these inbreeds, but have you won over me? Of course not, *silly*…" he allowed himself a brief chuckle that was unnervingly higher in pitch.

Sly got out of his chair, walking casually down the steps he traced a gloved finger across the dusty spindles, never once looking up while he spoke, "I have been waiting for you, Rob, for really quite some time and now here we are…"

He walked to the centre of the Court and slowly raised his head. Sly's eyes danced with fire as he removed his gloves, finger by finger.

"You see, young Rob, I know who you *really* are, let's just say a little bird told me."

Rob was swiftly losing his nerve, wondering who could have betrayed him? *Little bird?* In a blinding flash, memories from outside the Pye Shoppe flooded his mind, *Smidge, the Faux!* He recalled the message the repentant sprite had given him:

"The plot involves bridging the three peaks, look for the three peaks and you will know your enemy, but you must send urgent word to Buttercup, only she has the power—" warned the Faux, before he was burned to cinder ash by a dark magician.

Shit! Merlock has to know, thought Rob in a panic, *but how?*

"Aaaaah, I see you know who our little bird is, quite the talker isn't he?" teased Sly, as he approached nearer.

Rob recognised that same silver symbol again on Sly's uniform—three adjoining circles with centre points—

dazzling from the shafts of sunlight, breaching their way in through the weathered shingle. *What did Smidge say about three? Three Peaks and know your enemy? Wasn't the beheaded magician last night wearing such a symbol?*

A cold terror washed over Rob, realising the symbol *was* the Three Peaks, home to the Dark Fortress and the shadow Goblin government. When the Three Peak Mountains were viewed from above they looked like three circles with centre points.

Rob froze, as Sly moved closer to within earshot and quietly spoke, "You are more important than you could ever comprehend. Whatever you have heard about me, I can assure you it is not entirely factual, for to hold a certain position of authority it is imperative to have a reputation of sorts, do you understand?"

Rob barely nodded.

"The truth is I need your help, Rob. It is a simple enough task and would be achieved considerably less painfully with your full cooperation. As a show of faith I am prepared to release your friend Fingle and co-conspirators, whom I believe are watching from the gallery. Do we have an agreement?"

Rob was in total shock, how did Sly Slaughter know about him? Why was *he* so important? What is it he had to do? How did he know about Merlock and Clump?

"What happens if I say no?" said Rob with trepidation.

"Oh, I think you can use your imagination, Rob. After all, as I mentioned, I do have a certain reputation to protect." said Sly sinisterly.

Rob had no other choice but to accept the terms. It was in some ways the best outcome he could have hoped for, at least in this way they would all leave in one piece and alive.

"Very well, I will help you, Sly, but I want your promise that my friends are free to leave and will remain free and unharmed."

"Splendid. You have made the right decision, the *only* decision, Rob. I hope that during our time together we may even become...friends."

Sly turned to face the Court, raising his voice so that all could hear, "I have heard the Defence and I also acknowledge the seriousness of the allegations made against Fingle Froglick. I know you will all agree that Fingle's service to his own kind has transcended all expectation and as such he cannot be punished. The Court therefore has no just reason to detain him. So without further delay, I, Sly Slaughter, hereby decree that Fingle Froglick be released immediately and that everyone leave this dolorous den of dinginess to enjoy Build-Wall Day!"

Everyone cheered, clapped and jigged, eager to partake of the day's festivities. Merlock had not known what conversation transpired between the two of them, but it was evident some kind of bargain had been struck. But he did know with all certainty that Sly Slaughter would sell his own grandgoblins to the redcaps for their gaming pits. Fingle was astonished at the sacrifice the Human had made on his behalf. He realised his preconceptions regarding Humans were woefully inaccurate. Merlock watched in anguish as two of Sly's guards began placing manacles on Rob's wrists.

"Clump, we must activate plan 'B' now!"

Clump nodded as he stood, then sucked in as much air as he could muster. With an almighty effort he bellowed, "We have a *Yawner*!" and pointed directly to Merlock.

Everyone's attention instantly focused on the small wizard; Rob knew what was coming and cringed. A deafening silence followed as Merlock's jaws opened wide, the terror in the courtroom was tangible. Merlock issued a dramatic, lingering yawn to the masses. The nightmare had been released.

What happened next was a mixture of a poorly executed drill and unscripted chaos.

"Bolt the doors!"

"Send for the 'Break and Taker'!"

"Get the B.A.T.!"

"Close your eyes, nobody leave!"

During Rob's tutelage, Merlock had informed Rob how Goblins reacted to yawning and of the mortal dangers being caught within a 'yawning circle'. Rob did not believe any of it, until today. He knew from his own world that yawning was intriguingly contagious, but *lethal*, really? According to the wizard, the most dangerous job in the city was a 'Break & Taker', known colloquially as B.A.T.'s. In the extremely, unlikely event of a yawn ever being released in a goblic place, the heroic task of a yawn-breaker was to run directly into the affray and wait for everyone to close their eyes and release their yawns, thus avoid contracting the condition again from witnessing further yawns. When the last yawn was yawned, the yawn-breaker would allow it to infect him/her, then take the yawn to a place of safety where the yawn could not escape by being seen again, hence 'Break and Takers'.

When Rob enquired as to the fate of the yawn-takers, Merlock had said that if they hadn't managed to fall asleep—exhaustion from continual yawning—they would most likely die from starvation and dehydration, or worse still, explode due to a greater volume of air being sucked in than was blown back out. Rob had argued that it made no sense, *why didn't everyone just close their eyes and wait for the yawning to stop?* Merlock replied by adding, "Remember, Rob, you are in a magickal realm now, the rules here are very different to your own world. A simple yawn to you, is a very real danger for us Goblins. It is no exaggeration to say that a Goblin's yawn has its own agenda. It is born through complacency and thrives off the fear from others; it is in essence brought to life and will not simply go away. It constantly seeks out new hosts to ensure its survival by replication. If it wasn't for these brave souls willing to rush into a yawning building and being paid a crom load of gold pieces, we would all be looking at an extinction level event for our kind."

The main Court doors burst open and Clump galumphed in. Merlock had already sent him on ahead to take advantage of the chaos they had invoked.

"Fingle, Rob, follow me!" shouted Clump between yawns.

Fingle leapt out of his chair and pulled Rob away from the guards, who by now had their eyes tightly shut and far too terrified to open them. Everywhere Goblins were yawning, it was spreading like a bush fire, rampant and multiplying exponentially.

"So this was your plan 'B'?" Fingle screamed through yawns.

Clump sighed a crooked smile and shrugged. Merlock now joined them and the small party ran from the Court. Rob was largely unaffected, but still felt an unusually powerful compulsion to yawn and managed to suppress it, but only just. Standing in the corridor he looked back into the Court and could see Sly desperately fighting his way through the panic stricken Goblins, which were either yawning or stumbling blindly into one another. Fortunately, someone inside closed and bolted the Court doors, despite an outcry from Sly.

As per the plan, Merlock swiftly assembled the yawning-circle together in the Courthouse lobby, ordering each Goblin in turn to lose their yawn and close their eyes, until only Rob remained watching. Once Rob had taken the yawn, he heroically diffused the deadly contagion with an intense stifled grin.

"It's okay guys, it's gone."

They slowly opened their eyes and cheered, it was insane but brilliant! A terrifying thought vaulted from Rob's mind, "Merlock, how did you know I would not be affected like every other Goblin?"

"I didn't…oops." said Merlock stunned, realising he had completely overlooked the possibility.

As they ran for the main exit leading onto Lostleg Street, a distressed Goblin burst in.

"Where is it? I'm the B.A.T."

Merlock quickly calculated this chance encounter would buy some much needed time, "Everyone, shut your eyes, give it to him, Rob!" ordered Merlock, trying desperately not to laugh.

"Here it is…" said Rob, feigning a drawn out yawn, while hushed giggles were overheard.

The 'Break and Taker', although unsettled at their whimsical manner, performed her duty by collecting the virulent yawn and ran back outside, obscuring her own mouth by yanking over her emergency yawn taker helmet. She ran down the road screaming "Bat!" between yawns, which had the surreal effect of sounding like a constipated sheep hurtling past. Members of the goblic upon hearing the warning, immediately shielded their eyes and moved to the edge of the streets, leaving the central area free to allow the emergency service full access. Merlock had guessed correctly, the B.A.T. was heading for Sleepy Isle, but first had to retrieve the B.A.T. boat from the docks to travel there. Fortunately for them, Fingle's boat was moored at the same marina. The fugitives followed the B.A.T. closely, shouting additional warnings as nearby whelps clung to their mothers. After making good progress, they arrived at the busy dock, exhausted but determined.

"Which boat's yours, Fingle?" asked Rob, panting heavily.

"Crom, it's the one that's heavily guarded, how did they know?"

"They must have had orders to guard it if anything went wrong at the trial. Someone must have sent word to a standby team when they had sent for a B.A.T.?" Merlock said, rubbing his whiskers.

"Look, they have a second B.A.T. with them, we can't use plan 'B' again, we will have to turn back." said Rob.

"Not so fast, I 'ave another plan. They don't call me *Fingle the greatest Goblin mastermind* fer nothing."

"I have never heard *anyone* say that before, Fingle. Ever." replied Clump.

"Shut up yer big oaf and get yer clothes off. All of yer, snip-snap, clothes off."

Before Rob could argue, Merlock quipped in, "Do it now, Fingle might be many things and we heard most of them in Court, but trust me, he's as slippery as a dwarf's dump on wet cobbles."

They reluctantly removed their clothing and bundled it into the large backpacks that Merlock and Clump were carrying. Fingle then fumbled around the waistband of his breeches until he pulled out a large handful of very bright, colourful feathers. They all stared, confused, until Merlock gasped. "Nephew, you are not seriously considering—"

"Yep!" said Fingle, wearing a jubilant smirk.

"What in the hell is this?" contended Rob.

"This, my flappy friend, is our salvation. Yer need ta place a feather in both yer earing holes, we are going ta bend-walk our way onto me boat, masquerading as the 'Knot-Ear' descendants."

Rob was precariously close to convincing himself he was in some kind of elongated nightmare, a delusional state that had imposed itself while under the influence of those unusual mushrooms he had gorged upon at Cornfoot's supermarket. It was not entirely inconceivable he may be drooling in some padded cell and that all of this was just a very complex, alternative reality he had somehow self-generated. A sharp pain to his head brought him back to his senses, which of course made very little difference where his senses were concerned.

"Sorry, lad, you went somewhere else and we need you here or it's the noggin spikes for all of us." said the wizard apologetically.

"Okay, but can someone please tell me what the hell is a Knot-Ear?" stammered Rob, feeling tearful that his grip on sanity was now tenuous at best.

Merlock took it upon himself to answer Rob's question quickly, hoping that an explanation would help delay a full mental break down.

"The Knot-Ears, are a family of Goblins, recognised by the brightly coloured plumage they are allowed to cram in their earflaps by royal decree, but only upon this day and all other 'Build-Wall' days, past and future. It all began during the preparations to celebrate the first ever 'Build-Wall' day. To commemorate the momentous occasion, auditions were open to every Goblin in the Faerie Kingdom to find suitable acts to entertain the Goblin King and Council. Everything was going as well as could be expected, until a late entry appeared, butt naked, save for a coloured feather stuck in each hearing hole. Muckbeth Knot-Ear, squatted in front of a panel of Judges, resembling an oversized yet undernourished witchetty grub. The act consisted of Muckbeth wriggling his ear flaps to rotate his feathers in small circles—the movement was embarrassingly negligible. In concert, he straightened his legs, but painstakingly slowly, slow enough to make your mind mince itself. Eventually, once his creaking knees had locked into an upright position, the feather rotations ceased."

"How long did this madness last?" asked Rob, settling for serene disassociation over encroaching hysteria.

"It was said to have lasted six whole candle burns…"

"Six hours! How is that even possible? What happened to him?" questioned Rob, grinning unnaturally, blissfully unaware his facial muscles were twitching while he made loud clucking sounds with his swollen tongue.

"Well, the King's panel of Judges were so traumatised, they had no other alternative than to simply ignore him. To even hint at Muckbeth's existence would have required them to inwardly process what they had just witnessed as something real. No one was either willing or capable of such a feat, as their unhinging minds already teetered upon the threshold of insanity. So, the naked Goblin limped away, assuming he had been a great success, misinterpreting their catatonic silence for awe and respect. The highly anticipated first ever Build-Wall day took place. The grog was free, as were the hundreds of spit roasts that lined the crowded streets. The King was in high spirits, enjoying the acts that had been chosen for his entertainment and everything went splendidly well. When the King had believed the last act to have finished, an odd looking Goblin without a stitch of clothing, save for a coloured feather stuck in each ear, sidestepped in front of him. Unfortunately for the King, the unutterable act had returned, as no one had informed Muckbeth that he had been spectacularly unsuccessful during his audition...The historical conversation that was recorded in the Gobbledebook, went as follows:

'What is your name, Goblin?' enquired the King tentatively, wondering why his Council looked away in horror.

'My name is Muckbeth, Muckbeth Knot-Ear, my King. I am most honoured to share with you my greatest performance. It has taken many long cycles to perfect.'

'Welcome, Muckbeth, please continue.' replied the King, somewhat amused by his eccentricity.

After the passing of the first candle burn into his performance, the King had wished in earnest to know if Muckbeth's waggling feathers would serve him in some other way, specifically if he were thrown headlong into the

Waterfall of Outlandish Deluge, but pity had steadied the king's hand. After three candle burns, the King pondered the notion that he could enhance the overall effect by adding a further ten thousand feathers by stabbing them deeply and indiscriminately into Muckbeth's shuddering, sweaty flab rolls, then sell him to a local Gaudy-bird herder as a breeding companion—the males were extremely excitable at this turn of the wheel. But on this occasion, unadulterated revulsion had steadied his hand. When the act had mercifully drawn to a soul-destroying anti-climax, the King and his entire palace of guests were doing anything but look directly towards the triumphant Goblin. The king himself was filing his nails down to a bloody pulp while trying to whistle something uplifting, yet inside he wailed like a neglected new-born, mourning the loss of all life's meaning. From that day hence, the King decreed that any descendant of the 'Act that never was', while naked and wearing coloured ear plumage, may go about their business on Build-Wall day, completely ignored and unseen by all, on the condition they only utter the words 'Knot-Ear' and none other."

After his heart wrenching delivery, Merlock looked poignantly to Rob, who howled hysterically, almost giving up their position inside an old disused boathouse.

"You expect me to believe *that* crock of shit? I mean seriously, that really *happened*?" blurted Rob.

"Yes, uncle's right, now do as I say and stick these fracking feathers in yer oles, assuming yer can get them in under those dangling meat strips." scolded Fingle, conscious they had wasted enough time.

In the far distance, a loud commotion approached.

"It's Sly and his bungling bullies, they are heading here," snapped Fingle, "Clump, carry the bags, I will go first and everyone do everything *exactly* as I do, does everyone understand?"

They all nodded anxiously, leaving Fingle to exit the derelict boathouse first.

"There they are!" screamed Sly to his guards as they approached the docks.

"Where?" rasped an out of breath guard.

"There, they are right there and they…are naked…?"

Sly's voice trailed off as he tried to make sense of things. All four fugitives walked in a sidestepping motion, bending fully at the knees to a squatting position with each step. It was peculiar enough that they had large colourful feathers in both hearing flaps, but while naked? It was repugnant to behold. Each squat promised the onlooker an unsavoury image to be emblazoned upon their psyche for an eternity, never to diminish in its profane clarity.

"They are Knot-Ears, sir, we can't touch or talk to 'em, we can't even look at 'em, it's the King's law." puffed the overweight guard.

"Don't be stupid, they are *not* Knot-Ears." lectured Sly.

"No, Knot-Ears, *not* Knot-Knot-Ears." corrected the guard, feeling smug with himself for being right for once.

"Crom, I swear I am surrounded by gooch grabbing, sewer sucking, limpet licking fracklets!" screamed Sly, while his guards forcibly restrained him, for fear of breaking the King's law.

"Oh my good God, it's actually working..." whispered Rob, following Fingle's lead.

As they approached Fingle's boat, the guards were forced to casually look away, desperate to avoid eye contact with the Knot-Ears as if they didn't exist. The plan was going better than expected, until Fingle developed severe cramp in his left buttock. A searing pain reached down into his leg as he clasped a hand to his taught derriere. In sympathetic obedience, the others responded. Now, all four escapees hobbled towards the boat, yelping and clutching their clenched arses. Mimicking Fingle as accurately as possible, the announcement of their arrival had altered slightly to sound less like 'Knot-Ear' and more like 'No-tears', as they hissed their proclamation through gritted teeth. Fingle cringed at the irony of the unintentional bon mot. One by one they hobbled on board the empty vessel. Fingle limped over to where the rope kept his boat moored at dock. He beckoned Clump to help while maintaining the deception. Clump bend-walked over and thoughtlessly responded, using words other than those decreed, "Shall I pull it up now, Fingle?"

Everything stopped, Fingle's teary eyes enlarged, Clump realised he had given up their charade.

"Now, can we please just arrest them!" wailed Sly, deeply dismayed at his moronic troops. The guards turned around and quickly approached the boat.

Clump roared, "Knot fracking here!" and hauled the heavy rope from off the mooring point, swinging it into the oncoming Goblin guards. Those that weren't rendered unconscious found themselves floundering in the thick slime that clung to the port walls.

"Raise the cloth and get to the paddles!" shrieked Fingle as Clump used his mighty leg to push away from the port, while the blundering guards hurled insults. They of course reciprocated by taking numerous bows while facing in the opposite direction. There was something uniquely discomforting and furiously demoralising, seeing a naked, sinewy Goblin with a coloured feather jammed in each ear, rubbing his rump and meting out a one fingered salute. *Some gestures are wonderfully universal,* mused Rob.

"What do we do now, Sir?" asked the Captain of the King's Guard.

"I do nothing, *you* take a bath." said Sly, booting the Captain headfirst into the feculent froth. *I have a notion of where you are headed, let's see who gets there first Rob of Terra...*

Chapter 9

Fingle was not overly excited at the prospect of leaving his boat moored unattended along the river Oodles, but it was as close as they could get to Merlock's place. Fingle had listened while his uncle explained how they had found Rob and of the warning given by Smidge the Faux as he navigated his vessel up river. Although Fingle's expression remained largely inscrutable, he was impressed, entertained and deeply heartened by all of their remarkable sacrifices. By the time they moored up, it had been unilaterally agreed they were to seek out whoever this Buttercup was. But to do so, meant they would have to risk a return journey to the wizard's home and retrieve his looksee ball. Without it, they had little chance of finding Buttercup. After a sorrowful departure from his beloved boat, Fingle joined the others on foot as they all disappeared into the dense tree-line of Whisperun forest in silence, each to their own thoughts—Clump excluded.

"Something's wrong." muttered Merlock.

"What is it?" enquired Rob.

As Merlock tuned into his surroundings, a disembodied voice spoke.

"Theeeeey hafff come for yoooooou, Meeeerlock, yooou must ruuuuuunnn..."

"What is it, Spirit? Who has come for us?"

"The masked dark one, theeeeey have surrroundeeeed yourrrrrrr hommme…"

"Thank you, Spirit, but we must risk entry, without my looksee ball we have no chance of discovering the identity and location of the only one who can help us."

"What are we ta do then, Uncle? If what Rob says is true, then we cannot waste a single moment." said Fingle, looking intently at the wizard while he paced back and forth. "Uuuuussse the tuuuuunnelllls..."

"Crom! Spirit's right, we are standing above a labyrinth. Assuming Sly has not detected them, we can secret our way inside by using them. You're a genius, Spirit of the woods, we thank you."

"Waaasn't cleverrrrr enufff tooooo leeeeave a boggle's muuuuuuzle on..."

So confoundedly dark was the forest, that even during broad daylight it was difficult to discern anything other than a blurred shadowy blanket of indistinct greens and impenetrable blacks. A short while later Merlock exposed one of the few tunnel entrances, hidden within feral, thorny gorse and dense bracken. Upon entering, Merlock led the way using his druid egg, which radiated a soft blue light. It was bright enough to see by, but bereft of the glare that impaired night vision. It hadn't taken long for Rob's imagination to play tricks, flinching at the furtive shadows leaping and quivering around him. He had lost count of the number of twists, turns, jumps and crouches they had taken. As they passed adjoining tunnels, their own shadows would betray them, fleeing without warning and creating obscure demons that would cavort in an infinite variety of unsettling shapes and bewildering sizes. The stifling heat became overwhelming at times and in stark comparison becoming bitterly cold as they navigated around deafening underground springs. Rob was almost lost forever after slipping upon loose rock, but was caught and suspended by Clump's quick hand above the turbulent waters roaring from the gloomy inkiness far below.

Merlock stiffened, then whispered to the rest, "From this point onwards we must not talk, we use only hand gestures and we must choose our steps more wisely. We have almost reached my home, which means we have an entire search party above our heads."

Nodding, they continued, slowly, silently helping each other when required. Merlock stopped again and uttered a string of strange syllables, removing the enchantments he had set in place for the unwelcome. A hidden door revealed itself, then opened. One by one they entered Merlock's home then sat down while the wizard vanished to collect his magickal tools. While Rob sat in the warm silence, a sleepiness fell upon him. The culmination of prolonged physical exertion and sustained mental alertness had taken its toll. The tunnels had a strange effect, as if time had no place being there. He had almost lost his senses at one point, no longer certain of day or night, or even what they were trying to achieve. He had just focused on scurrying through the darkness without pause.

As he entered into a light sleep, a distant and familiar sound cruelly denied him the soft sweet relief his body and mind begged for. Grudgingly, Rob opened his eyes, becoming more alert upon hearing the same sound again. He looked up at Fingle who was already wide eyed and paused for breath.

Merlock rushed back in, "Those wretched meatballs, they have betrayed us!" spluttered the wizard angrily. "I don't know how, I have spells in place for them to never nosell out subterranean scents!"

Above ground, clustered around the concealed entrance of Merlock's home, a mob of noselling Boggles were running full tilt and smashing themselves into the foliage in a frenzy, foaming heavily in their muzzles and desperately trying to gain entry.

"How could they have known, it's imposs—" Merlock stopped mid-sentence, "where's Clump?"

Rob and Fingle shrugged, they were so tired they hadn't noticed him leaving the room. Fingle smelt it first. They ran into the kitchen and threw open the door.

"Don't worry, I've made enough for everyone." said Clump, flaring his nostrils over a large frying pan heaped high with sizzling hog bacon.

"Clump, what have you done?" shrieked Merlock.

"Oh, just bacon, but I can do some eggs as well."

"You fool, the stove smoke feeds outside!"

"Shhh, they will hear you." admonished Clump, turning the bacon with reverence.

The guards tried to encourage the Boggles to leave so they could rat out the fugitives. But the scent of salted hog bacon was irresistible and they promptly turned upon Sly's elite squad, thrusting their foaming muzzles savagely against them. The scene was both awkward and freakish. A horrified guard rooted to the spot, stood squealing with his eyes closed until Sly had cuffed sense back into him.

"Bring me the Guild." demanded Sly, unable to look upon the parody any further.

A group of dark cloaked Goblins made a solemn entrance, their faces hidden beneath their cowls. They understood what was required and in an instant Boggles were blasted apart by streams of crackling red fire, manifesting from the palms of the dark magi. Their cries were pitiful. Those that were not barbecued to a crust, rolled away in haste. The tasty aroma was now considerably less mouth-watering.

"This way, quickly." urged Merlock, hearing the muffled wails from his loyal defenders above. They ran through a bolt hole that led back into the tunnel system, but now in the opposite direction from which they had arrived. Merlock grabbed what he could, knowing that Sly would surely have them had they remained any longer.

"I'm sorry..." offered Clump, still chewing on a bacon sandwich.

"*Sorry*?" hissed Fingle, "if we are caught, the King's hogs will be chewing on *yer* backside."

Sly's guards were now in the tunnels and rapidly gaining ground. The escapees were forced to venture down a seldom used tunnel system, as the guards occupied all of the remaining tunnels around them.

"I don't understand. How could they know which directions to take, aren't there traps in place?" asked Rob.

"They are using a dark and powerful magick, I sensed its use against the Boggles. It possesses the same corruptible flavour as the magick used outside the Pye Shoppe. Listen carefully, the only escape we have available to us leads out into a small expanse that's closed off by the base of Sailor's Toof, a vast and impenetrable mountain that is far too steep to climb. Our only option is to head directly for the mountains base and find cover."

"Are you saying we'll be trapped? How can we survive against these odds?" implored Rob.

"Please do as I say, I will deal with the rest." Merlock panted, as they increased their pace.

"Move faster!" screamed Sly hungrily. He knew they were outnumbered and with the Guild at his disposal, outclassed. He had of course heard of Merlock and his abilities, he was formidable yes, but against six high magicians of the Shadow Goblin Government's own Guild? Not even a level forty-two druid could withstand them all. As Sly ramped up his pursuit, occasionally a guard would stumble into a crevasse, or trip into an adjacent tunnel, becoming ensnared in a lethal trap lying in wait. Sly considered them as an expendable resource, a means to an end, so that his own agenda may finally come to fruition *and* settle a long overdue debt with an old friend.

Merlock was the first to tumble out of the hidden entrance, swiftly followed by the others landing on top of him.

"Mfft, keep moofing you idiots!" blurted Merlock, spread-eagled.

They picked themselves up and ran for the steep base of Sailor's Toof. Although the grassland they traversed was not a particularly large distance to cover, it seemed to take an unbearably long time. Merlock flagged, but Clump swiftly scooped him up. As they neared the mountain's base, a loud cry came from behind them as the guards now spilled out into the field. Short of breath, Rob turned to face the impending threat, his adrenaline pumping hard. Fingle snarled menacingly, holding a terrifying knife in each hand and Clump stood resolute, calmly swinging a monstrous double-headed battle axe in a huge arc, while Merlock decided it was the perfect opportunity for a little meditation.

"What's Merlock doing?" stammered Rob, unable to mask his trembling voice as he watched the furious stampede approach.

"Unlike fatty 'ere, he's *saving* bacon, yours and mine. Now let him be and take this knife and if yer unsure how to use it, stick the pointy bit away from yer. Oh and stick some moss in yer flaps."

"Not again. Then I suppose we are un-pinchable and we sidestep away to our freedom." groaned Rob.

"Don't be witless, that would never work. What yer do is stick this green sponge in yer ears, real tight, then when yer hear a funny sound, copy it as best yer can, got it?"

Rob's fear was almost replaced by the deep despondency that settled in. It seemed like everyone else knew exactly what to do and when to do it. Like forcing moss in both ears, waiting to emulate a sound he had never heard, while an encroaching war party was about to approve his life membership to the choir invisible. Rob became aware of a strange scraping noise. He shrieked and literally held himself as hundreds of small grey stones scuttled past. Watching in horror, the stones rose up on little hind legs then began to vibrate...alarmingly loud.

"Fingle, Fingle, the stones are alive!"

"They ain't stones yer nugget." Fingle snorted.

"What did you say?" replied Rob, cupping a moss laden ear.

"I said they ain't stones, they is hum-bugs *and* it's *that* sound we have ta copy."

"Did you just say humbugs?*"* shouted Rob.

"Yes, they is bugs which hum. Uncle's been talking with 'em. Now start humming if yer wants ta stay alive."

Rob gave up trying to rationalise anything anymore and did precisely as he was told. His vision was blurring over and he felt acute nausea coupled with a horrific headache. As instructed he began to hum in tune, then immediately noticed his symptoms alleviate. As he fine-tuned his vocal vibration to resonate with the hum-bugs, he experienced an enormous improvement. Utterly astonished in his own ability to govern how he felt merely by humming, he almost failed to notice the dire effect it was having on the charging horde, which had thankfully ground to a halt not less than fifty meters away. The hum-bugs—although close to Rob—were standing directly in front and facing away. En masse, they produced a unified sound wave that crippled anything in their path possessing a central nervous system. Rob could barely watch while the guards fell to their knees, clutching their convulsing heads in agony. Many were vomiting uncontrollably, while others screamed until their lungs had emptied. During the bloodcurdling spectacle, Rob momentarily forgot to hum, until a searing pain between his temples had reminded him. The next thing Rob felt was a hand grab his arm, it was Merlock, drenched in perspiration and looking much older than he had a short moment ago.

"Follow me, our little friends cannot hum forever." said the wizard and led Rob away.

The humming entourage approached the flat base of the Sailor's Toof, while the hum-bugs remained steadfast.

"I need a few moments more." Merlock shouted, placing a shaky hand upon the cold ancient stone.

I wish I knew what he was up to now, thought Rob, watching the wizard gently sway with only the whites of his eyes exposed, which frankly did little to soothe his aching nausea.

"Get them! Blast them! Do something!" commanded Sly, banging his skull against the dry earth. The Guild had managed to regroup and manifest a frequency shield against the vibratory onslaught. They pressed forwards in deep concentration, allowing the squirming guards to recover once safely behind the Guilds defence, although considerably worse for wear.

"They are coming back." Clump bellowed excitedly.

Damn the Guild and their deviant sorcery, muttered Fingle, unsheathing a third knife and placing it between his bared teeth. Rob felt the stranglehold of panic once again as the sonic wall began to waver and the valiant hum-bugs were finally tiring from their supreme effort, some collapsing and scuttling back into cover. He looked behind at Merlock leaning against the mountain, still uttering a strange language.

Clump stood in front of Rob, "If they want to get to you, they have to get past me." growled Clump, like a roll of thunder.

As the humming decreased, it buttressed the advancing rabble, increasing their own courageous cacophony. Suddenly an enormous cracking sound tore through the grassland, accompanied by a blazing flash of light that blinded the guards and surprised the Guild, momentarily rendering them ineffectual. Rob almost put his neck out as he spun around and gasped aloud at what he saw. Merlock had somehow convinced the mountain to split itself open, just enough for them to escape through. Fingle ran over, catching his uncle as he fell to the ground, exhausted from his inconceivable feat.

"Run, yer dunderheads, run!" yelled Fingle.

Rob ran towards the impossible groaning fissure, threatening to slam shut at any given moment. Clump stood at the opening, holding his outstretched hand to Rob. He almost met it but fell short as a searing pain hammered into his lower leg. As he toppled, he observed an explosion of green sparks, the same kind he had witnessed at the Pye Shoppe when all hell had broken loose, or rather Clump's battle lust had. One of the Guild had recovered from his temporary blindness and struck a lucky blow to Rob's leg. The dark magician summoned a second sphere of malevolent energy, preparing to release it towards Rob for the deciding blow. Two things then happened very quickly. A tall hooded stranger leapt from the shadows, letting loose three arrows at a preposterous speed and unimaginable accuracy towards the unshielded magician. And Rob was airlifted by Clump and thrown inside the mountain's base just before the vibrating fissure crashed closed, sealing itself once more into an impenetrable agglomeration.

"Open it now, now, now!" ordered Sly thickly, unable to control his raw infuriation. He stumbled around half blind, lashing out at any poor soul who was close enough to receive it.

"On behalf of the Guild—minus the magus wearing three arrows for a hat—I'm afraid we cannot open a mountain, Master."

"Why not? Do we not feed your black appetites without question? Do you not hold high enough positions within the Council?" spluttered Sly, stamping on any remaining hum-bugs and nearby Goblin hairy bits.

"Yes of course, my Beloved Devotee of Debauchery, but it is an ancient magick that Merlock weaves, a magick we cannot wield. It is a natural alchemy, a partnership between the elements of which we have forsaken, in favour for conjury of a much darker kind, a kind that best suits the Council..." replied the overconfident magus with a touch of disdain.

Sly loosened his grip on a gurgling guard's throat and straightened himself, tugging his gloves tightly around his fingers, "What good is a fizzing green ball, when Merlock has mountains and bugs that do his bidding?" Sly spoke softly, as he walked over to the sneering sorcerer. "I sometimes think that we give you too much, almost as if it is *you* who are in charge and *we* simply exist...to serve you?"

Sly let slip a high pitched giggle, one that usually preceded death in some form. He pressed his curled black lips to the magicians trembling flap and breathed, "I think you have become a little bit self-important. I think that *you* think *you* are better than me. But I can help you, you see you have just...lost your way. I will let you into a special little secret I hold very dear, *no one* is better than me, not even that insufferable turd who calls himself King..."

The sorcerer's monobrow seesawed in shock, like a bewhiskered worm fending off a sky full of ravenous crows. Sly's mouth parted and his black tongue flicked at the sweat forming upon the magicians face. Sly savoured the salty taste of fear, then plunged a knife upwards into the base of his skull, letting him drop at his feet.

Twice you have bested me Rob, this is becoming a bad habit of yours, but with all bad habits, they have bad consequences. I will wait.

Sly licked his blade, allowing its cool edge to cut his tongue a little and with immaculate wickedness sparkling in his eyes, issued orders for his guards to head back into the tunnels. They would have no option but to march around the mountain's base until a more suitable terrain would enable them to resume the chase. Before Sly and his troops left the open grassland, he bent down and yanked free one of the arrows from the dead sorcerer's head, sniffing intently along its wooden shaft.

It seems someone else has an interest in you, Rob from Terra. Everything is going deliciously according to plan…

Chapter 10

"That was close." said Rob rubbing his leg, while Clump continued dragging him into a large underground cavern, not far from where the fissure had closed.

Fingle was already making a much needed brew of hot tar. Merlock was lying down on a blanket, having entered a 'wizard's snooze' to regain his strength.

"You can stop now, Clump, I can walk from here." said Rob, hugely relieved that thousands of tons of rock now separated them from that masked maniac and his mindless minions.

Fingle looked over to Clump, then back at Rob.

"Rob, how's yer leg?"

"Oh, it's not too bad, I can walk okay, see?"

Rob had a slight limp that seemed to improve by the second.

"Rob, I don't wish ta alarm yer, but yer were fully exposed ta a blast of dark enchantment that's created fer one thing, ta destroy. Can yer please tell me why yer are simply walking it off?" enquired Fingle, deeply suspicious.

Rob thought for a moment then sat down, *Fingle had a good point.*

"In truth, I have no idea. Maybe it was a glancing blow and I got lucky?" Rob offered, but deep down, he knew the fireball had been a direct hit.

Fingle was brewing a second cup when Merlock sat bolt upright, "Whazzat, curse you, Boggles, be gone!" the last two words echoing around the cavern like a portent of doom.

"My apologies, a wizard's snooze is deep and dizzying, but most replenishing nonetheless. Now, back there I had to act fast to save our skins, that was the good news, the bad news is that our options are once again limited."

As the echoing faded, Merlock caught Rob rubbing his leg and noticed his breeches had been badly scorched.

"Crom, did you get hit, boy?"

"Yes, yes I did, but it's merely a scratch, nothing more." replied Rob, standing effortlessly.

Merlock gasped, "Rob, I think you are something other than what you appear. It seems you have a natural defence against shadow enchantment. Whether this is because of your transition here, or whether it is innate I cannot say yet, but either way, you have magick in your bones. Let me think on this a little more when I have the time. But now, we have by my reckoning four options. We can stay here and eventually die; we can re-open the fissure and face the guards that have been undoubtedly left for us, or we can enter the Devil's Spit Bowl, which is suicide. Its towering walls have become completely smooth from tidal waves surging from underground rivers connecting out to the Great Wet. We'd all be stranded in the bowl until we drown."

"That's three, Merlock, what's—"

"Glad you asked, when we leave the other side of Sailor's Toof, we must head directly for the Black Line."

Fingle shook his head while his uncle continued, "Before you ask, it's a bottomless chasm of ancient doom stretching as wide as the eyes can see, from This-Way to That-Way. Mythical monsters were once cast into its depths, remaining there ever since the time of the Shining

Ones. Walking around its perimeter is out of the question, as going *This-Way* will take us to Sly and his horde and going *That-Way* will funnel us towards Fai Vale."

"Well that sounds pleasant enough." remarked Rob.

"F.A.I. Vale is far from pleasant. Fire And Ice, is a large training facility where nature's elementals are granted artistic license to practice their trade before visiting your world. They are, for all intents and purposes, solely responsible for your seasons. Fai Vale is far removed from the Faerie tale imagery it conjures up. Rather, it is a tempest of raw and frighteningly potent energies that tear through the valley in constant flurry of seasonal change, so much so in fact, that all four seasons, with all of their extremities can be experienced in under one minute of your time. But, as fortune would favour, not far from here there's a single place along the Black Line that a crossing is possible."

"Did yer knock yer noggin numb, Uncle? That bridge is guarded by Toesin *and* he ain't letting anyone cross."

"Who's Toesin?" questioned Rob, trying to keep up.

"He's the keeper of the Black Line Bridge. Every bridge in both our worlds belongs ta a Troll; it's simply the way of things. Some Trolls prefer ta hide under 'em, some of 'em like ta come out and scare folk, but the worst kind will mash anyone ta marrow that tries ta cross 'em." Fingle said.

"Which one is Toesin?" asked Rob, already having a fair idea of the answer. "Neither, he gives travellers a *fair* chance to cross by employing their wits. Of course, if you tried to cross uninvited, then you would get mashed." explained Merlock.

"Fair, fair? No one has ever managed ta out-wit Toesin, yer may as well take a running jump across the Black Line cos that's as far as yee's ever gonna get." spat Fingle, as several drops of icy water spattered on his shaking head.

"There's something I haven't told you, Nephew, when I was talking to the mountain she gave me a gift. I received a vision, it showed us all crossing the Black Line Bridge and reaching the other side safely. I am seldom wrong in these things as you know." said Merlock solemnly.

"I know, but if yer wrong this time, Uncle, we are as good as toasted slop slugs."

"First however, we must find out who this 'Buttercup' is, hand me my bag, boy." Merlock said, smiling at Rob.

Merlock reached in and produced a large smoky quartz ball. He placed it reverently upon an ornate wooden stand and in seconds his breathing had slowed as he gazed unblinkingly into its murky depths. The air was heavy and oppressive, it's cloying chill uncomfortable. The fire sputtered and hissed as icy droplets lost their grip from countless lime formations hanging precariously above their heads. Menacing shadows flinched and jerked throughout the cavern's unfathomable reaches. Merlock's breathing faltered, becoming more erratic and laboured. He began swaying in unsettling circular motions; Rob looked towards the others and judged by their startled faces this was not at all expected behaviour. The wizard juddered as he swayed and began grinding his teeth as a terrible measured moan escaped.

"Shall we stop this?" asked Rob, deeply concerned.

"Nay, let him be, it might be more dangerous." said Fingle darkly.

Abruptly, the swaying stopped. Merlock's head lifted, his eyes snapped open and were now glowing emerald green, "Look upon me and heed these words, if you do not give up your futile search, your souls will be in terrible danger!"

"What the..."

"Shhh Rob, let him finish." snapped Fingle.

"What danger?" Clump asked.

Fingle shot him a disapproving look. "It doesn't matter, you will just be in great danger, so you must all turn back and give up your impossible quest if you value your pathetic lives." warned the possessed wizard, in a squeaky, yet guttural voice.

"Are you saying our lives *and* our souls are in danger?" puzzled Clump.

"Yes, yes, both are in great danger, they are so in danger that I wouldn't want to be in your shoes, that's how much danger." threatened the demonic voice issuing from Merlock.

Fingle joined the bizarre conversation while Rob sat in silence, feeling very disassociated by the proceedings.

"Are yer saying that our *shoes* could kill us, cos the *soles* are dangerous?" said Fingle hiding behind a smirk.

"No! That is not what I meant, you *must* know what I mean?" seethed the devilish voice.

"I'm not sure that we do? I had these shoes made by the finest cobblers in Tawdry Hollow, so I fail ta see how they could endanger me life, or the lives of me travelling companions?"

"Forget the shoes and forget the soles, I mean remember the souls. Look, irrespective of your footwear, you are all in great peril and must turn back. Is that clear enough?" "Rob, is that clear fer yer?" enquired Fingle matter-of-factly.

Rob sat mesmerised, unable to shift his gaze from the green smoke trailing from Merlock's nostrils.

"How about yer, Clump, do...yer...under…stand?"

Clump nodded eagerly, then sank back down glumly shaking his head.

"Hmmm, I'm afraid we are struggling a little here, I think it may 'ave something ta do with taking threats, yer see we don't give a Faerie's fart wot yer say *or* do. If yer *ever* soul-seize uncle again and insistyouate that me shoes are not of the finest craftsgoblinship, I mean, fer crom's sake, look at the stitch work, I will hunt yer down and pilch yer pickles with nowt more than a blunted tuskpick!"

As Fingle delivered his colourful pledge, he loomed in closely to Merlock's abandoned gaze and at that same moment, several of the Guild in the Dark Fortress fell backwards upon seeing Fingle's ponderous snout and baleful eyes fill the whole of their scrying bowl. Fingle slapped his possessed uncle—ignoring Clump's irritating offers of assistance—until Merlock came back to his senses.

"Crom, my balls have been compromised!" coughed Merlock, immediately covering his Looksee ball in a black cloth.

"Who did this?" asked Rob shakily.

Enraged, Fingle replied, "I know exactly who, those incompetents in the S.G.G. We are on ta something big, big enough for them ta risk the balance of magick, this will not go without consequence." murmured Fingle, soothing his faint uncle.

"What kind of consequence?" pressed Rob.

Merlock sat up, taking a hot sip of tar that Fingle had made, then faced Rob.

"All magick here is in balance, watched over by those that dwell in the Crystal Mountains, it is how we have always existed. Unlike in your world where freewill allows anyone to use dark or light magick, of which the effects are of a more direct nature, only affecting the users and receivers at that time, or at a future time. Your world is not so much in balance; it is more in a constant state of struggle. But here, in the Faerie Kingdom, any excessive use of magick has an impact in ways we cannot foresee or control. It is no exaggeration that the fabric of our world could unravel if the balance of magick favoured any one pristine polarity, if only for times briefest of breaths."

"Couldn't you just counteract it? Do something good with magick? I don't know, feed the hungry or manifest a fluffy rainbow Unicorn?" offered Rob, eyes wide with enthusiasm.

Merlock chuckled, "I wish it was that simple. Imagine a pond and someone throwing in a pebble, the effect ripples outwards, yes? Now imagine another pebble thrown in by someone else trying to cancel out the ripples coming towards them. One of two things will happen. If fortuitous, both ripples will cancel each other out. But, if more pebbles continue to be thrown in, the water becomes more turbulent as the ripples join to create a larger wave. In the end it becomes a contest in who can create the largest wave. From a once serene pool of water that occasionally rippled, to a maelstrom of uncontrollable fury."

"What you are saying, is that *if* we fight back, we could unintentionally help to destroy the fabric that holds this world together?" spluttered Rob.

"Precisely! But only if we use magick, which is why it must be used sparingly…" Merlock replied.

"But, if we continue to let the S.G.G. use their dark magick, they will achieve their evil aims without any opposition."

"Aye, Rob, now there's the rub," sneered Fingle, "yer see, the bitterest grog that was ever drank, is that some think about the fabric and some only think of themselves. Now there's nothing bad with being bad, but when it stops yer being bad, or good, cos there's nothing left ta live in, well, that's just plain crazy. Magick's useful, but there are many more ways ta cook a Fidgeting-flea soufflé…" Fingle nodded over to where the giant barbarian gleefully sharpened his dreadful battle axe.

Merlock added, "We must therefore be careful in how much magick we employ, relying more upon our wits and brawn, between us we have plenty. Don't be down, lad, much can be achieved by Goblin spirit alone, it has its own kind of magick. It's indestructible, inspiring, and the hope it quickens in others is unstoppable, spreading like a fire that can *never* be snuffed, you will see." Merlock gave Rob a wink as Fingle helped his uncle back onto his feet, stretching out the cold cramp that had set in his legs.

"How do we find Buttercup now?" asked Rob, hoping that in doing so they might have a chance to set things straight.

"Well, I can't use my old Looksee ball anymore and the nearest place I know of, where a seer of reliable repute that could help us, can only be reached on the opposite side of the Black Line."

Fingle looked astonished, "Are yer talking about the Crone in the Cone, Uncle?"

"Yes, Nephew, she is undoubtedly the finest seer I know of, but regrettably difficult to ask."

Sensing one of Rob's relentless questions, Merlock continued, "She is difficult to ask, because to get inside the hill in which she lives, is to venture beneath a waterfall. Sounds simple enough I grant you, but you must wade through the water with pure intention and none other. I suppose it's a safeguard of sorts, it deters marauders from stealing her vast fortune gained from hundreds of years selling hidden truths of a time critical nature, or after all other means of enquiry have been exhausted."

"But what could be so difficult in wading through water?"

"It's not the water that poses the problem, it's the *Impenetrabubbles*. Yes bubbles, those most flimsy of transient things. You will see what I mean when we get there, but for now we have more immediate concerns than that of the Crone in the Cone of Certainty."

The small gang gathered their belongings and followed the wizard through the mountain's inner lair. On one occasion, Clump had almost brought down the entire roof after punching rock apart to fit himself through, forcing everyone to sprint blindly away as dozens of limestone skewers rained down upon them. After they had reached a safe enough distance, Clump waited patiently for Fingle to cuff him firmly behind his earflap—although he had to leap off a large craggy rock to do so.

The trek had been shorter than the tunnelling beneath Whisperun Forest and oddly, Rob began to feel very much at home deep within the mountains belly, he really was becoming quite concerned with his newly acquired tastes. Merlock had led them to a small natural opening in the far side of the mountain, by investing just a small amount of magickal energy for simple navigation. They shielded their eyes as they adjusted to the bright sunlight, which blazed in an azure sky unchallenged by any cloud.

"We head, Top This-Way." said Merlock, as they left the refuge of the Sailor's Toof.

Merlock picked up the pace, reminding them Sly would be in hot pursuit and eventually catch up with them. They needed to get to the Black Line as quickly as possible. Fingle had his doubts about Toesin the Troll allowing them to cross his bridge—the *only* bridge over the entire chasm—but the odds were palatable compared to facing Sly and his ever increasing army advancing their way.

Chapter 11

"Did he say anything, anything at all when you found him?" she asked, holding his charred ragged body close to her, feeling its weak and erratic heart beat against her own.

"Yes, my Queen, he said he had urgent news and asked specifically for you." replied her warden, taking a knee respectfully.

"Dern, please look at me, what else did he say?" she said softly, but with an authority that was impossible to ignore.

Dern raised his head and stood. He was her most loyal aid and fiercest protector. He straightened his powerful arms and stepped closer to his Queen, struggling to look into her piercing eyes, eyes that shone like amber held to sunlight.

"You were right, they have been plotting against you. Dream regulation has been compromised...by the regulators." he said regretfully, his jaw visibly tightening.

"And Jarett?" she whispered.

Dern nodded gravely, casting his solemn gaze downwards.

She walked over to the window that spread the entire width of the room. Running her hand through her cropped black hair she looked down upon the land she dearly loved. The lakes that glimmered, the vibrant forests and lush valleys that hummed and sang with life. She surveyed the countless mercurial rivers that weaved and wandered, sensing their coolness and vitality. Her gaze fell over the mountain ranges that spanned her Kingdom, her heart reaching out to the many races that depended upon her.

"See to it that the Faux makes a full recovery, it seems we have much to discuss."

"Yes, my Queen." replied Dern dutifully.

As he began to leave she added, "And, Dern, please summon the Defence Commander, tell him to mobilise our air and ground forces and that it is not a drill. Oh, and please give Jarett a personal message from me, tell him that Dream Control have a nightmare coming their way, they have pissed off the wrong Faerie. Tell him I am curious to know how far I can wedge my wand where the sun cannot reach!"

"My Queen, we cannot find Jarett. It appears he has been gone some time. One of the prisoners had been covering for him."

The Queen turned to face him and he could see the trace of tears that carried her pain, but her eyes presented a different picture. They were ablaze with fire, a fire so terrible he did not believe it was the same person that faced him, the Queen who did nothing but give and nurture to all those that needed it. As Dern closed the doors behind him, he heard a terrifying scream. He realised in that moment the rumours were true, the Faerie Queen, for all of her benevolence was also a formidable opponent. Chilled to his core, he left hastily to ensure that little Smidge's recovery would be as swift as possible.

Chapter 12

Although running at speed, Fingle and Rob managed to maintain a conversation while remaining vigilant for danger as they bounded over open ground.

"Who exactly is this Toesin character, Fingle? And what is it that we have to do to get across his bridge?" panted Rob growing anxious again. In fact, he could not recall the last time he felt anything other than anxiety.

"Personally, I think we have more chance discovering what really goes into Pat Thogens meat pies than ever bettering ol' Toesin. The tale told of 'Toesin the Trolls Tail', is a unique one fer sure. It is better known by 'Toesin's Tail-Tale' fer short, or T.T.T. and that acronym is by no coincidence, Rob. Yer think that yer Humans invented acronyms? Pifflepuke, it came from the faerie realm, as did yer alphabets and even numbers."

"Wow, that's incredible! But surely not everything came from your world Mr Froglick, what about the legal system?" said Rob grinning proudly.

"Aye, yer right there and look where that got us, all discomgoblinated. Now listen sharp, it was decided there was too much confusion, due ta the many uni-onions working ta maintain the balance 'ere and in yer own world, so everything became abbreviated to stop the mind muddles. It worked well until folk began ta forget what they had originally meant, so Toesin decided he would log all the acronyms in a single tome. He was a victim of his own success, as anyone who wanted an explanation on any acronym would ave ta go and visit him and if yer understood anything about Trolls, they likes ta be left well alone. So, after he had a belly full one day, he refused ta talk ta anyone any further. The only way yer could get a looksee in his tome was ta play him at *Tic-Tac-Toesin* and win. Now, he uses his tome ta stop walkers from crossing the Black Line Bridge instead. Because no one has ever beaten him, no one even bothers trying anymore and he gets left well alone."

"Tic-Tac-Toe? You mean noughts and crosses?" replied Rob, surprised it was known here as well.

"No. Tic-Tac-Toesin. It's a game of wits using acronyms that are collected in his tome. Folk seeking long lost descriptions of acronyms, or wishing ta cross his bridge must take turns in marking empty spaces in a three by three grid using letters. The first line of letters that are displayed in a horridzontal, fertical, or diagonalley row, is the acronym Toesin must know *without* consulting his tome first. Once he writes down a description, he proves it's right by showing it in his tome and he *always* lets the challenger go first."

"That's good of him I suppose?"

"Not really, cos when someone's thought of an acronym ta beat him, he usually lets 'em get two letters in a row, but on Toesin's second go, he adds a last letter ta the challengers line, changing it ta a completely different acronym the challenger first had in mind, crafty!"

"So Toesin has the *only* recorded work of *every* acronym in the land and there are thousands of them?" said Rob a little out of breath, trying to keep up in foot and mouth.

"Yes, and not thousands, but tens of thousands. Thirty five thousand one hundred and fifty two combinations ta be precise. That's including all letters, either in all big, *or* in all small, but never mixing the two letter sizes."

"Bloody hell! Well in that case, we must have a good chance of getting one of them right that he can't remember." said Rob encouragingly.

"Yer would think so, but Toesin's obsessed with 'em, he does nothing but read his damn tome and has done fer the past seven hundred long cycles. He's never lost. And yer can't use magick cos he will sense it and yer will have lost. Yer can't kill him, cos he's a Transforming-Troll and can shrink or grow ta whatever size pleases him and if you've ever seen a Transforming-Troll full size, yer would understand. Besides, his two brothers, Mish and Mash live under the bridge and yer do not want to mess with them, crazy as an Orc army with pyre-flies in their under-crackers and just as deadly. By my reckoning we are wasting our time, but the *wise old sage* reckons otherwise."

Merlock slowed and Clump scooped him up, propping him up on his shoulder as he was accustomed to doing so during long journeys. The terrain was forgiving enough, open grassland peppered with boulders and narrow streams. Merlock scanned the horizon from his new vantage point and could see no signs of Sly and his cohorts. Although the sun's heat was taxing, the sympathetic winds carried a coolness, washing over the grateful, puffing fugitives. Rob deemed himself to have a reasonably high level of fitness, but even with his new body, he had struggled to keep up with the Goblins. They were a hardy race, all muscle and sinew, tightly sprung with a stamina that was perfectly proportionate to their infuriating stubbornness. As Rob ran, he felt his hot blood coarse through his body, his chest heaving, his strong arms and sturdy legs pumping hard. Although a little short of breath, he felt strong and surprisingly vigorous even though they had been running at a considerable pace for what must have been around two hours. His mind wandered back to when he had once trained for a marathon, in honour of his late mother. His father didn't like to discuss the past and rarely opened up, but he was told his mother had died shortly after his birth, taken by some rare blood disease. The charity marathon he had taken part in was his way of dealing with the loss of a mother's love. He had hoped that in some small way, the money he had raised for the blood research charity may help another child to not share his fate. And hopefully his own mother, wherever she was, would love him for doing so. He recalled the race and remembered how he had felt when he had crossed the finishing line. He was positioned within the top two hundred runners and had given it his all, collapsing in a heap of emotions, unaware of the applause surrounding him.

His thoughts returned back to the present, as he leapt over a series of interlacing narrow streams. Rob knew with all certainty they had just ran not one, but two marathons in only half the time and felt he could do the same again. Being a Goblin came with serious benefits, but he dearly wished his bounteous earflaps would stop slapping his face like the hands of a belligerent personal trainer obsessed with victory by proxy.

"I see it!" yelled Merlock.

Rob scanned the horizon and could discern a dark smudge spanning the entire width of his vision. As he approached, the smudge became deeper and darker, until all that he could see was an enormous bottomless crack that not even the blazing sun could penetrate. Clump lowered Merlock back onto his feet and they followed him to where the ancient bridge began. They had gotten to within fifty feet, when a gnarled hand appeared, rising from out of the chasm. Toesin hauled himself out, standing steadfast between the intruders and his bridge, unblinking and very intimidating. He reached at least twelve feet in height, thickset and covered in black, wiry hair. Perched above his uneven teeth, sat a large, red, bulbous nose that had a tendency to wobble as he walked. His hands and feet were disproportionately large and a long, thick tail swished threateningly behind him, terminating in a dense, bushy tuft.

"Well met, Bridge Guardian, we come peacefully and wish to cross." said Merlock in a firm voice, bowing respectfully.

A tired gloat stretched across the Troll's leathery face as he pointed to his enormous tome he cradled within his muscular, hairy arm. Merlock nodded and stepped forwards to where a small fire was constantly kept aflame. Behind it stood a large slab of roughly hewn white marble. Toesin walked over to the white tablet, never once removing his stare and casually dipped the large tuft at the end of his tail into the charcoal that lay scattered beyond the flames. With unnerving precision, his tail came alive as it drew out a three by three grid on the standing tablet. When he was done, Toesin nodded back at Merlock.

"Let the games begin." muttered Fingle.

Merlock was no newcomer to acronyms either; most of his magickal education had consisted of them. He thought initially of trying out M.A.D., it was how he had first felt when he took up the study of the Arcane arts during his time in the Citadel of Light, with the woodland Elves and Faerie's at the school of H.E.X.—Hogspots Enchantment Xpandability—hidden within Ambershea Forest.

M.A.D. stood for 'Magicians Asinine Department'. It had been set up collaboratively by the Goblin, Elf, and Faerie councils, for recovering magicians at H.E.X., who had simplifried their intellectual and emotional capacities from voyaging the void—amongst other terrifying occultly endeavours. A place where he had feared he would end up more than once, as many often did! Merlock picked up a fragment of charcoal from the fires edge and wrote out the letter 'M' in his first grid square, mindful to keep it in upper case—only crom and Toesin of course, knew what M.A.D. meant in lower case? The wizard looked back at the Troll, who now appeared to be running some kind of computation in his skull. Toesin's dark brown eyes performed rapid circles while his enormous yellowed teeth ground together furiously. Rob was forced to look away, Toesin's thinking face was the stuff of nightmares. Mercifully his eyes rattled to a stop and Toesin's tail tuft dabbed the ash at his feet. The Troll deftly wrote out a letter 'P', on a separate line within the grid. The moment that Merlock wrote his second letter 'A' in his adjoining square, his hopes were dashed as Toesin moved in quickly to add *his* second letter 'A', in Merlock's final grid line square. The Troll's tail then spelt out the acronym and associated description below the grid with finer finesse than a fourth-century virtuoso Japanese calligraphist.

M.A.A. – *Maenads Alcoholics Anonymous*

Toesin then flicked through the tomes pages with lightning speed, stopping with a chipped black finger nail resting triumphantly upon:

'M.A.A. – Maenads Alcoholics Anonymous.'

Merlock had expected as much. He turned around to the others. "This may take a while, you had better get some rest, but take vigils between you. If you see Sly Slaughter then we have no other choice but to head for Fai Vale, understand?"

They all agreed. While Merlock battled on, Rob lay back, watching the most surreal war of wits he would ever witness. The speed at which they contended acronyms was staggering. He looked to Clump, who had taken up sentry duty watching That-Way Down, while Fingle had This-Way Down covered. Although feeling substantially inferior in comparison to the two logophiles locking horns, he was no stranger to acronyms either. During his study of Law as a graduate back home, he knew how maddening yet useful they were and had cause to employ them many, many times.

Immeasurable attempts later, Merlock was beginning to struggle, presumably exhausting his vast knowledge of acronyms. He also noted that Toesin had become noticeably more relaxed, arrogant even. He was now allowing Merlock to add his final letter within his grid line without even bothering to interfere. Toesin was truly a master of his craft and didn't care what acronym the wizard threw at him, he knew them all and would happily demonstrate his expertise using his cinder smeared tail and subsequent tome referencing.

Rob sat bolt upright, a distant memory of a past conversation entered his mind, a conversation he had during a law class in which the subject of acronyms and the sheer volume of them were in hot debate. He sprang an idea, it was a long shot at best, but they had nothing left to lose. Rob jumped up, walked over to the Black Line and coughed his presence. Nothing. He coughed much louder, adding an odd yelp to its declarative delivery. The two combatants stopped and looked over.

"May I have a go please?" petitioned Rob, beginning to wish he had thought it through properly.

Expecting to see Merlock display disdain or surprise, he instead smiled, as if he had been waiting for Rob all along. Merlock bowed to Toesin then winked at Rob as he walked away. Toesin nodded at Rob while stifling a yawn, such was his growing boredom and cyclopean confidence in his own game and grinned anew as he saw relief flood over the Goblins as a partial yawn had *almost* escaped. Rob picked up a charred stick and walked towards the marble tablet. Toesin's tail swished away the previous effort from Merlock. The grid had been re-drawn and Rob nervously added the first letter 'T' in his first grid square.

Toesin did his usual unsettling eyes and teeth thing, then added 'Y' to his first grid square on a separate line. Rob then wrote a second letter 'L' in his adjoining square. Merlock's eyes fixed on the tablet, waiting for what Toesin would do next. Rob held his breath, his chance at success hinging solely in what the Troll's next move would be and all three of them knew it. Toesin grinned as his tail hovered teasingly above Rob's third and final grid line square...

Toesin's tail surprisingly swished to his own grid line, adding his second letter 'A'. Rob's pounding heart launched into his throat, he couldn't believe the Troll had allowed him to add his last letter where he needed it! Whether Toesin was bored, curious, cruel, or compassionate, he didn't care, now would be his only opportunity to outwit the legendary Troll of the Black Line Bridge.

Rob squeaked out the letter 'A' in his final square. Immediately Toesin ran his abhorrent computation, then smirked while his infuriating tail wrote:

T.L.A. – *The Leprechauns Adversity*

Rob stood his ground shaking his head, stating boldly, "No, that is incorrect."

The Troll blinked, then flung open his tome. With awesome alacrity he highlighted the same entry.

Rob still shook his head, "No, Toesin, I am afraid that is not the correct acronym description."

Toesin snarled while his thrashing tail wrote:

t.l.a. = *teratosis lexiphanic alliaphage*

Rob didn't budge, although he was terrified of what the Troll might do to him. "No, I am afraid that neither are the correct acronyms."

The Troll strode out to meet Rob and thrust the huge weathered tome in his face. Rob could see the two entries clearly under T.L.A./t.l.a., but refused to acknowledge it.

"Rob, whatever point you have, I strongly urge you make it quickly, a Troll's patience is shorter than his guest list."

"Merlock, trouble." said Clump.

A cloud of dust developed in the far distance, it seemed that Sly had enlisted many more guards than they had last encountered.

Merlock spun around to face Rob. "Finish this quickly, lad, it's our last chance, make it count." urged the wizard, as Toesin stared down Rob.

"Your tome is regrettably incomplete, Mr. Toesin, you are missing an acronym." stated Rob, barely able to look the Troll in the eyes.

Toesin stepped back in surprise, dropping his tome. He then leaped forwards gripping Rob by his arms, raising him high into the air as the Troll transformed to his fullest height. Merlock and Fingle had to restrain Clump from swinging his axe into the Troll's toe. Toesin opened his enormous mouth and Rob recoiled from a pungent waft of wild garlic.

Then, a very deep gargle, gurgled from Toesin, "W.T.F.?"

Rob had forced Toesin to break his centuries of silence. Knowing their lives now hung in the balance, he peeked downwards at his companions, who looked very small and deeply concerned.

"Toesin, your knowledge astounds and your reputation precedes you, but T.L.A. also applies to *Three Lettered Acronym...*"

A worrying pause ensued while the Troll attempted to assimilate the information. Meanwhile, the clatter of ill-fitted armour fast approached.

"What I mean to say, is that all of your tome's entries fall under this single acronym, as all of them are three lettered acronyms. By this virtue, an additional T.L.A.

acronym *and* its definition, *must* be added within your tome."

Rob's face screwed up like a dehydrated lily pad as Toesin's eyes—now blood red—threatened to plop out of his throbbing skull. Gradually, Rob un-crinkled his expression and watched the Troll's features soften, then quite abruptly Toesin bellowed out a deep rumbling laugh. The Troll was forced to drop Rob as he clutched his sides, he hadn't laughed in an exceedingly long time. Thankfully, Clump managed to catch Rob. They then took immediate advantage of their incredible good fortune by making great haste towards the dilapidated rope bridge.

"Run yer pair of loopy letter lovers. If Toesin realises he's been duped we're all going ta take the plunge!" Fingle howled, cackling like a lunatic.

"Agreed, let's do this…P.D.Q." quipped Rob with questionable bravado.

What has 'Pyromaniac Dragon Quarantine' have to do with anything? mused Merlock, while adjusting his beard ring to see where he was running.

The bridge was badly worn by time's hand. Given the choice, no sane attempt would ever be made to venture across the dark chasm, especially upon a bridge that looked like it could collapse at any given moment. However, choices were in stark supply for the desperate Goblins, so they boarded the creaking bridge, trying desperately to avoid looking through the rotting boards, down at the petrifying blackness below. Merlock knew only too well what manner of beasts had been cast into the pit, those that never slept and those that always knew hunger. There was good reason why these primeval miscreations had been condemned to the Black Line. Though it was believed impossible for anything to escape its incalculable depths, the notion would keep you awake at night if you allowed for the thought to settle, for even as brief as a twinkle of the dullest star.

"Shouldn't we be taking turns, or at least spread out a bit? If we walk across together, our combined weight could snap the boards, or worse the ropes." stammered Rob, wincing while Clump did as his names sake suggested across the complaining wood.

"Unfortunately, we do not have that luxury, speed is our best ally now. Besides, the bridge has been unused for so long it's bound to grumble. It was built to last a thousand years." encouraged Merlock unconvincingly, gingerly stepping over a broken slat.

"Halt!" ordered the Captain of the guard.

"Sir, the bridge is just ahead and our scouts tells me Toesin may be sleeping, or having a nightmare by the look of it. Or he could be laughing, we just can't tell." said the guard apologetically, as he reported his sketchy findings to Sly Slaughter.

"Is he perhaps laughing at us do you think, Captain? Laughing that Fingle and his renegade friends have evaded us for so long and now, beyond all expectation have managed to gain passage across the *only* bridge that can *never* be crossed?" said Sly, barely constraining his frustration as he spoke.

"I don't rightly know, sir, you pose quite an interesting quandary for a lowly Captain to ponder upon." replied the Goblin, attempting to look thoughtful.

"It was meant to be rhetorical you slime sucking sycophant."

"What about that then, sir? Was that retardical also? No…that was meant for *me*, wasn't it, sir?"

Sly punched him in the throat and walked over to a large boulder, then hopped upon it. Removing his search-scope, he held it up to his eye. For once, his incompetent guards were right. Toesin lay on his back, but he couldn't make out if he was sleeping, dying, or laughing, they had to get in closer. He aimed the scope towards the bridge.

There they are, those pustules, continuing to humiliate me. Well, fools they are and fall they will.

"Get up, Captain! I want you to take the regiment as close as possible to the Troll without disturbing him. If we do not cross that bridge, they will have gained several days march on us and that cannot be allowed to happen. Oh, and that punch *was* meant for you."

The Goblin nodded holding his throat and got back up. After enlisting his Corporal's vocal chords to deliver the order, they moved out as quietly as a regiment of incompetent, armoured Goblins could.

The lunacy of crossing was marginally favoured against the prospect of being caught by Toesin or Sly. The escapees had however made surprising progress, as mid-point was in sight. The swinging now increased to an alarming arc, the prevailing winds not helping in the slightest. The wrathful gusts screamed through the chasm, causing the rope bridge to sway so substantially, they were in very real danger of toppling over the fraying hand rails.

"Only move when the wind dies down!" shouted Merlock above the gale.

"What did he say?" Rob cried to Fingle, who was creeping forwards in front of him.

"I'm not sure, I canna hear uncle too well. I think he said, '*Once removed was the King's shiny crown*'!"

Rob clung on for dear life, too afraid to look behind, below, or anywhere else other than towards Fingle. "Why did he say that?" Rob yelled back.

"I 'ave no idea!" shouted Fingle.

"What you saying?" Clump hollered, clambering up the rear.

Rob stopped and craned his neck over as much as he dare, "Merlock said, '*Flouncy moods warrant slinky gowns*'!"

"What does that mean?" boomed Clump.

Rob raised his hands in mock uncertainty and almost fell over the side, buffeted by the howling winds. Clump had struggled the most. His size and weight did not offer any advantages and now he had to contend with confusing messages about 'bouncy toads warning stinky clowns'? *It must have been important enough,* he thought, but he was the last in line and hoped that whatever the problem was, it would be dealt with before it had gotten to him. After all, he was having his own issues with balance, but had found it much easier to only move when the wind had died down.

Toesin had shrunk back to his normal size, although defeated he was still entertained by Rob's daring triumph and seemingly oblivious to his surroundings, but of course a Troll's nose is *never* oblivious. It not only smells at great distances, but smells downwind, upwind, underground, and around corners, all at the same time. But most importantly of all, it smells intentions. The guards had achieved the impossible; they had managed to creep past the laughing Troll and onto his bridge. Sly remained at a safe distance convinced it was a trap, allowing his Goblins to continue, suspecting their noisy approach was masked largely by the Troll's gargles, echoing horribly around the chasm. Sly seized his opportunity and ran towards the bridge. As he reached a short distance between Toesin and the crossing, he was stopped in his tracks by something resembling a large snake wearing a sooty wig. Looking along its length, Sly shuddered, seeing it disappear behind the Troll. Toesin stopped laughing and stared murderously towards the intruder. Slaughter was about to make a run for it, but Toesin wrapped his tail tightly around Sly's waist, then transformed to his fullest height.

"You think me a fool, Masked one?" rasped the Troll.

"You must be, if you let those four witless Goblins on your bridge." spat Sly contemptuously.

"They earned their right, unlike you and your ignorant swamp-dwellers, *stealing* your passage." asserted Toesin croakily.

Almost half of Sly's guards had already entered the bridge and were almost a third of the way across, some having already fallen to their deaths in their reckless haste.

"Shall I cut it?" said Clump, now standing on the far side.

He was holding onto a thick rope, looking very dejected at the prospect of missing out on a good scrap.

"No, Clump. As much as I am tempted to destroy Toesin's bridge. it's not our decision to make and as yet not our only option. After all, those bungling block-heads are only following orders." said Merlock with a wry smile, gazing along the fearsome, swinging bridge they had all managed to cross.

"What we shall do instead, is convince them that the Black Line legends are most eager to greet them…"

Merlock knew that caressing an illusion into life was not a particularly difficult feat for a level forty-two wizard and as such the magickal footprint was negligible in terms of the great balance. He sat down comfortably and emptied his thoughts. In moments, he submerged into his subconscious mind, creating only *crom* knew what.

"It's happening!" gasped Rob, as an enormous, writhing, black tentacle slithered out of the cavernous gloom.

It probed its bulging way upwards until it found the bridge, then snaked along it, heading towards the oncoming clumsy guards. Immediately, they ceased their pursuit and turned tails, piling upon each other as the front sought desperate escape, but the ignorant rear continued blindly onwards, disastrously oblivious to the impending threat. A second tentacle appeared, then a third. Shouts of panic echoed around the bottomless canyon, as Clump,

Fingle and Rob cheered, poking fun at their imaginary plight.

Merlock opened an eye and the other instantly followed.

"Come, we mustn't loiter and lollygag, it's only a matter of time before they discover it's all just a ruse, we really must make tracks."

"That was incredible Merlock and how exactly does an illusion do that?" asked Rob pointing at the bridge.

They watched as two sucker-tipped tentacles held aloft several guards and shook them violently apart, while a third tentacle swept a dozen more into the gaping darkness.

"That wasn't uncle, ruuuuuuun!" yelled Fingle, as blood curdling screams filled the Black Line's amphitheatre of death.

Toesin looked upon his bridge, or what was left of it, "You've woken ol' Jelly Legs!" cried the shrinking Troll, loosening his tail's grip, enough for Sly to slide out and fall to the sooty ground. It was now every Goblin and Troll for themselves, any outstanding debts would have to be repaid later.

"Run you pathetic Goblins, follow me away from this cursed hole of filth." commanded Sly, already making considerable ground and feeling not a shred of remorse, or sorrow, for the shrieking fates that were sealed so horribly behind him.

Mish and Mash crawled out of the chasm, each clutching a large bag of possessions and looking lethally incensed.

"Who has done this?" roared Mish.

"We gots to leave our home, can't have a home without a bridge!" screamed Mash.

Toesin's curled grey lips quivered uncontrollably as he pointed towards the tall masked Goblin fleeing in the distance. The three brothers snatched a final look at their home which had spanned almost a millennia and a ludicrously rare, single tear fell from Toesin's twitching eye as he watched his beloved bridge disappear forever.

Chapter 13

All were in attendance at the Hall of Sparkles, all except the traitors, most of whom had fled as soon as they had been exposed. The hall was used principally for hosting great celebrations and welcoming ceremonies for as long as those present could recall. It easily extended three hundred feet in length and half that in width. The décor was what one would expect from a royal residence, yet largely uncluttered by superfluous antiquity and unnecessary opulence. It had been constructed mostly from glass and crystal, which optimised the amount of light that could be captured and reflected from the dazzling crystalline features adorning its interior and dizzyingly high ceilings. Sadly though, the effect had been lost this day. During times of crisis it also served as a place of military strategy and serious discourse.

The tall, ornate entrance doors opened, the Faerie Queen appeared, flanked by an armed escort of her most trusted Elves. The murmurs quietened as she stood in front of her throne. The throne was not what one would have expected for a Queen, it was little more than a simple, cushioned wooden chair. It was deliberately designed to be less intimidating and approachable, like the Queen herself. Unfortunately, there were some who had taken advantage of her good will and in doing so underestimated her. She would see to it that they would know the full measure of their Queen. As she sat, those assembled did the same. Although the chair was modest in design, it was raised upon a small pedestal so she could survey all of the proceedings as she pleased. She carefully regarded those seated before her and noted several chairs empty; the one that hurt the most had been Jarrett's. She was genuinely shocked at his betrayal; *why had I not seen it coming?* It was no secret he was ambitious, but to use his position and influence for dark purposes? This was something she could scarcely bring herself to believe. What else had he intended, a coup? A murder?

"My Queen, we await your council. Please allow me to be blunt as time is regrettably against us and the traitors already have the upper hand. How shall we proceed?"

McGrath was always direct, but never wasted an opportunity to exercise courtesy as a means of excusing his candidness. He accepted he would often be seen as callous, but genuinely held no malice for those he held discourse, or felt the need to apologise by way of explanation. He saw it as being counterproductive, an unnecessary waste of time and energy for the sake of someone's inflated ego misinterpreting his brutal honesty for arrogance. The Queen looked fondly at her Defence Commander, although forthright, he always brought a sense of calm by adding reason to any situation. His approach was not to everyone's taste, but to her, she depended upon it. Conventionalisms and diplomacy were reserved for social protocol and political negotiation, but only served as obstacles where defence issues were concerned. She held a special place for McGrath. He had been a father figure for her when she was growing up in the castle. On several memorable occasions he had covered for her when her parents had accused her of disobeying their direct orders by allowing her to express herself and her magickal abilities without supervision, even though it had caused McGrath considerable trouble at the time.

"Commander, yes time is against us, but we now know of their plans a great deal more prematurely than they would have wished. I believe we are on equal footing." replied the Queen optimistically.

"And how may I ask do we know of such detail? Do we hold any prisoners?" enquired McGrath.

"Yes and more. Dern, can you please bring in the Faux. He has travelled long and far to give us his message. He is weak but recovering well."

Dern nodded. Opening the tall doors he beckoned in a healer, cradling a small body within her arms.

"I would like you all to meet Smidge. As you can see he is a Faux and more importantly he is sober." said the Queen with a smile, as laughter rippled among the attendees. "Smidge, if you are able, can you please tell everyone here what you told me, you do not have to leave anything out." She said warmly.

Smidge sat up, coughing a little. Fortunately, the Hall of Sparkles had been built to allow for anything spoken from the front to be acoustically amplified, this allowed the Queen to speak naturally and still be heard.

"Greetings. I am Smidge from the Faux clan McStewed. We live in Whisperun Forest, or did. A giant Goblin and a small Goblin wizard had destroyed my clan, but in truth, we had regretfully pissed on them for many years. They believed we had all been destroyed, but I managed to hide in their belongings while they journeyed back to the wizard's home, all the while seeking my revenge and plotting their deaths. What I saw in the wizard's home I will never forget. They had turned a Human...into a Goblin…"

Shouts immediately arose from the assembly,

"Preposterous!"

"Lies!"

"How can this be?"

Dern quickly interceded, expecting such a reaction and persuaded them to allow the Faux to continue.

"I stayed hidden while watching them, learning of their schemes. At first I thought it was going to be something terrible, well it must have been, they had a Human with them and made him look like a Goblin. But as time went by, I learned all they were trying to do was help release another Goblin from jail. His name was Fingle. He was the wizard's Nephew and the giant Goblin's best friend."

"This Fingle character, it wouldn't be Fingle Froglick by any chance?" asked the Captain of the Iron Cavalry.

"Yes, how did you know?" Smidge said, propping himself up further.

"He is well known to us. Many times my soldiers while out on military leave complained about being conned by a canny Goblin in the Goblin City's dockyards and Inns. And they all gave the *same* name. Why are we listening to this balderdash, my Queen?"

"Please, let him finish." said the Queen, then nodded at Smidge.

The Faux coughed a little more and settled himself. "After the Human, wizard and giant left their home in the forest to head for the Goblin City, I flew all the way to the Dark Fortress, to trade my knowledge for their help in seeking my revenge, although I knew in my heart it was wrong. I travelled there because I had heard there were those that lingered within its walls that would value such information and operate outside of the Goblin legal system. But they must have known I was coming, as they were waiting for me."

"How did they know? Can you elaborate?" enquired McGrath.

"Well, they said they were expecting me, so I put two and two together...Then I was taken to a large room, a bit like this one, only much, much darker. I told them everything I knew, but what surprised me is that they were not shocked, they just smiled."

"How many were there, did you hear any names?"

"Well, there were others, you know, other than Goblins, Trolls, Gnomes, even one of you…" said Smidge, feeling very uncomfortable.

"Elves? In the Dark Fortress?" balked the Captain, standing in protest at the outrageous slander.

Dern ignored the Captain's outburst, "Are you absolutely sure about this, Smidge?"

"Yes, I think his name was Jarwett or something?"

"You mean Jarett?"

"Yes! That was his name, he was saying something about dreams and how the bridge was almost ready. He said…he said the Queen suspected nothing."

Smidge looked ruefully towards the Queen. The room was in uproar, most were now standing, prodding accusatory fingers while others remained seated in shock.

McGrath stood, raising his arms, "Quiet! Everyone please remain calm. This is indeed grave news if it is even factual. It is never an easy thing to accept there may be others who are prepared to betray their own kind, but we must work together and *not* accuse one another. Infighting will not solve anything, it will only serve to divide us, which is *precisely* what the enemy wants."

"Can you please continue, Smidge?" said the Queen quietly.

"Yes, my Queen. They also spoke of a missing piece and how important it was to their plan."

"What plan?" pressed McGrath.

"I don't know exactly, but they intend to use the Human to invade Earth…"

Chapter 14

They had made good ground since their escape from the Black Line. As dusk settled, the four fugitives approached Hopper's Drop, a small hamlet of outlaws and scallywags. It was an ideal place to lay low. It was too far from the Goblin City to be bothered and too far from anywhere else to be of any strategic threat. In any case, the Black Line was usually enough to deter anyone bothering to travel to Hoppers Drop.

Merlock led them into a grove of mature Aspen speaking in hushed tones, "Well, after what we have just been through, a hot meal and rest is justly deserved. But we must remain vigilant. Although everyone here is hiding from someone else, it doesn't mean that *we* are safe. I am in no doubt we already have coins on our heads and there's a strong possibility that word has already reached the flaps of these motherless wretches."

"What do yer want us ta do, Uncle?" said Fingle, feeling jittery about Hopper's Drop, more concerned with the number of Goblins he had swindled over the cycles, than any bounty placed upon him.

"The weather's fair, I sense no rain; we will camp within these trees. You wait here with Rob, while I go with Clump to fetch some supplies. If I am not back soon, come and get me, we will be simple enough to find if you can recall the Pye Shoppe debacle." winked Merlock.

Rob watched them walk towards the hamlet's orange twinkling lights and muted laughter in the far distance. He sat down against a tree, plopping his aching feet into a small stream trailing lazily towards Hoppers Drop. He looked round at Fingle, watching him sharpen his blades, senses on full alert.

"Fingle, can I ask a question?"

"Can I stop yer?" snorted Fingle, then sighed deeply as Rob waited like an expectant puppy.

"If yer must, but do it quietly, places like these ave a way of nicking all yer knacks, then using 'em to finish yer off one way or tother..." warned Fingle, eyes glinting as brightly as the edges of his cold blade.

"Why is it that Humans have such a bad reputation?"

Fingle's eyes became two black moons, "Has someone scraped out yer skull boy? Everything that crawls, fly's, slithers, and springs knows that Humans are mighty dangerous beasts. Stinky-pinks make the Hopper's Drop lot look like a bunch of frolicking Faerie princesses."

"Has it always been this way?" asked Rob, feeling a little dejected.

"No. There was a time when we were close, I mean our worlds. Humans would talk ta us, seek us out, learn our magick even, but they have forgotten we exist. And that's the way Fingle likes it."

"But *you* like me, don't you? I'm Human. And in our world Goblins are thought of in exactly the same way. Maybe there are just good and bad Humans and Goblins and that's the meat of the matter." speculated Rob, wriggling his toes, enjoying the soothing current running between them.

"Yer talk too much, Rob from Terra." Fingle grumbled.

"Maybe so, but I speak the truth and not the hogshit you peddle, oh, great Fingle of Faerieland."

Fingle feigned astonishment and they both erupted into laughter.

"Fair enough, I admit I *may* have warmed a little ta yer, despite yer constant wind-baggery. And…I never thanked yer for all what yer did fer me, Rob."

"That's okay, it was nothing, you would have done the same."

"No! That's my point, I wouldn't have, Rob. I have only watched out fer meself, it's the Goblin way. Who'd have thought I'd be learning me headupdation from a Stinky-pink." Fingle chuckled, shaking his head in mock despair.

"Tar?" offered Fingle warmly.

Rob nodded keenly. He had become quite accustomed to its hot, sweet, treacly taste and how it soothed his mind and loosened his aching muscles. They stretched out, hidden within the grove on the babbling riverbank, watching the fading light merge into soft layers of crimson and purple, as the stars poked through the shifting canvas stretching beyond the gently swaying canopy of Aspen.

Rob awoke with a start, realising he must have drifted off. He had been moved closer to the small fire Fingle had lit. After dusk the air had become cooler and he was grateful for the crackling heat warming his tired bones. He propped himself up and could see the others had now returned, thankfully without incident. Clump was roasting what looked like pork over the fire, rotating the spit with his usual, ridiculous devoutness. Rob decided against questioning the origins of the creature that was sizzling so enticingly. The delicious aroma was enough to allay such concerns, the main thing, was that the creature's skin was not green and that was enough.

"Grog?" grinned Fingle in the firelight, extending a tankard towards Rob.

He took it thankfully, drinking deeply of the dark amber liquid. It was malty and bittersweet and immediately raised his flagging spirit. As they spoke about their escapades so far, the roasted meat was passed around, with Merlock adding his own leafy contributions from previously foraging the local area—although Rob passed on the mushrooms. Their wildly exaggerated accounts had been highly entertaining, with the increasing embellishment consistent with the refilling of their tankards.

Fingle tossed another log onto the glowing embers. Clump watched the red sparks spiralling skywards and said, "Play something, Fingle."

"That's a splendid idea, Clump, play something bouncy and Byzantine, Nephew, after all, the Hopper's Dropouts will never hear us, they'll be too soaked to see a hole in a ladder."

Fingle sighed dramatically, while sticking a thumb and forefinger deep inside a nostril. He pulled out a long brass pin with several notches etched into it. Immediately, all four of his nose rings fell out, jingling into his open palm with well-rehearsed effort. He tucked his weighty rings and brass pin carefully away inside his tunic—each nose ring was solid gold, essential for trade or bribery. The lengthy ring pin also served as a master lock pick, worth considerably more than gold, unless of course it provided access to even more gold.

Rob edged around the fire, fascinated to see what he did next. Fingle placed a thumb over each nostril and using his fingertips he covered the eight ring holes either side of his enormous bugle. Fingle's cheeks bulged a little and as he raised his forefinger he delivered a sweet sounding note! Fingle winked at Rob, then played his nose like the devil himself.

Good grief, thought Rob, realising traditional folk music must have originated here too. The masterful goblin continued to play the most complex and intoxicating melody he had ever heard. Without warning, drumming entered the melody. Rob looked over to see that Clump was holding his shield and skilfully pounding the inside with a small carved stick. He had never noticed before, but there was an animal hide stretched taught across its interior, just inches away from the handles. Exhilarated, Rob clapped in delight at the sweet, intricate whistling and deep rhythmic pulses of the drum.

"Hurry up, Merlock." said Clump.

Merlock had already untied his staff from his pack. After unscrewing the end, he gave it a tilt and two fiddle bows slid out. Producing two brass clamps, the wizard attached them both to the end of his long white beard. From the clamps hung two small stirrups which he thrust each foot into and stretched his legs out a little. The clamps split his face whiskers into two equal lengths, so that when tension was applied—by extending his feet—he had two fiddles to play.

Merlock joined the rhapsody adding his two fiddles worth and somehow managing to play two different, yet complementing melodies simultaneously. The overall effect was mind-blowing, a symphony of inescapable enchantment. The wizard's speed and dexterity was jaw dropping. Rob felt joyous and tearful, such was the inspiriting effect the profound harmony stirred up deep within his soul. The celebrations continued on for hours, the music pausing only to sink a grog or three. Rob had never felt so content or as happy as he had in these moments he shared. He would do whatever it took to protect his new friends, who now felt very natural to him, like family.

Chapter 15

"Get up, Lore-yer and do it quietly, we have ta move *now*. Clump and uncle were spotted after all. Can't really miss the big oaf now can yer?" whispered Fingle.

Rob sat up rubbing his eyes, then caught his breath seeing the creeping silhouettes making their way towards them in the early twilight. Merlock swiftly conjured a 'Wizard's Mist' to snake into life, while a heedful Clump crouched quietly, battle axe at the ready. Fingle beckoned Rob to follow him over a small rise, keeping low, with no sudden movements. They then maintained a rapid pace using tree cover whenever possible, confident the dense fog and dim light had hampered their pursuers and concealed their escape.

This had altered their situation drastically. It was not only Sly who was keen to track them down, but also any sell-sword who favoured gold above all else, which included half of the Kingdom. They followed Merlock's lead towards the Cone of Certainty where they might discover the identity of Buttercup. They all had their doubts, but they had to try, the only alternative was to hide out somewhere dark and smelly until they were either found, or worse, the Shadow Goblin Government achieved its nefarious aims.

"I had no idea you could all play musical instruments, Merlock, it was incredible." said Rob unexpectedly, recalling the previous night's celebrations.

"Everyone here can play, it's whether we choose to or not. We don't need to learn, it simply flows through us. Fingle is exceptionally fond of music. In fact, he once played in his own band as a whelp, I believe it was called 'Fingle Infection'."

"Did you try ointment for it, Fingle?" Rob teased.

"Funny fer someone who flaunts an Ogre's bowjangles fer hearing holes." said Fingle and they all laughed including Rob.

"And before yer make slight of me generous schnoz, at least it has its uses."

"Yeah, not only does it double as a whistle, it can smell what Clump's having for supper…tomorrow." said Rob.

Fingle grinned by way of concession, he had to admit, Rob was getting a handle on things.

* * *

The sun was at its zenith when Clump first sighted the Cone of Certainty. As they emerged from the tree line, the Cone came into view. The hill, with its steep slopes was much larger than Rob had imagined and was a spectacular example of nature's fecundity. A huge waterfall cascaded from the shimmering summit, gradually fanning out to seven tiers, each as mighty and glorious as the next. The hill was abundant with bracken and tall grass. A patchwork of pine dressed the Cone and a wealth of exquisite flowers, displaying their dazzling array of colours blanketed its slopes from top to bottom. Wondrous birds swooped and soared, merging their startling plumage with waterfall rainbows, each voicing their unique echoes of joy. Near the base, the seven flows re-joined to form a roaring eighty foot wall of crystal clear water. Although deafening, it did not detract from its beauty and oddly, its serenity.

The Goblins approached a large shallow pool of cyan water, which lead into deeper waters broiling beneath the cascade. To the left, beyond the rocky perimeter, the water funnelled back into the River Oodles. Rob looked at the foaming mouth below the shifting barricade of silvery shredded silk. The bubbling coalescence seemed harmless enough, iridescent and ghostly, shrouded in misty droplets. Two craggy arms stretched out either side of the waterfall, as exotic flora clung fiercely to the torrent sprayed boulders, all nodding in their approval, beckoning wearisome travellers to enter its domain and reveal its secrets.

"So, who's it ta be?" said Fingle loudly, irritated by the plummeting water behind him.

"Well, assuming that one of us can even gain entry into the Cone by getting past those despicable bubbles, they will then have to face the Crone. She is ancient and wise, as all crones are, but she is also a powerful sorceress. I cannot say it will be safe to enter and I cannot guarantee ever getting out again. All in all, it's a bit of a long shot I'm afraid." said Merlock, sitting down by the water's edge.

"Long shot? We got more chance of finding a stick with one end." griped Fingle.

"I've got one!" shouted Clump triumphantly, holding a stick high.

"Turn it around, Clump…" groaned Fingle.

"Oh…" Clump said, continuing to search for another.

"I will try." ventured Rob.

"How can *yer* do this? More stinky-pinks have crossed Toesin's bridge than jabbering lungwords with the Crone! You don't even come from 'ere, what would *yer* know, what would yer do if old fustylugs hexed yer? I will have ta go, shan't I? Clump's too deficient, uncle's too old and yer just a Stinky-pink, so that settles things."

"Be nice, Nephew, that was unfair." chided the wearisome wizard.

Fingle marched into the pool, splashing water everywhere while mumbling all manner of things.

"Ignore him, Rob, he's just tired. We all are and probably a little afraid. Goblins aren't what you thought they'd be, are they, lad? We have our flaws, as certain as each morn heralds a hog shit. But we are not immune to fear, worry and self-doubt, which is probably why we are so caught up with ourselves and not so much with each other."

"Thanks, Merlock, but things aren't so different back home, believe me..."

While Clump was busy, cutting the same end of a stick repeatedly and scratching his head, Merlock and Rob stretched out in the sun, enjoying the cool misty droplets settling upon their sun baked bodies and enjoying Fingle's clumsy attempts at advancing through the Impenetrabubbles.

"Why can't...I get past these...fracking bubbles?" shrieked Fingle, as his friends held themselves, howling with amusement.

"Empty your mind, Nephew, that shouldn't be too difficult." shouted Merlock, unable to proffer further advice for giggling so hard.

No matter how hard he pushed, the bubbles would gang up, melding and enlarging. Although transparent and maddeningly thin, they were indestructible. Brandishing a blade in each hand Fingle swung wildly, while his screams became a muffled gargle. All he could see was a myriad of angry warped self-reflections, a sudsy hall-of-mirrors tormenting him for his feeble efforts. Exhausted, he fell backwards into the water.

"Well, it looks like you have your wish, Rob. I know I can't do this; I tried several wheel turns ago and failed like a shoe salesgoblin at a mermaid convention. I got very close mind, but not close enough sadly, it doesn't help when you can barely see over the water! Clump would have been an excellent contender, emptying his mind comes naturally, regrettably he gets easily distracted, so this leaves you as our only hope."

Rob desperately wanted to prove his worth. He knew he was always at a disadvantage and it did not sit well with him. He felt like a liability, a burden to be carried. The others *always* knew what to do and he was always left playing catch-up. He thought that if *he* was fed up with it, how must the others feel? He would do this, if only this one thing, he would do it. Rob stood up as Fingle slumped down beside Merlock, gasping for breath and looking murderous.

"Don't...say….it, boy, just go…" rasped Fingle, pointing towards the waterfall.

"Rob, you'll need these for the Crone and good luck." said Merlock, tossing two gold coins to Rob.

"Of…course…he…fracking…will…"   sneered Fingle, shaking his dripping head.

Rob tucked the coins deep into his tunic pocket and entered at the water's edge. He felt the gentle lap of fresh water rise slowly as he ventured deeper into the lagoon. He was under no disillusion in the difficulty of the task he now faced. If Merlock and Fingle were unsuccessful, he knew his own chances of gaining entry were highly improbable. He berated himself for casting doubt and attempted to empty his mind. He realised the Impenetrabubbles were an impressively cunning way of filtering out those who were less desperate in cause and therefore less noble. The sheer magnitude of effort to empty one's mind while immersed in an environment that throttled every sense was surely unachievable and he marvelled at the genius behind its design. Rob was now aware he entered into a shallow film of tiny bubbles and couldn't resist a peek down at his thighs, watching them slowly cling to him. He looked up again and kept walking. Besides the increasing depth, the resistance felt normal, wondering momentarily if anything other than water impeded his stride. The distance had decreased to only ten metres from the blurry opening behind the waterfall. The water was now chest high, beyond his peripheral vision he distinguished a blanket of foam collecting around him. Rob cursed for acknowledging it and as he continued, he felt as if he were pressing against a flimsy wall.

Thoughts raced through his mind and in response he was being pushed backwards. *Damn it!* Rob's chest and neck were now covered in bubbles, increasing in size with every moment that passed. Pushing forwards he panicked, unable to breathe as his head was engulfed by the opalescent plasticity. In sheer desperation he ducked beneath the water's surface and tried to gain ground, but it was just as unyielding. He launched back out of the water gasping for air and as he did so his lungs filled with sparkling spume, sending him into a blind retching panic. He had no alternative but to turn back, he had been beaten by bloody bubbles!

Defeated, Rob knew he was their last chance, only chance of finding help that would determine all of their futures. Even Merlock had failed and in that he found some comfort, but he was *different*, maybe he just needed to try harder. He was always accused of being a quitter. 'Non-achiever', his father would say and this was just one more thing he gave up on.

"Come back, lad, it's okay, we will try something else." shouted Merlock from the grassy bank.

He almost did…

Rob stood perfectly still, placed his arms down by his sides and closed his eyes. A look of serenity replaced his insecurity and he allowed the sound of the crashing waterfall to empty his mind and wash away all doubt.

"What's he doing?" said Clump, sitting amongst a large pile of wood shavings.

"He's believing in himself." beamed the proud wizard.

Somewhere in the back of Rob's mind, he sensed the bubble barrier relent. His breathing became shallow and unforced. He was aware of his foot slowly moving forwards and let it continue without thinking on it. Again, his opposite foot moved and all the time his breathing was the only sound he heard, despite the increasing roar of the waterfall.

"Look! Look at how close he's getting!" yelped Merlock, jumping in excitement.

Fingle sat up, "Well, I'll be fodder for a stifferstuffer…"

Rob had mastered his mind.

The Impenetrabubbles had reduced to foam once more and clung limply around his chest as he slowly edged forwards. His pristine awareness was now as clear as the silvery avalanche plummeting just inches away, until a swooping Gaudy bird deposited a votive offering to the water gods. Rob shuddered to a halt, as perception of his environment returned rapidly—the temperature of the water, the crashing roar of the downpour above him and the smell...*what was that smell?*

"Rob's faltering, we must help him!" shouted Merlock, wading into the lagoon.

The others quickly followed, although Fingle was lagging, howling at the huge pile of steaming bird plop resting upon poor Rob's head. Rob opened his eyes and almost fell backwards, realising he was practically beneath the waterfall. He sensed something was wrong and felt his head, pushing his cold fingers into something warm and squishy. At the same time, he felt resistance rapidly build around him. Looking down he could see the bubbles becoming larger, with a sizeable, green, organic mass slopping onto them, which stank like rotten cabbage. He stared in horror as the bubbles continued to rise, carrying the mushy stench closer to his outraged nostrils. Rob felt utterly beaten and too exhausted to continue. As he turned to walk away he felt an enormous surge of pressure from behind, sending his arms high above his head and lifting him out of the water. Clump had charged his way over to push Rob forwards!

Suppressing the joy and respect he felt for his friends, he emptied his mind as best he could, doing his part to make this last ditch attempt count. Fingle had both hands clamped against Clump's generous backside, pushing and still laughing, while Merlock summoned a powerful wave of energy that pressed behind Fingle, forcing his smirk to assist his hands in the effort, much to his absolute dismay. Rob felt the water thunder upon his head, slashing his skin and driving his shoulders downwards. He couldn't breathe, his ribs were being crushed and the torrent completely smothered his numbing face. He became dizzy and his limbs went limp as his world grew darker. Clump sensed the danger and roared his way through the impossible barricade with every ounce of strength he could muster, until his hands felt nothing but water.

Rob choked violently, as he raised his head off the cold wet stone and looked towards the dazzling waterfall. He could make out three watery shapes jumping around on the other side. He had made it through.

Chapter 16

"The boundary still holds, my Queen. The riders have confirmed the Black Line Bridge has fallen, but nothing has yet escaped."

"More to the point, can we verify what the injured guard had witnessed, about the Goblins they were chasing, that made it across?"

"I have spoken with Toesin, he confirms this. He said there were four, a wizard, a giant, one with inappropriate ear flaps and Fingle himself. Toesin and his brothers now side with us."

"I want the fugitives captured, Dern and brought under our protection before Sly reaches them. If our intelligence is reliable and I see no reason why it is not, we must get to the Human first."

"I have already taken the liberty of sending out a rescue party, McGrath is leading the operation personally."

"McGrath? I need him here, what if Corona is attacked? I know you are more than capable, Dern, I just like having him around, you understand."

Dern moved in closer, she looked up and smiled, "I know I am not your *McGrath*, my Queen, but I will *never* allow you to come to harm, I took an oath remember? Besides, our moles have indicated the Dark Fortress is busy in preparation for the invasion of Terra and will not risk open battle for fear of losing their invading forces." said Dern, smiling back.

"Very well, *my guardian protector*, but we will still need to bolster our own forces, we must send word to all those who might aid us immediately and pray they will. Please stress that those who choose not to act, choose against themselves, we are all in this together." She kissed Dern lightly against his cheek.

As she pulled away, Dern pulled her back in tightly, they embraced with an urgency known only to true love.

*   *   *

The Kelpies inhabiting the black waters around the Dark Fortress were unsettled, as the invasion arrangements had intensified. AMOK—The Embittered Three and Two-Fifths—scuttled across the scaly debris to the balcony, peering through the stone ramparts as another incompetent physician fell to his death. The creatures born of night and claw wasted no time in mauling the gift. The gurgling screams did not last long as the thrashing moat waters settled once more to an obsidian mirror, concealing monstrosities that were far darker in purpose.

AMOK faced the high Elf and appraised his worth.

"I understand you can heal. Mafalda?"

AMOK scrambled around so its second head—Mafalda—could address the Elf.

"Before you deny it, think wisely, Elf. Odessa?" said Mafalda threateningly.

The creature turned again so that its third head could speak In turn, "If you cannot help us, Elf, you will die. If you do not try to help us, you will die. Only one of these choices will guarantee your life lasts longer than this conversation. Kassim?"

Again, the grotesque beast rotated once more so that the last and most distorted head lolled and leered at the shaken Elf.

"I do apologise for the candid approach, but my supplementary codicils are lacking in the propriety protocols. I however, would like to wish you the very best of fortune. Back to you, Alun." slurred Kassim, as mouthfuls of saliva oozed and dripped in revolting, stretching pendulums.

The abomination returned back to its original position and in doing so the Elf staggered backwards, as with each scuttling turn, a fresh release of mucus and powdery flakes scattered around its deformed legs.

"I see you have realised the calamity of our conditions, other than having three heads and two fifths of another. Mafalda?" remarked Alun, with an ironic sneer.

"Thank you, Alun. Yes, between us we are constantly shedding on each other. Odessa?"

Odessa turned to face the Elf, holding up two of their misshapen limbs in sympathetic appeal, "Malfalda speaks the truth. I am constantly clawing through skin, slime and droppings. I am completely at my wits end! Kassim?"

As Kassim pivoted into view, the high Elf was forced to duck under a thick yellow globule spinning his way.

"Dear, Odessa, let's not omit discharge from the list shall we darling? What my esteemed council of impurity are trying to impart, is that our individual maladies combined, in such close proximity to one another, is leading to a level of distress that may very well be the undoing of all existence. Please begin your preparations, Elf, the healing will begin at first light on the morrow, best of luck."

AMOK raised a crooked leg and gestured the Elf to leave. Stunned, the high Elf walked away. As he closed the doors behind him, he looked down at the congealed flakes that had glued to his boots. Jarett leaned heavily against the wall outside the room of horrors, hoping his sacrifice had not been in vain. His part in their diabolic agenda had now been played and he knew his time was short. He just needed to stay alive a little longer, or it was all for nothing. If he did not devise a way to improve AMOK's condition and quickly, he would be next to meet the fury of the Fortress's black waters.

Chapter 17

Rob couldn't help but grin as he made out the mercurial outlines of his jubilant friends, dancing idiotically in the lagoon on the other side of the waterfall. He turned the opposite way, peering into the cavern's dark entrance and shivered as a cool draft of air breathed over him. He quickly searched for the two gold coins he would need to conduct business with the Crone, sighing a relief they were still safely within his pocket.

Travelling deeper into the gloom, the roar from the cascading water diminished, until only his gritty footfalls were heard echoing across the cold hard corridor of basalt. The ambient light was fading and Rob struggled to see where his feet were landing. He stumbled several times, being forced to feel along the pitted walls for guidance. He wasn't afraid of the dark and his time spent beneath the ground was proving useful. After navigating a long bend, a strange luminescence appeared. He immediately recognised the undulating dappling as light reflecting off water and was proven right as a final turn gave way to a huge underground lake, surrounding a tiny island that shone brightly. The walls and ceiling were breath-taking; the whole cavern was an enormous glittering geode that radiated its chromatic brilliance in every direction. Rob let out a giggle at the absurd cliché, *a twinkling grotto, housing a powerful witch beneath an enchanted hill in Faerieland...give me a break!*

"Any chance of dialling it down a notch?" asked Rob, shielding his eyes from the intense light emanating from the small, central island.

"Why? Are you more accustomed to the dark?" croaked a reply, "Is this any better? Is there anything *else* I can do for you?" shrieked the irritated Crone, coughing up a significant amount of phlegm.

She had now come into view, the cliché did not disappoint.

"My apologies, I do not wish to offend, I have come here because—"

"I know why you are here, stupid, it's my job!" screamed the crouching, putrescent hag, slapping her face several times before regaining her composure.

Good lord, she's completely deranged, I must tread carefully, thought Rob, wondering how long it had been since she had last spoken to anyone.

"Please excuse my incompetence, Ma'am, this is my first time seeking a very wise and powerful seer such as yourself." said Rob, bowing respectfully.

"Well, I should think so too, stupid! Is that how you treat all your ladies?" leered the Crone, tussling back her last remaining clump of greasy hair to reveal a little more cleavage and her emaciated ribs.

"Er, no, of course it isn't, I suppose I am just a little nervous."

"Well that's just more stupid, I wouldn't hurt a Faux."

"Yes you would!" replied another voice.

"Shuddup!" screamed the old hag.

"Who? Me?" asked Rob confused, wondering who else had spoken.

"No, not *you,* stupid. Now come closer, so I can see you better, all of you..." grinned the witch, lying back upon a stone plinth.

Rob stepped to the water's edge, feeling utterly repulsed by her unwholesome wantonness, fearing that gold was not the only payment she desired.

"Ah, that's better. I wonder why a nice, young, firm Goblin like you has paid me a little visit? The information you seek must be very important to you, I should think. How much gold do you carry?"

"I have two gold coins, I believe that is the payment." answered Rob, trying hard to ignore the occasional hair mite she would snatch at and devour.

"Oh my, whoever told you that is a little falsity fish and needs gutting, no, the price is much higher I'm afraid, little Goblin."

"But that's all I have." Rob spluttered, recalling his enormous struggle just to gain council with the unhinged harpy.

"Well, that's not *quite* true is it? I mean, a woman has certain needs…" she said, smiling deliciously, placing the tip of her swollen grey tongue upon her last remaining tooth and wobbling it in seductive circles.

"Stop it, leave him alone!" cried a voice from somewhere behind the witch.

"I said shuddup, scaly squashnips! Any more from you and—"

"And *what* exactly? Without me you would be nothing, old woman."

Rob strained to see beyond the light. The voice had sounded like a young girl.

"What's going on, who is that?" demanded Rob, "No one said anything about *two* Crones."

The witch faced Rob again, "Right, let's wrap this up, give me the gold and a kiss, *with* tongues and I will tell you what you want. It's my final deal."

Depressingly, he could smell her rancid breath from where he stood and there had to be at least ten meters of water separating them. He had no other alternative. At least the others would never know, but *he* would...*What happens in the Cone of Certainty, stays in the Cone of Certainty,* he told himself and reluctantly waded into the icy cold water towards the salivating, personification of purgatory.

As Rob approached, the Crone wondered why he was pinching his nose. She placed a wrinkled hand in front of her mouth and breathed hard against it. Instantly, she became light-headed and her rheumy eyes watered, causing her to tumble from the plinth. As Rob climbed onto the granite refuge, the witch was desperately scooping up her distended teats—which had slipped from beneath her moth eaten blouse, resembling the valves on two deflated beach balls.

"Fancy a rummage do yer, whelp?" coughed the befuddled witch, heaving herself back onto her feet.

"Let's just get this over with please." Rob whimpered. Closing his tearful eyes and clenching both fists, his mouth parted, as he moved in for a Frenchie he would never, ever forget…

"You don't have to do this, Rob!" yelled a voice.

"Who *is* that?" demanded Rob, opening his eyes again.

"She's nothing, she's pondscum! Now come give granny some sweet, green sugar."

"Buttercup is the Faerie Queen and she lives in the Crystal Mountains!" shouted the disembodied voice.

"Curses! You, fiddlesome fish bait. You will pay dearly for this."

The hag swung wildly around, slipping on a puddle from Rob's dripping clothes. Seizing his chance, he leapt over the plinth, to become face to face with a beautiful young girl held captive in the water.

"Quickly, take my hand."

"I cannot, I am a prisoner here." pointing to the rusty chains keeping her enslaved.

Rob jumped into the water, feeling along the chains to where they were attached. He shrieked, jumping away from her, "You're a...you have fins, I mean a tail, a fish's tail." exclaimed Rob.

Despite their predicament, she allowed herself a smile, "Of course I do, have you never met a mermaid before, Rob?"

"No, never and how am I supposed to get you out of here? You can't even walk, what with your..."

"Tail?"

"Yes, your tail."

"I *can* walk, Rob, but I need to be on dry land."

"Of course, that's the answer! Your tail is too wide to slip from the chains, but, if you transform, it may be enough to slip free of them." said Rob excitedly.

He tried lifting her onto the tiny island, but the chains would not reach far enough.

"It's okay, Rob, I have tried many times before, I'm afraid it's no use." she said sadly.

"Wait here. Sorry, of course you will, but I have an idea." said Rob.

He jumped back onto the island and saw the old hag spluttering her way back to her feet. Immediately he ran over, apologising as he sent her reeling back into the water. He then moved to the large raised plinth and began pushing as hard as he could. He felt it budge, but his feet were slipping. He gained a better footing and heaved harder, a loud scrape was heard and Rob felt his end raise.

"Watch out!" he bellowed, as the plinth slid into the water next to the mermaid, causing a huge splash that sent waves slapping against the floundering witch.

Rob jumped back in the water next to the mermaid, praying the stone plinth was close enough. Carrying her, he waded to the submerged plinth, placing her tail as far up as he could reach and waited, but nothing happened.

His head hung in defeat, "I'm so sorry, I wasn't even sure this would—"

His apology was cut short as the rusted chains rattled on the stone and disappeared beneath the water. Looking up, he could see he was now holding legs, with not a single scale in sight.

"Quickly, hold on to me tightly." urged Rob.

She did as she was asked, placing her arms around his neck. Rob waded around the island and back towards where he had first entered the cavern, careful to avoid the wailing witch while she desperately sought the sanctity of her stony, mental asylum. He raised the mermaid as high as he could and rolled her onto the entrance floor.

"There's something I must do, be ready to move." panted Rob, then swam back to the Crone.

He had to reach into the water to drag her back to the surface. Rob carried the Crone back to the small island and placed her down, tilting her onto her side as she lay coughing up water.

"I'm sorry, but you cannot keep anyone locked away like this. I hope you will forgive me."

Satisfied she was recovering, he swam as fast as he could back to the entrance, grabbed the mermaid and ran without ever looking back. As they fled, the demented witch screamed and cursed after them.

"Well, she sounds better." joked Rob, the mermaid flashed back an excited smile.

As they approached the increasing roar of the waterfall, the unrelenting volley of insults were thankfully drowned out, but the mermaid had slowed her pace, "Forgive me, I am a little weakened, I will need more time."

"There's nothing to forgive. It's hardly surprising though, for being a fish out of water. How did you know my name?"

"I have known your name for a very long time and have been waiting for you ever since." She replied, with a frail smile.

He studied her face carefully, it was hauntingly familiar. Rob picked her up and carried her towards the gleaming wall.

"Are you ready?" he said, she nodded eagerly.

Jumping through the heavy curtain they felt its icy pressure for only an instant, then they were both basking in glorious sunshine.

"Taa-Daa." said Rob, holding a soaking, beautiful young woman in his arms, a woman whose legs had remarkably transformed back into a large scaly tailfin, flapping iridescently in the sun.

Rob walked forwards, blinking away water and searching out the lagoon. There was no sign of the others. How long had he been?

"Merlock, Clump, Fingle!" he shouted, with growing concern.

He lowered the mermaid carefully, she swam beside him shielding her eyes from the intense light while Rob walked to the water's edge.

"Where are your friends?" she asked.

"I don't know…."

Chapter 18

She had been right to dispatch an additional squadron of Drakite riders despite McGrath's assurances, as she watched the search party return with casualties. Dern appeared concerned, after receiving news from the squadron leader.

"My Queen, I am afraid it is not good news."

Her face paled, "McGrath?"

"He is still alive, but seriously wounded. The aerial report described it as a massacre. The search party were grossly outnumbered."

"I knew it! I told him to take added protection, but he insisted it would slow his progress, damn his stubbornness." she said thickly.

"He is now with the best healers we have in the Abbey of divine light, supervised by the more than capable Abbess Remi-Dee and her sisters of resurgence. If he was still breathing when he was taken there, which he was, then he will be healed. And I am quite certain Remi-Dee will not stand for any of McGraths nonsense." replied Dern softly.

The Faerie Queen nodded, taking a deep breath, while wiping her eyes.

"So they have them now and we are too late." she said, falling back into her chair.

"Not necessarily. Our riders reported seeing only three Goblins held captive, not four. We also identified two of the captives, the wizard and the giant, but we are uncertain on the third. It could have been Fingle, or possibly the Human. The riders also reported seeing several scout parties break away from the Dark Fortress army in every direction. This would imply they still sought out the Human, or they would have not bothered."

The Queen stood, "Well, we must presume he is still out there, somewhere. We can turn this around, Dern, prepare my Drakite and armour."

"My Queen, I understand how you are feeling right now, but I do not think—"

"Do as I command, I am your Queen. You will ride with me. Tell the Squadron Leader to prepare for flight once more and that this is not reconnaissance. I want every rider, excluding the home guard to take flight and they should be prepared for battle."

Dern knew there could be no dissuading her, it was in part why he admired her, why he loved her.

"My Queen, there is something else. When our riders rescued the survivors, a tall, hooded stranger was reported to have appeared from out of the trees. Several enemy Goblins were holding McGrath as Sly Slaughter himself prepared to deliver the mortal blow, but the stranger had let loose an impossible volley of arrows that all hit their mark. The guards fell, allowing McGrath to make good his escape.

"What happened next? Who was this stranger?"

"As our riders picked up McGrath and the remaining survivors, an unknown battle group of Orcs released several volleys of arrows to aid our escape. According to eye witnesses, the stranger and Orcs simply vanished back into the forest. Whoever they are, they appear to side with us."

"I once knew of such a stranger, he too had command of an Orc battle group, they called him *Archer*, but that was long ago. Either way, they saved McGrath's life and our riders, a debt I fully intend to pay. We leave now, Dern, this Human is still out there and needs our help, I can feel him. I sense fear, but also a determination about him. There is something else. I sense magick, Dern. He may be more resourceful than he realises."

Chapter 19

Together, they inspected the broken bodies that lay around them, only a short distance from the Cone. The larger number consisting of Trolls and Goblin guards, but also Elves.

"There was a battle here while I was inside the Cone, that's why my friends are gone. I can't see their bodies. Maybe they escaped?" Rob hoped, searching the mermaid's face.

"Maybe. Maybe the battle was over them in the first place. Didn't you say the Shadow Goblin Government were after *all* of you?"

"Yes. We became fugitives after rescuing my friend Fingle from jail and escaping the Goblin City. But there was something else, we unearthed a dark plot. That's why we came here, to find Buttercup the Faerie Queen, so we could enlist her help and find out what's really going on."

Heavy-hearted, Rob slumped down pulling at the grass, trying to collect his thoughts and arrange his emotions.

"Look, if they were hunting you all down just to kill you, why would they have sent so many soldiers? I'm sure you're very dangerous, Rob, but it wouldn't make much sense to send an entire army after four Goblins, unless you were of some value to them. Which means that your friends are most likely being kept alive, probably to bargain for your life."

Rob turned to face her, "Sly Slaughter did say to me in the Courtroom he needed *my* help. He also knows I would never help him if he hurt my friends."

"In that case, we just need to find out where they are being taken." she said, smiling enigmatically.

"That won't be a problem…" said Rob, pointing downwards. Someone had stuck one of Clump's shaved sticks in the sand, surrounded by three roughly drawn circles, containing inners circles.

"I'm not sure what that means, Rob, but I can tell you they are heading for the Fortress of Eternal Darkness."

Rob sat bolt upright, "How would you know that?"

"*I'm* the Crone from the Cone. Well, not *the* Crone, just an unfortunate mermaid who has served the witch for seven hundred long cycles." she said sadly.

"So you are a powerful seer then?"

"Yes, but don't underestimate the witch though. She *is* powerful, but she wouldn't 'see' a sign if it hopped onto her lice ridden head playing the trouser tuba. Her powers are only restricted to mortal inflictions and illusions, which is why she had managed to portray herself as such a comely vision of beauty to you…"

"What do you mean comely? You mean gruesome surely?" hesitated Rob.

"No…I mean attractive. Rob, are you telling me that you could see past her magick? See her *true* form? Do you know what this means, Rob?"

Rob felt a shuddering excitement rise within, a vague remembrance, a gossamer reflection of miraculous potentials locked deeply away within his core, demanding to be reawakened.

"Yes…yes, it means I too can wield magick!"

"No, Rob. It means you're gross enough to smooch a hog's ass."

Rob's face reddened, although she could not see it, he certainly felt it.

"Look, I feel as disgusted as you do, but I had no choice and it *was* with the noblest of intentions." pleaded Rob, looking ridiculously crestfallen.

A smile crept over her face upon seeing his indignation and chuckled at his seriousness. Rob was about to protest, but instead grinned.

"Sorry, Rob, I simply couldn't help myself, I don't really get out much." with that they both laughed.

"But with all sincerity, Rob, you *could* see through her illusions. I think there is much more to you than chivalry and funny ear flaps."

Rob waggled his ear flaps in mock dismay, "Hey, you know what they say about big earflaps?"

"If you must." groaned the mermaid, rolling her malachite eyes.

"They're bloody annoying."

"Well, Rob, I suppose we have ourselves three options. We can go on a mission of lunacy by attempting to save your friends. They will be expecting this and we will be crushingly overwhelmed. Or, we can attempt to find the Faerie Queen and petition her help, which makes much greater sense and judging by the Elves that battled with Sly's army, she is not only aware of your existence by now, but also aware of your importance too."

"What about the third option?"

"I was thinking we could invest your two gold coins and set up a small business in training novice jesters, calling upon your immense skill in humour and ear-flap wit. Then, fail spectacularly and be flung into jail for being so *unfunny*."

"Hmmmm, number two it is then." conceded Rob.

They left the Cone of Certainty with the mermaid leading the way. Occasionally, she faltered and Rob was there to help. Patiently he kept at her pace, knowing her strength would eventually return and was astonished in how much it had already. He admired her indomitable spirit. He could never have survived in the way that she had. Her legs may be weak, but there was absolutely nothing weak about her spirit. She was inspirational, remarkable.

"We should head top ways towards the Dolorous Heights. It will be a safer passage, skirting the Needles on route to the Crystal Mountains. It will give us plenty of time in getting to know each other, although I already know a great deal about you already, Rob, sorry old habits. I almost forgot. My name, is Siren-Dipity, but please call me Dippy, it's much easier."

Chapter 20

"Remind me again why we didn't just cut some throats and high tail it back there, Uncle?" complained Fingle, coughing on the dust kicked up by the horses.

"Fingle, I do not like this any more than you, but our capture has given young Rob the best chance of finding Buttercup, which will in turn help us all. It was our only choice." whispered Merlock, looking down as they walked in chains, surrounded by menacing guards on horseback.

"We don't even know if he made it out alive. Which means, Uncle, we just lost our only chance of escape and I strongly suspect no one else is coming ta help."

"Shut up down there, unless you want to be dragged the rest of the way!" yelled a mounted guard.

"Please, feel free ta try, fortress scum and my best friend here will happily throw yer horse on top of yer, like he did ta yer comrade earlier, if yer memory has forsaken yer." slammed Fingle.

The guard mumbled something, then galloped off further up the line.

"Fingle, you must not antagonise them and please do not encourage Clump to throw any more horses, especially those with riders still seated upon them."

Sly's warrior caste were considerable in number and a surprisingly well-disciplined bunch of Trolls, Gnomes and Goblins, the latter being the predominant.

An armoured rider thundered to a dusty halt removing his helmet, "Your Darkship, so far all of our scouts have reported no sightings of the other traitor, shall we widen our search?"

"No, it is not necessary. We have the next best thing, his wretched friends. Although worthless to us, to him they mean much. We shall simply wait for *him* to come to us."

* * *

After several days into his new appointment, Jarret still struggled masking his revulsion while applying healing energy to AMOK. All Elves are taught the basic tenets of healing and those who displayed a natural predilection would invariably join the great Elven healers within the Abbey of Divine Light, Jarret was not one of them. Fortunately, the vile creature did not know this and Jarett was forced to employ inventiveness to make up the significant shortfall.

"I'm afraid your herbs and tinctures are either unsuitable or ineffective. I shall require a fresh supply if I am to continue treating your very unique and advancing maladies." said Jarett, in a sympathetic, professional manner.

"We have been reliably informed that the agglomeration of healing prescriptions we have readily available are not only fresh, but also specific to our requirements." spat Alun.

"Forgive me, AMOK, my intention was not to question, but if you will permit me to ask one...?"

AMOK scuttled around and Odessa glowered at Jarett, "Of course you may ask a question, Elf, but be aware, it may well be your last."

Jarett gulped and continued, "Your healing concoctions and herbal remedies are vast and rare in type, a most impressive collation, of that there is no doubt. But I wonder, has it genuinely helped to cure or even alleviate *any* of your conditions?"

There was a long uncomfortable silence as all heads turned inwards to debate this very moot point.

Kassim faced the Elf and answered dispassionately, "The verisimilitude of our current moribund state would lend credence to your contemptuous appraisal, therefore you get to live, for now…"

AMOK wheeled around, disburdening its various forms of waste in a wide arc, narrowly missing Jarret.

"Runner!" yelled Alun, while eyeing the Elf with undiluted malice.

The door knocked once and in ran a panic-stricken young Goblin, "Yes, my Viscount of Filth, how may I serve you?"

"Find the scribe and bring him back to my quarters immediately. In addition, prepare a team of foragers for *suitable* remedies. Oh, and I wish to consult with Slaughter. Inform him I demand an immediate update on our progress, my patience wears dangerously thin." ordered Alun, never once removing his crusted gaze from Jarret.

After the runner had vanished, AMOK finally looked away, scuttling into an adjoining chamber, leaving Jarret to sigh a momentary relief. *This could be useful,* he thought, *if I can gain any strategic information from their conversation, I must bring it to the Faerie Queen's Attention immediately.*

The diminutive scribe was badly out of breath as he crept in AMOK's room. His timid eyes searched out the Elf, then nervously approached.

"Greetings, Healer. I am here to take notes for your herbal requirements, to pass on to our foragers, shall we begin?"

"Yes, but I will need to think on the matter, this is not something that can be rushed, you understand."

The scribe nodded gloomily, dispirited his attendance was likely to last longer than he would have hoped. As the Elf and scribe settled down at a small table near the entrance to the antechamber, Sly Slaughter marched in, the amassed detritus discarded from AMOK muting his urgent footfalls.

"I am in here, Slaughter; pray you have good news for us."

As Sly approached he glanced down at the Elf and scribe, who were in deep discussion and continued past, closing the chamber's doors firmly behind him. Jarett quickly and quietly ordered the scribe to find a competent picture painter, insisting descriptions alone would be inadequate for the necessary ingredients he would require. The scribe gratefully scampered away, while Jarett carefully walked over to AMOK's door and leaned in closely to detect their conversation, satisfied the scribe would not hurry back any time soon.

"My Lord, as you know we do not have the Human, *yet*. He evaded us at the Cone."

AMOK slowly clacked across the floor, remaining within the shadows, "We asked for news on progress, this does not sound like progress. The Guild are confident the bridge is now ready, but without the Human, as you know, our plan cannot succeed. Please remind me how he managed to escape *Sly Slaughter* and a whole legion of Fortress guards on horseback?"

Sly's mouth went dry as he shifted uncomfortably, "AMOK, as I previously informed you, we did not come back empty handed, we still have the rest of the company, his friends, who have been rotting in our cells ever since our return. I believe the Human foolish enough to attempt a rescue; my recommendation is to wait until he does."

"Your recommendation is to wait…? We *have* waited and nothing! Your recommendation is flawed, we no longer have time to wait!"

AMOK leapt from the cover of darkness to land at Sly's feet, its jagged claws embedding into the wooden boards. The creature extended itself to its fullest height, withdrawing and straightening its crooked legs until its grotesque heads were now level with Sly's.

"We have waited twenty long cycles for the cosmic alignment. We have clandestinely enslaved thousands of sleeping Human minds to create an energetic substructure of our own Fortress, while our Earth allies are poised for complete takeover of their home world. And *you* think we have time?"

Sly edged away from the large pulsing thorax that served for its torso, like a spider's abdomen, covered in oozing ulcerations and knotted tufts of greasy hair. AMOK skittered around in uneven circles, unable to decide who should rebuke him further, all the while covering the high guard in slime of differing pigment, odour and viscosity. Although shrinking in disgust, Sly's anger unleashed as he reached for his sword. Instantly, he was thrust hard against a stone wall and raised high above the ground by some unseen force pressing against his crushed body.

"Letch mee dow yoo dishgushting monshroshity!" spluttered Sly, unable to move even his mouth, while pinned tightly against the cold rock. Every limb was rigid, he was completely restrained against his will.

"YOU DARE TO UNSHEATH YOUR WEAPON TO HARM US? WE ARE AMOK THE EMBITTERED, THREE AND TWO FIFTHS! WE ARE THE JARKANOUGHT MALSKIPERRON, OVERLORDS OF ALL THAT WRITHES AND WEEPS IN THE DARKEST OF NIGHTMARES, PATRONS OF FEAR AND EFFLUENCE OF FILTH, DEFILERS OF

INNOCENTS AND CHAMPIONS OF WOE, WE WILL TEAR AND RIP AND CLAW AND GNASH AND CLEAVE YOUR SOUL APART!"

"Will thish affectsh my promoshion?" garbled Sly imperiously.

"This means your services are no longer required, guard. You think me, *us*, are so self-absorbed that I, *we*, do not notice your yearning for grandeur, for power absolute? You do us a dishonour and yourself a calamitous injustice by flagrantly proclaiming your self-inflated authority in *our* name, *dammit*, names! As we speak, our entire army is positioned south of the Dark Fortress, ready to march through the portal and invade Terra. The pathetic world of Humans will be crushed and we shall rule over them all. Your campaign ends here and now, *Sly the slaughterer*. Tell us, how does it feel to be on the other end of the blade?" taunted Odessa with unrestrained relish.

Sly began to laugh, laughter that compelled Odessa's sneer to slide from her face. AMOK released its hold with a circular movement from one of its extended claws and Sly crashed to the floor, causing a billow of uncongealed matter to disperse further.

"I am intrigued by your insolence, even when you must surely recognise your imminent demise?" quizzed Mafalda.

Sly raised his head and stood to face the abomination, "Your arrogance is your undoing, AMOK. You think I have just glorified in your name, hiding behind your authority? Ask anyone in the great Goblin City whose name they fear greater. Ask anyone in the lowlands, the highlands, the mountains, or the forests whose name they are afraid of. I have travelled the four directions and left *my* mark. Who fears a creature that hides away in a fortress, hides away from itself, never to be seen or felt? Yes, you have guided my fist, but it is my fist that is felt!"

The high guard walked over to face AMOK, seething and indifferent to the creatures power and weeping pustules.

"You underestimated me, AMOK, for I too have plans and there is no place in them for a nauseating parody of an oversized decomposing crab. You think you can rule over the Humans? I used to think that way. After all, magick is all but forgotten to them. But they have a *new* kind of magick. I have seen it and its power is beyond anything we know. Which is why, you festering coagulum, that they, the Humans, with a little help from me of course, are waiting on the other side of that portal, ready to invade *our* world, not theirs!"

Sly let slip a series of unsettling high-pitched giggles and unbuttoned his shirt. A bejewelled amulet swung out from around his neck. Immediately, AMOK shrieked and skittered into a dark corner wailing in terror.

"Something wrong? Do you find my new ornamentation distasteful? I consider it rather captivating. Quite by chance, while enforcing our allegiance throughout the Kingdom, I happened upon a very industrious Goblin who had managed by sheer luck to have traversed the Breeze Blunders. He was also very talkative, an amiable little fellow who had somehow lived long enough to tell his tale, of how he had appropriated this powerful charm, but of course, lived only long enough to tell me his tale…This amulet, as you are aware by now, is one that protects the wearer from their opponents' magickal ability. Oh, that's me isn't it?" chuckled Sly.

Crom, I need to act fast, thought Jarett, edging away from the chamber door, then creeping over to the main door as quietly as he could, silently closing it behind him. The high Elf walked swiftly and authoritatively, heading directly for the Fortress dungeons. This would be his only chance before a full scale coup would be imposed, time was fiercely against him. Jarett knew enough of the Dark Fortress layout by now to find the cells, hoping that was where the captured Goblins were being held. Fortunately, he had previously planned out his escape route, hoping Sly's coup may provide the advantage he desperately needed, if he hurried.

Chapter 21

"I thought you said they never venture this far out of the mountains!" shouted Rob, running full tilt around a craggy bend, being pursued by a company of ravenous Trolls.

"That was seven hundred long counts ago, I guess things have changed a little." shouted Dippy, leaping over a series of jagged rocks.

After an uneventful two days march around the base of the Needles, Rob and Dippy had become so absorbed in each other, they literally stumbled into a hunting party of Rock Trolls at a river bank. Dippy had previously assured Rob that mountain Trolls never left the mountains and the fact that mountain Trolls were virtually indistinguishable from the enormous grey boulders that littered the river's banks, she really shouldn't be held accountable for their current situation.

"I thought you could see the future," argued Rob, ducking a huge timber club hurtling towards his head.

"I can, usually, which is why I'm still running!" she screamed back, then fell abruptly onto her backside after bouncing off a Troll's bulging belly blocking her path.

Rob slowed to a stop, as did the Rock Trolls behind him. The Troll in front of Dippy signalled for his hunting party to gather together.

"What do we do now, Dip? Shall we run again?" urged Rob.

"No, we wait. I have seen this, I think this needs to happen."

"Think?"

The huge Troll in front roared at Rob, forcing him to look away, conscious not to upset it any further. It then roared over their heads at the Trolls amassing behind them. They roared back. Then both parties began a heated guttural exchange.

"What are they doing?" whispered Rob.

"Well, from what I can gather, one hunting party are Rock Trolls and the other are Stone Trolls".

"What's the difference?"

"In truth, there is none, but I would strongly advise to never ask that particular question."

"Okay, but what are they arguing over?" said Rob, pulling his ear flaps taught to drown out the jarring clamour.

"They are deciding which clan has the right to invite us for tea."

"Ooh, that's sounds better than I expected."

"We are the main course, Rob."

"Oh…"

The climb had taken several hours and the sun was now falling behind the imposing ridgeline of the Needles, casting long cold shadows and bathing them in occasional bursts of warm, orange light. It had been a pleasant enough journey tied to a pole, carried up the rocky terrain, but with the declining temperature, Rob was beginning to feel the chill and encroaching fear set in. Eventually, the two opposing hunting parties spilled out into a large plateau that was concealed on all sides by the ridgelines above, splitting in two and encircling them. Small fires were lit while the Trolls howled bizarre sounds into the invading darkness. An enormous cauldron—which had the appearance of serving countless generations past—had been filled with water and put to boil above a large fire pit.

A Troll grunted at Rob then jutted his bloated finger at him, then to the pot and finally back to his toothy grin while rubbing his belly. The gesture was sadly lacking in misinterpretation.

"Well, Dippy, I guess this is it. I always wanted my life to have meaning, to experience adventure, to be special I suppose, but the way it's looking right now, maybe I should have just been more cautious."

"You *are* special, Rob, but more like a chef's special."

"How can you be so *flippant* right now, let's hope they love seafood."

They both giggled despite their plight. Although Rob struggled to suppress his terror, he found great strength in her, she gave him the courage he needed.

"Dippy, is there anything you are not telling me, about our future?"

"Who me? What would I know…even if I did, telling you could be catastrophic. Our futures could change incalculably if you or I did anything different than what we would normally do. Besides, where would be the fun in knowing?" she replied with a bewitching smile.

A loud horn resounded around the plateau, signalling the two clans to enter. Gradually, they filled the outer edges of the entire tableland and still they continued to swarm in, until only a central space was left free where Rob and Dippy were held. A second horn blew and the shuffling Trolls parted. Upon a third horn, two enormous, battle-scarred mountain Trolls—one representing each clan—lumbered in, one shouldering the other as they muscled their way along the passage. When they eventually stopped in front of the blistering fire, they faced one another, dramatically framed by flaring yellow lances and blood red sparks. The rock Troll raised his cudgel high and roared towards his opponent, one half of the plateau went wild. When the stone Troll held both arms aloft, the rest were whipped into a delirium, bashing stones off their thickset foreheads. Rob identified a rudimentary chant being sung, presumably to intimidate the rock tribe.

And so it began. Whatever exchanged between the tribal leaders could not have been pleasant or decent. The hand and body gestures alone were certainly adult rated. Rob had witnessed his share of heated disputes back home and frankly they paled in comparison to the barbaric obscenity that was now being displayed. He knew unreservedly, that after tonight—if he managed to survive—he would never be quite the same.

When he thought he could endure no more, the fever pitch escalated even higher. Rob was about to scream against the madness, but as he opened his eyes, his world was upside down. The rock Troll, in a frenzy, had seized the pole that Rob was tied upon and held it high above its head. The stone Troll immediately responded by grabbing at Rob's head. He could feel its greasy, fat fingers squeezing his skull and stretching his neck from his shoulders. A fleeting image of a past Christmas, of just him and his father—which could have been any of his past Christmases—filled his fading mind. A memory of when they would pull apart the only Christmas cracker set upon the table and for some reason he had always lost. Waiting for the inevitable 'crack' and usual disappointment to occur, Rob heard another sound. Sluggishly, he clawed back some of his senses when the pressure had lessened and became aware of a dramatic silence, save for the crackling fire and hissing cauldron. Rob dared to open his eyes once more.

A monstrous misshapen face filled most of his vision, but its blinking eyes looked skywards. Rob followed its gaze to a terrible looking club suspended above them. Hanging from the club were two crowns, one of each belonging to the tribal leaders. They were held in place by a hefty black arrow that had embedded deeply into the cudgel's scarred wood. The next thing Rob experienced was falling. Still bound to the pole, he thumped brutally onto his side against the hard plateau floor, knocking the wind from his lungs. Rob heard a wave of gasps as a single set of footsteps approached. He strained to see the stranger but had fallen the wrong way.

A tall hooded figure emerged from the blackness, carrying a longbow and quiver slung across his back. As he walked, every Troll grunted and moved aside. When he reached the tribe leaders, they bowed. Next, a brief exchange of barks and growls took place, whoever this was, they were fluent in Troll tongue. The tall figure then pulled an arrow from his quiver and traced the symbol of the three peaks in the fire's ash while the two leaders watched intently. He then traced a line to each peak forming an inner triangle and finally three straight lines each moving away from the triangle's corners. The Troll leaders looked at each other in surprise, then the stranger pointed the arrow towards Rob.

Amidst the chaos that erupted, Rob was quickly untied and brought back to his feet to stand next to Dippy, who was as usual frustratingly cool and smiling in that enigmatic way she did so well. The mysterious stranger had his back to him as did the clan leaders, who were shouting something together that sent the whole plateau into pandemonium. The Trolls had set aside their grudges as they hugged, danced and kind of sang together.

"Dippy?" questioned Rob, she squeezed his hand tightly.

Encircled by the celebrations, the stranger turned and walked over to Rob and calmly introduced himself, "I, am Rob-in-Hood." pulling his cowl from over his head.

Rob almost passed out, "Hey, I recognise...Dad? Dad!"

Chapter 22

Jarett ran down the main stairwell leading into the Great Hall. Droves of excited Goblins were already tearing down title banners and flags of the previous ruler. Jarett was almost crushed by a Goblin platoon marching past in double time, displaying Sly Slaughter's insignia. It was anarchy as small pockets of Goblins still loyal to AMOK were desisting and putting up a good fight. Some looked confused, while others took advantage by looting what they could. Jarett was virtually invisible as he weaved his way through the political uproar, heading towards the dungeon's entrance. As he approached, luck was with him. The gates had been abandoned and left wide open. He ran swiftly down the worn steps, careful not to slip on the slime formed by dripping water seeping down from the fortress moats—he had to concede it was a sobering feat of engineering, particularly for these feuding lunkheads. He arrived at a second set of gates, but they were guarded by two Goblin jailers who looked like they had never seen the light of day.

"Halt! Who are you and wotcha doing down 'ere?" declared a podgy guard gruffly, his hand fastened upon his rusting weapon.

"I am the official Dark Fortress healer and member of the Strategic Council, I have orders to interrogate the prisoners." replied Jarett formally.

"No one said anyfing abowt dis did they?"

The other guard shrugged.

"I take it you are aware of the current situation here?

AMOK has been usurped and Sly Slaughter has now taken overall command of the Dark Fortress."

"Hmmm, we don't get much involved wif any poultrytics, or nuffin else, 'cept torture really."

"Well I think you'd better, otherwise your new leader may question your loyalty and then it would be *you* for the chop." warned Jarett.

"Mubee he's roight, c'mon let's goes and shows our loyaltee."

Jarett quickly added, "Wait, if Sly sees you still holding the keys to the cells, he would know you had left no one guarding them, which means you would lose your jobs and your heads. I will guard these rats until you get back. Quick, hand me the keys and hurry."

"Fanks 'eeler, you're alwight for a pointy ear." said the guard, handing over the heavy ring of keys and disappearing out of sight.

Pointy ears? Better than limpy lobes, muttered Jarett, searching for the fugitives.

Most of the cells were empty, presumably because death by torture was preferential to incarceration by both parties, or the cells that did contain prisoners were already dead and in some cases, a very advanced state of decomposition. The Elf approached the last cell and slid open the wooden shutter, then jumped backwards as a long green nose sprung out with two beady eyes perched above it.

"Took yer time, Elf. By my reckoning, this coup will be over and order restored in about, ooooh, the time it takes fer us ta escape, so please, if it ain't too much trouble, *open this fracking door*!"

Jarett fumbled through each key but nothing seemed to work.

"Elf, see that gold pin over there, go fetch it snip snap."

Jarett searched around, then spied a large golden pin sitting on a shelf with four gold rings; he snatched them up and quickly passed them over.

Fingle's fingers got to work and in seconds a loud click clicked.

"Uncle, Clump, we move now. Stay close, Clump, no brawling."

"Wait for Merlock, he's still slarfing." warned Clump as the old mage returned from his wizard's snooze.

The heavy door screeched open and Fingle ran to where their equipment had been stored. He handed Merlock his bag and staff and Clump his battle dress, shield and axe. He then picked up his own items and a little extra that was lying around that no one probably needed— after inspecting it for moss.

Jarret took the lead, "Quickly, this way, I have planned out an escape route. It is vital we get away and find the Faerie Queen, I have information she will need if she is to stand a chance in saving the Kingdom."

"What *about* our Kingdom?" demanded Fingle, following the Elf.

"It seems that Sly Slaughter has lived up to his namesake and reputation and if he ever gets hold of your friend, we will be overrun by Humans, Humans harbouring ill wishes for us all."

Fingle shot a look at Merlock, still groggy from his inner voyage.

"Uncle, are yer alright, shall we slow?"

"No, no. We must be as quick as a wink. The second sight has just shown me where we must go, it is where we shall find Rob. He will be on the other side of the Tin Fence where the Tundra mines begin, next to Plague Peak. Clump give us a hand will you?"

Fingle stopped running, "What? We can't go in there; it's worse than here! The whole place is teeming with Red-

Caps; they control the Tundra mines and anything that goes through Winter's Gate."

Clump clutched the shaken wizard in his left hand and brandished his battle axe in the other, smashing anything that was in his path to smithereens. As they ran for the dungeon entrance, the heavy iron gates had been locked shut.

"Crom! Those incompetents hadn't been as incompetent as I'd first thought. Fingle, have you your lock—"

Clump hadn't seen them stop up ahead, he was busily concentrating on the green sludge that coated the steps. Fingle and Jarett parted just in time to avoid Clump loping full tilt and continuing to do so, long after the iron gates had been wrenched free from their hinges.

"Look up, Clump, we need to wait for the others, but good work, my boy." praised Merlock.

"Eh? Oh..." Clump sheepishly replied.

"In Oberon's name! Your friend is remarkable, why didn't you escape earlier?"

"We wanted ta give Rob, our friend, his best chance of finding someone called Buttercup, we have vital information ta pass on." said Fingle, sidestepping the skirmishes still in full swing around the Great Hall.

"Did you say Buttercup?"

"Yes, whatsamatter, yer pointys been enfeebled?"

"I'm trying to find her too, because she protects the same Kingdom that's about to be taken from her."

"You mean ta say Buttercup *is* the Faerie Queen?"

"Yes, only Buttercup is what her closest allies call her, it's what I once called her..."

"Crom. No wonder the Faux said only *she* can help and I suppose it was safer ta use her secret name. There was I locked up, enjoying me notoriety, when it was always about Rob." said Fingle in disappointment.

Jarett grinned, then beckoned them all over, "Listen, keep close now and follow my lead. There's an escape route from the Fortress's internal herb garden, leading directly into Shadow Haven woods. From there you can ride to the Tin Fence where it meets the Dark-Cloud Crags. I have collected plants with the foragers and know the woods are unguarded. The foragers have their own stable where Shadow Haven begins, I'm sure Sly wouldn't mind you borrowing a few horses."

They ran the length of the Great Hall keeping low, avoiding the odd chair and goblin thrown in protest.

"Through here." instructed Jarett, directing them to a small door revealing a long corridor.

They ran through, waiting while Jarett closed the door. As he did so, he saw Sly marching down the stairs at the far end of the hall, surrounded by guards cheering the successful takeover.

"We don't have long, Sly is heading our way, follow me!"

They ran down the corridor as fast as they could, discarding all caution, recognising this as their only chance of escape. Jarett grabbed a burning torch hanging from outside the entrance to the herb garden and they disappeared inside.

Panting hard, the Elf stopped running, "The exit is on the far side, once through, the stables are only a short distance to the left. You cannot fail to see the tracks leading into Shadow Haven woods."

They looked at him in shock. "Why are you not coming with us?" asked Merlock.

"There are only three horses kept in those stables, besides, you have a much better chance of escape if I hold them off, even if only for a short while."

They knew he was right. In any other circumstance they would have refused, fighting everything the Dark

Fortress could throw at them, but their mission was simply too important to risk failure.

Jarett looked them squarely in the eyes, "You must inform the Faerie Queen that the entire S.G.G. army is positioned to the south of the Dark Fortress, probably hiding out within Doom Forest and that Sly Slaughter has overall command. They will most likely use their army to stop anyone attempting to thwart the Human military invasion. Tell Buttercup that Sly has double crossed us all and is aiding the invasion into *our* world, but is unable to, unless he has Rob. You must do this, go now."

They reluctantly agreed and shook his hand.

"We will come back for you, Jarett and we will tell the Queen that you never betrayed her, but instead had only honourable intentions. Farewell, high Elf, may the shining ones show mercy upon you. Thank you, brother." choked Merlock. A deep understanding passed between them all, of the sacrifice Jarett had just made.

As the Goblins ran for the exit, a shout came from the corridor outside the herb garden, "The Elf ran in there, your Darkship."

Jarett watched as the brave trio ran towards the stables, then walked over to where he had previously hidden a large barrel of pitch behind a toxic creeper. Removing the lid, he kicked it over towards the doorway. He waited until a guard burst in and stepped into the black ooze before he threw his torch upon the expanding black puddle. The guard was immediately engulfed in flames, as was the internal entrance to the herb garden, stopping anyone who wished to stay alive from entering. Jarett watched the screaming guard stumble back into the corridor, then callously pushed aside by Sly Slaughter. Sly stood at the doorway, glaring through the smouldering inferno at Jarett. The Elf could see flames dance in the Goblin's eyes and wondered if they were more than just a reflection.

"Uncle, there are six horses, not three." said Fingle, after they rushed into the stable house.

"Good, I'm taking two." Clump said cheerfully.

Merlock looked towards the walled herb garden in the far distance, with black smoke now rising from the vented windows. He could make out Jarett through the blaze, fighting fiercely against several Goblins that had dared to jump through the flames. The small wizard almost ran back to help, but with a heavy heart he decided against it.

Merlock faced the other two, "Jarett had never intended to save himself when he knew of our existence. We *cannot* fail him, for he has given his life for our own. We must ride like thunder..."

Chapter 23

"You knew didn't you?" said Rob to Dippy, as he was being untied.

"I am *so* sorry, Rob, it's the burden I carry. I am cursed in keeping the future to myself, otherwise the future could be changed and this was our best outcome." replied Dippy, feeling his confusion and sense of betrayal.

"Best outcome? Being pulled apart like a Rob shish kebab, then discovering your father isn't Mr. Robert Swindlar, but is in fact Rob in-bloody-Hood!"

"Please calm down, Son, I understand this is all very odd, frightening even, but it will do no good for your asthma getting all upset and offending the nice lady present. You simply got in the way of the Tatterdemalions and the Slubberdegullions, causing a minor clan dispute." replied Rob's father.

"Odd? Noooooo, there is nothing *odd* about any of this, *off the fracking scale*, well, that's wholly more accurate. Please believe me when I say I do not give a crap about slobbering gulls or tatty onions and for your information, *Dad*, I have not had an asthma attack since I was eleven, but since you're never around I don't suppose you even noticed!"

For the first time in Rob's life, his father looked exposed. Rob saw him unravel and ran over to support him.

"I don't know what to say, Son…" offered his father meekly, tears rolling down his cheeks.

Rob hugged him tightly, "It's okay, Dad, really it is, I have just missed you so much."

His father hugged him back, "I love you more than you will ever know, my beautiful boy. I never once believed you'd be in any danger, but because of me, because of my past you were almost killed…"

"I understand why you never told me, you were doing what every good father should by protecting their child. Hey, we might both have green skin, but I'm hardly a chip of the block with *these* ears?" choked Rob, wiping his eyes.

As Dippy watched, she felt a longing to be back with her own family and to be a part of the love she once shared with them. But Dippy was needed here and Rob needed her, even if he didn't fully realise it. Rob's father, Robert, had arrived earlier at the plateau with a band of loyal companions he knew of old. He had also the foresight to bring along several large carcasses ready for the spit. Robert had known it was not only impolite to turn up at a Troll gathering empty handed, but also foolish. As more fires were lit and sizzling meat passed around, the atmosphere had become considerably more relaxed. Rob, Robert and Dippy had found a suitable place to sit undisturbed next to the fires warmth, yet far enough from the cauldron that nearly parboiled them.

"Son, to say I owe you an explanation is beyond ridiculous. I understand how insane this all seems, but if you let me though, I will try. No doubt you have many questions, it is good I think, that some things never change…"

Rob smiled, holding his father's hand as Robert took a deep breath, "There have been many things I have been forced to keep from you, Son, for your own safety. Every single moment of every single day we have been watched by a secret department of our government."

Rob cringed, *they must have enough on me by now to throw away the key*.

"As you have already surmised, this is not the first time I have been here, to this world. In fact, this is only the second time. Initially, I too was transmogrified from a Human to a have a Goblin's appearance, so now, every time I pass the threshold between our worlds, I instantly undergo the change, it's how the magick is intended to work. The first time was long before you were born. I was approached by secret government agents who wanted to enlist my help in protecting Earth. Our governments have long known about the Faerie realm and all of its inhabitants. Naturally, at first I thought it was some elaborate prank, until I was taken to a top secret underground facility containing captured creatures from the land of the Fae, from here."

"Why did they show you all of this, what did they want from you, Dad?"

"They said they needed a spy, someone who could infiltrate their kind and report back any threat to our way of life. Our government knew that the Shadow Goblin Government wanted total control of all Goblins, but to achieve this they needed to convince the free Goblin clans of the benefits in living and working together…"

"The Goblin City!" shrieked Rob.

"Yes. AMOK knew the success of his dominion relied upon total control of all feuding clan Goblins. In galvanising them together, they could be used as a formidable resource when required. The S.G.G. had learned that some of Earth's governments had incorporated such a control and wished to replicate it here but lacked the expertise. This is where I came in. Our government knew I was a fully practising solicitor with many victories under my belt, notably so for such a young man. They also knew I was single, without children and had an appetite for adrenaline, no doubt from documenting the many dangerous sports I enjoyed in my spare time. It seems I had unwittingly *ticked every box*." said his father cynically.

"But not *all* governments impose total control. Besides, without some structure, society would be in utter chaos." added Rob, struggling to look past his father's pea-green complexion.

"Yes, Son, you are correct. But imagine a society where it 'appears' civilised, but its judicial system is rigged in favour of the court and *not* the individual, then you have real power, actually, absolute power…"

"So, our government sent you here to help the S.G.G. establish a rigged legal framework, so they could then establish complete control of the Goblin clans, placing them all under the watchful eyes of AMOK."

"Precisely, and in return our Earth government would have an inside man, or rather Goblin, that could determine any risks to our world after implementing such an enterprise and of anything else that may be of strategic value."

Rob looked quizzically at his father, "*But,* the S.G.G. did not know you were a mole. So what did they trade your legal expertise for?"

"Divmatronium. A ludicrously rare source of immense energy that can only be found in the Faerie Kingdom. Here, it is quite inert, without any known use, but on Earth, its atomic structure alters significantly, I suppose a bit like us when we cross over. One ounce is the equivalent of the total annual output of all the Earths nuclear reactors and then some. Can you imagine what this could do if it ever got into the wrong hands?"

"We cannot let that exchange ever happen, Dad."

"Well it kind of did and kind of didn't. A microscopic amount was allowed to be analysed to prove its worth. Our scientists had absolutely no chance though of ever synthesising it, as they did not know its original atomic structure before it passed between worlds. So the only way to use it on Earth was to first synthesise it in the Faerie realm. AMOK insisted that once the clan wars had ceased and the majority of Goblins were contained within a vast city with a legal framework in place, then and only then would there be a full exchange of Divmatronium and the opportunity to study its properties."

"But the City *is* built, the Goblins *do* all live there and the law courts are in full swing, believe me, I know." laughed Rob.

"Exactly. Our governments were tricked. The S.G.G. never intended for the exchange to take place, realising it could endanger their own world. It was not long after this betrayal I returned to Earth and that was twenty years ago."

Rob realised his father had no idea of what was really being planned. "Dad, there's something else, something that has been happening here ever since you left. The S.G.G. has somehow managed to build a portal, a bridge large enough to allow for a full scale invasion of Earth. I am unsure how it all works, but I do know they are finalising their preparations to invade."

"Good heavens! Are you quite sure?"

"Yes. This is why we must find the Faerie Queen, only she has the power to stop them."

His father stood, paced back and forth then gestured into the darkness. In seconds, a battle group of Orcs appeared. "Son, I trust these Orcs with my life, they have saved it often enough. Meet my faithful band of Orchi, they are Oalnor, Kalanna, Fairran, Riellernon, Rielog, Nororciousand Ormia. And this stout fellow is Kang, their Commander."

As the Orcs acknowledged Rob, he tried hard to mask his fear, these were no ordinary Orcs, not like the few he had seen so far. These were enhanced, considerably larger, with a cold look in their eyes that not only knew bloodshed, but welcomed it.

"Very pleased to meet you all. Forgive me if I forget your names, I forget my own sometimes. And thank you for looking after my father, I hope in time we too may become friends."

Kang turned to his warriors muttering something, they all laughed loudly, including his father.

"What did he say, Dad?" enquired Rob, half smiling.

"He said he would find it difficult to like someone who had coin bags for ear flaps, it's really a complement, of sorts…"

"Funny! Unequivocally, I can assure you all, I did not ask for these. Dippy, I can't believe your laughing too." Rob blurted.

"Sorry, I think they are very cute, although in a tough, Goblin warrior kind of way."

Rob belted out a war cry, turning his head quickly from left to right, allowing his ear flaps to slap hard against his forehead. They laughed louder still and he figured it was a good enough ice breaker and had to be content with that. Rob marvelled at his father as they sat together in a tight circle, forming a plan of action. He knew his dad was confident and authoritative, but he had no idea he was a natural born leader and military strategist. He would have to wait for the right time to bombard his dad with his infinite questioning, regarding what really transpired twenty years ago, but that was a story for another time.

They spoke in great length about a vast chain of subterranean prisons in the Tundra region which were ruled over by a cruel race knows as the 'Red-Caps'. They were a particularly vicious breed of Gnomes and it was said they dipped their caps in the blood of their victims to stain them red. If that was not troubling enough, it was also said that if the cap dried out, then the creature would perish, so through necessity they required a fresh supply of blood on demand. For this very reason they had been the perfect choice as wardens for the imprisoned races that refused to co-operate with the S.G.G. Rob's father explained that without the thousands of prisoners that were held captive by the Gnomes on the other side of the Dark-Cloud Crags, they would hold little chance against the Dark Fortress Army. Rob understood these kinds of campaigns relied crucially on numbers, but he also sensed something else about this rescue mission. Something his father was withholding and that they all seemed to be aware of. All except him?

After a suitable plan had been agreed upon, they bade each other a good night. They slept together in the company—and now safety—of the mountain Trolls. The Archer had told the Troll tribal leaders that the long awaited prophecy had arrived and that all those who were either imprisoned or ruled over by the flaky fist of AMOK would finally be freed. This included many absent members of their own mountain clans.

Rob remained deeply unsettled. He knew he needed rest and he knew they would be up at first light for a full days march, but he simply couldn't sleep. What a night and what an adventure. Only a few hours ago he was about to be eaten by Trolls and now they were protecting him. His father had miraculously appeared as a legendary Goblin archer and military leader and at long last he had finally found a girl he really liked. Rob realised he really *did* like her. He opened his eyes and Dippy was looking straight at him, smiling.

She moved in closer, "It can get awfully cold up here in the Needles. Makes sense to keep warm." she said grinning.

Rob agreed and held her hand as she snuggled into him. Although he felt his heart begin to race, he was too overwhelmed by the night's events. Very soon, he had fallen into a deep and restful sleep.

Chapter 24

The Queen enjoyed the cool rush of air and exhilarating speed, sitting astride her Drakite. Behind her flew an entire war party from her Air Armada. She was heavily flanked, with Dern riding next to her. She had decided against taking further risks, opting to go in heavy if they located the Human. They needed to be able to protect him at all cost. Despite the rhythmic whomp of its powerful wings, she managed to calm her mind, sending her senses out into the land far, far below. Her essence became an antenna reaching down, discovering the joy of flowers and insects as they danced together. She heard the song of the water as it trickled and roared, nourishing all living things. The Queen felt the hopes and dreams of all that existed, all was sentient on their own unique journeys of experience.

She experienced a tugging sensation, barely perceptible, but unmistakable.

"Dern, we head for Oak Seat Forest, within it lays Night Glade, we must land there, the Human still lives!" she shouted, breathing fiercely.

Dern returned her smile, signalling the Armada to bank a hard left and descend towards the glimmering green forest in the distance.

Kang stopped abruptly, "Archer, find cover."

After the long walk down from the Needles, Rob, Dippy, his father and Orcs had headed directly for Oak

Seat Forest in a bid to keep concealed as they ventured towards the great Tin Fence of the Dark-Cloud Crags. They had reached a section of the woodland where an enormous glade opened before them. They were confident enough to navigate across the broad expanse, until Kang had spied something in the skies heading in their direction and it was big. They swiftly found refuge, hidden within the lush ferns that grew at a safe distance from the tree-line. The woodland was dense enough to shroud them in darkness and they were virtually impossible to be seen, particularly from the glade where the sun shone brightly. The dark smudge came further into view. Before long, it seemed the whole sky had turned dark.

"Keep low and do not move, a Drakite war party approaches, unlikely a coincidence, so be ready to run." warned Kang.

Rob couldn't stop his legs from trembling, telling himself it was the squatting that caused it. He found it difficult to keep his breathing shallow, as his heart was pounding in his chest. The glade blustered wildly from the downbeat of air as the huge, winged beasts landed. Everywhere it seemed, Drakites were thrusting their enormous powerful talons deeply into the soft earth as they settled. Every available space of the boundless glade was now occupied. It was only until they had landed that the riders could be seen. As the nearest creature enfolded its wings, the Faerie Queen slid from off her saddle, landing gracefully upon her feet, as did half of her Elven riders, quick to secure the area.

"You may come out, we wish you no harm!" Buttercup shouted towards the trees in which they hid. Kang was about to counsel against doing so, but Rob's father had already began walking towards the glade.

"Dad!" cried Rob leaping forwards, Dippy caught a hold on his arm.

"It's okay, you trust me don't you? Leave him, he knows what he's doing."

Robert emerged from the trees, walking a little way into the sunlight.

"We believe you travel with someone of great import, you must realise we both have his best interests at heart." said Dern sincerely.

Robert did not reply, but instead approached the Queen, ignoring the Elves that stood in his path wielding swords, "Hello, my Queen, you may know me better if I remove my hood."

As he did so the Queen felt herself whisper his name beneath her breath.

"Yes you are right, Elf, he's very important, he's my son."

Dern spun around to face the Queen, each sharing one another's shock.

"Robert? *Robert*, is that you?" she instantly ran to him, hugging him tightly.

"Easy, Buttercup, I haven't been away that long have I?" he laughed.

"We heard the rumours, but I dared not believe them, I feared you dead, but I always sensed you were alive, somewhere. And after our reports mentioned a mystery archer saving McGrath's life, I hoped beyond all hope it would be you..." she squeezed him again and laughed joyously, it had been the best news she had received of late, rekindling the hope she had almost allowed to wither away. *Could this be the time that has been foretold*, she thought, *a time of great peril where two realms hang in the balance?*

"What about us? He doesn't execute rescue missions alone." shouted Kang, as the others emerged from the treeline, revealing themselves to the Elves.

"Well met, Kang. I have heard many astonishing tales of you and your legendary battle Orcs. Truly, it is a great honour to know you." said Dern, gripping the Orc's heavily muscled forearm in a warrior's clasp.

"Hmmm, I am afraid I do not know of you so much, maybe that is a good thing I think…" replied Kang with a wry smile.

Dern laughed warmly, "I quite agree."

Rob and Dippy walked over to where his father stood, facing the Faerie Queen. She was breathtakingly beautiful and yet there was also a resilience that was immediately obvious; she too had the warrior's way about her, an intoxicating blend he couldn't ignore.

"Your Queen." declared Rob, lowering his head, conscious of his dangling lugs more than ever.

"Please, you needn't, but it is gratefully received. Would it be acceptable if we escorted you back to Corona, in the Crystal Mountains? It is where we live, maintaining the balance of magick, the essence of all life. Although it seems of late we have become a little complacent…" said the Queen, her gaze shifting towards the distant snow-capped mountains, with her words trailing softly.

"It would be my honour." replied Rob proudly, pulling her back to the moment.

"My Queen, as much as it appeals returning back to your magnificent home and reacquaint our relationship, we are regretfully headed elsewhere." said Robert respectfully.

"Where is it you intend to go, Archer? Will you require any assistance?" replied the Queen puzzled.

Rob's father smiled, "I'm glad you said that…I was rather counting on it."

* * *

Sly Slaughter left nothing out. He had exhausted every method of torture he could imagine, yet still he was unable to extract any information from the Elf. He had to admit,

Jarett was a tough nut to crack, which did not sit well, it only served to enrage his tormented mind further.

"Curse you, Elf, if I can't get you to talk, I will leave you to the rats!" he seethed, ordering his guards to hurl his limp, broken body into a filthy pit, set in the centre of the Great Hall.

An iron lid slammed shut above Jarett and was chained up noisily. Sly never intended to open it again, at least not until the rats had resorted to eating each other. Sly had lost the only leverage he held over Rob after his friends had escaped and he was furious. How could he persuade Rob to return to the Dark Fortress now? He still had the Elf scum—for now—but held little hope they would be foolish enough to rescue him and even less, risk involving Rob in the attempt. He had only one play left, but for it to work, certain pieces would have to be in position. He knew at some point—assuming Rob would be under the protection of the Faerie Queen—the Human would be kept at Corona, most likely within the Citadel itself, nested high in the Crystal Mountains. A notoriously difficult place to penetrate, but not so difficult to escape from. If only he had inside help, a spy or two perhaps…

Sly chuckled to himself while making his way up to the tower where his Guild were busy at work. He needed to send word at once in preparation for a little game of smash and grab.

This is far from over; this is where it all begins…

Chapter 25

Dern asked Archer to wait while he took the Queen to one side, "I appreciate you wish to pay back a debt of gratitude and I understand that you wish to help, but this is a fool's errand. We have not conducted any reconnaissance of the area for quite some time and at best we can only guess the level of resistance we might encounter. It is an ill thought-out and highly dangerous mission, I must strongly advise against it."

The Queen took his hands, "I appreciate your concerns, Dern, but sometimes we are left with no other option but to act. The Archer is right; we do not have the military might to contend with the Dark Fortress Army and it is only a matter of time before they will attack Corona in search of Rob. If we can release those imprisoned behind the Tin Fence, we will have our army, an army that is hell-bent on retribution."

Dern studied her for a moment. He knew he couldn't dissuade her and she had presented a strong argument.

"Very well, my Queen, but first I insist you send for reinforcements."

"I already did and thank you, Dern"

"For what?"

"For being here, for being you."

The Queen walked over to Rob, "You will ride with me and the rest of you can double up. All Drakites are fitted with double saddles, half of our squadron have riders teamed up with archers, which we have found makes for a very effective combination."

"You want *me* to sit on *that*?" spluttered Rob.

Dippy giggled, "Oh, Rob, I thought you were my brave rescuer, ready to do battle and save mermaids in distress."

"I was just making sure I had the right bird, dragon, thing, that's all." he replied unconvincingly.

The Queen had already leapt into her seat, pulling the reigns in tightly, while the Drakite eyed up Rob then snorted loudly, making him jump. He found the foot hold and hoisted himself up to sit directly behind her. She pointed to a leather strap which he then pulled around his waist, buckling in as tightly as possible.

"You may wish to hold on to me, Rob from Terra, I will allow it on this occasion..." she said with a wink.

"Riders, ascend in battle formation!" cried the Queen and gave a sharp tug upwards with both reigns.

The Drakite responded immediately, letting out a piercing cry as its huge wings beat forcefully against the ground, in moments they were airborne. The power of the beast was astonishing. Rob felt its muscles and tendons, wrenching and tightening beneath him, while its wings pounded the air with colossal force. Rob dared a peek and really wished he hadn't, the ground was disappearing at an alarming rate. The towering trees that had hidden them so easily, quickly became a vast collection of small green points. Rob squeezed his eyes shut—seriously regretting his decision to climb aboard—and held on for dear life while the Drakite's wings compensated for the increasing air turbulence.

"It's okay, Rob, you can relax soon and maybe I will be able to breathe again."

Rob reluctantly loosened his grip from around her waist. Although still ascending, things had settled considerably. Despite the invigorating rush of air, it seemed reasonably calm and he felt brave enough to snatch a second glance and gasped. As he surveyed the sky and land around him, his fear was all but forgotten. Still keeping close to the Queen, Rob could see all of the Elven riders in magnificent formation, dominating the sky in every direction. The sight was extraordinary and to' be a part of it was beyond thrilling. A little way ahead, he could make out Dern. The Orchi were to his left and right. Beyond them, he could see the horizon, an azure blue canopy sinking to a hazy white line. Beneath that lay the extended grey patina of the Dark-Cloud Crags—the mountain range was better known as the Tin Fence as the rock contained high quantities of tin ore and would scatter an unusual silvery-white brilliance on clear sunny days.

Although still buffeted by the wind, the sun was pleasantly warm, allowing him to see for hundreds of miles with ease. He looked behind to make out any landmarks he had just left. Instantly Rob recognised the Needles, which was simple enough. Then looked to his right for the great Goblin City. It was too far for any discernible details, but he thought he glimpsed the shimmering waters of the Great Wet beyond. He saw Dippy pointing to her right, he followed her direction and saw a large mountain range, taller than it was broad, but what really stood out was the way in which the sunlight reflected off its peaks. It resembled coloured mirrors from this vantage point, a beautiful chromatic display that could only be the Elven City of Corona, heartland to the Faerie Queen. He hoped soon he may be fortunate enough to view it much closer. Dippy caught his eye again by pointing downwards and to her left. Searching, he could only see open plains and woodland with flashing glints of winding rivers and voluminous lakes. He looked a little further...then saw it. Three black peaks grouped tightly together, like an unwelcome stain on a map. From this height it looked small and insignificant, but he knew it was a snake pit of vile intention and nefarious activity.

"Have you become more accustomed to travelling by Drakites?" shouted the Queen.

"Yes, thank you. It's amazing up here!"

"Don't get too comfortable, you know what we face ahead. But don't be too concerned, we will ride the winds while your father, the Orcs and my warriors land. After they have secured the area, we will land."

"Will there be any fighting when they first land?" shouted Rob.

"I wouldn't expect any less, the Red-Caps will not be welcoming in the slightest."

Rob considered this for a moment. He accepted he was not much with a sword, or any other weapon for that matter, but he would not see his father risk his life while he remained at a safe distance.

"Faerie Queen, can we land first as well? If my father's fighting, then I will fight by his side."

There was a pause, then she looked over her shoulder, "That's a shame, I will have to dismount as well." she replied grinning, with a steely air etched into her Elven features.

As they flew onwards, Rob wondered what lay in wait. *Would we be lucky and the place deserted? Unlikely. Perhaps the Red-Caps would see the air battalion and turn tail, running for the sanctuary of the Tundra mines.* His thoughts included his journey so far, from waking in Pardonme Marsh on the back of a green monster, to his time spent at Whisperun Forest, learning about Goblins and as much about himself. He then recalled Fingle's farcical Court case and the bizarre way in which they had managed to escape from Sly's evil clutches and of the standoff at Sailor's Toof, where the small wizard had communicated with hum-bugs and even the mountain itself. Rob smiled at how he alone had not only bested

Toesin the Troll, but also the Crone in the Cone and walked away with a beautiful mere-girl that he was falling deeply in love with. Whatever the Tundra mines held in store for him, he knew he could deal with it. It was time he believed in himself, he had not come this far to fail now. There was a future for him here, a real future. It was everything he had ever dreamed of. He seriously doubted he could ever return to his own world and surprisingly, it hadn't bothered him at all.

As he looked down, he could see the Tin Fence. They were almost above it, the prevailing icy winds swirling up from the Tundra were now whipping about them. Dern trailed a large blue banner behind him and the squadron responded by plunging into a rapid descent.

"Hang on, Rob, this will all happen very quickly. Try to stay calm and keep your wits about you. And remember to breathe!" shouted the Queen, as they left flight formation in preparation for a combat landing approach.

Rob felt fear rise in the pit of his stomach again, tasting the bitterness of bile as it burned his throat. He took one last look around him and felt buoyed by the sheer number of seasoned warriors surrounding him, yet oddly, he would have felt safer if Merlock, Fingle and Clump were with him right now. He missed them beyond words and prayed they were still alive. If he had to fight every last Red-Cap to save his friends, then it would be this single thought that would be enough to carry him through this alive.

Several dozen Drakites from the front broke away, accelerating into a hard dive as the Tin Fence gave way to the icy Tundra flats and snow laden mines. The difference in temperature was alarming, the enormous Tin Fence, living up to its namesake, had literally penned in the bitter northern climate from the rest of the land below, much as the Goblin City did the same with the warmer southerly climate. Rob watched intently as the Drakites became smaller, circling once above the proposed landing area, then into another hard dive. This prompted half of the remaining squadron to begin their descent, leaving the Drakites with rear archers to follow at a lesser angle and speed, to expand outwards and provide the landing party with critical air support.

The Queen peeled away, initiating an aggressive dive herself. Rob caught sight of the Elves flanking them, they had not been expecting this maneuver and quickly raced after them. Looking above her shoulder, Rob could see the advance party had now landed and the Drakites were being positioned in a large circle facing outwards. He couldn't see any activity around the mines. All looked eerily still and deserted. As Buttercup's Drakite came in to land, Rob felt the huge thrashing of its wings as it slowed to almost a hover. The Queen swiftly dismounted as the beast landed safely within the large circle of riders. Rob unfastened his straps and jumped off too, following her over to Dern and the Archer. The Elves and Orcs stood protectively, weapons in hand, scouting for any signs of life.

"My Queen, why have you landed? I cannot allow this, you know it is forbidden!" balked Dern.

Buttercup knew she was acting against protocol, but was inflamed by the public reprimand Dern had just given her.

"Must I remind you who has overall command of our Forces? However, this is not the time for petty dispute."

Dern tightened his jaw and bowed his head, "My apologies, my Queen, I am as always, merely concerned for your welfare. It is my position to do so, a position that *you* appointed."

He looked up and she could see the frustration wrestling within him. She walked over, placing her hand upon him, "And I thank you for it, always."

Rob's father ran over, "My Queen, I respect your right and decision to be included in the ground assault, but I do not wish my son to be involved, he is not ready."

Rob walked out from behind her and faced his father, "You are right, Dad, I am not ready, but that is not a bad thing. Given the choice, I would prefer to never be ready, but that choice is part of a much bigger one, one where I must decide if I can carry on living by losing everything I love because I did nothing to protect it. If that is the choice, then it has already been made. Sometimes, there are much bigger things happening around us, things we cannot ever fully understand, but understand enough that we are *all* vital pieces within the great struggle. If we didn't struggle together in the name of love, if we just gave up, then everything we value, everything that matters and makes sense in all the madness would be taken from us. I choose to fight because I choose you, Dad, and I will die protecting that love before it is taken from me."

Robert placed his hands on his son's shoulders, "I understand, really I do, but I am just afraid for your safety, it's kind of my job. But please know this, Son, I have never been *anything* less than proud of you, even when you *literally* caused Mr. Cornfoot to develop a hernia. From what I hear, it was long overdue." said his father thickly.

Rob laughed and hugged his dad, "Never fear. I will stay close to the legendary Archer, but c'mon Dad, Rob-in-Hood, seriously?"

"Ha ha, fair point, it just sort of happened. I know it's already been taken, but *they* don't know that." replied Robert, flashing his son a wicked grin. "When did my son become the philosopher anyway? It appears you have grown a little wiser perhaps."

"All I needed was the opportunity I guess. Being here and being accountable for every decision I have made, has forced me into seeing things *very* differently."

"Sorry to break up the party, but we are in serious trouble here, my Queen" said Dern after talking with the Squadron leader and Orchi.

"How? Not a single life has been taken since our landing, surely that is a good thing?" replied the Queen.

"No, it is far from good. We *need* the Goblin prisoners if we are to stand any chance against the Dark Fortress, so far we have not seen a single prisoner and equally as worrying, any Red-Caps."

Kang stepped forwards, "Perhaps they had been forewarned ahead of our arrival? Or previously considered that we might rescue the prisoners to boost our own Forces? We have to face the possibility the prisoners may have been executed."

Dern thought for a moment, "No. I know we have been lacking in reconnaissance lately, but we have moles also, it is an unavoidable necessity. We would have heard if something of that magnitude had taken place. They must still be here, somewhere. We will keep the archers circling above for support while we split into teams and begin a search of the mines for signs of life, agreed?"

The agreement was unanimous. There was little else that could be done, as time was also their enemy. They needed to act fast.

"This feels wrong, something is very wrong about this place, Dad?" said Rob nervously.

"I agree, Son, it reeks of deception. We must maintain a high level of vigilance at all times."

The grounded Drakites remained in circle formation, while the search groups had each been allocated an area to scout. Rob, his father, the Queen, and Dern had identified a cluster of five mine entrances, approximately six hundred feet from the landing site. The group spanned out evenly, each primed to react if needed. Rob carried a sword given to him by an Elven rider, it was surprisingly light and looked dangerously sharp, but felt its burden adding to its weight. The possibility it could be the only thing standing between him and certain death filled him with dread.

Craning his head, Rob paused, "What's that? Can anyone else hear—"

Before he could finish, his world erupted into billowing dust and great shards of rock!

"Incoming!"

In a daze, Rob looked around and was thrown hard against the ice as the ground exploded several times. He opened his eyes and saw his father's mouth move.

"Son, we are under heavy attack; we must get back to the Drakites now!"

Rob was hauled onto his feet and tried to make his legs run. Robert was practically dragging his son across the open Tundra, as huge rocks crashed about them, some landing so close that the dust filled their lungs, with shattering fragments causing deep lacerations to their exposed skin. Rob tried to focus on reaching the landing area, but his vision was a shaky blur. Frightening sounds of rock smashing rock, intensified by screams and shouts all added to his confusion. The loyal Drakites were thrashing and screeching, suffering horrible injuries from the hurtling projectiles while obediently waiting for their riders to return. The Queen had made it back and so too the Orchi, huddled together watching skywards, trapped between the mines and the Tin Fence.

"We are caught within a killing zone. There are catapults on either end of the ice flats, they were hidden beneath huge snowy sheets resembling rock." yelled Rielog to Kang.

Kang nodded gravely then turned to Dern. "If we stay here, we will all die. We can try to fly out, or head back towards the mines."

Dern looked at the Drakites, half of them were now mortally wounded, an easy target due to their size and ironically their discipline. Leaving them grounded in the direct line of fire had proved a devastating oversight. Dern assessed the situation, if anything the aerial assault had intensified, showing no sign of abating.

"My Queen, if we attempt to fly through this, some will survive, but I believe our Elves will stand a better chance of survival if we head for the mines."

Buttercup watched the poor creatures, caught between loyalty and agony. Her sadness mingled with rage.

"We send up the Drakites that can still fly and we run for cover." she yelled, then dived into Dern as a boulder narrowly missed her.

He picked her up, her head now bleeding, "Are you okay?" he cried.

Dazed, she barely nodded.

"We run now!" shouted Dern above the noise, as the Elves regrouped, helping those who were injured to move away from the devastation.

The order was given to release the remaining Drakites that could still fly. Rob's heart sank, watching several of the riders permanently end the suffering of their wounded Drakites. The Tundra's white expanse was stained heavily with the blood spilt from the fallen. Elven riders lay twisted and bent next to their dutiful winged comrades, amidst debris that did not cease, as huge rocks continued to plummet down. Some of the beasts managed to escape unhurt, while some limped into the sky, beating their battered wings, searching for an escape through the bombardment. Some—not so fortunate—were forced back down, defeated and crashing haphazardly into the unforgiving ice.

The Drakite archers circling above could not get in close enough for fear they too would be pummelled from the sky and even if they were able, they had no enemy to fire upon. A small aerial group had cut away, heading for the catapults, but the catapults were deeply entrenched, never intending to be mobile. In this way they were substantially fortified and any attempt at rendering them inoperable by the Drakite archers were simply futile. A ground force invasion was the only way they could be neutralised. A long ragged line of Elves and Orcs' sprinted towards the numerous mine entrances dotted along a rocky mound spanning the entire length of the frozen territory— ending where the catapults were positioned at the distant ends.

As they approached the mine openings, the ground took on an incline, making it difficult to traverse as the surface was little more than compacted sheet ice.

"Haaaaaaaaalt!" yelled Kang as loudly as possible, everybody immediately responded.

Kang studied the ground, then looked up towards the scattered mines, now only a few hundred feet away.

"Regroup, regroup, make ready!" bellowed the seasoned Orc.

Every warrior reassembled to form a defensive stance, grouping tightly together with their weapons made at the ready.

"Kang what is it?" said Rob's father.

The veteran Orc pointed down, "The ground here has been made smoother than anywhere else and we are now on an incline. The terrain outside of the mine entrances is different, instead it is littered with small rubble which has been placed there very recently, maybe even earlier today."

"Chaaaaaaaaaaaarge!"

Kang's observations were well founded, as swarms of vexed Red-Caps poured out from the mines. The Archer caught his breathe, realising had they continued any further, they would have been cut to ribbons while desperately seeking to gain a solid foot hold on the glassy ice. The Red-Caps had never intended to fight on the ice, but Kang's experience had compelled the Gnomes to take the fight to them. This provided a merciful reprieve from the aerial assault, for the Red-Caps had no other option but to enter the killing zone and in doing so, forced their own catapults to stop firing.

Rob was kept back from the front line, but he could still see the venom on the pinched faces of the Red-Caps as they slashed and thrust their swords at the Elves in fury. Although shorter in stature, the Gnomes were thickset, tough and notoriously cruel. The Elves and Orcs were easily the better fighters, seasoned and deadly, but for every Red-Cap felled, two more would take its place. The Gnomes began to edge around the defensive formation, until eventually Rob found himself trapped centrally within a large circle of Elven warriors, all fighting outwards. As the mines continued to haemorrhage reinforcements, the Elves and Orcs were already beginning to tire. A large cluster of Elves protecting the Queen, manifested a magickal defensive shield to safeguard the front line against the incessant stabs and strikes.

The Drakite archers upon seeing the attack flew in immediately, assisting where they could, aiming toward the outer regions of the surge. But the catapults began to fire again, having altered their trajectory so that the angle of fire would only impede their aerial support and avoid the ground forces altogether. During the melee, Rob was squeezed to the rear of the circle and was now facing the base of the Tin Fence. A spiteful, gnarly face jumped into view and lunged forwards. Before Rob could raise his sword, an arrow struck the Gnome, leaving it standing limp while being jostled in the skirmish and staring lifelessly at Rob. He was immensely relieved his father had his back and was now ready for the next attacker. Between the frenzy of arms and clashing steel, another seething Red-Cap forced his way through, Rob buried his sword as hard as he could into its chest. The Gnome screamed in fury as Rob was sprayed with bright red blood as he withdrew his sword. If Rob had any time to consider his actions, he would have been physically sick. His world was spinning fast, sounds and smells, emotions and colours all tangled together. He wanted to stop, he wanted it all to end, but a calm voice somewhere within was telling him, "Stay alive, Rob, keep going and stay alive…"

Dippy could scarcely watch from the back of a Drakite, *such a needless waste of life.* She couldn't see Rob, but she knew he was still alive. She wept for him, deeply saddened he had to play his part in the eternal struggle, in all its brutal ugliness.

"Abranth, they have left."

"All of them…?"

"Mostly, only a few remain. There is talk of a large battle taking place, right now above our heads."

"The prophecy…"

"What?"

"Never mind, you must send urgent word to all section Goblins, the time we have prayed for is finally upon us. We move together and we move now."

As the skinny Goblin galumphed away down a dimly lit tunnel, Abranth had to steady herself at the realisation of what she had just said. After surviving the mines for almost twenty years, their moment of freedom was finally upon them. She pulled herself onto her feet using her staff. Although limping, she moved swiftly along the dark passage. When she approached its end, the prisoners were already amassing in a fever pitch. She glanced over to where a Red-Cap was being relieved of his duty by five pick axes and to her right was another Gnome being strangled with a set of leg irons.

Keys were passed around and more prisoners were being set free. A deafening cheer arose, filling the entire cavern. Abranth took her rightful place, standing upon a central rock so that she could address all the prisoners, *her* clans, a place where she had imagined this moment countless times, while subjected to cruelty beyond measure. The torture over time had broken her body, but ironically, it had also ensured her survival, forging an unbreakable spirit that no whip, blade, fist, or boot could ever touch.

"Goblins, this is *our* time! We will have no other. We must seize it and make it count. We fight now, for our lives and for our freedom, are you ready to take it back? Are you willing to follow me and make these devils pay for all they have done to us?"

The reply was thunderous, thousands of crazed Goblins demanded blood that would not be denied. They looked to their leader, to Abranth. She had been there from the very beginning, the last of the free clan leaders. She too had suffered the indignity and brutality at the hands of the Red-Caps. She had been their pillar, a beacon of hope by refusing to let her spirit be broken, their rock to cling to in the dark tombs of horror for almost two decades of hell…

The Goblins helped down their leader and picked up shovels, pick axes, anything that could be used to slaughter their captors. She led the way, up and out towards an emancipation they craved, yet were almost too afraid to imagine. She hadn't gotten far when the advance had been staunched. A panic stricken Goblin pushed through the crowds of emaciated Goblins, all with vengeance clawing away within their heaving chests.

"Come quickly, we are unable to leave the mine." he cried in dismay.

Abranth was swiftly helped along the widened tunnel as the Goblins parted. As she hobbled into the light, she dropped her staff to shield her face against the severity of daylight. Abranth was led up to the huge gates that kept them all from escaping. She studied it for a moment and almost sank to her knees. She could see that even with the weight of a hundred raging Goblins pushing against it, it would not be enough to break free, they would only crush themselves to death. The gate was built of solid iron bars, all at least eight inches thick. The enormous hinges were also forged from solid iron and set deep into the surrounding rock. Nothing was going to move them. A thick bulky padlock—that could be reached by hands, but not by tools—had been locked securely through heavy chains that wound around the central bars. It was the only obstacle standing between them and their freedom; it was agonising to be so unbearably close, the ultimate final cruelty imposed by their captors.

Abranth cried as she peered through the gate. She could make out the fringe of the battle, watching the outnumbered Elves bravely fend off the determined attacks. She looked upwards and saw the sky peppered with hurtling rocks, blocking the desperate Drakite riders from entering the fray. The fierce pain in her leg had returned and her heart was heavy, it took every last ounce of strength to remain standing, when all she wanted to do was collapse. But she was the last, great clans' leader, their *only* leader and she would stand tall for every last one of them, for whatever happened this day, whether freedom reigned or death called, she would stand tall.

As Rob fought valiantly, he looked over the heads of the amassing, snarling Red-Caps to the outer edges and still the circle was widening. How many had he killed? How many more would he have to? How many more could he? Amidst the clamour of battle, an alarming "crack" reverberated around the Tundra, yet Rob seemed to be the only one who had noticed. He soon realised why only he alone had noticed, because only he alone had heard it once before. He pulled back a little from the skirmish, enough to allow him to scan the base of the Tin Fence. He couldn't believe his eyes...a huge cleft had wrenched apart in the rock face and his friends emerged from it!

"Wait you fools." scolded Merlock, a little uneasy on his feet—convincing a mountain to make a doorway was not for novices.

The small wizard took Fingle's hand for support and continued, "It seems the Gnomes were expecting them, they were well prepared. No doubt we could make a dent in them, but there are just too many, see how they spill from the mines."

"I thought yer said the Goblin prisoners were thrice as many, Uncle and yet I canna see any?" said Fingle scratching his head.

"Therc." said Clump, thrusting his battle axe towards a gated mine entrance on the far right, where dozens of green arms frantically reached out.

"Crom! He's right, well done, my boy. The Elves need our help, so we must free those prisoners. I just hope there are enough of our brethren still alive behind that gate. Do you think you two can manage it? I *would* help but—"

"It's okay, Uncle, get yer strength back and don't yer dare move from this spot. We'll 'ave 'em all out quicker than a gold toof from a fresh corpse."

Smiling proudly, Merlock lowered himself down, then groaned as Fingle clumsily skidded onto his belly, while Clump continued thundering forwards.

"Clump, Clump, get back 'ere yer galumphing Troll-tit."

Clump slid to a halt and peered around, "Wot you doing, Fingle? We gots to help them, now!"

Gingerly, Fingle got back up, muttering all the way over to Clump. "Look, I am having difficulty 'ere, can yer...yer know."

"Yes?"

"Can yer *please* pick me up?"

"No problem." said Clump, switching his axe to his left hand and scooping up Fingle with his right.

"Listen, if we ever get out of this alive, we *both* ran together, yer got it?"

Clump nodded eagerly and winked.

"What does *that* mean?" argued Fingle, but Clump had already launched away, his large feet and heavy weight giving him the distinct advantage over the icy ground.

Rob now fought with renewed vigour, his friends were alive! But where were they going? He followed their direction and saw they were heading towards a distant mine by the look of things. He squinted hard and then he saw it, dozens of small green hands desperately waving from the obscured entrance; *it had to be the prisoners.* He searched for his father and found him close by, working his sword fiercely against the Gnome horde.

"Dad, the clan Goblins, they are being held over there!" yelled Rob as loudly as his lungs would allow.

The Archer immediately looked over at his son and then to where he pointed. The Goblins had not all been killed, hope for them remained. Regrettably, the Red-Caps had also overheard Rob. A secondary battle now commenced. Rob's father swiftly gathered the Orchi away from the front line while relaying the information. Meanwhile, a large swathe of Gnomes from the outer edges had left, heading back to where the prisoners were being held. The Gnomes knew that if that gate was ever opened, it would mark the beginning of a rapid and permanent decline for them all.

In seconds, the Archer and Orcs had carved a pathway through the circle, eventually escaping from where the line had thinned from the migrating Red-Caps. The Faerie Queen remained with the bulk of her Elven fighters, maintaining the magickal shield, which by now was beginning to weaken. The effort to protect her people from the concentrated malevolence was taxing and yet still the bobbing river of red continued to swell around them. Rob managed to muscle his way through to join the rescue attempt, fortunately for him Nororcious and Kallana had been assigned to watch over him. The veteran Orcs helped to break him free by cutting down any Gnomes in his path.

The race was on.

Rob caught up with his father and the rest of the Orcs, with Nororcious and Kallana at the rear. Behind them, was an ever increasing army of Red-Caps hot on their heels. Running full tilt, Rob looked ahead to see the huge swarm of sprinting Gnomes that had first peeled away, desperate and determined to reach the prisoners before anyone else. He was literally sandwiched between the enemy, *what would happen when it all came to a crashing halt?*

Breathing hard, Rob looked ahead and to his right and saw the hulking frame of Clump striding through the blizzard, a monstrous shadowy form showing no signs of slowing. Rob could see that at some point—very soon—Clump would undoubtedly collide with the Red-Caps in front of him and be unable to beat them to the gate.

"Can't yer run any swifter? Yer slower than yer wit!" complained Fingle shakily, clutching onto Clump's heaving chest for dear life.

"I can't...sorry...Fingle." gasped Clump, between large gulps of air.

Fingle knew the fate that awaited them, if the detestable Gnomes managed to secure the mine, or worse, kill all the prisoners within. Without the clan Goblins, they were insanely outnumbered and despite a respectable culling spree, their journey would end at the hands of these callous sonsofwitches. Fingle's eyes narrowed, he had a cunning plan, not his best by his own admission, but Boggles can't be choosers during times of crises.

"Clump, remember that game we like ta play, when uncle isn't around?"

Clump thought hard, then grinned, "Boggle... Bowling."

"That's it. But I need yer ta pretend *I'm* a Boggle and that gate up ahead is really just a mob of Boggles who are drinking down by the stream, next ta Merlock's home, just like in our game, yes?"

"I like...this game. Hold on, Fingle...I will try not to make it...hurt much..."

Hearing Clump's parting words, Fingle immediately regretted his master plan. Clump's mighty arm—that held Fingle—drew back fully, until all that Fingle could see was the blur of Clump's feet pounding beneath him. Fingle had *just* enough time to curl into a tight ball before being launched forwards with a velocity that bested the boulders catapulted above their heads.

Fingle's world exploded and imploded at the same time, as he tumbled at break neck, back, arms and legs speed. Drooling uncontrollably, he was vaguely aware that friction was taking place. His eyes should have remained tightly closed were it not for the gravitational forces thrust upon them, coupled with the Tundra winds whipping mercilessly across the icy terrain. His vision consisted solely of an extremely rapid slide show of black and white, framed by little sparkly lights, as if an inattentive God toyed with the switch of creation. Derangement spun into delirium as he relived his own birth—a difficult and hesitant affair, his poorly mother lacking the strength to push her son out from the darkness and the determined effort of his uncle attempting to pull him into the light.

Most of those running for the mine had now seen the mysterious large green ball rolling at high speed—never abating, aided by the slippery surface it barely touched—while emitting a peculiar spiky howl as it rocketed past. The Red-Caps ahead increased their pace in response. Rob glanced behind and saw their pursuers slowly gain ground, yet despite their hatred, he also saw fear etched into their faces for the first time. After hurling his best friend as hard as he could towards a solid iron gate over sheet ice, Clump had the full use of both arms once again and managed to pump his body harder. Although approaching the mine from a different angle, he knew he now had the edge and would beat the Gnomes before they could reach Fingle. As he thundered closer, the corners of his stretched black lips began to twitch of their own volition, while his hand squeezed firmly on the thick oak shaft of his terrible axe. *Two of my favourite games, in one day,* Clump thought joyfully.

"Everybody, get back at once, protect yourselves!" shouted Abranth, stumbling for cover as the large irregular sphere tumbled into view. A painfully loud clang was heard, as the projectile ploughed into the Iron Gate. The Goblins rushed forwards to meet a jumble of green limbs on the outside and a quivering nose on the inside.

"I..feeeel…shickk…" gurgled the limp body, sprawled haphazardly outside the gate—which was still reverberating.

"My…noshe…pull…it…out..."

A Goblin reached down and yanked his hooter hard.

"Aaarrrgggh, not my noshe…what's...inside it."

The prisoner recognised the glint of gold and pulled out the pick. Impossibly, Fingle managed to force up a quivering hand and catch his gold nose rings, despite the clicking resistance his arm gave him.

"A lock pick! Who can pick a padlock? It's our only chance."

A straggly prisoner scuffled past the crowd of malnourished bodies and swiped the pick away.

"Giv' it 'ere, thieving's a dying trade and a dying shame it is, y'all shud be ashamed of yerselves."

He was lifted up to the padlock. Two other Goblins reached through the bars to orientate the lock towards him, as much as it would allow. His feeble cold hands shook with the effort, but his features remained unflinching.

"Abranth, the Gnomes, they're here!" screamed a prisoner, falling to his knees.

"I just need, a little, more…"

A tide of red capped maniacs were about to collide with the gate, but were prevented by an enormous circle of shining steel. Clump's terrifying battle-axe cleaved through the onslaught, decapitating a score and six in a single sweep. The frightening barbarity did not falter, the horrific arc of death continued mutilating crowding clusters of dumbfounded Red-Caps.

"I've got it, I've got it." sang the triumphant little Goblin as the padlock and chains clunked heavily to the floor.

It was the most unsettling of pauses, as if all the heavenly hosts held their breath, looking away in sympathetic understanding of what must come to pass. In the eerie silence of the Tundra, the only sounds were of those still running—ignorant of their appalling fates—and the lamenting icy blizzard that weaved and wailed its requiem throughout, until a long sonorous creak from the opening Iron Gate shattered the silence. It was heard by captives overcome with an unquenchable blood lust that had festered for an eternity and by captors who knew a quick death was now their best hope.

Bespattered in lumps of crimson flesh and splintered bone, Clump stood over Fingle and roared, no one challenged him. The Orcs, Rob and his father were forced to run to the refuge of the Tin Fence for fear of being trampled to death by a stampede of retreating Gnomes and a legion of berserk Goblins hunting them down. Rob felt the sadness and bitterness within the furious screams of the Goblins, but above all, he felt their rage. The ensuing massacre that transformed the Tundra from a spectral white to scarlet, was a forever nightmare of awaited release made manifest. A brief and dreadful beginning, necessary in clawing their way back to finding some semblance of what they once were. It was terrible, yes, yet no one could pass judgement upon it. It was born of the Red-Caps, a hellish retribution they alone had spawned and reaped upon themselves.

Hundreds of Goblins seized the catapults to the left of the mine they had just escaped, there was no resistance. The Goblins aimed the projectiles towards the catapults at the far end and in moments they had been destroyed. As the remaining Gnomes tried to flee back into the mines, they were rounded up and hacked to pieces. There were no prisoners taken and again, no one had questioned it.

The Archer placed his arms around his son, letting him weep until he was ready to let go. The Drakite archers and reinforcements were finally able to land. Dern and the Queen—with the aid of the remaining Elves—treated the injured and provided the prisoners with clothing and food where possible, prioritising the young, injured and elderly first. Although spent from sustaining the magickal shielding, the healing energies the Elves applied had the beneficial effect of replenishing their own flagging bodies and spirits.

Rob searched everywhere for Dippy, but could not find her. He suspected she would be helping those in need somewhere, but *he* needed her right now, more than ever before. He walked the short distance over to Merlock. The old wizard climbed to his feet and embraced him firmly.

"I am so sorry you were a part of this, my boy. You have a pure heart, such a shame, such a terrible shame…" he choked, as tears explored his crinkled cheeks and hid amongst his dusty beard.

"Hey, we're still alive aren't we? And we have saved the prisoners." smiled Rob.

"Yes, yes of course, you are right." replied the sniffing wizard, managing a smile.

"Was it your idea to turn Fingle into a bowling ball?"

"Sadly, I cannot take the credit, the stupidity was all of their own making." Merlock chortled.

Clump bounded over, holding Fingle lovingly in his blood soaked arms. "Merlock, Fingle's broken, please help?" asked the giant, shaking with worry.

"B...bowling Boggles, is my spec...special, is my thing...my nose...yes my nose will never play again, but...it saved the day..." mumbled Fingle, distorted and hunched, weakly resisting his body's desire to transfer back into a ball.

Well, for starters, Clump, the blood's not his and he's just a bit discomgoblinated. I have a splendid remedy for that and all will be as rotten as rats once more." reassured Merlock. The giant nodded, beaming his dreadful smile back.

As Rob's father walked over, Rob began the introductions, "Dad, may I introduce—"

"Merlock, you old sorcerer!"

"Rob-In-Hood, you're a sight for sore seers!"

Rob watched in disbelief as they both embraced.

"Merlock, how long have you known?" sputtered Rob, dismayed and utterly confused.

"My boy, my dear, dear boy, I confess I had my suspicions, but until this day I could not be certain. We have much to talk about, but now is not the time and the Tundra certainly not the place. My old bones are chilled to the, well bones." offered Merlock apologetically.

"Anything else you think I should know, Dad?" Rob said, entirely stunned.

"Yes...there is, Son. Abranth, could you please come closer. This is Rob, Rob, this is the last, free clans' Goblin leader."

Rob's father squeezed her hand and she nodded hesitantly, "Thank you, Archer...you kept to your promise, thank you." smiling, she kissed him tenderly, both tasting each other's tears.

Those present parted and with his father's help, Abranth limped over to see the young Human-Goblin.

"So, *you* are 'Rob from Terra'. Do you know how long I have waited for this moment…to see you?"

Rob felt unsteady again; all eyes seemed to settle on him. What did she mean *wait*? There was something familiar about her, despite her grace and strength, something else?

Abranth continued, "Rob, whatever your father has told you, it was only ever to protect you, do you understand?"

Rob felt himself nod despite not fully understanding her words, it was as if her words, no, the *sound* of her words were ringing inside his head.

"You may have heard talk like 'prophecy' mentioned and this is true, for you are the prophecy we have all been waiting for, but none more than I, because you see, Rob…you are…"

Abranth collapsed and began to weep, Rob quickly bent down and held her cold, shaking body.

"Abranth, tell me what else, what else am I?" he urged, choking on his words, terrified to deny or surrender to a distant emotion tearing its way out from a long forgotten place.

Trembling, she looked up into his eyes, tears streaking her dusty, tired face, "Rob, you are my beautiful son…"

Chapter 26

"He's in a state of shock and will need time and space to heal. I do not believe seeing you will be of any benefit to his recovery!"

"I appreciate that, Sister, but he's my son and he will want answers. That is if he is to ever speak with his father again."

Rob was already awake, but chose to appear asleep. He could not talk about his feelings with his father, not yet anyway. He waited until he heard the door close and their footsteps disappear. Slowly he opened his eyes and found himself sandwiched between crisp, clean linen sheets. It was by far the most comfortable bed he had slept in since his adventures first began. Rob sat up and swung his legs over the side. Across the sparse room, there was a large circular window, bright with sun light. The room was built entirely of white marble—which enhanced the light within, creating a serene and ethereal atmosphere, perfect for healing. Gingerly, Rob placed his feet down and was pleasantly surprised at the warmth of the marbled floor.

Walking over to the window, he attempted to push all thoughts aside, curious to investigate his new surroundings. The view was startling. A glorious vista of natural beauty in all its wondrous aspects. He remembered what he had glimpsed of the Crystal Mountains from riding upon the Drakite, but this was profoundly more spectacular. Gazing downwards he saw the great crystal shards illuminated by the sun, dazzling intense colours bursting in every direction. Further below stood a magnificent city, ancient yet pristine, set within the rainbow hued precipice, a living testament to existing in true harmony with nature. It was lush, exciting, exotic, and miraculous. It was difficult to discern whether the city had been built first, allowing for nature to flourish around and within, or perhaps it had been the other way around, so intrinsic were Elves with the elements.

"Corona..." Rob gasped in awe, uncertain he had left his bed at all and was perhaps still dreaming.

"If yer gonna jump, be quick about it, only some of us are trying ta get some rest."

Rob spun around, "Fingle!" he cried, running over to his bed which had been next to his all along.

"Steady on, Rob, watch me breakages, that cyclopean softskull Clump is to answer for me feeblyness."

Rob laughed and sat down next to him, "From where I was standing, the *pair* of you were responsible for saving pretty much everyone in the Tundra and possibly everywhere else, feeble Froglick indeed."

"Maybe so, but Clump hasn't saved his backside from me boot if ever I get out of 'ere."

"It's good to see you again, Fingle. Merlock *and* Clump too. I missed you guys, a lot."

"I suppose I might have missed yer yammering and yer stupid quest-onions. But mostly, mostly I just missed yer. I thought fer a moment back there, I was never going ta see yer again and…" Rob saw him struggle and hugged him tightly.

Fingle hugged him back using his good arm. "Right! Enough of this sillymentality, what's important now is that we keep yer away from Sly and his cohorts of doom and stop the Stinky-pinks invading 'ere, no offence."

Rob smiled while Fingle hurriedly dabbed his face.

"Has a young girl been to visit me, Fingle? Her name is Dippy, or maybe Siren-Dipity? She's a mermaid."

"No, only Elves and Goblins. Why? You been *wooing* while we've been stewing?" grinned Fingle.

"I rescued her from the Crone in the Cone, a story I will tell later. But for now I have questions that need answers, so I will let you rest. Is there anything I can get you?"

"A new arm maybe? Otherwise just get the answers yer seek lad and I will always have a spare flap for yer in case yer need Fingle's advice, discount for yer of course..."

Rob opened the door, looked fondly at his friend once more, then closed it softly behind him. He turned around and ventured down the long marble corridor. Although feeling much better for his stay, he still had a large knot in the pit of his stomach. He remembered enough of what had happened before he passed out. *Is Abranth really my mother?* It certainly made enough sense and explained why his father had always refused to talk about his mother, other than saying she had left them when he was very young. Perhaps this was why his father had never found anyone else, choosing to remain alone?

Rob had always assumed his father was simply too busy in his work to be romantically involved with other women and that whatever had happened between his parents had left his father bitter and reluctant in forging new relationships. Knowing what he knew now, *if* this clan leader was also his mother, then his heart went out to his father. For whatever reason they had to separate, it was born of necessity and most likely to be because of him. His father had never found another partner, simply because he still loved Abranth and had clung to the hope that one day he would again be reunited with his lost love. Despite being lied to, Rob understood it had been with good intentions. He knew he couldn't blame his father, especially when considering the crushing, corrosive guilt he had been shouldering for so many years. What was important right now, the *only* thing that mattered, was to become a real family. Although the knot remained, he felt his heart blaze with uncontainable love he needed to share with a mother he thought he would never have.

His thoughts returned to Dippy and how he longed for her. She would have known about his mother and had to conceal the unbearable pain of not being able to tell him, for fear that Abranth may have been killed during the Tundra rescue. Rob increased his pace, eager to re-join his parents and Dippy and to tell how much he loved them all. He leapt down a set of wide steps and almost careened into a young Elven girl carrying a bundle of fresh linen.

"I'm sorry, are you okay?" asked Rob, feeling foolish.

"Yes, I'm fine thank you. Hey, is your name, Rob?" she enquired, smiling prettily.

"Yes, why do you ask?"

"I was told that if you left your room, I was to escort you to the Queen, she is waiting patiently to talk with you."

"Oh? Well in that case I would be delighted, please show me the way."

The girl took him down another set of steps and led him down a corridor to his left. Rob thought it a little odd leaving the main route in favour of a more discreet passage and presumed it was a quicker route. She continued to take him along more corridors and around several bends until she stopped at a small door in a darkened corner of a narrow passageway.

"If you go through here and follow the stairs to the bottom, there will be someone else to guide you further." said the smiling girl, holding the door open for him.

Rob thanked her and began to descend the stairs. As the door above closed he heard it lock. Immediately he sensed something was amiss. *Maybe I should not have been so trusting,* he thought, but this *was* Corona, surely he had nothing to fear? He had little alternative than to continue down the narrow, winding staircase, until someone blocked his way.

"Greetings, Rob, we have been searching for you for a very long time." spoke a menacing voice from out of the shadows. Rob was about to run back up the stairs, but his world dimmed as a heavy club was brought down hard against his skull.

Chapter 27

"My Queen, we are sending aid to the Tundra mines. The clan Goblins, for now, are better left where they are. Strategically, they are safer too. We have set up guard posts on either side of the Tin Fence and a regiment of Elven warriors remain on standby. We also have Drakite air sentries on watch. The Goblins have been issued with weapons and armour, should the Dark Fortress decide to march upon them, *or* us."

"Thank you, Dern. I don't suppose it matters where they are, as long as they are safe, warm, fed and free. However, the sooner we can find them a more suited home the better, but that shall have to wait, we have more pressing issues at hand."

"Yes, my Queen. Also, Merlock the Goblin wizard has something of great import he insists he must deliver to you personally."

"Please bring him in."

Dern bowed, leaving the hall of Sparkles, shortly re-entering with the small Goblin.

"My Queen…" declared Merlock, bowing respectfully.

"Thank you, Merlock, the respect is mutual. It is not a common occurrence to have a mountain open and three heroes emerge to save the day!" she exclaimed as she ran over and hugged him hard, causing his feet to lift slightly.

"It's been a long time, too long. Please, come over here where we can talk better." she gestured towards two comfortable chairs near the panoramic window.

Merlock sat down, still blushing from the unexpected welcome, "My Queen, first I must warn you we are under great threat, all of us. AMOK, as you know, intended to invade the world of the Humans and in doing so disregarded the sacred universal laws and cast our collective reputation as the World of Fae to the four winds like dust. But, while we were being held captive at the Dark Fortress, there was a successful coup staged by Sly the Slaughterer..."

"Why would he choose such a crucial time for such a thing?"

"Because, my Queen, Sly has a different agenda. It appears he has been working closely with the Human militscary machine and if ever the Dark Fortress portal bridge is opened, then the Human army will invade and conquer *our* world."

"What! How do you know this? What do they want from us?" spluttered Buttercup, unable to control her outrage.

"This leads me to the second part of my message. We had the good fortune in meeting a high Elf while we were imprisoned at the Dark Fortress, his name was Jarrett, I believe you know of him?"

"I do and he is a traitor. Do not trust him, Merlock. I thought we were once friends, good friends, but he betrayed us all. He works for them, the S.G.G. and all of their hell-spawn." she fumed, looking away to compose herself.

"No! No he doesn't. He told us you would think ill of him and that was the price he was prepared to pay. Jarett infiltrated the S.G.G., providing false information so that he might learn of something useful and he had. He had no idea that dream control had been interfered with and by the time he discovered it, it was too late. He decided it was critical to *appear* to be of use to the S.G.G. in order to discover their plans, as opposed to a dead Elf without a great deal to report back. It was Jarett that warned us of the impending Human invasion and he suspects the Dark Fortress Army to be hiding out in Doom Forest, employing dark magick to remain undetected."

The Queen faced the wizard and leaned in closely, taking his hands in hers, "But *how* do you know he hasn't just given you false information too?"

"Because he gave his life in doing so."

The Queens hands dropped away as she shook her head, then she collapsed into her chair. Merlock leapt forwards and held her, placing his hand upon her forehead while reciting an unintelligible incantation. Immediately the shock left her face and she slumped against the wizard.

"Quick, somebody help please!"

Dern was already there, supporting her limp frame against his body, "What happened, *Goblin*? What have you done?" charged the Queen's protector.

"I have done nothing, *Elf*, besides soothe her mind against the pain she holds. I gave her news of Jarett and how he has only served your best interests, in how he bravely became a spy, gaining vital information he managed to pass on to me after he had broken us all out of the Dark Fortress. And in doing so, giving his own, *unworthy* life away in the process." balked Merlock, more than a little exasperated.

"I am sorry, Wizard, I should not have spoken harshly, it's just…"

"I know, in love."

"How?" replied Dern, eyes wide, certain they had been so careful together in hiding their forbidden love.

"The same way I knew Jarett was truthful. The Queen will recover soon, best she returns to her bed chambers. In the meantime, we might do well to prepare for an attack here at Corona. Sly has only a few days left until the celestial alignments alter, then it will be too late, whether he has a Human or not. How is young Rob anyway? Has he spoken with Abranth, his mother?"

"As far as I know he is healing from his trauma and has not yet left his room. I will check in on his progress with the Abbey sisters and also send word for McGrath and the other Commanding officers; we *must* be prepared."

Abranth could wait no longer, she was concerned Rob was unable to recover from the shock and was perhaps already awake and confused, or maybe too afraid to see her?

"Robert, I am going to see our son, you are welcome to join me or stay here." she stated, heading for the door.

"I understand how you feel, really I do, but the healers warned against it, they said he needed more time." replied Robert.

"You are wrong. The longer we wait, the deeper his trauma will become, he needs to come to terms with it and quickly. *Then* he will be able to heal." Abranth opened the door and left the room, Archer followed.

By the time they approached their son's room, they saw Dern running out.

"Have either of you seen Rob?" he shouted anxiously.

"No? We were on our way to see him, to see if he had awoken...?" trailed Abranth, already suspecting the worst.

Dern stopped short in front of them, his heart racing, "I have just spoken with his friend, Fingle. He told me Rob left several candle burns ago, apparently to see you two."

"They have him..." stammered Abranth, looking through Dern as if he wasn't there.

"Maybe so, but we know he's being kept alive and we know where he is being taken to."

"It will be too late, we have all failed him..."

"No! The only way they could leave is on foot or horseback. The entire air region between here, the Tin Fence and the Dark Fortress is watched over by our Air Squadron. Since we took custody of Rob, we implemented such a strategy in the event of his...capture..." said Dern, intensely frustrated and increasingly uncomfortable.

"Well, maybe you should have implemented a better strategy for guarding him!" shouted Robert, banging his clenched fist hard against the wall.

"You are right, Archer, this is unforgivable. Clearly the dark will stop at nothing. We must be extra vigilant; it is most likely these walls still harbour traitors, unless they escaped with Rob. But for now we must assume otherwise. Only the very closest of the Queens allies will convene in the Hall of Sparkles, immediately."

As they hurried away, a gangly figure hobbled out of a room at the far end of the corridor, "Wait fer me!" hollered Fingle, becoming twisted within his bed sheets and falling flat upon his already bloated and significantly bruised snout.

*   *   *

Some distance away, in the darkness, a small group of Goblins rode their mounts mercilessly. Before first light they would make it as far as the Leaning Root, then begin skirting the Murk-Sun Marshes.

"Don't worry, whelp, they can havs you back, as soon as we is done wif ya." teased a burly Goblin, the others laughed cruelly.

"Wot's that? Snarler's got ya tongue?"

Rob could only glare back in anger as he was bound, gagged, and plopped astride a galloping horse led by the rider in front. Occasionally they would stop and exchange their exhausted horses for fresh ones, which had been previously tethered along the route to gain the fastest ground possible. Rob wished he had more experience in riding, he fully expected after the journey that the question of his fertility would be in some serious doubt. It was pointless attempting to dismount, it would only hurt, a lot and incense the brutal guards. Rob did not feel afraid for his welfare, but was afraid in being a failure and angry for allowing himself to be so naive. He hoped by now his disappearance had been discovered and the cavalry were on their way. *At least I hadn't travelled by air,* he thought, *it will give them a chance in catching me up*, he hoped.

Chapter 28

"Do you think this, 'Dippy', had anything to do with Rob's kidnapping?" wondered Buttercup, anxious to root out the rot.

"No, my Queen. One of the Drakite riders relayed a message from her soon after the Goblins had taken the Tundra mines. She said she had to take leave immediately and that she was sorry in doing so. She also said she had no other choice and that Rob would understand in the *greater scheme of things*, whatever that meant." replied Dern.

"Hmmm, I'm not convinced; it sounds as though she may be complicit."

"I have seen them together, my Queen. I have heard the way they talk and look at each other. Unless I am very much mistaken, they are in love." replied Rob's father

"Very well, Archer. I will take your word for it. They may genuinely care for each other, but love can cause you to do all manner of strange things, especially if that love is threatened."

"His word is also good with me." declared a gruff voice.

Everyone turned to see McGrath stride into the meeting, larger than life and very much recovered.

"I must thank you, Archer and your courageous friends for saving my life, a debt I intend to settle when I get my hands on the Dark Fortress scum."

The Orchi grunted their appreciation and their approval.

Robert nodded too, wearing a grim smile, "You are most welcome, but may I ask a favour in return?"

"Anything within my power, Archer."

"I must insist that Sly Slaughter is left to me, alive…" it was delivered in such a way that no one would contest.

"Very well, you have my word and the word of my Elves."

McGrath walked over to address those assembled around a large table, preferring to remain standing—as always.

"My Queen, our Elven mystics have sensed a large presence hiding within Doom Forest, just as Jarrett's intelligence had suggested. Merlock has also verified this. Merlock?"

Merlock stood, introduced himself and continued to explain his findings, "I projected my essence to the boundary of Doom Forest earlier today. All had seemed well, but the moment I entered, I felt an extremely powerful, yet subtle magick in place, a spell of concealment, concealed within itself. I know the signature well, as I use it for my own protection. I carefully unwound the spell cords and a flurry of images bombarded me. Images of thousands of rogue Goblins, Gnomes, Trolls and Dwarves, all ready for battle. I peeled it a fraction further and became ensnared, enmeshed in its energy and sustained an immense psychic attack. The Guild in the Dark Fortress had sensed my presence interfering with their magick and the entire lodge of dark magi threw everything they had at me…" said Merlock, looking down at the floor.

"My goodness, are you alright? What happened?" pressed the Queen.

He looked up, flashing a wicked grin, "I may have accidentally disabled their entire army, oh, and the Guild as well…" Merlock's eyes glittered in undisguised mischief as they held her astonished gaze.

McGrath was the first to break the silence, "Merlock, I do not wish to patronise or underestimate you, but you must be clear on this matter. If there is any doubt in this we must know, our lives depend upon it."

Merlock nodded and continued, "Magick requires a level of confidence for it to manifest as a working resource. Too little and it will simply not work, but too much, well, then you will leave yourself open to catastrophic causality. The Guild have too much confidence. They wallow in self-aggrandisement, disrespecting all natural laws and have paid a hefty price. Once they had detected my presence, they made a fatal error of judgement. Instead of untangling me first from their concealment spell, or rather removing my energetic entanglement from their energetic manifestation, they simply attacked me in reckless fury. Their arrogance was their undoing. Every level one wizard at Hogspots knows, that if you are entangled in another's energy and they then attack you, then you are effectively shielded, as they cannot attack their own magick, using *their own* magick. But, what can happen, is that if the spell you have weaved is powerful enough, such as the concealment spell at Doom Forest and then you inadvertently attack your own spell while trying to attack something else connected to it, the original spell acts as a mirror and the negligent attack is returned to whoever is energetically linked to the magick…*thrice fold*!"

"Hang on, you said *you* were linked to their magick?" said McGrath.

"Yes, I was, but you don't think I go snooping around without adding a little protection for myself now do you?" grinned Merlock, looking devilish once again.

"Are you saying that the Guild have killed their own Army?"

"No. Not quite. A most peculiar and may I add, entertaining reaperconcussion has taken place. The concealment spell has reversed itself, in a way…"

"In *what* way is it entertaining wizard? And aside from now being able to see them all, how has that rendered them ineffective?" replied McGrath, irritated by the confusing conversation.

"My apologies, I do not meant to rant in riddles. In truth, as you say they are now visible, but with one crucial difference, they are only visible to themselves and not each other."

"Hold on, are you saying that the entire Dark Fortress Army and the Guild cannot see anyone else around them?" spluttered McGrath in disbelief.

"More so even than that, they cannot see *or* hear anyone that was connected to the concealment spell."

"Crom! We must take advantage of this, my Queen, we will not have a better opportunity."

Everyone stood, debating loudly. Merlock had caused quite a stir and felt a little pleased with himself, even if he wasn't entirely responsible for the incredible good fortune bestowed upon them.

After McGrath restored a semblance of order, Buttercup addressed the Commanders and other members present, "Not that I doubt you for a moment, Merlock, but we must be certain this has come to pass and be prepared if it has not, *or* that they may have since identified a solution? In your opinion, Merlock, if they can reverse the reverse spell, how long might it take?"

"My Queen, it is very difficult to co-ordinate anything when you cannot see or hear those you need to co-ordinate with. I have no doubt they will unravel their mess eventually, but it will take a fair amount of time. I would say several days at least before they are again at full strength."

"Then we must embrace our good fortune and put an end to this madness. Our first priority is to rescue Rob. We will send air scouts to verify the Dark Fortress Army is still disabled. We must alert the Goblins and Elves at the Tundra mines, I understand they are on standby, equipped and ready to march with us. McGrath, I will leave the details to you, but I want to move as soon as we can, within the wither of a wick."

As the commotion continued, Merlock left to fetch Clump and Fingle, but was stopped by the Queen. She bent down, hugging him again fondly.

"Merlock, you really are quite something. If we make it through all of this, I hope you and I will get to know each other a great deal more."

As he bowed she held his fluffy face and kissed him softly on his cheek, which became very warm, very quickly. He smiled proudly, stumbling out in a daze.

"Uncle, are yer alright? What did they do ta yer in there?" demanded Fingle, peering through the open doorway to the great Hall of Sparkles.

"Oh…nothing…everything is just splendid, Nephew…" said his uncle softly, holding his glowing cheek above a crooked smile.

Fingle caught Buttercup smiling affectionately, waving at the little wizard.

"Buttercup kissed him." giggled Clump.

"Seriously, Uncle? I know yer both well over a hundred, but yer look it and she don't. Besides, yer old philanderer, she's already taken so I hear, even if she's cast a spell on yer. *Merlock the all-powerful sorcerer, felled by a kiss from a Faerie Queen,* puuuuleeeeeease."

"Well, if you've got it, flaunt it, my boy. Anyway, how's your arm doing? Can you move it properly yet?" hurried Merlock, conscious of his pathetic resistance to Buttercups charms.

"No, it's dysfunctional and I needs it ta be healed snip-snap ta be of any use ta Rob. But I reckon I have more chance of platting me own piss than me arm being fixed by then." said Fingle miserably.

"Hmmm, we should allow for the healing to take place naturally. There may be another way, but there are no guarantees." Merlock warned, stroking his whiskers.

"If it means I get ta rescue Rob, so be it and so it is."

"Are you quite certain?"

"Wot's a matter, got bugs in yer lugs, Uncle? Yes I'm certain."

Chapter 29

"Sir, we can confirm we now have a visual on the Dark Fortress portal. The co-ordinates are 50.6960° N, 3.8114° W, Sir!" the sergeant reported to his superior officer.

"Excellent, Sergeant, I want our forces on full standby. If our sources are correct, the bridge to the Faerie Kingdom will soon be visible. When I give the command, we unleash a sustained artillery strike. On my second command, we send in the ground forces to conduct a sweep of the area and neutralise any survivors."

"Yes, Sir!"

The sergeant from the armoured battalion ran back to the front line, while his commanding officer breathed across the silver pommel of his swagger stick, polishing it to a brilliant shine. Smiling, he studied its reflection, admiring the military might positioned around him, prepared to act at his behest without question.

*　*　*

"Your Darkship, two more of the Guild have reversed the reverse spell, that totals three. We now have enough magi to maintain the bridge, but not without the Human."

Sly turned to face the Goblin officer, "Do you honestly think I do not know that, Mumblecrust? Perhaps I have been chasing him all over the kingdom for a jolly old lark and a spot of fresh air, while enjoying an enchanting picnic, *or fifty* in the fracking process, perchance? You unctuous, congenital toad."

"I am truly repentant, my pernicious President, of course you know, how stupid of me..." grovelled Mumblecrust.

"Adopt the position please." commanded Sly, removing his right glove.

The officer quickly spread his legs apart, used his quivering fingers to force his eyes open and then extended his black tongue out as far as it would reach. When Sly had counted to five, he rammed two fingers into the officer's eyes, followed by yanking his tongue—so hard it bled—and finished by swinging his armoured shin pad forcefully into the officers dangly bits. Although over in less than two seconds, it was brutally effective and provided Sly with a rare moment of quietude.

Sated and content, Sly added, "For your information, muck-scum, we already have the boy. A whole regiment has been dispatched to bring him to me. Very soon he will arrive to fulfil his destiny, as *the boy who betrayed his world...*"

"Blut woth aboth ow armee?" drooled Mumblecrust, nursing his family's fixtures and fittings.

"I have no idea what you just said, you blithering intestinal sculpture, but unknown to those meddlesome do-gooder Elves, I have a second army. They are almost in position, just a short march up from the Howl and Hullaballoo Caves. Always have a contingency, Mumblecrust. In your case, adoption would now be your best option."

Sly walked away chuckling, confident all was as it should be, but he had long forgotten about the pit in which he had just stood above, or he had simply not cared.

"If you help me, I can lead you to safety. You will be pardoned and can start over." came a raspy voice from the sealed pit beneath the Goblin officer.

"Who saith thath?" spluttered Mumblecrust, half blind and writhing in agony.

"I did, down here."

The Goblin felt for the hatch, working hard to see through his tears.

"Dith you thay you canth protecth mee?"

"Yes and not only that, I can help you get far away from here to begin anew, vindicated from all previous crimes. But you need to help me escape and fetch two horses, can you do that?"

Mumblecrust didn't take long to make his decision. He was sick of the way Sly mistreated him and he knew it was only a matter of time before Sly would snuff out his existence, probably because he had scuffed his boot, or a fortress cockerel misjudged the sunrise. The Goblin high officer yearned for something more than just killing things, Mumblecrust's dream was to have his own livestock, so he could butcher animals to make a living.

"Yeth, waith here, I will come bacth, ith I can sltill bloothy walk."

Jarett had been privy to most of the events that had happened recently. Hearing news of how the Guild and a secret Dark Fortress army had been rendered useless, had revived him greatly. With luck, he may yet live to explain his truth to Buttercup. Sly had certainly lived up to his namesake, no one had known about a second army. He *had* to warn his Queen.

*   *   *

"If yer laugh any more, Clump, I vow ta cover yer in wrangleroot leaves and feed yer to infinitesisnails, it will be a very slow death."

"I think he means it, Clump, best to ignore it, I suggest we all *get a grip…*" said Merlock, doing a poor job at masking his mirth.

"Oh, yer as well? Sometimes, Uncle, I wonder if yer do these things deliberately?"

"Look, Nephew, I did what I could, you knew the risks involved and accepted them. Besides, it's a fleeting thing so don't be such...a *baby*..."

Merlock could not contain himself any further, as he and Clump roared with laughter. Fingle slumped, surveying his new arm. Sure it worked fine and for the most part was all but identical to the previous one, but it terminated with a hideous hand, a hand that was no larger than that of a new-born. Even a child sized hand would have been a marked improvement, but this, what was he supposed to do with this?

"Uncle, seriously, I canna fight, I canna climb, cook, catch, or cling and will struggle riding anything bigger than stunted Dwarf, I am no better off." moaned Fingle, wriggling his stumpy fingers like hungry green grubs.

"Well, there *was* something in that spell about rejuvenation and youthfulness, I suspect I may have over emphasized the youthful part? What I do know, is that it will return to its full size, maybe in a week, maybe overnight? In the meantime, I'd wager it would be wonderful for picking pockets or even locks?" offered his uncle, trying to raise Fingle's descending mood.

"Or use it for sign language, for little Faeries?" added Clump helpfully.

"Hee hee, stop it, Clump, har har har, sorry, Fingle, I mean fingers, hee hee—"

"Fine, yer all have yer laugh now, but when it grows back, I'll use it ta rip off both yer arms and lash 'em ta yer backside, then throw yer both ta a pack of Centaurs in season!" spat Fingle before storming off.

"Were sorry, Nephew, honestly we are, aren't we, Clump? We promise to never again make slight of your weird baby hand."

As Fingle walked away, he raised a one fingered salute to his tormentors, but disastrously forgot he was using his new hand to do it. He could still hear their laughter from a considerable distance away.

*   *   *

Jarett looked up when he heard the clinking of chains. He had to shield his eyes from the light when the hatch was prised open. The Goblin officer had returned as he said he would, despite his pronunciation deficiency.

"Quith, come owth, I hath the horthes waithing."

He helped Jarett climb out of the stinking pit he had been left to rot in. His aching muscles had lost some strength and his buckling legs were cramping.

"Thank you, but we must leave immediately if I am to keep my end of the bargain."

Tongue lolling, the officer nodded leading the way. Jarett couldn't help noticing how the guard was escaping, he wasn't running exactly, more of a brisk walk, hunched, with his knees knocking together. Jarett had difficulty too, opting for a swaying motion, afraid his legs may seize up completely. Between the pair of them, it was a spectacularly lacklustre escape, as though they had just dismounted the horses they awkwardly approached, after riding bareback for six months without respite. Fortunately, they had the cover of darkness to hide them and the way out appeared clear. After a poignant mount, they rode away quickly and quietly, all things considered.

From a tower, Sly watched them both, *run, run, and keep on running little rabbits, until you can run no more, then I shall make your world a frothy crimson...*Sly enjoyed the chase, he savoured the foreboding he could fester in others, *go tell your perfect Queen, it matters not, let them worry, let them fear...*

Not long into their journey, Jarett heard company heading their way and beckoned Mumblecrust to seek cover. They managed to hide amongst dense scrub just before a regiment of Sly's guards thundered past. Despite the blurred imagery, Jarett made out a Goblin in the centre of the pack, not holding reigns and heavily bound in rope. It *had* to be the Human born. Jarett knew he alone could not help him, their best hope was in reaching Buttercup and fast.

Chapter 30

The Faerie Queen opted to travel over land with her entire Elven Army, instead of riding the skies on her Drakite. The bulk of her forces were on the ground and it was important the Queen was seen amongst her people as they marched towards battle. Her air armada filled the skies, ever watchful for trouble. Although her Drakite fleet had been reduced to two thirds its original size, it still posed a formidable threat to the enemy. Half of her ground forces rode upon armoured horses, taking the vanguard, while many scouts were sent on ahead in all directions, scouring the land for enemy forces or ambushes. The remaining Elves marched behind the cavalry. Trailing behind those, was an assortment of battering rams, an armoury and vast supplies to include food, water, and medical equipment, all of which were heavily protected by cavalry guards and a squadron of Drakite archers. Dern, Abranth, Archer, and the Orchi kept close quarter to Buttercup, as did Merlock, Clump, and Fingle. McGrath took his place at the vanguard, stirringly courageous and ever vigilant.

Thankful for the arrival of the morning sun, they had marched throughout the night, determined to make good time. The Faerie Queen's army—even on a forced march—was too slow to intercept Rob's captors, so she had dispatched an advance party of her fastest riders and Drakite scouts. Buttercup had not received any news all night, until now. The cavalry moved aside to allow two escorted riders through. The first rider held aloft a white cloth in surrender, he wore armour that bore the three peaks insignia; it was one of Sly Slaughter's guards. The second rider looked vaguely familiar. As he neared, Buttercup's eyes filled with tears. It was Jarett, only not how she remembered him. He was slumped over his reigns, hair matted, with dirt streaked down his gaunt cheeks. His body was all sinew and bone, instantly reminding the Queen of the prisoners' plight at the Tundra mines. Jarett had suffered deep lacerations and multiple burns, half of which were infected.

"Jarett!" she wailed, jumping from her horse, "Help him!" she ordered.

Jarett was carefully carried from his mount and placed onto a healing cart from the medical attachment. She summoned for Merlock to assist. The wizard managed to rouse him in such a way that pacified the rawness of his wounds, while a team of healers attended to his battered body, cleansing and applying ointments where needed. Jarett slowly opened his eyes, his cracked lips stretching to a painful smile.

"Here, take this." offered Buttercup softly, supporting his head while pouring a sweet amber liquid gently into his mouth.

After some coughing, he managed a reply, "My sweet, Buttercup, I hope you will forgive me…"

"There is nothing to forgive. I know why you did what you did, because you are brave and loyal and because you are *you*." then kissed him tenderly on his forehead.

"My Queen, there is something else."

"What is it? Tell me if you are able, Jarett."

"Sly, he has a second army, they will be waiting. They came up from the Howl and Hullaballoo Caves and Sly has the Human…" his words, strained and fitful.

Buttercup froze, an icy cloak of dread bound tight around her.

"Hush, you must rest now my brave, brave, Jarett. You are safe. We will make Sly pay for this, *I* will make him pay."

She stroked his head, waiting for the liquid to take effect. Once sleep had fallen upon him, she gave orders for Jarett to be taken post haste to the Abbey of Light, uncertain he would even survive the journey. Jarett had earned his rest a thousand fold. Buttercup shared her devastating news with McGrath and the other officers. They altered their plans accordingly, sending Drakite riders along the passage that divided Ambershea—home to the mysterious woodland Elves—and Doom Forest. If anything had left the Howl and Hullaballoo Caves, it would almost certainly pass through this region. It was pointless marching on Doom Forest in search of a second army, as Rob would be held at the Dark Fortress. Besides, there were hundreds, if not thousands of Fortress soldiers slashing blindly against each other, still under the reversed concealment spell. Presuming of course they had not already killed each other, or worse, wandered into much darker places—places that should *never* be wandered into within Doom Forest.

* * *

"Let me see him." spat Sly, as his guards unsaddled Rob, disturbing a murder of crows that flew in fractured angry circles around the Fortress towers as dusk crept in.

Rob raised his sagging head and looked up at the imposing stronghold, a disorienting inky nightmare, all points and angles set within the craggy confines of the Three Peaks that merged effortlessly with the onset of night.

Sly Slaughter strolled over. "Greetings, Rob, it's been quite a frolic hasn't it? And how crushingly disheartening it has all been for nought…but then, doesn't *everything* come to end? Have you any last words of Earthly wisdom to convey, that is before you help to destroy this ridiculous world."

"Yes, I do. Whoever invented horse riding, may their balls forever rest in peace."

"I see...and there was I thinking you had none, interesting...Guards, please show our guest to his new accommodation. I think he will find it, most fitting." Sly twirled around, skipping happily back inside the Fortress.

"Does he always dance like a little girl?" croaked Rob to a gloating guard.

"Only when he's 'appy, which means trouble for you."

The guards dragged Rob inside, hauling him across the stone floor to the centre of the Great Hall, which had been emptied save for a single seat. Rob was forcibly sat down and secured in place by thick leather straps with heavy buckles. Rob felt his hands and feet grow cold with the tightness of his bonds.

He looked up at his captors, "I suppose this is the part where you try to get me to talk. Well I can tell you, I know nothing more than what you already know I know, so it will be a complete waste of everybody's time."

Sly slunk from the shadows to stand behind him, "Goodness no, Rob, we are not Gnomes! Besides, I wouldn't be much of a host now would I? All I require from you is to...sit. I am sure even you can manage that."

"Why? Am I bait? Why not place me somewhere out of sight? I shall be easy to find and rescue, sitting out here in the open."

"I'm afraid it is too late for bait, dear Robin. I have no doubt your friends are coming to rescue you, but this has never been about you, it's always been about *where* you came from." replied Sly, relishing his moment.

"Well, I suppose I am really from, here...?" as he spoke, the words rang in his mind. He had not yet fully processed this; he was born *here*, in the land of Fae!

"Yeeees, that's right, Rob, but can you guess what makes you so succulently special, so delectably different?"

"My father, my father is Human and my mother is Goblin?" he stammered.

Rob searched inside himself, why was this so important? How could this affect things? Who was he exactly?

"Correct. Now suppose I tell you that *our* world is governed by magick, it's what keeps the balance between good and evil, blah blah blah. Your Human world however, remains in a constant state of struggle, as the forces of light and darkness are never in equal measure. Instead of magick, Earth is governed by the freewill actions of all who live there. This governance thing has caused me a big boring problem, it inhibits the passage between here and there. As you have already discovered, we *can* portal between our worlds, but sadly, only a few at most before the portal closes."

Sly feigned sadness then walked over to Rob, waiting until he had caught up. Rob's eyes widened, "*I'm* the bridge aren't I?"

"Bravo, Rob. Go to the top of the class. Without *you* a portal cannot be sustained, they only remain accessible for a teensy moment and then 'poof', it collapses in on itself. Can you now see how important you are, Rob? Because you are half Human, half Goblin, you can sustain a portal between both our worlds...Together, you and I shall make history."

Rob felt sick, maybe if he had known this earlier he could have stopped this from happening? Why didn't anyone warn him? "Wait, I may be able to sustain a portal, but you need a portal in the first place and a portal large enough for a full scale invasion."

"Aaaaah, now that's the meat and marrow isn't it? This is the beautiful part, Rob, so pay close attention. Did you know that Human souls originally came from the Faerie Kingdom? Our creator, in all its divine wisdom decided to create a sister world, a world where freewill existed for incarnated souls to have a different experience, how fascinating, how boring! Source wished to see how light and dark would self-organise, I suppose a bit like letting the whelps go off and play unsupervised and what a grand experiment that was...Tell me, Rob, when you dream, do you dream of Unicorns, and of monsters and Faeries?"

"Sometimes, I suppose, but thankfully nothing as foul as you."

Slaughter ignored his comment—for now. "Of course you do, for when you sleep, your soul often returns back to the place it was originally forged, it simply can't help itself, silly really. Now we, both you and I, have the power of creation within us, literally at our fingertips. The difference is, *we* call it magick and as I have previously mentioned, *ad nauseam*, our use of it here is regrettably governed. But, and this is *key,* Rob, it is *not* governed in the world of Humans."

"Rubbish. If that were true we would all be using magick."

"Yes, you would think so wouldn't you? But in order for your freewill experiment to work, you must all pass through the proverbial river Lethe and forget who and what you really are. You have all simply forgotten just how powerful you are, how hilariously cruel." Sly laughed aloud banging his fist into his palm, his guards shifted nervously.

"Now back to the portal, Rob. Unbeknown to the ever optimistic Faerie Queen, her dream control had been...tampered with, never enough to raise any concerns you understand, but just enough for our needs. Every night for the past twenty of your Earth years, a random selection of Human souls have been, 'encouraged' to work for us. Such a pliable and co-operative resource Humans are when in their dream state, bless them. By harnessing their creative abilities we managed to construct a duplicate energetic substructure of our Dark Fortress to manifest on Earth. It has however only existed in the fourth density dimension, which is why it has remained invisible to the Humans, that is until now. We knew celestially on a specific future date and time, the veil betwixt our worlds would be sufficiently attenuated to allow for a large enough bridge to exist. Well, masks off to all those unsuspecting Human souls working so diligently during their sweet slumber, we now have such a bridge. The stars are finally in alignment for the portal to appear and you, dearest Rob, sweet Rob, *you* are the final piece we have been waiting for, the real star of the show."

"You will never win, Sly. You *may* have magick, but we have technology and numbers and organisation. If you *ever* tried to invade Earth you would be blown to Faerie Kingdom come, quicker than being outfoxed by Fingle Froglick. Our powerful armies are immeasurably more equipped and outnumber you vastly. If you honestly believe you will succeed, you are away with the fairies!"

Slaughter looked genuinely surprised, then after a brief pause he clapped his hands, "Oh…oh, Rob, this is priceless, you really don't know do you?" Sly leapt over to crouch in front of him, clasping his gloved hands upon Rob's knees. "It was no accident a portal opened in your room so you were brought here instead of your father, my Guild made certain of that. And you haven't been brought here to help invade Earth, AMOK always believed this was so, but I had other plans for you. I struck a bargain with your militscary powers; they are to invade *here*, the world of Fae…"

Looking through the slits in Sly's mask, Rob could see a terrifying mixture of simmering spite, fanaticism and maniacal glee churn in his wild eyes.

"You would betray your own kind?"

"Of course, silly, but the Humans in their greed have forgotten one crucial minutiae; they are conducting business with a Goblin. Sometimes you have to lose in order to win, Rob. The Humans intend to plunder our Divmatronium as a source of virtually limitless energy and in return they are offering me a prominent position within their own ranks. The changeform spell as you know works both ways. But answer me this, what if magick could not only change your form to resemble another race, but also another's face…?"

Sly paced around Rob's chair, bristling with anticipation.

Rob gasped aloud, "You *are* invading Earth, but over a longer period and in a covert way. You get your feet under the table and then gradually bring in more and more of your own kind to replace our kind. By selling out to your own race, you appear as if your allegiance is to the Humans."

"Naturally, but let's not forget, Rob, without the governance of magick on Earth, we shall be invincible. I have waited twenty long cycles for my opportunity, so what's a short while longer in the grand scheme eh? And as for allegiance, I'm afraid you are mistaken, the only allegiance I hold is to myself, obviously." Sly chuckled.

"That's sick! Without the restraint of your magick, the whole of Earth would fall into total darkness, which *you* caused."

"I know, isn't it breath-taking? At this juncture, I really don't know what else to add. Look, I appreciate this does not absolve me in any way, but come on, Rob, I was born evil and I happen to be going through a very difficult period right now, I am simply trying to do the best I can."

Rob was consumed with anger, displaying open contempt for his captor sneering above him. "You have underestimated Humans, Sly and greed is sadly what nourishes many of our societies. It has been become a sickness of our people, a pandemic that has distorted the truth of who we really are. Our lives have become so preoccupied with material gain, we have lost sight of where real importance resides. We wage continual wars in the name of greed. We work ourselves into spiralling debt and crippling depression in the name of greed. We gossip and slander against our own kind because we covet which they have and we do not. You think because you are a Goblin you are any different?"

"Well, if your world is so similar, Rob, it will be all the easier for me to *tweak* it to my particular tastes. A world consisting of ready-made slaves, hmmmm, I like the sound of it already. Anyhoo, as much as I have enjoyed our enchanting discussion, I'm sure you will appreciate I have much to do and so regrettably I must take my leave. But please, do stay and enjoy the show, it promises to be most memorable…"

As Sly skipped away, Rob continued, "When I first arrived here I was terrified I would not be accepted. I was wrong, very wrong. Goblins for the most part a despicable, violent bunch of thieving back stabbers you wouldn't trust to wash your socks, or their own socks for that matter. But I have also witnessed as much Humanity, compassion and kindness here, as I have anywhere else on Earth. There will always be *types* like you in any world, clawing their way to the top whatever the cost is to others. But in the end, the greatest cost is to yourself, because once you have achieved everything you think is important, you are still left with a gaping hole of nothingness gnawing away inside of you. Until of course, the next fool comes along and takes it all from you anyway, that is, all except your infinite dissatisfaction that continues to consume you until you become nothingness as well."

After a long difficult pause, Rob heard leather gloves scrunch tightly behind him, then feet running up steps,

"Watch him closely!" barked Sly from a balcony at the far end of the Great Hall before disappearing through a door.

Chapter 31

The long march so far had proved uneventful. A slow, deliberate undertaking, taking its toll on mind and body. A teetering balance between the laborious advance, forging ahead in full battle dress and weaponry, yet still maintaining a high level of alertness, ready to attack or be attacked. Despite the fatigue, the tension was tangible. Although the Elven warriors marched in silence, the long snaking advance—with its rhythmic thump—could be heard and felt from great distances. The time for subterfuge long passed, replaced by decisive action and military might.

An erend-rake, flanked by two riders, urged his mount through the ranks. "My Queen, it is as Jarett had claimed, there *is* a second army. It has assembled along the banks of the river Gurgles and defends the approach to the Dark Fortress!"

"Thank you, Rider, please tell me your name?"

"I am Allanon, my Queen"

"Tell me, Allanon, what number do they count?"

"I estimate seven thousand strong, a third are on horseback."

"Thank you, Allanon, for your bravery and service." she said, smiling.

Allanon bowed then rode away. The Queen signalled for her commanding officers to rally around her. When they had done so, she gave them the grave news.

Dern was the first to react, "Crom, that amounts to double our own forces. How in Oberon's name did the S.G.G. manage to hide this from us?"

McGrath reined in his horse and spoke next, "My Queen, this is most unexpected and highly disturbing. As Dern stated, how we have not known of this before astounds me. But let us consider, we also have the clan Goblins rescued at the Tundra. As we ride upon the Three Peaks so do they and they number almost three thousand strong. They may be undernourished and undisciplined, but they carry a terrible retribution in their hearts."

"I know, thank you, McGrath, but we still fall short. And what if the Humans do manage to cross over, what then?"

"Then we shall boot the trundle-tails right back! I have *never* held anything against them, but if anything comes here uninvited with ill intentions, then they will taste Elven steel." said McGrath, spitting at the dirt.

As the day pressed on, Buttercup received further reports, none of them good. Rob had been seen by a scout inside the Fortress' Great Hall, tied to a chair. The Fortress itself, although surrounded by a large moat, had a huge steel drawbridge which had been lowered. The scouts also reported that a substantial part of the keep's entrance, leading directly into the hall had been removed, presumably allowing for great numbers of bodies to enter *or* exit. The strategy however, had largely unchanged. Rob had always been their main focus, if you removed Rob, the portal would fail, it was the only decisive way to stop an invasion, or at worst stem an ongoing assault.

The natural lay of the land lent to a gradual decline from the Murksun Marshes, onwards towards the Three Peaks. The peaks could be seen in the far distance as black claws thrust upwards, threatening to tear asunder the black clouds permanently looming above it. The Dark Fortress itself was hewn in part from the three black mountains surrounding it, but to the encroaching Elven army, it was not yet fully visible—their current altitude obscuring the lower region of the infernal stygian spikes.

As the hours passed, the sense of foreboding grew and in sympathetic response, the sky began to churn upon itself. A distant rumble overhead heralded broiling cloud formations, twisting and rolling as if in agonising torment. The sudden change in weather was alarming, the entire skyscape fast becoming a vortex of malice, heavily oppressed by colossal thunderclouds, pregnant with rage. The first swollen drops of rain fell, tiny platinum explosions littering the vast dusty terrain. As the Elves continued to march with grim determination, a quickening of the blood suddenly spread throughout the ranks, as the ground had now dropped sufficiently to allow the Dark Fortress to come into full view.

"Halt!" cried McGrath from the front, the command continuing down the line by officers from their respective troops. The Queen and commanding officers conferred, surveying the parched grasslands. Although the lumbering, wrathful storm had stolen much of the light, enough remained to observe the monstrous army of the Shadow Goblin Government that amassed around the shadowy keep, stretched along the banks of the river Gurgles. The army was much larger than expected and would take a considerable effort to breach, if at all possible.

"My Queen, the clan Goblins are almost in place." said Dern, pointing towards the far side of Shadow Haven woods.

"Very well. We shall rest here and prepare for the final descent. Merlock is in agreement with our celestial professors, that soon the heavenly bodies, as predicted, will be in complete alignment. We have ran out of time, we must take the fight to them in an effort to stop this madness."

All heads were in agreement; there was no other option than to take the keep by force, whatever the cost. Buttercup cursed she had let things escalate for so long, shut away within her ivory and marble tower. Her compassion and forgiveness had allowed for complacency to exist, then finally deception to slither its way in. She still held enormous faith and love for all of the races, but never again would she be so easily fooled. The Elves took advantage of the brief respite to replenish their energy and spirit through simple food, ale, and prayer. A final check on armour and weapons, and a sharing of goodwill was passed around regardless of rank.

The Elven army re-organised itself as the commanding officers rode back to the front line. The Queen, McGrath, Dernand Orchi were all at point, preparing to march towards their destinies and ultimately the fate of their world. Clump was on the largest chariot they could find, being pulled by three Shireflame horses. Beside him, his best friend Fingle and the wizard Merlock sat astride their impatient mounts. In front, were the Archer and Abranth.

The last Goblin leader of the free clans turned to face Robert. He caught her wintry eyes flash with vengeance, "Archer, let's go get our son."

Robert nodded and gently kissed her scarred hand; grim set, he turned to face the Dark Fortress, narrowing his eyes. The drizzle had now become a deluge. The ground was a bubbling soup, driving upwards a writhing blanket of cold mist, in which seething mercurial splinters from the punishing rain would shred apart in humourless irony. Sodden banners of the Royal Elven House were held high. Once resplendent, now reduced to silhouettes that whipped and wrapped themselves around their stout poles in angry strangleholds. The Elven Army lurched back into life as a formidable serpentine contortion, an unyielding inevitability of horrors it would be forced to unleash.

* * *

A soaked guard sploshed his way over to Sly Slaughter. Wiping his eyes, he sprayed his urgent message, "My Ambassador of atrocities, the Elven army approaches from This Way on high and the clan Goblins have assembled along the upper banks of the Gurgles behind Shadow Haven!"

"Yes, yes, thank you, Lickspigot, I had already seen them myself from the tower. It's a good job we don't have you to rely on for anything *important*!" screamed Sly, sending the guard face first into the squishy mire.

"Now go and fetch me the Guild like a bad little Goblin, or what's left of them. I need to know precisely when this egesta of a portal will open."

Rob continued to work away at his bonds despite the bleeding sores now developing around his aching wrists. He knew his friends were close; the atmosphere was palpable, bristling with the despairing anticipation of impending battle. The raging storm created dramatic, panoramic bursts of white electricity, flashing across the rain swept land between the two armies. The only sounds heard above the torrential rains were the fractured roars of thunder that shook the ground, as if to appeal for reason and resolve. Rob stopped wriggling and his blood turned cold. Above the rebuking tempest, he could hear the unmistakable horns of Corona. He had first heard them beyond the Tin Fence when the Elven war party had been surrounded by Red-caps, only this time there were considerably more sounding off. In retaliation, deafening war drums were beating out their defiance from the Fortress, as the rogue army jeered, screaming their warped battle cries, cries birthed from a twisted marriage of dark bloodlust and berserk barbarity, gasping for its life and demanding nothing less than death. It was a terrifying audible prelude to the bodies that would be smashed and butchered once the armies engaged.

Rob was afraid and sickened by the guilt that he alone had made it possible for the land of Fae to be invaded and destroyed. He knew it was not directly his fault, not by any decision he had ever made, right or wrong, nonetheless he suffered its crushing responsibility and cursed the day he'd been born. And what of the personal loss he now faced? The loss of his new friends, of his father and the love of a mother he never knew? What of his life with Dippy, a life he yearned for, that would now be stolen from them? Where had she gone when he needed her the most? Rob prayed that wherever she was she was safe and vowed if he ever managed to escape, he would find her, or die trying.

Chapter 32

Raising his deep voice above the blustering elements, McGrath rallied the troops on his armoured steed, galloping along the immense, intimidating line of Elven cavalry. He did not need to rouse them, they were highly disciplined, courageous and loyal to a fault. He held great pride in knowing that whatever the outcome, his warriors would fight with fury and valour until their dying breaths. Eventually, McGrath returned, taking his rightful place next to his Queen. Buttercup sat atop a magnificent white mare, its nostrils snorting visibly through the cold downpour and frothing mouth chomping at the bit. Buttercup had exchanged her riding armour for full parade armour. It was of a lighter weight and polished to a mirrored sheen. The plate edging was embellished with gold trim and her gleaming chest plate boasted a large engraving of the house of Corona. Against all advice, Buttercup had refused to wear a helmet; she had argued the importance of remaining visible for her allies to find strength and for her enemies to cower from. Upon her cropped raven black hair, she wore a simple gold coronet, designed to resemble a chain of spring flowers—a symbolic tribute of her affection for and connection to the land.

"I know yer a grown Goblin, Uncle, but if yer don't get in Clump's trundling death chair I'll be too worried about yer and no doubt receive a belly full of steel quicker than sidestepping Maw Wallop's slop buckets. Besides, I want me baby hand ta get back ta full fat and without yer it may never happen."

Merlock peered over the front of the chariot, his sodden snowy hair clinging to his head.

"I do not intend to go anywhere, Nephew, *someone* has to keep a close eye on Clump, he's never been in a fight before…"

They all laughed, although Clump's was laced with hysteria and continued for much longer than was comfortable. The giant was transfixed upon the potential carnage calling out to him. It was no secret Clump was different from other Goblins, but no one talked about it, Clump was just Clump. Merlock looked at them fondly, then abruptly looked away, swallowing hard and gripping hold of the chariot for support.

"Uncle? What is it? Look, no one would think bad of yer if you backed out, yer too old for fadoodling." said Fingle, deeply concerned for the grief stricken wizard.

"No, no, it's quite alright, my boy, I was bashing bonces before you were…born…It's something else. It's about Clump…"

Fingle's face dropped, he sensed where it was leading, he always knew something about Clump was amiss, something not quite right. "Uncle, what is it? Yer must tell me and be snip-snap about it." insisted Fingle shakily, wiping the rain from his face.

"Yeah, what is it, Merlock? Is it about the Boggles, cos I didn't mean to—"

"No, Clump, it's something I should have told you both a long time ago. Fingle, your mother thought it best that certain things were kept from you, truths that could jeopardise your relationship with her and with Clump."

Fingle jumped from off his horse and walked over to the chariot, "Go on." he said, eyes wide despite the downpour.

The small wizard appeared vulnerable, he paused, then looked into their eyes, "Fingle, your Father was a scoundrel, a repulsive Goblin with a big reputation for being as such."

"I already know this, Uncle, but thank yer for yer kind words." replied Fingle sincerely.

"But you, Clump, your Father, he was an Orc, *not* a Goblin…"

Fingle and Clump stared together in shock.

"Of course! That makes perfect sense doesn't it, Clump? I mean, yer have the size, strength and battle skills of an Orc, only much bigger and stronger. But that doesn't account ta why yer looks like a Goblin. Why is that, Uncle?"

Merlock reached out to clasp their hands. Clump's hand engulfed the wizards. Fingle reached out too, Merlock slapped it away, "The other hand, Nephew, the baby one makes me a little queasy, sorry."

"Listen to me, boys, Clump is the way he is…because his mother is a Goblin. And her name was *Tipsycake Froglick…*"

"Hey, that's the same name as *my* moth…" Fingle's words fell short, replaced by a timely rumble of thunder.

Merlock squeezed their hands tightly, "That's right my wonderful, Nephews, you are brothers." said Merlock, clasping their trembling hands and crying unashamedly.

The two best friends turned to face each other. Fingle's jaw slackened, as he mechanically mouthed *brothers*. Clump hugged him tightly.

"Fingle, we are brothers!"

Fingle's desire to continue breathing brought him back to his senses, "Put me down yer witless blimp."

Clump dropped him immediately, his beaming grin withering to an uncertain smile. Fingle slowly got up from the sticky mud and splurged back to his mount, never once looking up.

"Well? Say something, Fingle. Say *anything* for crom's sake." shouted Merlock, consumed with guilt and shaking from the disclosure of what he had locked away for an eternity.

After an excruciating delay, he finally turned to face them as the haunting horns of Corona echoed far across the land, signalling the Elven army to charge upon the Dark Fortress. Fingle's face was dark and sleek, his mouth pinched, and his eyes aflame with wickedness and cunning. As he spoke, his penetrating features were framed by blinding flashes of apocalyptic lightening, "Well, what are we waiting for, *Brother*, we have a war ta win!"

Overcome with relief, Clump grinned deliciously and cracked his whip, roaring at the enemy as his chariot leapt forwards. For a brief moment, Fingle's horse reared in response, his striking silhouette captured against the raging sky—a terrifying harbinger of death and destruction—until his baby hand lost grip of the slippery reins and promptly fell into the brown gloop his horse had churned up.

He sat in the mud, forlorn and feeling foolish while Clump and Merlock disappeared into the teeming obscurity along with the entire Elven army, including his own horse.

"Hogsplops. What's a Goblin ta do ta have a decent bloodied brangle around here?" he muttered to himself.

He clenched and unclenched his tiny fist, wondering how in Faerie Kingdom he was ever going to fare in hand to hand combat. Standing up, he closed his eyes and faced the wrathful firmament, allowing the rain to fall into his open mouth, *brothers...brothers...* His eyes blinked open, *Crom!* Fingle launched into a hard run, he knew he was at a disadvantage, but still, he had his wits, he also knew as sure as Shuffle's shifted slabs, that he outfoxed everyone. He would swap his blade for brains, his grasp upon strategy was significantly more reliable than his grasp on a knife, reigns, or anything other than a pacifier right now. Being the last to enter battle had its obvious benefits, his chances of survival had increased, but he could also see how events panned out. He was confident uncle and Clump would be significantly better than fine, undoubtedly scaring the rabbit raisins out of anyone foolish enough to get in their way.

Fingle slowed, studying a huge surge of Sly's soldiers amassing around the Dark Fortress entrance where the Elven army spearheaded its attack. Fingle winced as the Elven cavalry thundered towards its mark, waiting for the inevitable crunch...it did not come. Instead, a huge expanse gave way as nearly two hundred horses disappeared! A loud cheer came from the Fortress. The S.G.G. had dugout deep pits and concealed them all along the river bank leading up to the keep's entrance. Fingle watched in horror as the sky above the pits grew even darker, as an enormous blanket of arrows were let loose from the battlements. He had to look away, unable to witness the carnage, but instead of screams a second cheer arose. Fingle turned to see the arrows burn to ash, as they collided with an arched, glowing shield, manifested by the Elves, but only long enough to protect them. The effort would claim its price, but better to survive depleted than die.

Return volleys by the Elven archers—sat upon Drakites, circling above the keep—allowed enough time for the majority of fallen Elves to clamber back out of the trenches and continue their attack, although with a reduced number of horses. The remaining cavalry were forced to navigate the length of the trenches until they could re-join the main thrust once more. Fingle marvelled at the ingenuity of the S.G.G., the pits had served a sneaky secondary purpose, they forced a bottle neck to form and in this way the defenders could stave off a direct attack much more effectively.

The clan Goblins now joined the affray, but disastrously the bottle neck had only served to slow things up further. As they poured down from the upper left side of Shadow Haven woods, they could only enter into a long queue that had formed. This proved devastating, they were now all stationary targets, only able to view the main battle from over the heads of hundreds of frustrated Elves.

McGrath forced his way through to the Queen, "We *must* regroup. If we remain like this the enemy will pick us apart as they wish and the Drakite archers cannot keep the Fortress archers on the defensive indefinitely."

"We cannot turn back now, McGrath, every moment we waste is another moment the portal strengthens, we must push on. As for the Fortress archers, leave them to me, I have a plan..."

Stern faced, McGrath nodded, he knew she was right, "I will inspect the Gurgles banks farther down and see if we can cross. The river's current is slower there and shallower too. We may be able to attack at the rear of the fortress. Or at least divert some of the archers away. I will need five hundred riders to make it count, my Queen."

"Very well, I hold my faith in you, McGrath, but *please* be careful, I don't trust these devils."

McGrath bowed, pulling his charger around heavily, shouting his way back through the melee.

Clump's chariot thundered up and down the muddy river banks, inadequately steered by Merlock, who could barely see above the carriage's front-guard. Their bones rattled from the jolting wheels as they thudded over small rocks, weapons and fresh corpses. It was all the brave wizard could do to maintain a straight line at high speed during the storm, while his eyes were being shaken like dice in a tablinghouse.

Clump however, was in high spirits. He sang aloud as he leaned out as far as he could, brandishing his hefty battle axe, "Fingle is my brother and Merlock is our uncle, my mother's Fingle's mother and our fathers did a runner!"

Merlock's concentration faltered frequently as he tried in earnest to avoid decapitated heads, limbs, or torsos tumbling into the air, while Clump continued to scythe a wide bloodied path through the terrified rogue army.

"Sir, look! That crazy giant Goblin has cleared the way." alerted an excited platoon leader to McGrath, pointing towards the hurtling chariot weaving haphazardly through the screaming hordes.

Even McGrath's blood turned cold. Clump never seemed to tire, if anything, he was hastening into an unstable frenzy as the death toll increased exponentially. Many of the S.G.G. warriors and guards wisely decided to leave the river banks to join the main effort, swiftly making their way to the relative safety of the raging Fortress battle. Clump and Merlock had now secured a great length along the river's banks, conveniently allowing the Elves to attempt a crossing.

"Follow me!" ordered McGrath, heading for a shallower region.

The Commander knew if they were to stand any chance of stopping the Human invasion, then this had to be it. Having successfully crossed over, they *may* be able to breach the rear of the keep, or at least cause a significant diversion, providing the Drakites kept the Fortress archers pinned down long enough. Hundreds of Elves dismounted and led their nervous mounts into the dark swirling waters. The river was shoulder-deep and icy cold—coursing down from the snowy Tundra. McGrath stopped, upon hearing a scream in front of him. He signalled the other riders to stop too while he shielded his eyes against the stinging rain.

A second scream and this time McGrath had seen an Elf disappear beneath the water, then his horse followed.

"Quickly, get back, get out of the water!" yelled McGrath, but the treacherous currents made their movements painfully slow.

Several more screams were heard and McGrath could now see what new enemy they faced. A terrifying twisted shape, as dark as night leapt up effortlessly from beneath the water's surface and plunged its huge talons into the side of a horse, bringing it down with disturbing ease. As the horse thrashed around, struggling to breathe, the shadowy creature kept it submerged, then cocked its head towards McGrath. Using a single hand to drown the floundering horse. The living nightmare slicked back its long ebony hair, revealing a pallid sickly sneer and cruel mocking eyes which cast a repelling luminosity about them.

McGrath recognised it in an instant, "Kelpies, retreat, retreat!"

Some of the Elves that had ventured too far out had little choice but to fight, but the Kelpies would avoid their weapons with lightning speed, then vanish beneath the water, only to reappear from behind and drag the riders under, never to be seen again. The Elves—although formidable warriors—were no match against these aberrations of nature and were at a distinct disadvantage in the turbulent inky water, water that would sweep the sturdiest of feet aside in a single misjudgement. The fortunate majority regained temporary sanctuary on the banks once again. McGrath looked out into the broiling darkness, cursing the Godless creatures. A sudden lightning strike illuminated the river; scores of wrathful Kelpies were lying in wait, bent, cruel and hungry for more victims. The Commander looked towards the keep, it was heavily protected by an enormous, seething mass of guards and could clearly see they were outnumbered and strategically at a significant disadvantage. A blood curdling battle cry emerged from behind them. McGrath swung around his steed and his heart sank. Infantry, at least a thousand strong had broken free from the cover of Doom Forest. It was the remainder of the first S.G.G. army, the same army they'd hoped were still rendered ineffective under a concealment spell that had backfired. Whether the Guild had managed to lift the spell, or whether it some kind of ruse was unimportant right now.

"What do we do now, Sir? If we head towards the keep along the river bank, we will be caught between the front and rear, fighting in both directions. If we charge the first army down, we may manage to disperse and weaken their advance, but we do not know how many more may lay in wait within Doom Forest and we will be further away from the main effort. We certainly can't cross the river, or jump the trenches."

McGrath struggled to make a decision, the Elven officer had made salient points but offered no practical solution to their dire predicament.

"We stay here. We help the Queen by keeping those motherless devils at bay. Quick, I want battle formations at the ready."

The Elven cavalry positioned themselves ten ranks deep, with the Gurgles on their right and the trenches to their left. The first army were closing in fast, running savagely towards the Elves.

"Steady yourselves, for Queen and Kingdom!" inspired McGrath.

"Sir, only a smaller group heads our way. A greater number is breaking off to run around the other side of the pits."

The Platoon leader was right. Again they had been out-manoeuvred. They would be forced to stay put, as the might of the S.G.G. first army circumnavigated them, to attack the Queen from the rear, while the deep pits kept

McGrath and his cavalry confined along the river banks. It was a guileful strategy he had to concede; clearly they had all underestimated Sly to their detriment and ultimately their doom.

"My Queen, behind us!" warned Archer. Buttercup followed his gaze and saw the reformed first army heading their way.

"How is this possible?" said Abranth.

"I don't know, I *thought* they were all bewitched. Unless we move now we shall be hacked to pieces. My Queen, what orders do you give? My Queen…?"

Buttercup's world ground to a muted halt. Everything became distant, even the heavy rains had numbed to nothingness. Listlessly, she sought out McGrath; and could see he too was trapped, fighting fiercely both front and rear.

How has this happened, so quickly, so easily…?

In their reckless haste they had allowed it to unfold, but time was a luxury denied to them. If the Human invaders arrived they would be completely overrun, it was a simple game of numbers. They were fighting for their lives on all borders, praying the main spearhead could somehow breach the Fortress and rescue Rob and prevent the cursed portal from ever opening. Buttercup knew the gateway was dangerously close to full materialisation, as a mysterious purple light was now pulsing from inside the keep. The Queen instructed Dern to assemble half of her remaining army to face the new threat from the rear and Abranth asked the same from her clans. Buttercup watched her Elves and the stout-hearted Orchi battle furiously towards the fortress and offered a silent prayer.

Fingle was the first to notice, as he approached the Queen's personal guard after witnessing their disastrous change of fate. He became aware of a deep rumbling he initially thought was the just the storm, but it did not yield, if anything it was increasing. The ground around them began to tremble, as though a monstrous, underground beast clawed its way up to the surface. Fingle looked over his shoulder, towards the dead ground he had just ran down and needed to blink several times. Against the sooty skyline, a lighter impression gave way, a vast, bobbing, grey shadow grew in size, as did the rumbling beneath his feet. Fingle slowed to a walk, squinting through the murkiness, his heart racing with the dread of an advancing peril threatening to engulf everything in its path. Uncertain whether his trembling body was of his own volition, or from the shaking ground, a tiny speck of hope rattled its way out. Straining his eyes further he caught his breath, could it possibly be…?

Chapter 33

"Trolls! They're...every...where...hundreds of 'em!" screamed a hyperventilating Goblin guard, running in the opposite direction to the stampeding horde.

Fingle jumped up and down—albeit at a safe enough distance—while the towering mountain Trolls galumphed past, breathing heavily, looking outrageously antagonised and brandishing absurdly oversized cudgels.

"Crom, I never thought they would come…" muttered the Archer.

"My Queen, look to the hills. Let it be known, upon this day, the Trolls of Thunderbone Ridge fight alongside Goblins and Elves!" exclaimed Robert, feeling the flame of hope blaze anew.

"And Orcs!" yelled Nororcious.

Robert laughed, "Yes and Orcs too, and I doubt we will never hear the last of it."

Buttercup felt a measure of relief tainted with unsettled sadness, as she watched the first army being indiscriminately pulverised to a fleshy pulp by the barbarous mountain Trolls.

Meanwhile, Clump's chariot had long been ditched after losing its wheels. Merlock, having lost all sense of propriety, was concentrating on maintaining a magickal shield while being flung around wildly, tucked under Clump's left arm. Elated, the giant continued swinging his wide curvature of death almost casually, trying to ignore his growing irritation at the dwindling numbers advancing towards him. Suddenly something caught his eye, causing him to look across the trenches and towards the hills. It was then he saw the most magnificent, most alluring vision of beauty he had ever beheld. Clump ogled as Pumice swung her bulky cudgel with consummate ease, a dreamlike specimen of battleship-grey perfection. He was awestruck in the way she moved. Although cumbersome to the ignorant, to him she was lithe and ethereal in delivering her mortal blows. A momentary shaft of sunlight breached the storm's defences and favoured her celestial image, emblazing itself upon Clump's soul. Illuminating her craggy features, the golden rays captured a straggly knot of flaxen hair mid fling, freeing her vehement stare to transfix upon her next victim. Clump envisaged a majestic eagle swooping down upon fleeing vermin, but with talons replaced by elephantine feet.

Pumice was born to the tribe of stone Trolls and was the Tatterdemalion's tribal leader's niece. She was a simple thing, unfettered by fashion—or any clothing for that matter—thoroughly disinterested in social affairs with all its trappings, opting to grunt in two ways and not the cultural norm of three. The only thing she had ever displayed any enthusiasm for, was in collecting stones and making bad things bleed. That was, until her derelict eyes slid over Clump, who was looking directly at her, drooling heavily and carrying a small Goblin wriggling angrily beneath his arm.

Pumice became aware of a pain developing around her changeless mouth. Her waters broke by way of a large gobbet of saliva hanging from her bristly chin, while her face contracted during the birth throes of her first ever smile. It swept across a leathery landscape like an inverted rainbow arching across an ashen sky. Never before had Pumice experienced such a wondrous string of emotions, shuddering excitement, anxiety, warmth, and giddiness.

The giant Goblin warrior had awakened something primordial, as the aroused Troll's heart began to pound desperately fast at almost four and a half beats per minute.

"Hur hur." she laughed aloud—in her own exquisite way—and began bounding towards her green demigod of unrestrained virility.

She felt a lightness, a delightful fluttering inside her loping form causing her to catch her foul breath. She ran to him, relishing his image standing atop a pile of contorted bodies littered all around, like fragile petals of a fragrant flower, open and revealing its innermost prize.

"Clump, Clump, can you hear me? Please release me now, that's an order from your uncle!"

Clump placed Merlock down without ever shifting his gaze from the heavenly and agreeably buxom she-Troll pounding towards him. He savoured every contracting muscle, every flexing tendon, mesmerised by her flapping teats—all six of them—her ample toenails, graceful, yet wild in the way they left deeply splayed imprints in the mud *and* his heart. Clump marvelled in the way the storm winds whistled between her blocky, uneven teeth, inspiring her voluptuous jowls to fully inflate, like a descending parachute of forbidden love hurtling towards him at a perilous momentum.

Merlock swiftly leapt aside as the two collided and embraced. Their entwined muscles and flabby bits rippling in waves of impact energy, serving to heighten their wanton passion.

"Clump, I am delighted you have finally found your life mate and equally disturbed I have to say, however, we *are* in the midst of a battle for the survival of all races."

Clump eventually managed to prise away from Pumice, albeit begrudgingly.

"I love you, can we kiss again after we chop up the naughty ones?"

288

Pumice didn't fully understand Clump, but shoved him behind her as a large clot of rogue soldiers edged over, hoping to take advantage of the bizarre infatuation. Hoisting her eight foot long cudgel high above her, she launched into them, felling half in a single sweep. As Pumice stamped out the life of the last chancer, Clump shed a sincere tear of authentic love for her and her slaying prowess.

"Commander, have you seen them?" yelled an Elven rider to McGrath.

"How could I not and just in the nick of time I would say! Who'd have thought the Trolls would have ever left their mountains?" said McGrath as the Elves cheered them on.

"No! Not the Trolls, look to the river."

McGrath reined his restless horse around to face the Gurgles. Something was happening in the water, something big. He nudged through the cavalry, getting as close to the river as he dared. Searching through the rain, he saw the river's dark surface boiling and spitting like a cauldron's brew. He thought at first it was localised to a single area, but as he surveyed the rivers length he could see the water churning all along, with violent bursts of white spume splashing everywhere. Screaming was now heard coming from the river as the Trolls' killing spree had distanced further away from them, forcing the remaining rogue guards to flee for their lives, back towards Doom Forest.

Are the Kelpies under attack? wondered McGrath, in hopeful anticipation.

Their cries were unnerving, a blood curdling screech that filled all those in earshot with dread and loathing. Their unyielding wails sapped all the strength from McGrath, he was uncertain how much longer he could endure. He watched his troops and the enemy fall to the ground, contorted in pain. Only the Trolls seemed immune, which suited them fine, as their victims were now easier to catch and mulch. McGrath managed to focus his blurred vision upon the turbulent waters despite the overwhelming agony. Just because the Kelpies were under attack, it didn't necessarily mean it was fortuitous, they had to be prepared to move quickly if a greater threat revealed itself. The ear-stabbing screams reached a discordant crescendo, a prolonged high pitched siren forcing the horses to thrash around wildly, dismounting their riders to the sludgy ground as they clutched their smarting skulls.

Then, without warning it stopped.

Dozens of enraged Kelpies made swift their escape towards the sanctity of the Dark Fortress moats. The Elven cavalry—over four hundred of them—were left stunned and deeply apprehensive. They continued to study the black waters for any indication of what had happened and then the surface began to stir once more.

"Brace yourselves, make ready!" ordered McGrath, his sword drawn high.

What appeared to be a head emerged from the water, followed by another, then another, until the river banks were teeming with muscular creatures. For the most part they resembled Elves, but broader and larger.

"Commander, why do they not leave the water?" questioned a Calvary officer.

Grinning, McGrath had already sheathed his sword away, "Because they choose not to, see behind them, they are not legs that splash."

McGrath climbed down from his horse and walked over.

One of them spoke first, "We hope we are not too late. We thought you might need a little assistance. I am Aquadya, leader of my people. We seldom reach this far inland, preferring the space and quietude of the Big Wet."

"We welcome you gladly, Mere-folk. I confess, I have seen your kind just twice during my life and only from afar and yet here you are in your hundreds, at only an arm's reach! We are profoundly indebted and humbled Aquadya, our people have always held your kind in the highest regard and your deeds this day will continue to consolidate our sincere respect." replied McGrath, taking a knee and clasping Aquadya's hand firmly.

"Thank you, your words are well received. We have always considered the same for the race of Elves. Despite the obvious differences, we are similar in deed and conviction. I believe you have met one of us before, but her true origin was concealed to you."

A young girl swam over beaming widely.

"Dippy! Crom...all along you were a Mere-folk? I must be getting old, my eyes aren't what they used to be. We were concerned, wondering why you had left so hastily after we had rescued the clan Goblins from the Tundra mines."

"You are not *old,* McGrath, just wise enough to admit your limitations. Yes, I am sorry for leaving like that, goodness knows what Rob must think of me. I didn't even say goodbye. It's complicated, but I knew we had to be here at this time, I hope he will forgive me when this is all over."

The veteran commander saw her pain, "Of course he will, he is a rare breed himself that one. But for now please excuse my brevity, we do not have much time before that accursed portal opens and hell is unleashed upon us all."

Aquadya replied, "We will keep the river safe for your riders, if that is what you wish. Rob gave us our Siren-Dipity back, we had thought her all but lost, so in return we gladly offer our services to you."

"We thank you again, Aquadya. Dippy, we need to cross this river in an attempt to gain entry to the rear of the

Fortress. We shall need the river and rear of the moat to be free from those infernal creatures, can you manage that?"

"Consider it done. We wish you the best of luck, Commander."

"We need it, we all do."

McGrath signalled his riders to dismount and lead their horses as swiftly as possible through the cold, violent waters. The Mere-folk had formed a solid line downstream to act as a safety net for any riders losing their footing in the strong undercurrents.

"Wait, were coming too!" yelled Merlock, with Clump and Pumice in tow, both exhibiting an unsettling mix of bloodlust and, well lust.

"Thank you, Merlock, we need all the help we can get." said McGrath, gawking at the unlikely couple holding hands while wading through the powerful currents as if splashing through puddles.

Merlock shrugged a sigh before climbing upon Clump's shoulder. "Where's that brother of yours got to, Clump? I do hope he's alright."

Merlock may just have just been talking to himself as he looked at Clump. Even though no more than a few feet from his ear flap, the fool was completely smitten, hearing nothing but the sweet sound of chirping birds, war cries and Pumice's alternating grunt.

Hundreds of Mere-folk had already departed, swimming at impossible speeds against the waters turbulent flow, heading directly for the keeps moat.

"My Queen, Fingle wishes to speak with you most urgently."

Buttercup looked around to find Fingle seated behind an Elven rider.

Fingle jumped from off the horse and walked casually over to the Faerie Queen, "My Queen." he offered, bowing deeply.

"Fingle, you do not need to bow to me, but I thank you all the same. What news do you bring, good I hope?"

"We will never breach those defences in time, so I propose I am smuggled in as far as yer Elves can get me ta the front line, I will do the rest from there, M'lady."

"What do you intend to do, Fingle?"

"I'm a Goblin, fer the most part *they* are Goblins, all I need is a fortress guard's armour and yer help in getting me in as close as possible. Yer Elves on horse or heel have as much chance stealing Rob, as I would stealing Shoggy Whiffpits bath steam."

"Who's Shoggy?"

"Yer don't want ta know, M'lady. Shoggy was thrown in the cells fer a whole wheel turn fer causing air pollution from his armpits. Folk were dropping like flies just breathing around him, and fer a Goblin that's takes some doing."

"I see your point. I will get you in as far as I can towards the Fortress entrance, but you will be on your own from there, Fingle."

"I don't need protecting, not from those lame brained boot lickers, I'll have our Rob out snip snap, you'll see."

Buttercup leaned in close, "Fingle, there is something you should know about Rob, there is a message you *must* give him, it may save his life and hopefully all of ours…"

As she whispered, Fingle's eyes widened. When she was finished, a combination of sadness and grit determination lined his face. Fingle had his pick of armoured suits displaying the three peaks insignia. Although the notion of covering himself with another's sweaty and bloodstained apparel was repugnant, he had little choice if he wished to pass as a loyal guard to the S.G.G.

A small band of Elves then secreted him as far to the front line as possible, one of them taking a mortal blow during the effort and another seriously wounded. Fingle vowed to himself it would not be in vain. Buttercup watched from afar offering a silent prayer for her noble warriors and the brave little Goblin.

"McGrath is leading his riders across the river, my Queen, the Mere-folk have claimed the river and beaten back the Kelpies!"

The platoon leader's words could not have come at a better time, the battle finally seemed to swing in their favour. She sent Dern to relay the incredible news back to the front line effort. In short time, she observed a strong surge from the Elves as the fighting intensified.

"Get 'em, stick 'em!" yelled Fingle waving his sword wildly, while surrounded by Dark Fortress guards.

He continued to edge his way backwards while facing forwards. No one had noticed a thing, Fingle was just another of Sly's guards wiggling a weapon and shouting obscenities at the enemy. *This is embarrassingly simple,* thought Fingle, looking over his shoulder to see what gap he could muscle into next. It was a laborious endeavour, but it *was* working. Every now and then, Fingle experienced a powerful tingling sensation within his baby hand. At one point he even untied the leather cord around his glove and removed it, checking for signs of change, but nothing…until remarkably there was...

His floppy glove spontaneously filled itself, but before Fingle could leap for joy, it cruelly shrank back again. Although deeply frustrated, Fingle remained optimistic. His hand was still tingling and harboured hope that soon he would have his hand returned back to normal. If ever he needed it, it was now.

* * *

A commander from the Air Squadron landed in an opening near the Queen. Jumping from off her saddle, she ran over to Buttercup's ring of protection, "Let me through, I seek council with the Queen immediately!"

The Squadron Commander was allowed through and presented to Buttercup, "What is it, Commander?"

"It's McGrath, I mean the Cavalry Commander, my Queen. He's under heavy attack at the rear of the Fortress, from the upper battlements. The Fortress archers number too many for our efforts and are too well protected from above. Our archers are finding it increasingly difficult to hit their targets and we are taking on casualties too."

Buttercup had suspected this might happen. Before they left Corona, McGrath had advised her she would need to find a way to neutralise their bows, or it could cost them the battle.

"Squadron Commander, I need your squadron to maintain an air presence, but slowly and *discreetly* distance yourselves. Watch for my hand, when I give you the signal, I want you and your archers to fly back again as swiftly as possible and engage anything that's still attacking us. Have your archers replenish their arrows from the re-supply wagons immediately."

"Yes, my Queen, on your signal."

Buttercup watched her run back to her Drakite and leap onto its back. In moments she was airborne holding out a red flag from her saddle bag, hoisting it high. A circling rider acknowledged the communication and relayed the same message. Before long—and each in turn to avoid suspicion—all Drakite's had landed, re-supplied and took off again. Buttercup admired their discipline and courage and relied upon them as equally as any other element of her forces, if not more. The Faerie Queen could not see how McGrath fared from her viewpoint and prayed their magickal shielding would hold long enough before the S.G.G. penetrated it. She watched the circling ring of Drakites begin to fan out, until they were at least twice the distance they were originally, leaving a large area above the Fortress to remain clear. The Fortress archers had not altered tactics, continuing to let loose their arrows above and below. *Good,* thought Buttercup; *they have not suspected a thing.* She pulled her robe around her armour and settled into herself, closing off all distraction with a formidable discipline that had been honed over many years of diligent practice. Her inner ring of protection were accustomed to their Queen entering a meditative state and continued to provide her with the security she relied upon. Although her eyes were closed, she invoked her inner sight and could see everything that surrounded her, all at once. This had taken some getting used to at first, but Buttercup had been a natural. Her gifts were passed down from her ancestors; it was in part why she had been chosen to rule over the race of Elves and the Kingdom. It required great love and respect to be able to communicate and work with the natural world, so in turn, this strong connection also ensured a strong and compassionate leader.

Her spirit—now free—soared high above the keep, looking down at the tragedy below. From this height all seemed trivial and meaningless, but she remembered what was at stake and proceeded to summon the Sylphs and wind Elementals. An enormous drifting, curling, grey configuration, divided into individualised cloudy forms before her. One considerably larger than the others, approached and waited patiently. Buttercup sent out her love and her understanding in why they were so angered. She created an image in her mind of what she needed from them. She felt the cool response of their departing ghostly forms flow through her spirit. It was done.

"I take it you're responsible for this?" enquired Dern, smiling as Buttercup opened her eyes.

She looked upwards and as requested, the raging storm continued, but not above the Fortress battlements and towers. The charcoal clouds had miraculously parted, allowing the blazing sun to shine down fiercely.

"Forgive me, my Queen, but why? Surely the Fortress archers can now improve their aim. How is this helping McGrath or any of the others? And why has air support moved away?"

As expected, hundreds of Fortress archers now turned their attention away from the skies and increased their rate of fire upon the Elves below. McGrath knew the Queen had a hand in this unexpected turn of events and encouraged his warriors to maintain the shielding for a while longer, despite their failing magick.

And then it came…

From out of the swirling black vortex above, a lone black cloud seemed to drift independently, descending from the gloom and into the light. Several of the Fortress archers had noticed the strange cloud, but were unable to discern any detail due to the sun's glare and so returned back to their savage ground attack, emboldened by the weakening Elven magick as the blue domed shields crackled and sparked less and less with every arrow fired upon it. Buttercup watched the solitary cloud continue to descend, relieved it had remained ignored. By the time anyone realised it was anything but a cloud, it was regrettably too late. A vast mesh of Faux had linked together to form a nebulous cloudlike shape. The nebulous part was not overly difficult as they were completely inebriated, but keeping the Boggles held aloft was another matter entirely, having to rely on bravado and brawn.

"Get a load of this pish!" bawled a crotchety winged sprite, as he and his companions let the first Boggle drop above the archers—ensuring its restraints had been released in the process.

The un-muzzled and highly confused Boggle attempted to transform mid-flight but there was nothing available for it to resemble. So on it fell, contorting and twisting into a number of amorphous identities, until eventually plopping upon the battlements, barking and noselling its impatience loudly. A Fortress archer looked behind at the harrowing noise and immediately the Boggle replicated his identity, thus commenced the deadly monologue.

The condemned bowgoblin would have gladly ripped away his ear-flaps, but was utterly disempowered to do so, or do anything other than listen to the dullest, most colourless, platitudinous drivel he could possibly endure until his imminent demise. As more of the homicidal haggises were released, the greater the number of archers became locked into utterances from Hades. Some of the archers not yet entrapped attempted to fire their arrows at the jeering Faux, but the glaring sunlight obscured their aim and the gloating Faux universally agreed it was a splendid opportunity to relieve their aching bladders, with extreme prejudice. It hadn't taken long before the entire battlements resounded with a mumbling mix of lethal diatribes. Those who managed to escape being Boggled to death, were pissed upon and chased away by the hovering hooligans. Although small in stature, in large groups they were a toxic, destructive force to be avoided at all costs and maddeningly difficult to kill owing to their size, speed, and astonishing drunkenness.

"Lower shields!" ordered McGrath, his Elves responding in cheer.

Aside from an irritating, mumbling monotone, nothing else seemed to be coming down upon them. Aquadya signalled to McGrath it was now safe to cross the rear moat. Fortuitously, the waters current was negligible in the moat, but its depth required them to leave their horses and most of their armour to swim across. The Mere-folk had kept to their word, the Kelpies were nowhere to be seen or heard. The Elves—exhausted from their magickal endeavours—tired further, swimming through the deep freezing waters. Clump swam past them effortlessly with Pumice in tow, churning up a turbulent wake that choked several exasperated Elves. Clump exited the water and walked over to a heavy wooden door beset with heavy black iron work. McGrath—already out of the moat—had begun searching for an opening, perhaps a lock that could be picked or smashed. Before he had even seen Clump, a monstrous double headed axe split the door completely in two. McGrath dived out of the way, showered in splinters and sparks.

"Crom! You might have warned us first." complained McGrath, lying on his back in the mud.

Pumice shoved Clump aside and lowered her cudgel to rest upon McGrath. He was uncertain whether he could have moved it from off his chest even if he had dared. The Troll leered in, baring her headstone teeth as she growled. McGrath quickly apologised, she then prodded her club deeper—forcing the air from his lungs—while pointing at Clump. McGrath looked over to the giant Goblin, wheezing out a second apology.

Satisfied, she took Clump's hand and together they entered the keep, kicking away the heavy debris as if it didn't exist. McGrath got up sighing heavily, *I am too old for this.*

"Shall we…?" said the weary commander, gesturing dramatically for his stunned Elves to follow the happy couple.

* * *

The replica Dark Fortress was now fully manifest. It was as real on Earth as it was in the Land of the Fae. Every stone block, every iron rivet, every single artefact that had been focused upon by the souls of sleeping Humans had been duplicated, nothing had been left out. The only difference 'Earth side', was the dismantled rear wall, supported and ready to feed through heavy artillery and thousands of infantry troops. The army General stood in the duplicate Great Hall, watching intently as a large, scarlet membrane revealed itself, then appeared to dissolve away from its pulsing centre. As he peered through, a Goblin guard peered back causing him to jump.

"General, I have been informed the portal will soon be fully accessible. Are we to proceed with project 'Black Rainbow'?"

"Yes, have your men on standby, Lieutenant. On my orders, send the tanks through first, followed by the infantry. I want those savages to grovel at the might of Earth's military power."

* * *

Fingle had wriggled his way backwards into the Great Hall itself. Even he had to admit he was a slippery customer, clearly aptitude tests were not part of Sly's recruitment process. Not only could he see Rob, he also saw something that made the hair on his palms stand on end. A pulsating, scarlet portal was opening and beyond it were Humans, many, many Humans and they did not look like fairy-tale enthusiasts. After edging his way down the side wall, Fingle inched closer towards the centre where Rob was tied to a chair. Those that weren't gaping at the portal were watching the Elves outside the keep, desperately fighting to gain entry. Fingle managed to sneak amongst a group of guards shielding Rob. Standing directly behind his chair, Fingle pretended to look elsewhere as he worked away at the leather straps holding Rob, with his sharpest blade. *This is too easy,* he thought as he cut through one, then shuffled to the next strap, no one seemed to notice. *Done it!* All he had to do now was to get Rob's attention and escape the keep, which easier said than done. In truth, he hadn't thought this far ahead, this was the best he could do under the circumstances.

"Psst, Psst, Rob, it's me, Fingle."

He tugged on Rob's arm, but nothing. He pushed him more urgently, again nothing.

"I see we have an admirer in our midst."

Fingle spun around to see a tall slender Goblin removing his helmet, revealing a leather mask beneath it.

"That's right, little Goblin, I have been watching your futile efforts for some time, although expertly *executed*, oops, insensitive choice of words. Although expertly *performed,* it was ultimately pointless, but nevertheless most entertaining. You see, Flangefull Fartfit, we have all been watching you. I'm afraid your predilection for lavender gave up the game quite early on, did you not see my guards retching?"

Fingle's jaw dropped as the guards laughed cruelly. He had been allowed to enter and never once seen as a threat, "I thought your guards...I thought they were..."

"Scared? Against that rabble out there? Hardly. Your friend, *our* friend, is quite catatonic. Initially bonds were required, we had to wait until more of my marvellous Guild had recovered from their embarrassing predicament, but now my magi hold Rob beneath a powerful spell. Incidentally, I really must afford your wizard companion my utmost respect, the reverse concealment spell was inspired. And credit also to young Rob, by all accounts my magi were forced to go to considerable lengths in controlling his mind. In another time perhaps, he may have made a useful addition to my Guild, such a pity, such a waste of raw talent."

Fingle trembled with fury as a guard slapped a pair of manacles over his wrists.

"I hope you don't mind, Fagflap, it's precautionary, you understand…"

"My Slimelord, the Humans are preparing to come through."

"Yes they are and tell me, Dungsponge, *why* am I your Slimelord?"

"Because we are slime and you are our lord?"

"Correct, now go out there and die for me."

Fingle watched the obedient fool sprint through the defences without even a weapon. How sad he thought, that minds could be so easily led without question. As he appraised the rabid assemblage of mercenaries preparing their invasion from Earth, he realised that things were not so different elsewhere.

"General, something's wrong. Our tanks were operating without fault until we drove them into the duplicate Dark Fortress and now all of them are defective."

"Damn!" seethed the General. *There was always a risk this might happen,* he mused. "Very well, Lieutenant, tell your troops to fix bayonets and prepare for close quarter battle."

Sly realised there was something wrong with the Human technology, for some reason it wasn't working for them. He cursed at their misfortune, but remained positive upon seeing the enormous swell of soldiers poised to charge through the portal.

Sly saw this as the perfect opportunity to display *his* importance and addressed his own guards, "Listen in you steaming mounds of rat's puke, I want you all to pull your flesh spades out of your quivering gobs and grasp them around your meat jabbers, let's show these stinky-pinks we can be killers and mincers too!"

Sly's guards stood in shock.

"Begging your pardon, Duke of death, but what exactly do you mean by *mincers*?"

"Okay, that came out wrong. Look, when they invade, just stand aside and *try* to look tough, do you think you can all at least manage that?" pleaded Sly, his voice inflecting to a higher octave.

The S.G.G. guards edged to the outer walls and began posing awkwardly. Some folded arms menacingly, then unfolded them, then folded them back again, quite unable to make a decision. Others were in deep concentration, attempting to display every weapon they owned and subsequently dropping them, then picking them back up only to drop others. And a small group broke away to begin arm wrestling and push-up competitions. Sly inwardly wept at the staggering display of incompetence and prayed in earnest that his guards were accidentally obliterated in a 'pink on green' attack by allied forces.

Then finally it happened, the unthinkable had begun.

McGrath stopped running down a Fortress corridor with the other Elves close behind as he felt the thunderous roar of boots below his feet, mingled with foreign battle-cries. They were too late.

Chapter 34

"You must leave, now, Buttercup, we have lost this day. If you are captured, there will never be any hope in saving our world, you know this."

While Dern attempted to reason with the Faerie Queen, his words became inaudible, all she could hear was the terrible struggle, the deafening clash of steel, the screams of the victors and the fallen.

"I don't want to lose you, Buttercup, I love you…"

Buttercup looked up, his eyes imploring hers, as tears merged with blood upon his desperate face. She managed a smile and allowed him to take her reigns. Buttercup knew if she refused he would not desert her and would die for his loyalty, for his love. Dern deserved better.

"Retreat, Retreat!" came the cries from the exhausted Elves, overcome by the onslaught. Hundreds of Human soldiers became thousands, pouring out of the Fortress as a torrent of hate, killing anything that lay in their path. The Humans' weapons by some miracle had been unable to fire, like the rest of their war machine, but it hadn't stopped them from advancing. On the contrary, forced to fight with bladed weapons only enhanced their murderous appetites. Abranth and Rob's father swiftly led the clan Goblins to the temporary safety of Shadow Haven woods, prepared to head back towards the Tin Fence if need be. There, they could dig in, taking strategic advantage of the natural features the Dark Cloud Crags and Tundra mines would offer them. The allied army lost half their number during the Dark Fortress attack and the rest would undoubtedly be killed by the invaders if they remained. Several of the Orchi had been slain too, those that still lived continued to fight valiantly against the invaders, allowing more time for the clan Goblins to gain a greater distance. The Drakites hardly made a dent, as wave upon wave continued to arrive; they fired every arrow they had, now unable to restock. Signals were given for a third of the air fleet to send urgent word to all races and warn Corona, so that they may fortify themselves. The rest of the Drakites would stay close to the retreating Elves and their Queen, ready to attack, or stall the enemy by any means necessary.

Fingle slumped against Rob's chair, his world a blur of charging bodies. He looked up. Rob was still clearly unreachable, whatever spell he was under, he had no way of breaking it. He looked behind at the landing, above the portal opening towards the far end of the Great Hall and could see the Guild magi in deep concentration. He sat up a little more, shocked at how much they were struggling. Fingle's sharp mind jolted into action. Sly had said that Rob's mind was difficult to control and as sure as Dingle Dogspit couldn't convince a clan of Faux to leave the Bleeding Beetle during happy hour, the Guild *were* struggling. All he needed was to find a way for them to break their concentration, but how? The Guild were heavily guarded and out of reach, but if he could disturb their spell, enough to rouse Rob and pass on the message Buttercup had given him, there was still a chance they could stop the portal from haemorrhaging further.

"We meet again, Sly the Slaughterer, it would have been useful to know our rifles and missiles do not function here, but no matter, my men have secured the area and are neutralising all remaining resistance."

Sly clapped his hands in delight, walking over to the military Commanding Officer, "Yes, General, an unfortunate by-product of portalling to other worlds, no two worlds are ever the same, or behave the same. Take Divmatronium for example, to us it is worthless, but to your world, well, that is why you are all here."

A soldier stood to attention, then showed the General a laptop computer screen and a notebook with something written down. The officer grinned then sent him away. The General left Sly and sat around a large table where other important looking Humans were sitting.

Sly was left standing alone, angered and publicly humiliated by being excluded from the proceedings, "I can see you are all conducting important discussions, but what about me? I have held my end of the bargain and presented you with our Kingdom on a plate. You are now free to plunder as much Divmatronium as you can carry."

The General turned to address him, looking irritated, "Yes, Sly, you have and we thank you for your assistance, but there have been some changes to the original plan." then returned to his discussions with the men around the table.

"What do you mean, *changes*?" demanded Sly.

"Look here, Goblin, there is no way we can ever risk an extra-terrestrial, such as yourself, to occupy a responsible position within our governments. Our agendas may be very different and that is a risk we are not prepared to take. As for plunder, see these men I am talking to, they are called *scientists*. They are here to run tests on Divmatronium. We have just verified our computers can cross the portal threshold with their data intact, so all we need now is the atomic structure, then we can produce Divmatronium in our own laboratories back on Earth. Look on the bright side, Slaughter, you get to keep your Divmatronium and your position as slum lord in this asylum, that is, after we have cleansed it of everything we deem as a potential threat, which regrettably means most of it…"

As the General turned his back on him once more, Sly exploded, "Who are you to come into my world and betray me? You think yourselves so powerful, so perfect, you're nothing!"

"I strongly advise you to gain some self-control, Slaughter, see these other men, they have orders to kill every last one of you, should you pose a threat to this mission. As for betrayal, you got what you deserved. You should have been more careful in who you made bargains with, Goblin. We have a saying on Earth, all is fair in love and war and believe me when I say, *this is war*!" the General stood and ordered his soldiers to arrest Sly.

The grossly outnumbered S.G.G. guards were about to protest, but were quickly kept in line. The Guild, after witnessing their superior threatened, momentarily lost their collective concentration and temporarily lessened the spell's power.

"You up there, keep the Swindlar boy under control or you will be the next to die, along with your faerie prince." balked the General.

The frantic magi nodded and redoubled their combined efforts. Fingle, although being placed under military supervision with the rest of the S.G.G., began to hatch a despicably cunning plan, hopefully more successful than his last.

*   *   *

McGrath had no other option but to head up towards the battlements. He knew the outside perimeter would be under careful observation by the invasion force. He hoped that by gaining a higher perspective, he may be able to find another way to escape. The Elves that followed their veteran commander were nimble and quiet in their movements, years of forest training and daily hunting expeditions had honed their remarkable skills. Clump and his new girlfriend were another matter entirely.

"Shhh, lad, if they hear us it will be your fault and no amount of magick will stop ten thousand jittery Stinky-pinks with murder on their minds." cautioned Merlock.

Clump nodded, then attempted to communicate this back to Pumice. She either ignored him or it hadn't registered, she was far too busy trying to squeeze up the winding stone staircase. It hadn't helped there were no windows, as Pumice became increasingly troubled in trying to comprehend *why* they had seemingly not gotten anywhere, despite her spiralling, upwards plod? After what seemed like several lifetimes—at least for the Elves following Pumice and her denticulated derriere—the spiral staircase finally concluded at a doorway leading onto the battlements.

Upon entering the expansive open area, they immediately crouched, ensuring they would not be seen from below, weaving through the Boggles and Bogglee's—a *Bogglee* being a moribund unfortunate, who becomes engaged in a one sided conversation with a Boggle, they are literally living on Boggled time!

Clump and Pumice were led to the central area, while Merlock unconvincingly convinced them to remain, keeping well out of sight from the ground. Fortunately, the happy couple were content to sit together, gazing adoringly at one another. Whereas Merlock, unable to ignore the elephants in the room, had been in far better places, Pardonme Marsh seemed a preferable alternative.

After looking out from the battlements in every direction, McGrath returned to the front facing wall. It was worse than he had hoped. By his reckoning, they had three options; head back down the tower steps, stay put on the battlements, or attempt to jump onto the mountain that surrounded the rear of the Fortress. The first option was out of the question; the keep was now heavily secured and escape an impossibility. The second option related to the first option, it was only a matter of time before they would be discovered. The third option, although a possibility, was also borderline suicide, the rock face was near vertical, loose and unsuitable to climb. The Elven commander observed the invaders through a crenel in the battlement wall. He watched how disciplined they were. Although the Humans were no tenderfoots, he knew his warriors would best them in battle. The Elves had a distinct advantage in speed, agility, and strength. They also had magick to aid them. But in this instance, the sheer size of the Human army, in addition to their strategy, training, and aggressive determination would prove unconquerable. McGrath had to face the facts of the situation, they could either fight to the bitter end, dying with honour, or surrender, hoping for clemency. But from what the old commander knew of Humans, they could be a very cruel and ruthless race, his optimisms were not particularly high.

He felt a sharp tug on his sleeve, a young Elven rider whispered to him urgently. McGrath went rigid, then looked through the crenel once more, this time much farther afield. Although the battlements were bathed in sunshine, the rest of the land as far as could be seen, was still cloaked beneath the baleful clouds, continuing to remonstrate the profane proceedings. McGrath's eyes— like his intellect—were still as sharp as ever. He searched like a veteran bird of prey, never blinking nor distracted and through the downpour he began to make out something moving in the remote distance and it was beyond measure.

Crom, the young Elf was good! he muttered.

He signalled for Merlock to come over and offer his opinion. The wizard quickly entered a trance and in a few short moments his eyes blinked back open. For a while he just stared at McGrath in disbelief.

"Well, what is it? It can't be Trolls, they are already here. Besides, what moves is ten times their size!" pressed the commander.

After gathering his thoughts, Merlock spoke, "You are not going to believe this, but if I am not mistaken, it appears the entire gobulation of the Goblin City, is heading our way…"

Chapter 35

The very same wall that had been the focal point of their most celebrated festival and the reason for their unprecedented success now imprisoned them. The Goblin City guards—under the ultimate authority of Sly Slaughter—were ordered to invoke a City-wide curfew after the Dark Fortress coup. Sly had the foresight to ensure there would be no last minute surprises for his guests, so he had every last Goblin living in the city and the surrounding shanty towns, rounded up and forced to remain inside the City as prisoners. Several enraged Goblins had tested the guards' resolve and earned the privilege of having the best views of the sprawling capital, courtesy of fifty foot spikes that lined the perimeter.

This had always been part of the original plan by the S.G.G. from the very beginning, unbeknown of course to all those that had settled there. If the social experiment had ever failed, because Goblins were unable to cohabit in large numbers, or perhaps social unrest gained momentum over an unfavourable S.G.G. policy, then in such an event the masses could be controlled by using the 'walled in City' as an enormous prison camp.

The Goblins had seen no reason to suspect anything and continued to venerate their founder 'Shuffles' and his wonderful tale. After all, the wall *did* keep out the worst of winter's bite and they had greater security by way of guarded entry—there was simply nothing worse than finding your domicile had been robbed by a drifter after you had arrived back home from a hard days thieving!

Sly had also ordered several garrisons to patrol the docks in case anyone attempted to escape by plunging into the Great Wet. The Goblins were instructed to go about their daily business and all would be well, providing no attempt at escape was made. Although no one had any idea why they had to stay within the City, as a collective they had decided the wisest course of action was to continue with their routines, despite being held as prisoners.

That was, until Siren-Dipity had arrived with her family and some friends and their friends…

Once the Mere-folk had taken control of the dockyards, they swapped their fins for feet to walk around the city. It wasn't difficult to find pockets of unrest and from these, galvanise them quickly into a sizable resistance. Although initially astonished upon seeing them, especially on land, the Goblins knew enough of the Mere-folk to know they were honourable allies and would never wish harm upon them. The Mere-folk had informed the Goblins why Sly had kept them imprisoned and what was happening at the Dark Fortress. When they heard of the impending invasion, the gobulation were outraged, especially that one of their own kind could commit such a heinous crime against Goblinity, after all, there was still *some* honour among thieves.

With the support and guidance of the Mere-folk, the rebellion gained momentum at a rampant rate. From the moment Dippy had arrived, it had taken less than a candle burn before the remaining guards had fled for their wretched lives.

Every City gate had been heavily chained together, but the sheer mass of Goblins had demolished the outer City walls in large dusty ruptures, demanding their freedom and justice. From Dippy's perspective, there was nothing else left to do, other than remain at a safe distance while tens of thousands incensed, weapon wielding Goblins scrambled over the rubble baying for blood, both green and red, they were not in a particularly picky mood it seemed.

The Mere-folk, jubilant and equally relieved their work had been achieved so successfully, had dived back into the gleaming waters of the Great Wet and swam hard towards the mouth of the Gurgles. They too had a battle to wage at the Dark Fortress, if Dippy was right—and she was seldom wrong—McGrath and his cavalry would need their help against the Kelpies.

Chapter 36

Eventually, Dern had convinced Buttercup to sit behind him on a Drakite—the squadron always kept the fastest available for the Queen should she ever need it. It was the safest way for her to travel during battle. Although initially she had protested, stating her place should be on the ground with the bulk of her army, Dern reminded her, the Elves would be much happier in keeping their Queen alive. Shortly after ascending into the sky, high above the acrid air—thick with smoke that reeked of tar and burning blood—Buttercup became grateful beyond measure she had done so.

Dern's Drakite swooped in low above the waves of crazed Goblins that continued to race towards the direction they themselves had just retreated from. An unstoppable ocean of green and glinting silver washed across the land. The elementals above reacted accordingly, altering their mood, the black clouds unrolling as quickly as they had coalesced. The rains slowed, as if a river had been dammed and in its place glorious sunshine shined forth upon the hills and muddy flats.

"What is it now?" snapped the impatient General.

The quivering soldier tried to remain calm, "Sir, sorry to bother you, but you *need* to see this, it appears we have company, lots of it."

"What do you mean, Soldier? Aren't you equipped to deal with this? You, like everyone else on this mission were briefed upon the dangers of what to expect. What are we paying you for?" The commanding officer stood abruptly, staring down the man, "This is what you get when you hire soldiers of fortune. This had better be worth my time…" then he marched over to the keeps entrance to look for himself.

After his eyes had adjusted to the bright sunlight, he gasped.

The entire region of land, right up to the crest of the distant hills on the horizon were teeming with angry Goblins, continuing to spill over the ridgeline without reprieve.

"Oh shit…"

The General ran back inside, snatching up any data they had managed to collect, then ordered the frightened scientists to head back to Earth post haste. They were to inform Command and Control, *the rainbow had broken, operation 'Faerie Dust' must now be invoked.*

The soldier, visibly afraid, spluttered, "Sir, what do we do now?"

"You do what your bloody well paid to do, which includes holding these monsters at bay until we can fumigate this whole bloody cesspit!"

The General, after losing all self-assurance, hurriedly snatched at papers and laptops then disappeared back through the portal, deserting all of his men and his ill-fated mission. Fingle recognised his opportunity to rescue Rob and hopefully put an end to the madness. He didn't know what new enemy the Stinky-pinks faced, but it was enough for their leader's bladder to burst. *Hmmmm, maybe wearing this uniform wasn't such a good idea after all,* he mused, while restrained by two of Sly's guards looking identical to himself.

*　　*　　*

McGrath knew that no army alive existed, save for the Orcs—who had left the land to voyage into the Great Wet many wheel turns ago—that could withstand a stampede of this magnitude, armed only with steel.

"Elves, listen in. This day is not yet lost. Our green brethren have joined us from their great City, *all* of them! This will be our final chance to fulfil the prophecy, to rescue the boy born of both worlds and close this infernal portal. For the Queen, for our people, for all races!"

The veteran warrior unsheathed his sword as did the others and together they cheered, calling out the ancient battle cry of Corona. Renewed, McGrath sprinted across the battlements and back towards the stairwell, eternally grateful he could finally escape the legion of babbling Boggles—who had not stopped for air since their magnificent arrival. The Elves scrambled after him, eager to join their leader in battle and ensure Pumice's rear was at the rear this time.

"Did you hear that, Robert?" said Abranth, holding her ear flap to the wind.

The Archer pulled in his horse and listened, "Crom, the horns of Corona, they call again?"

"Whatever's happening, Robert, the Elves are on the attack once more, we cannot desert them, we owe them this much."

"Agreed, but what of the clan Goblins? This could mean the end for every last one of them. Are you prepared for this?" warned Rob's father.

"We both know they would rather die fighting for something, than die as a prisoner in a pit, which is precisely what would have happened if it were not for the Elves. Is it my people, or is it *me* you are afraid for, Robert?"

The Archer's smile betrayed his words, his tired eyes revealing the adoration he held for her, "Both. I love you, Abranth, just give me your word you will stay alive. I have not waited twenty years and crossed two worlds to lose you again."

"I do not intend to go anywhere, Archer, other than rescue my son. Do not forget, I too have waited, only mine was for an eternity. Let's finish this." she smiled, then galloped away to corral her clans and rally their support.

As Robert watched her ride deeper into Shadow Haven woods, he called his Orchi war band together, now half in number but full in spirit. "I want Slaughter's head on a plate." he spat.

The Orchi roared their approval as they sped back towards the Dark Fortress with many hundreds of clan Goblins following in their wake.

Although the mercenaries had bolstered their defences, it was woefully inadequate, knowing very shortly they would be completely overrun. If they had use of their rifles it *might* have been a very different outcome, but crossing dimensions came at a price, a price that they could not afford. As fear spread throughout their numbers, so did thoughts of mutiny.

"No amount of money is worth being ended by these unnatural things!"

"Why should *we* stay here when the General has turned tail?"

"I was told we would easily out number them, I should have known it was bullshit!"

"If I can't fire my rifle they won't be needing a marksman, I'm off."

"*Be a soldier of fortune* they said, *visit exotic places* they said, *meet foreign people, then kill 'em* they said. No one said anything about Goblins!"

Dissent ran riot through the ranks like dysentery. What they had all been briefed and what they were now experiencing were two very different narratives. It wasn't long before large groups of soldiers decided to scarper and attempt to cross back through the portal. Fingle watched the rising insurrection taking place, he understood its significance and became enlivened at its growing panic.

The General thrust his reddened face back through the pulsing membrane, "Get back traitors, don't forget, our weapons work perfectly well this side. We need you to keep them busy while we get the gas. Those that abandon their posts and come back through will be shot where they stand!"

The soldiers had no other choice and returned back to the front line defences. The General's warning was made clear to all the trembling troops.

Taking full advantage of the increasing rebellion, Fingle got the attention of the S.G.G. guards holding him, "Listen in, nuggets, yer know what's happening here don't yer? They have no intention of staying any longer, like yer have no intention of ever washing yer hairy bits. It won't be long before yer will be all alone, facing that other lot that's coming 'ere…"

The two guards didn't take long to think upon it and let go of Fingle. Very slowly they backed away, then disappeared down a dark corridor. Fingle allowed the manacle to slide over his gloved baby hand and held the dangling cuff with the other.

Crom, these devils have something else planned fer us and it don't look like an apology. Fingle knew now was the moment to act. Clearly their leader did not care if his soldiers lived or died and that made the stinky-pinks far more dangerous than he had initially judged. The General had been just as ruthless as Sly, but even Sly would not have deserted his own. Maybe killed a few of them, maybe betrayed his entire world, but caught in a fist fight he would have fought on to the bitter end, he was a Goblin and it was in his nature.

Sly was cuffed, gagged, and chained to a back wall, being kept well away from the proceedings. This time, no one but Sly had seen Fingle sneak towards him—no other creature on two legs could sneak like a Goblin, which was a well-known and widely respected fact. While hidden within a shadowy recess at the far end of the Great Hall, positioned just below the groaning Guild, Fingle removed his nose rings and used the pick to remove his own dangling cuff, holding it up to Sly's face.

"Do yer see this? This is yer chance ta do something right fer once. I'm not going ta ask fer yer promises, as I have more faith in frying sizzlepops on a wooden pan, but revenge, now there's a dish fit fer a fascist fosterer of villainous vermin, like yer bad self..."

Before Fingle removed all of the cloth in Sly's contorting mouth, he spat out the rest in fury.

"Listen to me, Fumble Lockpicks, this doesn't make us friends, I still want you to gargle the contents of my Grandgoblins piss-pot and personally shave your sweetbread satchel with a cracked centaur's hoof. But...you are right. More than anything I want my revenge. If I stop my Guild from spell casting, can you get Rob away from my Fortress?"

"I can try. Oh, and just out of curiosity, how did yer know I likes to keep things tidy down below?"

"For the love of crom! If you must know, Fingle, I read it in court, it was logged on your charge sheet. Just get Rob out of here and take yourself too before I vomit."

"Right yer are, I'll have him out lickety-split. Hey, yer finally got me name right."

"I've always known what it is, moron. I was merely being disparaging, an integral component of any despot toolkit. It was actually covered during my first week when attending the highly acclaimed course in '*How to be an effective Oppressor*'. Damn you, Fingle! The second week covered, '*Never disclose personal information to your intended victims*'!"

Sneering satisfactorily, Fingle unlocked Sly's manacles then made his way back to Rob while keeping a beady on Slaughter, his level of betrayal was legendary, a great role model to all aspiring Goblins. Sly, in keeping with his own agenda, kept to his word and Rob came back around as if from a deep slumber. Although his bonds were still untied, two hulking Humans pinned him down. Fingle was uncertain in how he would be able to free Rob. All weapons had been taken from him. He needed an angle, perhaps a distraction and all the luck of the little people. A familiar and supremely timely tingle prompted a rescue plan. Removing his glove he sauntered over to Rob as the two mercenaries growled.

Fingle bowed theatrically, then said, "Pardon me, but have any of yer perchance seen a weird baby hand before…?"

Chapter 37

Sometimes there is a moment in time, when that time suspends itself. An acceptance of what must come to pass, despite anything else that desired otherwise. When the summation of all life's adventure flashes before you in a serene blur. A phantasmagoria of experiences, bereft of emotion, leaden by the impassive silence of inevitability yet laced generously with uncertainty, a tentative fear born of its own impending conclusion.

When the Human defences were obliterated with what looked and felt like the landscape sliding into them, the first few waves of Goblins landed twenty men deep, clambering over their heads and burying their weapons into anywhere that would allow. It was nothing short of a massacre. Hundreds of mercenaries tried to escape using the river and were helpfully directed back by the Mere-folk. Several troops thought to run towards Doom Forest, but the Trolls—having dealt with the rogue army—were now heading back, swinging their bloodstained cudgels high as they roared. The Elves and clan Goblins could not get a look in. In truth they had already fought valiantly, very nearly defeated by the invading army, but now it was time for the civilised City Goblins to unleash hell and maybe let off a little steam. Dern winced as the carnage increased, speculating that Goblins co-existing on a large scale, while living under too many rules may have created some deep underlying social tensions. As the invading troops were forced back to the entrance, Fingle could hear their shouts and screams clearly and knew the battle was dangerously close to spilling into the keep.

"No, not out there, look at me, look at me freaky hand, woooooo…"

The soldiers turned their attention back to Fingle's outstretched hand as he wriggled his mesmerising, minute digits in a hypnotic manner.

"I 'ave *never* seen anyfing like that before, 'ave you Dave?"

Dave didn't say anything, he was completely enthralled and a little smitten. It took him down memory lane, back to when his own hand had looked almost as tiny when he squeezed the life out of an unsuspecting worm, his first ever confirmed kill.

"Come…look ye closer." enticed Fingle.

Rob was now looking up too, head lolling to one side and no less confused as he had ever been. As bleary eyed Dave and his gormless comrade loomed in, the tingling sensation reached its zenith. Fingle, upon sensing the change, immediately clenched his baby hand into a tight fist.

"Awww, it looks like a Brussels sprout, ain't it cute, Dave?"

Before Dave could agree, Fingle's hand transformed to its fullest size at lightning speed. Oddly, Fingle hadn't felt anything during the exchange, but the mercenary's nose suggested otherwise. What was left upon the unconscious man's face wasn't worth salvaging. Just as rapidly, his hand shrank back again, allowing Fingle enough time to reposition it in front of Dave's inquisitive features. Unfortunately, his unresponsive companion had fallen against Dave and in turn sent Dave floundering forwards, resulting in Fingle's baby hand becoming lodged half way up Dave's conveniently flared nostril. Before Fingle could react, his hand expanded, resulting in less of a splatter and more of a detonation. By the time Fingle had persuaded Rob to stop vomiting over what was left of Dave, hundreds of soldiers—fearful for their lives—had retreated back into the Great Hall for protection.

"C'mon, Rob, I need yer ta get yer head straight. It's not the Humans we need ta fear now; it's what their planning ta send back through that pink 'ole. As long as yer are still within the Dark Fortress, *it stays open*!"

Sly and his Guild had long since vanished, but Fingle spied a large door left ajar, where the magi had been standing on the far balcony.

"Right, lad, come with me, we're gonna have ta make a run fer it, do yer think yer can manage?"

Rob straightened himself, looked Fingle squarely in the eyes then said, "You could high-five a faux with that hand."

"I ought ta slap yer with it, but it has a mind of its own. It's good ta see yer back ta yer old self, yer bluttering breedbate. See those stairs leading up ta that door, we need ta make 'em now."

"I thought you said we had to escape? Surely that's going upwards, not out?"

"Well, we can stay put and ask the nice killers if they will let us play outside, or maybe make a wee visit back home ta yer other world, with a welcoming party ta die fer?"

"You made your point. I will try and keep up, but I'm still a little groggy." said Rob, sneaking a peak through the shimmering portal.

"Fingle! I know what they are planning to do. I saw hundreds of barrels stacked on crates, being unloaded on the other side. And I recognised the symbol on the barrels; we're in *big* trouble."

"Crom! What does it mean, lad?"

"It's a symbol we use for chemical agents that are scientifically engineered to become biological weapons used for mass destruction!"

Fingle blinked, "Yes, yes, but what does it mean, lad?"

"It means anything living that comes into contact with it will die, horribly."

"Sacred crom, we need ta get moving."

"Stop those Goblins, bring them back immediately, the portal cannot close!" ordered the General teetering over the portal threshold, ready to leap back in an instant to the sanctity and sanity of his own world, surrounded by weapons of total annihilation.

"Quickly, through that door." urged Fingle, half dragging Rob across the balcony. He shot a glance down the hall to see scores of murderous mercenaries in close pursuit, driven by the terrifying prospect of becoming stranded. Fingle slowed, from his new vantage point he could see a maelstrom of advancing city Goblins outside the keep, so close in fact, he could even identify one or two from the sprawling melee.

Isn't that Mungus Murfles, the reluctant fishergoblin who has a severe shellfish allergy? It was! And Pilgwyn Wobblybobble, the farming Hobblegoblin! Fingle began calculating how many gold pieces Pilgwyn still owed him after convincing him he needed to buy an ancient hog he found snuffling around the dockyard. He advised Pilgwyn that he must ride upon the animal to curry favour with his contemptuous chickens. Fingle further explained to Pilgwyn, the sole reason his chickens—that Fingle had also previously sold him—were not laying, was on account of his club foot. Adding that the chickens refused to lay any eggs because they felt ridiculed by their new owner while he hobbled around, convinced he was taking the piss as they bobbed and pecked about his yard. Lost in thoughts of gold and genuine wonderment at the stupidity of his peers, Fingle forgot the dire need to avoid his own demise at the hands of the Stinky-pinks, until the door he reached for vaporised.

Pumice, with Clump in tow, entered the Great Hall right on cue by Clump's reckoning, as he launched his iron shield into five soldiers climbing the stairs, then leapt spectacularly over the high balcony, while swinging his axe in a crescent of extinction before him. He was forced to admit that being in love suited him, mindful in how his battle form was now imbued with a superior elegance and a certain sentimentality that was hitherto lacking. Fingle gawked upwards at the lumbering she-Troll. Pumice looked down at him and as she smiled, he caught a surreal glimpse of his own grave nestled between her uneven chipped headstones, gradually rising above her tightening, quivering lips. Not unlike Clump, smiling was something Pumice needed to work on.

"Braathaa…in…lorrre…" she rumbled then snatched Fingle up for a rare show of affection. It was apparent to Fingle that love did indeed do strange things to folk from all walks of life. Never one to waste an opportunity, Fingle had immediately seen the potential of trading with the mountain Trolls; after all, he was practically family. He just needed to wait until he was released from being squished between six leathery mattresses before he could acquaint himself in a more appropriate manner.

"There you are, my boys, great turnout today isn't it? I was thinking of taking a refreshing dip in the Castle's moat, will you join me?"

"Are yer okay, Uncle?" queried Fingle.

"Why, thank you for asking, I'm ravishing. Speaking of radishes, my boots need a shine, Runner, Runner! Tsk, never a whelp-help when you need your fiddle tuning."

"Rob, keep an eye on him, seems he may be suffering from a bout of M.A.D. He has these occasional turns, a throwback from his days of wizard training at H.E.X.

where he simplifried himself too often. Looks ta me all the excitement has taken its toll, it don't usually last too long."

Rob nodded and took Merlock's hand, as the three of them escaped through the hole in the wall where the door once lived.

"Clump, make sure no one follows us!" yelled Fingle.

Clump held up a thumb, never once looking round, "No problem, Brother!" he shouted back, while spoilt for choice as he cleaved apart countless soldiers of ill fortune.

Fingle liked the sound of that. Given the choice, would he have preferred an equal as a brother? Someone that had more to offer cerebrally? Conversations with Clump were at a premium and despite a disparity of character that was further apart than the poles, Fingle knew in his heart that nobody else could ever replace Clump. He realised the word brother was just that, for they had always been brothers. His mother, Tipseycake, had brought them both up in the best way she could with what little she had. She had taught them to accept one another as brothers and so they had done just that. Clump had quickly developed his Orcish physique and Fingle just as swiftly developed his cunningness. Any sibling rivalries between them that involved physical confrontations would usually conclude in a trip to the local healer, so early on Fingle had learnt the art of manipulation, which was now fully in bloom. Who knew, without Clump he may never had been able to sink so low as to flimflam a faerie of her worldly possessions—most though, not all. Tipseycake had taught him he wasn't entirely bad, he had an awful lot to thank her and Clump for.

"Oh and, Clump, be careful Brother." As soon as the words had left his lips he cringed.

Fingle was not one for open affection, yet still he meant what he'd said. After a second thumb appeared, Fingle led the woozy lawyer and scatter-brained wizard down the corridor. It wasn't long after McGrath and his Elves appeared, almost flattening them.

"Thank crom it's yer lot. Listen, can yer Elves keep them below from following us, we need ta find another way out, do yer know how ta reach the battlements?"

McGrath nodded, "Yes, we have just come down from there, it's full of Boggles mind, but it's safe enough. We couldn't find a way out from up there though and we have searched everywhere else but no luck I'm afraid."

"It matters not if *we* can't escape, but we all need Rob ta leave this cesspool and he can from up there. Can yer help us and secure a path, maybe leave half yer Elves to help Clump out below?"

"Yes of course, but I warn you, this is the last time I intend climbing those stairs, the only time I like long hikes is when they are taken by those that irritate me. I really am too old for this and no one seems to believe me." resigned the veteran with a tired wink.

After dispatching half his Elves to assist Clump and Pumice—although strongly suspecting they would just get in the couples' way—McGrath ran on ahead, ensuring Fingle's path was kept free from nasty surprises. Fingle had to push Rob harder, ever mindful of what new weapon the invaders had in store for them, it was nothing short of extermination. Fortunately, with every step Rob became stronger, while Merlock was preoccupying himself, taking on the role of a tour guide to any that would listen. After an upwards, clockwise slog, the dazzling glare of sunlight finally welcomed them. Fingle left Merlock with McGrath, then ran with Rob to a small clearing on the battlements, desperately trying to ignore the deafening Boggle waffle.

"How are yer now, lad? Are yer back with the living?"

"I am, thanks, Fingle, those dark bastards put me somewhere I couldn't get out of, but I never stopped trying." Rob said with a tired smirk.

"I know yer didn't, I could see 'em struggling with yer, hee hee. Look, I need ta tell yer something, it's the most important thing I have ever had ta say ta anyone and I wish it could have been someone else, but it ain't, it has ta be yer Rob."

Rob studied his friend closely, becoming unsettled in the way Fingle struggled.

"What is it, Fingle? You can tell me." said Rob gently.

"I wish it could be done another way, I wish we had more time…Buttercup gave me a message ta give ta yer and only yer."

"Whatever it is, it's okay, I can deal with it." said Rob, hoping he sounded convincing despite his stomach churning with fear.

Fingle looked up and took Rob's arms, "The Faerie Queen told me that yer are more special than yer realise, than anyone does. She said the problem is, the only one who needs ta realise it, is *yer*. And the only way ta do that is ta shock yer into believing it…"

"How? How, Fingle?" demanded Rob.

"By jumping off the fortress."

Chapter 38

Rob stumbled backwards, almost tripping over a Boggle. How could his *friend* ask this of him? Why would he say such a thing? His head began spinning and his stomach knotted into a tight fist of terror.

"I...I can't, I can't..."

Fingle felt terrible and was deeply afraid for him. "Yer know I would *never* lie ta yer, not ta yer, Rob. Yer put yer neck on the block and fought nail and toof fer me in that festering court when yer didn't even know me. Yer are me friend, me truest friend..." spluttered the Goblin, choking on his words.

A sudden light blinked on in Fingle's head, a majority part of him seriously wished it hadn't, "Rob, I believe in the Faerie Queen and I believe in *you*, that's why we will jump together."

"What? You can't do that! I won't let you!"

"It's my decision and it's been made, now it's yer turn and I'd hurry else we'll all be snuffed out by yer bio-illogicals."

"What else did Buttercup say? Anything, anything at all?"

"As a matter of fact, yes. She said if yer don't jump, we'll all be done fer, but if yer do jump then we might all be saved."

Fingle was right, he *had* to do this, what right did he have to allow this incredible world, with all of its amazing characters and creatures to simply perish because he was too afraid? And if he did die by taking a leap of faith, then at least all those he loved may be spared.

He took a deep breath and cleared his mind, "Fingle, you are my truest friend also, which is why I must give you this…"

Rob put his hand into his pocket and pulled out something he held within his closed palm. Fingle moved in closer as Rob brought his foot up hard between his legs.

As Fingle dropped to his knees, Rob kissed his head, "Please forgive me, Fingle." with his parting words, Rob sprinted to the battlement wall and leapt over the side.

"Truuuueeee frieeend…" groaned Fingle, as two types of tears filled his eyes.

McGrath and the Elves lowered their weapons, standing in a state of shock. Rob had sacrificed his own life for a world he barely knew. They all took to a knee in honour and admiration. Robin Swindlar, the boy from both worlds would forever remain in their memory and hearts, for this act would never be forgotten, not by the turning of any wheel for as long as the race of Elves existed upon their world.

Rob's fall defied time. He could see every detail in astounding clarity, stretched out far below, as if he were looking through something other than his own eyes. He felt an inner tug, prompting his vision to cast upon the Fortress moat and instantly recognised Dippy, he knew without any doubt she was smiling back, how was this so?

His vision then shifted towards Buttercup, she was riding upon a Drakite in the far distance and yet he could feel her somehow? A surge of love and intense pride she held blanketed over him. As time held its breath, he felt another tug, towards the Fortress entrance, it was his parents. This time he felt their despair and horror, watching their only child plummet to his death. Only he wasn't plummeting. He could look upon anything he chose as if observing a single moment captured in time. His thoughts were clearer than they had ever been; his pristine awareness finally afforded the room to expand after every last drop of fear and doubt had been removed. He recalled the time trapped against the Sailor's Toof, when he had received a blast of dark magick, he knew then he should have died, but he hadn't. He also recalled his struggle at the Cone of Uncertainty, in how he had managed to overcome the Impenetrabubbles, even when Merlock had failed, he had then suspected something more of himself. He remembered the faces, suspicious faces that whispered of *prophesies*. He had tried to ignore it all, but a nagging intuition had always preserved the truth of such things. Finally, Rob recalled his inner battle that raged against the Guild. In truth, he knew why the magi had struggled to control him, because he was more powerful, even then he refused to believe it. He tasted their dark magick, venomous, serrated, intoxicating, and silken, they threw everything they had at him and still he did not yield.

In an unexpected flash, an avalanche of images and realisation flooded his consciousness, strange geometric shapes and long forgotten knowledge unlocked their secrets. Buttercup had been right, she knew, the Faerie Queen had always known. Rob closed his eyes extending his arms outwards, sending his senses in every direction, like thousands of scattered spores drifting on a summer tide's breeze, all individual, yet all embracing the same essence. He felt the caress of cool air cradling his body and entering his lungs, smelt the cloying, acrid smoke from the pit fires and vitalising sap from mature pines in Shadow Haven woods. He tasted coppery blood and crisp, metallic ozone that hung in the air after heavy rainfall. His awareness expanded throughout the battle below, feeling around fear and anger, then further still to the land itself, to her unconditional gifts and forgiving benevolence. After his essence entwined with all that was, he simply, imagined...

Whomp!

Rob was uncertain in how it had looked, but was certain it felt undignified, as he landed upon a huge swooping animal catching him shockingly close to the ground. There was a moment of confusion when he studied its form and then he almost fell off with laughter. It was evident he required more practice, but essentially the nuts and bolts were there, but for now he had to be content with that.

"Did you see—" gasped Abranth.

"Yes, yes, that's our son!" rejoiced Robert.

The Faerie Queen flew alongside Rob, her Drakite putting up some resistance. The erratic flight of Rob's strange beast—that had materialised from out of the aether—unnerved the Drakite, but Buttercup smoothed its neck plumage, gently encouraging it to continue.

"Rob, are you alright?"

"I think so, thanks, Buttercup. And before you say anything, I was not thinking of a flying pig."

Buttercup was unable to conceal her amusement, "What *were* you thinking?"

"Pegasus. I was thinking of a majestic Pegasus, only, It seems I have conjured a Pigasus?"

"Hey, it worked didn't it? I concede we have a little work to do, but it was a magnificent first effort!"

Rob supposed she was right, of course she was right, but he knew he would not hear the last of this. If he were a gambling man, he would bet odds on he would become vegetarian before the year was out.

"Rob, the portal will be closing and the Dark Fortress will be destroyed. I will need to get everyone away from it immediately. I want you to get far away from here, please depart for Corona and remember, nobody but yourself saved your own *bacon*."

And so it begins... sighed Rob, as Buttercup peeled away with a parting wink.

By the time she had swung around, heading back towards the keep, she could see her Elves assisting the Faux on the battlements. They hurriedly helped to muzzle the Boggles before the Faux heaved them skywards in small groups and away to safety. She smiled at how even the troublesome, drunken sprites cherished all life—the Faux however, would tell you that without it they'd have nothing to antagonise. Buttercup said a silent prayer for all those who were Boggled in battle. She expected most of them had died long ago, but that hadn't dissuaded the Boggles, which had been beyond fortuitous, as they would have attempted to engage the Elves.

Landing on the battlements, Buttercup jumped from her saddle, "McGrath, as we speak the portal is closing. I need your Elves to force the invaders back to their home world, then get far away from the keep before the portal seals shut. Send them back down to the Great Hall, you ride with me."

"Very well, my Queen, but what of Merlock and Fingle?

"Yes, there is room, but for only one more."

Fingle limped forwards, nursing his jacobs and holding his uncle's hand, "Take him please, his jibber-jabber is making me upstairs ache more than me downstairs."

Merlock was delighted to accompany this strange woman on a flying bird, dragon thing, it was an impressive part of the tour and he fully intended to leave positive comments in the visitors' book. Buttercup managed to land considerably closer to the keep's entrance than she had anticipated; it seemed the Humans did not wish to outstay their welcome. The clan Goblins, Elves and Trolls were forced to remain on the periphery, as the City Goblins continued their unrelenting assault. There was no way through them, so Buttercup was forced to take flight above the fighting. From her vantage point, she could see into the keep and felt enormous relief upon seeing the portal finally receding. The mercenaries were literally diving back through. In terror, struggling to get past their comrades, some had attempted to dart around the opening, until Clump and Pumice discouraged them. As the Elves arrived from the battlements, spilling out from the upper corridor to the Great Hall, they found themselves with nothing to do, other than watch the concluding mayhem ensue.

Satisfied with the turn of events, Buttercup landed on the periphery once more, gathering in her strategic command. "Listen carefully, the fabric of our world that was torn apart was too vast and too protracted to be stable anymore. When the portal seals completely, the Dark Fortress will collapse in on itself, the fabric which previously held that portal space is now severely weakened. We must therefore evacuate everyone away in the short time we have available, but we must also wait until the last moment, ensuring as many invaders, if not all, have left our world for good."

They understood and immediately began evacuating where possible. It had taken considerable persuasion in convincing the City Goblins to cooperate; such was the intensity of their bitter crusade. Gradually, greater numbers relented, moving away to a safer distance. Fingle had long given up trying to get Clump's attention and left the pandemonium to find his uncle and congratulate Rob.

No one had seen the small wizard wander into the Dark Fortress, he didn't know how he could become invisible to others, or how he managed to protect himself from being trampled upon, but he did it anyway and with éclat.

Merlock happily ambled over to Clump who was perspiring heavily, still perfecting his swing.

"Clump, do an old Goblin a favour will you, and sit me on your shoulder so I can get a better view of the performance."

Clump looked down, "Uncle. Where have you been?" shouted Clump above the skirmish, sitting Merlock in his usual place.

The wizard rubbed his hands together then spoke into them. He launched his arm forwards, releasing an imperceptible ball of energy. Merlock looked delighted as it landed bang on target. A mercenary, fleeing for his life, stopped mid-flight, dropped to the floor and proceeded to perform push-ups. Those that hadn't seen him fell over his extended frame and in moments a frenzied heap of bodies were piling high. Merlock marvelled at the discipline of these sell-swords, regardless of the current state of affairs, if they were given orders, they foolishly complied. So he tested them again.

After he had formed another ball of energy, he spoke into it in an authoritative tone, "About-turn, quick-march!" and threw it at another scarpering Stinky-pink.

As ordered, the mercenary turned about and marched proudly into his retreating comrades, sending them sprawling in every direction. Clump's belly shook with laughter; taking a well-earned respite, he leant on his battle axe to enjoy the show.

Pumice was otherwise engaged, chasing a lone mercenary around the rear of the Great Hall as he screamed for his life, she didn't understand why though; his life was worth very little to her. Absorbed in their own amusement, they had no idea how much time had elapsed, but the lack of targets suggested it was time to wrap things up. The remaining Human invaders were spared, as they clambered through the diminishing gateway, leaving their dignity on the way out. The Elves and Goblins swiftly departed the Dark Fortress, making their way back to the hills to join the tens of thousands that sat cheerfully in the late afternoon sun, anticipating the celebrated collapse.

Spirits were high, laughter and cheering echoed across the land, never before had so many races in such numbers joined together in joyous harmony. Rob sat with his parents after a tearful reunion. He had been allowed to fly back and venture closer to the keep now the threat had finally passed.

"Have yer seen Clump and Uncle on yer travelling?" said Fingle, walking up to Rob while flexing his full-fat hand, hoping it would *never* shrink again.

"I thought they were with you?"

"The fortress!" they shouted in alarm.

Before they could run, a deep grinding blare issued from the keep as it shook violently.

"No!"

Rob ran screaming towards the shuddering monolith, tears falling down his cheeks, then Dippy appeared. "Stop running, Rob!" she screamed, pulling him back by his tunic.

He slowed, then pulled her close to him, sobbing hard. He couldn't bear to watch the fortress collapse as Buttercup said it would. The intimidating towers and turrets, part forged from the Three Peaks, tore away and thundered into its foundations, sending up voluminous swathes of black dust that blotted out the late golden light quilting the land. When the rubble had finally settled, a sorrowful and deafening silence lingered. Not even the roosting birds heralded the approaching twilight with their familiar chorus.

"Look at me, Rob, it's okay. You can't save them, because you don't need to…"

He looked over her shoulder still holding on tightly, afraid he would fall apart where he stood. McGrath began an ancient air, an ode that was sang to honour those who sacrificed themselves for the greater good. It was not Elven in origin, for the ballad was universal. The song soon fell gently from every mouth, as the bittersweet melody wept its flight across the grieving hills.

"Never give up, Rob." whispered Dippy, kissing him tenderly.

"Over there, what's that?" coughed a blubbering City Goblin, pointing at the moving rubble in the distance.

Rob quickly wiped his eyes as more voices raised. Then he saw it too. What looked like a large wooden beam forced itself upwards between the stone blocks.

"Go to them..." urged Dippy, smiling through her tears.

Rob sprinted towards the ruins, his heart thumping hard, focused only upon reaching the trembling masonry.

"Grrrrraaaahhhhh!"

The heavy stone blocks erupted as a dusty cudgel forced itself free. Pumice dragged herself upwards through the debris, carrying Clump with her free hand, while Merlock nested within Clump's arm.

By the time Rob had arrived, Pumice had already laid them out with great care, looking extremely distressed as she spoke. "Saaave..."

"I will try." said Rob wiping his face and placing a shaky but determined hand on both of the still bodies.

Burying his own emotions deeply, he went back to that place of knowingness he had now rediscovered.

This is new, he thought, leaving his body and looking down at himself. He felt a pull towards a soft pearlescent light and followed. Rob raised his arms yet he could not see anything, only light where his body should have been.

"Clump, Merlock, where are you?" his voice rippling through the opaque luminescence and in response a blurred shape wavered into view.

"Who is that? Clump? Merlock?"

"Rob, is that you? Where are we?" came back Clump's reply.

"We are in no-space, boys, a void of in-between. I have been here many times, but not quite like this."

"Merlock, you're alive! Why can't I see you?" said Rob excitedly.

"You can, you just have to ask."

Rob instructed an inner part of his essence to sharpen his sight and promptly he was standing in front of his two very good friends.

"I don't know where I am right now, or how I got here, but you need to come back with me. Back to the world of the living. This is *not* your time to die, I won't let you, neither of you. Clump, you have a lovely young she-Troll waiting for you and I do not want to end up in that cauldron. Merlock, Fingle will never forgive you and I will never hear the last of it, he will likely spin headlong into a fit of manic depression and refuse to refill his potpourri bowls that he pretends he doesn't have. I also refuse to leave this place until both of you leave with me."

Merlock moved closer, "My dear boy, I don't doubt that you would, but we will all be leaving together anyway, this isn't a place between lives, this is a place between dreams, we're just unconscious, Rob."

"Ah, another interesting observation, I can feel like a moron in dreams too."

"I suggest you go back, Rob, perform some ridiculous pomp and ceremony, like any self-respecting wizard would, then wake us up. Usually a wet finger shoved discreetly in the ear-flap does the trick."

"Look, I found a stick with one end!"

They both looked over and smiled at Clump, sure enough he had finally found one. A most surreal thing to behold, sadly they only existed where dreams came true of course. *It may prove difficult in rousing Clump from his prize.* mused Rob.

As Rob's eyes snapped back open, he was brought back to the living by the sound of lament, it seemed the entire kingdom was draped in despair. As he stood above his unconscious friends, everything went eerily silent. Trying to look as serious as he could, despite being aware he was bullshitting on a scale he never thought possible, he waved his arms dramatically in the air then stiffened, while chanting a deep incoherent mumble that terminated with a chilling scream. Rob fell to his knees, but not before licking both forefingers and jamming them into the flaps of his flaked out friends as he collapsed theatrically over them.

"Where's my stick gone…?" said Clump drearily, as Merlock sat bolt upright, coughing out a chuckle.

The entire valley went wild! Hundreds of Goblins ran over to the resurrected heroes, hoisting them high above their shoulders, despite Merlock's disapproval—Clump was dragged slowly, still searching his empty hands—while singing and dancing broke out everywhere.

"Behind you!"

Rob turned just in time to flatten against the hands that passed him around, as an enormous black tentacle swept across the top of the crowd, narrowly missing him by a witch's wart whisker. The Goblins quickly sought to protect Rob, taking up a fighting stance to combat the new menace.

Toesin and his two brothers emerged from the Gurgles sitting atop ol' Jelly Legs, the ancient sea beast that escaped from the Black Line. As it lurched forwards, its tentacles stiffened sufficiently to be used as rudimentary legs, although appearing unstable, it moved with relative ease. Toesin was frighteningly high, perched above thick, suckered, muscular arms extending to their fullest lengths. The towering Kraken, slitherstomping around with its huge bulbous eyes and writhing black form was utterly horrifying, scrutinising the ground in relentless exploration for tasty tidbits.

Rob's gaze followed a single tentacle that was held high, a Goblin was wrapped several times over in its fleshy arm. A quick command by Toesin and Jelly Legs lowered her gift, Rob instantly recognised the mask.

"G.A.S., Rob, we captured the one who broke our bridge. O.M.G, I caught him trying to run away, thought you might know what to do with the S.O.B. seeing how smart you are. Best make a decision P.D.Q. as Mish and Mash have recently developed a very exciting method of revenge, employing a single barrel of ravenous Feel eggs on the verge of hatching and a well lubricated magickal bean!" shouted Toesin, while his toothless brothers nodded eagerly.

"Your generosity overwhelms me, Toesin, but I must decline your esteemed brothers' kindly offers. As it happens, I have just the thing for Sly Slaughter, he will be in very appreciative hands."

"L.O.L, very well, F.Y.I, if you are ever looking for a job, I was considering updating my Tome. I.M.O. it seems it may be in need of a revision."

"Again, I am all gratitude, but I strongly suspect I will be needed elsewhere for the immediate future. You take good care of yourselves and O.J.L....ah, I did it again didn't I?"

The Troll grinned, then bowed his head respectfully, "Well, if you ever change your mind, master of T.L.A.'s."

After some coaxing and having to transform himself to his fullest size, Toesin eventually convinced O.J.L. to release Sly Slaughter and hand him over to the Elves for safe custody. Toesin thanked Rob again for his part in saving his world by way of handing him a very unusual talisman.

"Take this Rob, H.T.H, found it on Slaughter, it may come in handy one day. Sly mumbled something about it being able to control magick. I.A.C., it didn't mean much to ol' Jelly Legs, so she just grabbed Sly and juggled him around for a bit. B.F.N., saviour of worlds and crosser of bridges." he said warmly, then whistled for Jelly Legs to hoist him back aboard next to Mish and Mash. Rob watched the drooling sea monster lurch back into the Gurgles, heading upstream. He had a strong feeling their paths would cross again someday and was grateful for it.

With the Archer's permission, McGrath had been asked personally by the Queen to deal with Sly Slaughter and ensure he settled well into his new home. McGrath would gladly tell anyone who asked; how ludicrously far away from the Cone of Certainty, he was still able to hear Slaughter's screams. After losing the powerful seer— Siren-Dipity—the old crone didn't see any reason for maintaining such a high level of security and was delighted when her new play thing had arrived and wearing a leather mask too. S*aucy,* she thought, *more to unwrap.*

Chapter 39

Never wishing to waste an opportunity, the Goblins stirred up an impromptu celebration of epic proportions upon those historic hills that same evening. The Faerie Queen had allowed the use of her Air Squadron to return to Corona and fetch as much Elven ale and mead the beasts could carry. Scouts had been sent out to local villages to procure all the grog the inns and taverns had in supply. In fairness, Goblins never travelled light, the thousands of skin flasks that were passed around were a testament to that fact. The Elven army's winding caravan had harboured large supplies, which were gratefully distributed to all those that had fought in the battle. As spit roasting fires were lit and pockets of spontaneous music played, exaggerated tales were told of heroic endeavours. Great legends were born that day and long forgotten ties of old alliances were forged anew during the celebrations. The revelry had lasted until the sun was seen again. By early morning most of the weary, yet highly spirited races had left the hills, heading back to their homes on land, caves, mountains, or sea. The fallen had been counted, honoured and buried, the injured cared for.

Once back at Corona, a long discussion had taken place, regarding the future of Robin and his father Robert. The agreement had been unanimous, it would be far too dangerous for them to return to Earth and if they so chose, they would be more than welcome to live with the Elves in the Crystal Mountains as guests of honour. A further discussion took place deliberating Rob's newly acquired magickal abilities. It seemed he exhibited enormous potential and that one day he may even become a great wizard. After much persuasion, he reluctantly agreed to enrol at the school of H.E.X., at the White Path Keep in the Citadel of Light, dwelling deep within Ambersheah Forest—home to the mysterious Woodland Elves and Faeries.

The apprentice wizardry course would last five long cycles, unfortunately there was no way around this. Dippy had promised to wait for him, she was after all over seven hundred years old, which of course was but a drop in the Great Wet. Rob bade his friends, parents and Dippy farewell as he embarked upon his new adventure. He hadn't seen anything of the illusive Fairies or Woodland Elves since his arrival and was eager to meet them. They were extraordinarily secretive, existing ever so slightly out of phase with all other races. Like turning the frequency dial on a radio between channels, they *were* there, but tantalisingly just out of reach, unless of course you raised your own frequency—'joy' was a particularly splendid method—then...oh what wonders awaits the curious!

Chapter 40

Two long cycles later…

"So very sorry, Rob, dragging you away from your studies and all that, it's Fingle, he needs your help again."

As Rob emerged from the glittering golden light, Smidge shielded his eyes until it faded, returning once more to autumnal woodland.

"What do you *mean* he needs me? Is he in trouble? Where is he?"

"He's back in his cell, the same cell he was first imprisoned, back at the Courthouse."

Rob groaned, "What has he done this time? Have you flew off the wagon again, Smidge?"

"No, course not! I'm as sober as a Goblin judge. I can't say any more, it's far too dangerous. The woods have ears don't you know? I will fly on ahead and meet you there. Merlock and Clump are waiting there too, fare thee well, young Robin."

As Smidge flew away, he noted that Rob was somehow different. He looked older, obviously, but something else. He had a confidence and calmness to hitherto been lacking. Smidge continued to ruminate on the matter, hiccupping while he swigged from a tiny brown bottle. Rob watched the Faux haphazardly dart away, blinding himself within a yellow haze, as he slapped hard against a needle laden branch of a late pollinating

Yew tree. *What in Faerie Kingdom had Fingle done this time to end up back inside a cell?* Rob wondered.

Although the walk had taken several days before he reached the great Goblin City, it had been pleasant enough. His stay at H.E.X. had never seen seasonal change. It was forever in summer and he now felt great relief upon entering autumn once again. Rob savoured all of his senses, watching the caramel leaves as they tumbled back into life by brisk autumnal notes, rousing them from slumber, requesting a last wistful dance before a wintry embrace would stake its claim. He had walked for the most part along the coastline, navigating the Thorn Slave Cliffs. As he looked beyond the crystal waters of the Great Wet, his thoughts returned to his one love. Despite what lay in wait for him, he hoped that Dippy would be there to greet him, he had missed her the most.

And there it stood.

A vast labyrinth of streets and huts, alleys and buildings, all crammed tightly together and spanning such a distance, it seemed to be in real peril of spilling into the glimmering water as it teetered on the peninsula's edge. As Rob approached, the first thing that was apparent was the wall, or lack of it. During his absence, the great wall had been taken down and in its place, the same blocks had been used to create sturdier homes for the impoverished Goblins living within the shanty towns surrounding the city. He felt genuine admiration for the improvements, which benefitted the elements of Goblin society that needed it the most, something his own world still sadly lagged behind with.

After hiking down the long winding path that led towards the main entrance, the second thing Rob noticed was that the main gate had been removed. In its place, hundreds of colourful stalls lined either side of the busy thoroughfare, selling everything imaginable. Fortunately, the internal layout had remained largely unchanged and it wasn't long before he had found his footing and made his way through the bustling crowds to the courthouse in the city's centre. The final, significant change Rob noted, was that the courthouse, was no longer a courthouse.

"Ah, I see you made it okay. Just follow me, Rob, all will be explained." said Smidge, flying inside the large building through the open door.

Rob looked upwards where the courthouse sign had once hung, it had been replaced. It now read, 'The Robin Swindlar'. Rob stood speechless, watching his name swing back and forth with a painting of a bent over Goblin carrying a large sack of gold. The painting looked suspiciously like Rob. Next to it stood the gallows. Rob was extremely relieved to see that Gimple Fleablotch was not still hanging around. Instead, a fragrant, crowded basket of chrysanthemums now welcomed the appreciative.

"Hurry up, Fingle's waiting for you!" yelled Smidge, fluttering back out to see where Rob had gotten to.

As he entered the courthouse, the interior was much the same. Highly polished dark wooden panelling, accentuated by stone pillars and mosaic flooring. It all looked formal enough, except for the merry atmosphere, intense aroma of lavender mixed with hops and conspicuous consumption of grog, by the cart load.

"Good...to see...you, Rob."

Rob spun around and shrank. Looming over him stood Pumice, grinning inanely and grasping her cudgel—which had now been polished smooth and bore the engraved words 'Please come again' in gold leaf.

"Hi, Pumice, good to see you too. Your language has improved remarkably. What are you doing here?"

"Helping husband, stop bad ones coming in. Uncle Merlock touched my head, now I talk better."

"That's good. Well, keep it up, see you in a bit then."

"My sister, Ambergris, she likes you..."

Rob shuddered as her sister came into view, she was an exact replica of Pumice, but a brunette. Their disastrous experimentation with makeup only enhanced their roles as intimidating door-Trolls.

"Ambergris, pleased to meet you, but unfortunately I am already taken. However, if circumstances change and *I pray they do not*, I know exactly where to find you." smiled Rob, tearing away from her unhinged gaze.

The two Trolls giggled gutturally together, watching Rob speed away.

"What happened to the Courts, Smidge? Where are the clerks, the guards, the Judges?" said Rob in disbelief.

"Fingle bought the place on account of it not being used any more, he ploughed all of his ill-gotten savings into it. Quick, follow me, his cell is down here at the end of the corridor."

Rob tried to keep up with the Faux, his mind racing, he had no idea that Fingle had hoarded away so much gold to buy such a place. It was an enormous building and built to exacting standards, prime real estate slap bang in the city centre. As Rob emerged from the gloomy corridor, he arrived at a cell door that bore Fingle's name upon it, with 'Proprietor' written beneath.

Before he had a chance to knock, the door swung open, "Greeting and salutations." extended Fingle, with that same devilish glint sparkling in his eyes that Rob had missed.

"Greetings? Are you *insane*? I have just left my apprentice three long cycles early to help free you again, only *this* time you don't need freeing, as you appear to own the whole fracking courthouse!"

"Come, come, young Rob, maybe the message sent could have been a little disin-genius? Or perhaps the messenger had a momentary mentimutation? Whatever happened, happened, Rob, but now yer here, back with old

Fingle and he don't mind telling yer he's missed yer something rotten."

There was a long pause while they both studied each other. Fingle's mouth pinched at the corners first, Rob could not help but grin back.

"I'm not sure what mum and dad will say about this, or Buttercup, after convincing H.E.X. to finally accept me and what of your uncle?"

Merlock popped his wispy head around the door, "Ah yes, shame about having to leave prematurely, I wonder how Smidge could get so pitchkettled, the message was simple enough. 'Fingle needs help urgently, he is back in his cell in the City Courthouse'."

Rob looked at the pair of them shaking his head, "And *what* exactly do you need help with, Fingle? Choosing a new colour scheme for the bar? Stuffing your mountain of gold beneath your luxurious mattress?"

"Well, as it 'appens, I have another little enterprise. The bar out front's a nice little earner, but yer know me, always on the lookout fer the big scores. Come in…"

Rob walked into his cell, it was immaculate. The walls were white washed and blemish free. Rob could see his reflection in the gleaming floor tiles and the entire cell reeked of scented potpourri. In the centre stood a large chestnut table, no doubt once belonging to an important Judge. Fingle sat down behind it and produced a name plate from a desk drawer, placing it proudly upon the polished desk top.

Gold-Fingle
Entrepreneur, Bon Vivant, Revolutions Inspired,
Civilisations Saved.

"Gold-Fingle? Are you serious?" exclaimed Rob.

"Oops sorry, wrong one, this one…" replied Fingle sheepishly, swiftly switching name plates.

F.B.I. - Fingle's Bureau of Investigation

"What do yer think? Unlike me unambitious brethren here, I don't want ta be tied down ta a lucrative, legitimate business watching the honest coin come in, it's unnatural. *Adventure*, that's what we're made fer, Rob and as it so 'appens, I have me very first case."

Rob's eyes narrowed, "Do you now? And I suppose this is why you sent for me?"

"I don't know *what* yer mean. What are yer implying?" feigned Fingle in mock surprise.

"Fingle! For the love of grog, speak your mind and stop wasting my time."

"Right yer are. I need yer, Rob, let me explain. After yer left, the Archer's—I mean, yer dad's band of Orchi approached me, thinking I may be able ta help them. As yer probably know already, over forty long cycles ago, most of the Orcs set sail across the Great Wet. They knew enough from their ancient 'eritage, they were once sea voyagers and had settled here long, long ago. But as time passed, they felt a burning ambition ta return ta their sea faring roots. It was decided they would leave as a race together, echoing their motto, 'all or nothing'. Since then nobody and I means *nobody*, has seen or heard of 'em since. The Orcs that still live here on the mainland continue ta protect their homes and 'eritage in the Hollow Hills, a little up from the Breeze Blunders. When I enquired about their 'eritage, they mentioned sacred artefacts, historical wotnot, yer know…"

"You mean gold."

Fingle coughed, "Well, yeah, from what I have been told, they are sitting on a king's ransom."

"So, why do you need me?"

Merlock walked over, looking up at Rob apologetically, "Please forgive me, I didn't want you to become involved, but, well I have to be there to look after

349

my nephews. I'm not a whelp anymore, Rob and I have no one who has the *gift* about them, someone I can trust to pass arcane wisdom onto. You, are a sensitive. I have no doubt H.E.X. would have prepared you well, but sometimes it is better to jump in feet first. If you will allow me to be your tutor, I will teach you all I know. Do not forget, I have already passed my apprentice at H.E.X. and as valuable as it was, I found it to be lacking in any…*real* magick. This is what I can offer you, while I'm still around that is…"

Rob paced around the cell, rubbing the dark whiskers on his chin he had cultivated during his time at Ambershea.

"Let me get this straight. Both of you and Clump, are going on a sea voyage across the Great Wet in search of an entire race of Orcs who may even be dead for all we know? You have no idea what dangers lie in wait, I presume you have never set sail out of the coastal waters and you intend to be paid with a mountain of Orc gold for your troubles. Oh, and you want *me* to go with you."

"Yep, that's about the rub of it, are yer in then?"

"No! I have a new life now. As much as I would leap at the chance of becoming your apprentice, Merlock and watch Fingle drown in gold coins, I have been given a second chance with my parents and I am in love with Dippy, how could I risk losing that?"

"You won't have ta, they're coming along too." grinned Fingle, as they entered the cell behind him.

"Mum, Dad, Dippy!" Rob ran over and embraced them lovingly, then quickly pulled away, "Did you know about the message Smidge gave H.E.X.?"

His mother smiled warmly, "Yes, I'm afraid we all did, Rob, but we missed you so much. Learning how to manipulate magick is important, if that's what you truly want, but magick is everywhere, it is the stuff that binds us together. Our life has been less magickal without you. I'm afraid we have been a little selfish, please forgive us."

She was right, maybe he'd been a little selfish too. Rob held her again, "Just as well I left H.E.X. anyway, it was all a bit fluffy. All the fairies wore permagrins and never complained about anything, ever. Don't get me wrong, I learned a great deal and the things I witnessed were incredible, but it was not me, not who I am right now. I am not quite ready to swap my flying pig for a Unicorn."

"You mean Scobblelotcher? Someone had to name him after you left, he's snawking around out back." said Dippy bashfully.

"Hmmmm, it seems you have all made up my mind for me."

His father stepped forwards, "Son, no one is making your mind up, your life has been meddled with enough, but it is yours now and yours alone. Not even the likes of Sly Slaughter can interfere any longer, besides he has his hands full at the moment. Oh, and I heard about you and the Crone. Don't worry, what happens in the Cone stays in the Cone." he said with a wink, while everyone did a lousy job of masking their amusement.

"Dippy! Thanks for not telling everyone." blushed Rob, with a crooked smile.

"Very well. I will accompany you marauding bunch of buccaneers and take the case. But I expect a fair share of the proceeds, Fingle, assuming we will live long enough to collect it."

"Great crom, yer will not regret it. Let's celebrate by toasting our agreement with the finest grog ta ever be drank this side of the Great Wet."

Everyone followed Fingle out of his cell and into the bleak corridor. Fingle stopped abruptly, closing his eyes, reliving the moment he was first dragged down the same corridor, he really didn't expect to have ever seen the light of day again.

He turned to Rob and placed his rangy arm around him, "I will never forget what yer did fer me, Rob, never…" croaked Fingle, quickly turning away and clearing his throat.

"Come, come and taste Fingle's finest grog. But be ye warned, it packs quite a punch and a head-butt or three."

They walked into the main Court together, to where the original Judge's bench had been—replaced now by a long oak bar top—and the Inn was packed.

"All the dregulars from the Bleeding Beetle, the Wilting Table, and The Burnt Pan now drink in 'ere." boasted Fingle, standing proudly with a thumb hitched in either side of his ostentatious, leather chest plate.

Rob looked around the courtroom, he had to admit, Fingle had really gone all out. It was strange recalling what had previously transpired and now he was about to sup on a grog where he was once face to face with that awful judge.

"Fingle, what ever happened to that judge, the one with the bulging eye and serious drinking problem?"

"You mean 'Pickled Peeper', he's over there and not much has changed." Fingle pointed to a table near the entrance. The judge that once tried Fingle for treason was now sat singing merrily away, having clearly more sail than ballast.

"What can I get you? Dark or light grog?"

"Clump!" cried Rob, jumping over the bar to give his friend a big hug as far as his arms would reach.

"Good to see you, Rob, I missed you a lot. Me and my brother have a busynest together"

"I can see that, Clump, it looks amazing and it's packed with customers."

"It's the grog, Rob, it's the best in the Kingdom, but its recipe's a family secret, shhh."

"Really? I didn't know you and your brother were into brewing as well."

Fingle quickly stepped forwards, "Thanks, Clump, yer said enough." he said in a cautionary tone.

Fingle gestured Rob to follow him. They walked away from the noisy crowded bar and into the busy kitchens.

"Hey, isn't that—"

"Yes, AMOK the embittered three and two fifths. As it turned out, AMOK is an excellent chef. Alun is the executive chef, Matilda the sous chef, Odessa the pastry...well yer get the idea and the speed it, they, can cook is phenomenal. Granted, the menu ain't exactly highbrow and yer average Elf might turn his already upended snout away, but fer this city, it is by far the best on offer."

"What did happen to AMOK? The last I heard, it was overthrown by Sly and his guards and yet here it is." replied Rob, relieved it was wearing hair nets.

"It was and then presumed dead after the destruction of the Dark Fortress, but it had been miraculously saved by flaky snot. Where it had been locked up in the lower dungeons, it had no other place to scatter its body waste than where it sat, which by sheer luck had served as a germ infested cushion against the tumbling masonry, strange ol' world ain't it..."

"But isn't it still dangerous? Doesn't it seek revenge?"

"Well, a deal was struck. Yer dad, with the help of his Orc friends risked a last visit to Earth ta fetch as many beauty products as they could carry back through, skin lotion, saline sprays, incontinence towels, oh and a little 'eau de parfum' fer yours truly. As it turns out, the only reason AMOK had wanted ta invade Earth, was ta visit a health spa anyways. So in answer to yer question, AMOK is happier than ever doing something it loves, but of course it still has homicidal tendencies, after all, who doesn't? Well, except maybe yer."

"Hmmm, I thought everything that passed between our worlds changed, or didn't function as it should."

"Well, that depends on what it is, something the Stinky-pinks never understood. There are universal laws that all worlds are bound, so if an object is brought over that is intended for harm, then it's usually changed, sometimes *remarkably* so, follow me…"

After walking past AMOK, whistling away as an incomplete quartet, Rob continued to follow Fingle to a part of the courts he had not seen before. They emerged from the rear of the kitchens, took a few turns through some more dark corridors, until they eventually arrived at a large steel door, heavily bolted and locked.

Rob watched Fingle's nimble fingers unlock the various mechanisms, "Isn't this a bit over the top?"

"Nope. What I 'ave behind this door is the secret ta my success, the secret recipe of the grog that keeps 'em coming, by the cartloads."

Rob's curiosity had the better of him. He helped Fingle to push open the heavy door, then followed him down a long set of stone steps. At the bottom, Fingle lit a wall sconce with a flint, then two more. Looking around, the room seemed ordinary enough, as cellars often are, a couple of dozen barrels and a few smaller casks stored in the far corners.

"So this is it huh? This is your great secret recipe for the grog that Goblins can't get enough of."

"Not exactly." said Fingle, rubbing his hands together from the chill of the cellar.

He walked over to a loose brick in the far wall and pulled upon it, as he did so, a scraping noise came from the opposite corner. The pair walked over to the shadowy alcove and Fingle lit a fourth torch, removing it from its holder. The vulpine Goblin jabbed a spindly finger into a hidden recess, triggering half of the stone wall to slide away from the adjoining brickwork.

Rob gasped aloud, "A hidden door!"

"Yep. What I'm about ta show yer must remain our little secret, Rob, do yer understand?"

Rob studied his friend's face in the flickering orange light. Although his countenance was serious enough, his playful nature still danced across it.

"Of course I will. I like to think I have earnt your trust."

"Ha ha ha, do yer think me dim witted? Yer a Goblin now." he chuckled, then nodded for Rob to enter the secret passage.

Trembling with anticipation, Rob followed down the silent passageway, sensing the torchlight dim as the confines of the narrow corridor opened up into a vast underground chamber. Fingle continued walking, lighting torch after torch that hung along the endless walls while Rob stared in absolute horror.

Eventually Fingle returned, "I know what yer thinking, but so far there's been no reaper-concussions. I couldn't miss the opportunity now could I? So there was I, back at the docks minding me own after the battle, when I sees one of these things floating past, then another and another. It took quite a few trips I can tell yer, but with Clump, Pumice and Ambergris 'elping, we managed ta hide them all in me warehouse at the dockyard. I reckon they came down from the Gurgles. Why'd yer think I bought the Courthouse? I wouldn't have sunk me coin into this place, unless I *knew* I could make it work and yer seen how successful it's been. Goblins love this stuff. Now I've got coin coming in regular and I don't have ta cheat or steal for once, which doesn't exactly sit right with me, but nonetheless, I am surviving comfortably. This leaves me time ta go fer the big one, Rob, that's why I want yer ta come with us, on me new ship and find the Orc's. Are yer still with me?"

After Fingle had illuminated the entire chamber, Rob had done some basic arithmetic, the barrels had easily numbered a thousand in total. Each one also displayed a bright yellow symbol, with five words emblazoned beneath:

'WARNING BIOHAZARD LEVEL - 4
MILITARY GRADE'

"Well? Speak up, laddie, are yer still in…?"
"Fingle…you can't…you just...can't…"

15013076R00213

Printed in Great Britain
by Amazon